HARLEQUIN'S DAUGHTER

When journalist Brigit Flood sees Conor Byrne's paintings of his wife Hannah, she simply can't get them out of her mind. When she meets Hannah at Conor's studio home in Kilnaboy, on the coast of County Clare, she begins to understand the tensions that made Conor's paintings so memorable. Hannah, clearly unstable, is a thorn in the side of the small artistic community Conor has formed. Apart from Conor, no one seems to want Brigit at Kilnaboy, but, drawn to the charismatic artist, Brigit is determined to make the most of the opportunity, little knowing what she is stumbling into...

HARLEQUIN'S DAUGHTER

HARLEQUIN'S DAUGHTER

by

Mary Joyce

Magna Large Print Books
Long Preston, North Yorkshire,
BD23 4ND, England.

British Library Cataloguing in Publication Data.

Joyce, Mary
    Harlequin's daughter.

    A catalogue record of this book is
    available from the British Library

    ISBN   0-7505-1644-5

First published in Great Britain in 1999 by
Headline Book Publishing

Copyright © 1999 Mary Joyce

Cover illustration © Melvyn Warren-Smith by arrangement with
Headline Book Publishing Ltd.

The right of Mary Joyce to be identified as the author of this work has
been asserted by her in accordance with the Copyright, Designs and
Patents Act, 1988

Published in Large Print 2001 by arrangement with
Headline Book Publishing Ltd.

Magna Large Print is an imprint of Library Magna Books Ltd.

Printed and bound in Great Britain by
T.J. (International) Ltd., Cornwall, PL28 8RW

This book is dedicated to those good-natured people who responded to my inquiries while I was researching this book. Some were friends. Some were complete strangers who received phone calls out of the blue. Others – like Dr Charles Nelson who identified the flowers in the garden of *An Fear Gorta* – were experts in their field. No one was ever too busy to help.

I am immensely grateful to all of you.

ONE

Talking now about what happened, I maintain it was the paintings, that those landscapes of the west acted on me like a magnet. It's simpler to explain it that way and, after all, it's true – they did. The paintings, haunting and unsettling, were seductive and enchanting.

But other factors played their part at the onset of summer. The Rat's obsession and persistence. The memories I had of Joe. My own affinity with danger.

The heat had something to do with it too. With temperatures at ninety-two, London had become an oven. No clouds relieved the monotony of the low, anaemic sky out of which, at seven on that Monday morning, a ruthless and acidic sun focused on the city's faults, exposing grime on unwashed cars, dust on weary, cracking doors, and spiders' webs on window frames.

'Very stuffy,' said Mr Mehta the newsagent when I went to buy the paper.

'Aw, come on. You love the heat.'

'For you, it's stuffy, I was thinking. For me, it is a perfect day. Like our winters in Madras.'

'*Not* the place for me in summer!'

'In Ireland now it will be cooler. Probably it will be raining.'

'It's boiling over there as well.'

But no pollution, I said to myself – well, not as

11

much as there is here. And not so many people, either. Suddenly, I longed for home.

'They're taking bets on it,' Mr Mehta said. 'It may reach one hundred yet.'

I left the shop and went outside, brooding on that gloomy prospect. The morning rush had already started and the cachinnation of rows of cars, bumper to bumper along the road, added to the sense of pressure. In front of Style Antiques, bare-chested men, whom the sun had transformed from pale, shrimp-like, homely creatures into foreign feral beings, were loading furniture into a van. I smelled their sweat as I walked by.

'Hozzit, gorgeous?' one called out.

'Gorgeous' was a malapropos. I have my mother's looks but I do not have her beauty. What was exquisite in my mother, Meriel Flood – the oval, clear-complexioned face, the small, straight nose and full red lips – are slightly coarsened and stretched on me. Size and weight-wise, I am average – five feet six, size ten or twelve, depending on what I've been eating. My hair is brown, thick and straight, worn to the shoulders and cut in a fringe. My eyes are nearer black than brown. Oh, and I have ugly hands, with nails that tend to split and peel even when they're manicured.

Gorgeous, indeed... Ignoring that banal harassment, I walked on down the High Road and reached the corner of the terrace that led to my flat, stepping aside as a jogger went by. In the street into which I turned, several shops were opening up, the fishmonger, the greengrocer and the butcher across the road, and early risers in shorts and T-shirts, with shopping baskets in their hands, were forming into straggling queues. To all intents and purposes, Chiswick was a village still, just as charming as it had seemed when I first set foot in it. I reminded myself for the umpteenth time that I was lucky to be living here.

The flat, first floor, one bedroom, looked out on to Chiswick Common. Inserting the key in the front door lock, I thought, as I so often did, I must paint the sitting room.

The thought, finding no response inside me, faded as it always did. Moving in three years ago, I'd told myself it needed painting, convinced that I would see to it. At that stage I had few possessions – a bed, the camel-haired rugs that I'd bought in Omdurman after haggling with the traders, a herd of wooden elephants transported in a basket from Natal, and two hanging lamps of Spanish punched tin. The rest had been obtained from junk shops. The sapele table from the Old Stables in Camden Lock. The bamboo folding chairs from Northcote Road. The green velvet sofa from the flea market in Brick Lane which had begun its voluptuous life nailed to the deck of an ocean liner. The base of a treadle sewing machine converted into a coffee table.

Not a lot. Not enough to tie you down, which was how I wanted it.

I put the percolator on, took the paper into the bathroom, switched on the taps, sat on the loo and digested the morning headlines. 'Adams Plays the Democrat'. 'Queen's Tour Turns Sour'.

'MP Denies Infidelity Claims'.

In the features section, under the heading 'But for Grace', the editor of the women's magazine of the year, Grace Wilson, was explaining how she'd upped the dipping sales and ruminating about herself: 'I'm at ease with myself now. I have everything I want.'

Grace Wilson was thirty-one. We were the same age. We were both journalists. There the similarity ended. Grace Wilson had a husband, a two-year-old daughter and legs the length of Naomi Campbell's. Grace Wilson was pleased with herself. She didn't have a jaded feeling.

I did. To make matters worse, I had no justification for being so dissatisfied and restless, or none that I could verbalise. I was a fully-fledged producer, part of a team of thirty people working on an arts programme which went out four nights a week on BBC2 and wasn't under threat of cutback. In my time with the show, I had taken risks, survived a flood of criticism, triumphed over rivalry, acquired an assistant of my own and made some reasonable films. My future in the media was as secure as anybody's could be these days.

I wasn't hankering after a husband – not consciously, at any rate. I wasn't craving motherhood. My legs, though not in Naomi's league, were not in dire need of traction.

So what on earth was the matter with me? Why was it that the possessions I'd acquired, designed to play a vital role in the making of a home, had failed to carry out their task? How come that, though my clothes were hanging up, in a purely

14

emotional sense, none of my cases had been unpacked?

The bath was almost overflowing. I hastily turned off the taps and drained the excess water off. End of self-reflection time. I had piles of work to do.

I was working at home that day, as I did from time to time to get away from phones and chatter. I had reading to catch up on – biographical notes on the young German violinist Antje Weithaas whose forthcoming performance with the BBC Symphony Orchestra was to feature on the programme, and a four-thousand-word article on the controversial American choreographer Bill T. Jones whose work *Still Here* was to be staged in Edinburgh on the twenty-fifth of August.

I reined in my coltish self, the one that wanted to buck and bolt, and worked steadily through lunch. At four I went outside again, intending to buy milk and eggs. On the steps, I paused, dismayed. The Rat was walking slowly along the other side of the terrace in the direction of Turnham Green Terrace.

He was a small man, no taller than myself, dressed in flannels and a short-sleeved shirt, with short black hair and lily-white skin and a long, porcine nose much too big for his manikin's face. A visual nonentity, inscribed too clearly on my mind.

I'd seen him first in February, when weather conditions were very different. The wind was vicious. It was pouring. Locked in battle with the flu, I drove the short distance from my flat to

Sainsbury's in Chiswick Green. It was a Wednesday afternoon but the car park was almost full and I was forced to circle a second time before I spotted a parking space.

It was right down at the far end of the car park, necessitating a long, damp walk back to the supermarket. As I turned the engine off, I thought how deserted the car park was, how car parks generally were like that, with shoppers either inside the store or sealed inside their vehicles, oblivious of all else but the need to head for home to unload their acquisitions.

In my haste to get out of the rain I selected a trolley that veered to the right. Struggling with it inside the store, I dropped the list that I had made.

'Oh, God!' I said aloud. But almost at once I spotted the list. A small boy with blond curls had set his foot on it.

'Excuse me, but I need that paper.'

The small boy's mother, reaching out for salad cream, turned round to glower at me, the way that mothers do in London when strangers come too near their children.

I tried to set the record straight. 'It's just my shopping list,' I said.

The woman didn't smile at me. Someone else, however, did. He was a short, unattractive man whose trolley was stopped beside my own. His smile demanded recognition. Did I know him? No, I didn't. Conscious that my nose was running, I fumbled in vain for a handkerchief.

The man was still observing me, his trolley almost blocking mine.

'Excuse me,' I said again.

He didn't move. Perhaps he was a foreigner who didn't understand English. I reversed, narrowly missing the mother and child, swung my trolley to the left in the hope of straightening it and consulted my shopping list.

Cheese … I couldn't see beyond my nose – I'd been down that aisle already. Retracing my steps, I eased the trolley between an indecisive, elderly man and a toddler in a rage and scanned the shelves for Camembert.

Yes, there it was. But there, too, with his trolley next to mine, was the man who'd smiled at me. He wasn't smiling now and, looking into his lily-white face, I saw that his eyes – pale blue, milky eyes – had no warmth in them at all. A little shiver went down my spine. I knew then that he was Trouble.

He was. Every time I glanced around, the man who had smiled was close to me. Sometimes, when I rounded an aisle, he was already there, with his almost empty trolley.

When this had happened eight or nine times, I decided to seek assistance. A young man, obviously a Sainsbury's employee, was stacking bath oil onto a shelf. I went up to him.

'Someone's following me,' I said, aware that this sounded silly, that women were followed along dark streets and narrow alleys, not inside the supermarket.

'Really?'

'Yes, really,' I said. 'He's–' I cast my eyes around for the man. But by then he'd done a bunk. '–somewhere in the vicinity.'

17

'Has he been following you for long?'

'Since I got here, I suppose.'

'Well, let me know if you see him again.'

'Oh. OK. Yes, I will.'

He must think I'm a nutter, I thought; that I'm looking for attention; that, in these benign surroundings, I could surely look after myself.

I told myself not to be such a fool, to concentrate on my shopping list, to find the Kleenex, for a start. I needed to stock up on groceries. To that end, to give myself the time to buy them, I had worked the night before.

I did my best to think about food and not about the white-faced man. But I knew he was somewhere close, waiting for me to reappear, that when I left the store he'd be out there in the car park. That he'd also have a car. That he could follow me home in it...

He was over by the bread racks but he wasn't buying bread. He was simply standing there, confident of my arrival.

I thought of accosting him but a wave of flu came over me, so hot it nearly scalded me. I wasn't up to confrontation. There was nothing for it but to enlist the help of the young man six aisles back at the bath oil shelves. Trundling my unwieldy trolley, I returned to look for him.

He was no longer there – I couldn't see him anywhere. The till then. I'd tell the woman at the till what was happening to me.

I sought a sympathetic face, someone who was middle-aged and might have a daughter of her own.

The woman to whom I eventually spoke

18

responded by calling Security. A man in uniform appeared and I told my tale again.

'Can you describe this person for me?'

At that moment the white-faced man, having abandoned his own trolley, shot past me and out of the store.

'That's him!'

Spurred on by my agitation, Security rushed out after him.

He returned alone. 'There's no sign of him now.'

I half expected to be abandoned to the hazards of the car park.

'I'll walk out to your car with you.'

'Would you?' Tears of relief welled up in my eyes.

'You'd better let me push that trolley.'

We were weaving round the side of the store when the white-faced man came walking back.

'It's him – *look!*' I cried.

And then the action speeded up. The white-faced man, seeing I was under escort, ran inside the shop again. Security ran after him.

I waited for a while, then, presuming myself to be out of danger, set off alone across the car park, propelling my dysfunctional trolley past the rows of empty cars. I was within ten yards of my GT Golf when a black Mazda drew up on the throughway to my left. Even before I laid eyes on its driver, I knew it was the white-faced man.

I froze, hypnotised by his stare, like an animal caught by blinding lights.

We remained there, the two of us, for what seemed like hours to me. Then, mercifully, another car drew up behind the Mazda and its driver, impatient to make a getaway, sounded his horn indignantly. The Mazda was forced on towards the exit and into the traffic on the road outside. I memorised its number plate. Later, having driven home on a circuitous route just in case I was still being followed, I got in touch with Sainsbury's.

'We'll report him to the police,' Security said. 'There's not much that they can do. He's committed no offence. But you're right, the man is odd.'

'Well,' I said, secure within my own four walls, 'he's probably the kind of person who gets his kicks from frightening women. He won't come back to Sainsbury's or not your branch, at any rate. Maybe next time he'll try Tesco's!'

But next time it was Marks and Spencer, the Chiswick High Road branch. When that happened, I realised that the man was not, as I had hoped, a stranger to my area, someone who, having tried his luck in it and had his cover blown, was forced to move to other ground, but someone who was living near me. It was a depressing realisation.

Still, I thought, I couldn't be his only victim. He must follow other women.

'Maybe he did. Maybe he made a habit of it, drifting round from store to store, terrorising women shoppers, but whatever else he did, he went on stalking me as well. He turned up in Waterstone's Bookshop, lurked outside the Midland Bank, loitered by the Chiswick Restaurant. He seemed to be everywhere.

As the white-faced man persisted, I tried my best to shake him off. I asked to exit through back doors. I dodged and dived through other shops. I caught a bus to ride a block. In an effort to confuse, I drove all the way to Chelsea.

At least he didn't know where I lived. He hadn't got as far as that...

Apart from those in whom I was forced to confide when he followed me into their shops, I spoke to no one about his campaign. Talking about it would make it worse, I thought. To acknowledge him was to draw him further out of the shadows. And, surely, it was only a question of time before I was free of him. Sooner or later, I told myself, the Rat would grow weary of his pursuit and find himself another victim.

Casting him in the role of Rat, I was thinking back to childhood, remembering that other rat, the white rat which a boy, an admirer of my sister's (even at the age of nine, Darina had attracted boys) had let loose inside our house and which, in the week that followed before it was caught, had scampered onto my bed at night and right across my recumbent form.

The white-faced man was the Rat let loose again, fattened up to human size, clothed in men's apparel but as albescent as ever. And now he was there again, just across the road from me.

The saving grace was that he didn't appear to have noticed me standing on the steps but was intent upon his errand. Perhaps he needed milk himself, or a late edition of the *Evening Standard*. But he was living closer to me than I'd realised. Living with his mother, I imagined – a repressive,

21

elderly woman who laundered his clothes and cooked his meals and didn't permit him a life of his own, so he had his fantasies. His fantasies concerning me...

At least he hadn't spotted me this time. For safety's sake I'd have to postpone my shopping trip until he'd fetched his milk or paper and gone home again to Mama.

Which meant he was controlling me, dictating my movements. It made me wild. Retreating crossly inside the building, I slammed the front door in vexation.

There was a message on my answering machine.

'Brigit, darling, this is Mike. Give me a call when you get in. We should get together soon.'

Translated, this meant, as you'll be working with me this summer, we should put our heads together. My own programme was due to go off air for three months within the next few weeks. For the last two years, a short secondment to Radio 4 had taken care of the summer for me. In the past, this had seemed like a good idea. Mike Mabey was not unpleasant but he wasn't an ideas man. Which was why he needed mine. That made me wilder still.

And I didn't even have milk for tea.

That same week I saw the painting. When Louise suggested going, I thought that I'd be irritated. The artist, Conor Byrne, was Irish, 'the O'Casey of the art world'.

'Paddy-whackery,' I said.

'No, it's not,' Louise insisted. 'His last show

22

was a sell-out, Brigit. Brian Sewell raved about it. Waldemar Januszczak...'

Louise and her husband Tom owned a gallery in Barnes. They knew all the art reviewers.

I gave in.

The exhibition was on at the Janice Seton Gallery in Cork Street, convenient for lunch at Fenwicks.

Weather conditions hadn't changed. Wearing shoes that seemed to have shrunk, I emerged from Green Park Tube into unrelenting sunshine. Above the Ritz the Union Jack was hanging limply. The short walk from Piccadilly through the Burlington Arcade into Bond Street might have been a marathon, so exhausted did I feel when I reached my destination.

Inside Fenwicks, customers, abruptly transferred from the discomfort of the street into air-conditioned surroundings, were wandering around like bemused zombies. In Joe's Restaurant Bar, Louise, small and freckled and curly-haired, was waiting at a corner table.

We'd known each other since our schooldays but we were a class apart and couldn't then be described as friends. Meeting up in London later, we bonded like a pair of twins, although we were very different. Louise was stable and matter-of-fact, settled and focused and deeply committed. Reticent about herself, she was a delicious gossip.

'I ordered you a Perrier.'

'You're an angel. What did we do before mineral water?'

'Swallowed chlorine by the pint. I never even

23

tasted it. I'm dying to hear all your news. How are things with you and Simon?'

'We're not an item any more.'

'Aw, no, Brigit, not *again?*'

'Shall we order?' I said quickly.

But as soon as we'd done that Louise returned to the attack with the zeal of one who, having found *her* ideal partner, wants the world to emulate her.

'What happened?'

'*You* know. It wasn't going anywhere.'

'Meaning you got bored with him?'

'Not bored so much as... He's not dull. It isn't that. It – it didn't work between us,' I said, wriggling madly.

'He was crazy about you.'

'Oh, come on. He wasn't really. Anyway, that's not the point. I simply didn't fancy him. Or not enough to hang on in there.'

'Do you ever?' said Louise. The expression, three parts concern and one reproach, wasn't exactly unfamiliar. We'd been down this road before. It was strewn with the wreckage of my love affairs, none of which lasted for long.

I hastily turned the subject round. 'How's Tom? How's the gallery?'

Louise and Tom adored each other. She beamed at the chance to talk about him. 'He's fine. We're showing pottery now, you know, and it's going down a bomb.'

I was off the hook. For the moment, anyway.

Over lunch, Louise regaled me with the gossip of the art world. The artist Gerald Stewart had set up house with two women, one of whom was his sister-in-law. Muriel Tanner the sculptor had left her husband for a woman, a teacher at her daughter's school. The Parker Gallery was in trouble. Tony Parker had gone missing.

After lunch, we made our way back towards Burlington Gardens, past a British Gas lorry emitting the stench of propane gas and into Cork Street, where scaffolding over two of the galleries provided the shade that we were craving.

Our destination, a self-consciously modern gallery, was further down the street on the left-hand side. In the window three paintings had been judiciously placed to catch the eyes of passers-by. In front of one was a card which said 'Conor Byrne: The Island Paintings'.

Then it happened – just like that. The paintings cast a spell on me. I was magnetised, sucked away from sticky London into another, cooler place, where the air was fresh and pure and I was the only one breathing it.

Set in a sea that raged and glittered, the islands Conor Byrne depicted were splendid, wild and isolated. The rocks rising out of that volatile sea were black and blunt and menacing. Golden strands shrank back from them, fringed by deposits of carrageen moss. Above them purple cliffs loomed up. In the distance were ancient ruins – a medieval abbey and a star-shaped fort, a tumbledown cottage and a boat at anchor.

It was a land of astonishing contrast, bleak and rugged and mystical, tinted with the subtle shades of the tiny flowers that flourished there, blue and mauve and milky-pink, and the gaudier tone of the emerald grass.

'Louise, *look!*' I wanted to say. But delight had taken my voice away.

'Come on, Brigit. It's hot out here.'

I mutely followed Louise inside.

'Louise Cairns! How *are* you, darling?' An all-blonde woman – hair and suit and legs and shoes – wafted forward to greet Louise.

'Hi, Janice. How are *you?*'

A kissy-kissy scene developed. I left them to it and looked around. The paintings displayed on the gallery walls, suspended from steel wires and illuminated by tungsten lights, were larger than the three I'd seen in the window. But here again were the rocks and sea, the flowers and the ancient ruins. Here was a deserted strand. A sturdy, austere, stonework cottage. A currach and a sailing boat.

The work was unashamedly naturalist. I thought of Gauguin's words of advice: 'How do you see this tree? Is it green? Then use green, the most beautiful green you've got. And this shadow, does it look blue? Then make it as blue as you possibly can.'

Conor Byrne's shadows were grey, not blue. The way he used them startled me, for his shadows were of unseen people and objects outside the picture frame. I know that isn't a novel device. Many famous artists used it, long ago, like William Collins. And shadows, too, have been distorted. Think of Grandville and van Veen, whose shadows tell a different story from the figures that they painted.

The shadows Conor Byrne employed were less distorted than uncertain; undefined. You knew

26

that something was going on outside the limit of the picture frame but there was a smoke screen round it, creating mystery and disquiet.

I stopped by an untitled picture. Sea and clouds and dipping gulls. A whitewashed cottage, thatched – of course – standing on a grassy slope.

Predictable? Romantic? Charming? It might have been, without the shadow.

The shadow ran across the foreground. The shadow of a tree, I thought – or was it of a crucifix? I couldn't make out which it was, and that was unsettling. I shivered without knowing why, only knowing there was pain within the landscape I had entered.

It wasn't a myth, this place. The islands Conor Byrne depicted, Inishbofin and Inishark, lie off the coast of Connemara, a short distance from the mainland. No one lives on Inishark and very few on Inishbofin. No wonder they attracted me away from stuffy, sticky London. Particularly Inishark. No people. What a luxury, I thought, shifting my mind away from the pain so I needn't think about it and quickly moving from that painting.

There was so much else to see. So many other marvellous pictures.

Amongst them was another painting that stood out from all the others. It was of a seated figure, a red-haired woman dressed in green, positioned on a rock outcrop. You couldn't see the woman's face – she had turned her back to you – only her exquisite hair, long, with golden lights in it. Renoir painted hair like that, flowing down the model's back. But Renoir's women were plump and happy, with pearly bodies and artless ways. This woman was thin, very thin, almost emaciated and, though I couldn't see her face, she seemed too tense to be content.

She was painting. 'Hannah Painting' said the card on the wall beside the picture.

Was she painting the sea or the rocks, or the unseen source of the shadows? Again, the shadows were not defined. But they were shadows of little people. That, at least, I could make out. Little people playing games. Restless children gambolling, hopping, turning somersaults. Because they were so boisterous, I decided they were boys. The artist's family perhaps?

It was an idyllic scene – the rocks, the sea, that gorgeous hair – but, as with the picture of the cottage, something bothered me about it. That woman, Hannah, I concluded.

Whatever Hannah's problem was, she wasn't happy out there painting. Her back was much too tense for that. Maybe it was just her children, ruining her concentration. Perhaps the picture was a satire, commenting on family life. But it was a marvellous painting. I gazed at it and heard the sea pounding on those stark, black rocks. I thought of Ireland. Ached to be there.

'Give us your opinion, Brigit. Do you like the show?'

Louise, detached from Janice Seton, had finally caught up with me.

'It's wonderful,' I said sincerely. 'And you were right. We had to see it.'

I waited for Louise's comments. But Louise

was hesitant.

'Don't *you* think so?' I asked.

'Ye-es. I do. He's very clever.'

'But he doesn't knock you out?'

'Not exactly. You know, I saw his other show, the one he had a year ago, and...' She paused.

'And?'

'I think he's being repetitive. That cottage with the tree in front – the shadow of a tree, I mean...'

'I thought it was a crucifix.'

'Well, whatever. He pulled that one on us before. He's got a thing about it.'

'Artists are obsessive people.'

'Tell me about it!' Louise exclaimed. 'But it isn't only that. It's not so much the repetition...'

'Go on.'

Louise was tugging at her hair. She wrinkled up her nose and, after an even longer pause, said slowly, 'I think I felt this way before. When I saw the other show. But other things diverted me.'

'Lou,' I said, 'stop dithering. Tell me what you felt before.'

'It's just...' Another of those maddening pauses. Then, finally, 'The paintings are un-finished, Brigit.'

'Unfinished?' I looked again at 'Hannah Painting'. 'That is an *unfinished* picture?'

'I'm not talking technique, Bridge. That's not what I'm getting at. I mean, there's something missing from the paintings.'

'Missing?' I thought she was talking nonsense. 'You told me Brian Sewell loves them.'

'The last show – that was what I said he loved.

29

Maybe he likes this show too. If so, I'd agree with him. Conor Byrne's a major talent. But...'

'But what?' I was feeling quite indignant.

'He didn't say the guy's a master.'

'The show's a sell-out, all the same. Look at all those nice red stickers. Janice Seton must be ecstatic.'

'Oh, she is,' Louise said dryly. 'Hannah, on the other hand–'

'Hannah?'

'That's her, in the painting. Hannah Byrne. He's married to her. Well, in theory, anyway.'

'It's an open marriage, is it?'

Louise shrugged. 'He plays around. She drinks a lot.'

'So what else is new?' I said.

Louise discreetly dropped her voice. 'He's screwing Janice Seton,' she said.

'God!' I looked over to where Janice Seton was once more doing her kissy-kissy thing. So Conor Byrne is bedding her, I thought. No wonder Hannah's back is tense.'

I went back to that painting. I heard the sea and smelt the air and I was out there again. Back home, where I longed to be. And why not? I asked myself. Why can't I go where I want to be? Why can't I go back to Ireland – for the summer anyway?

No reason not, I said to myself. And then and there I made up my mind.

'Her husband knows,' Louise was saying. 'He doesn't care. Mind you...'

At that moment I didn't care much about Janice Seton either. I was ensorcelled, after all, and I'd other matters to think about. Plans to make.

'Louise,' I interrupted. 'Listen. I've just made a big decision...'

TWO

It felt like a huge decision, even if it sounded small – turning down that short secondment to Radio 4, going to Ireland for the summer. Putting it into practice proved comparatively simple. In less than a week it was all sorted out and I was free to go to Ireland.

Before I left I called Darina and she asked me down for lunch. My sister lived in Haslemere. The tranquil charm of rural Surrey, countrified without being wild, suited her extremely well. The unschematic windswept west, which had such appeal for me, was anathema to her. Forced to live in such conditions, I've no doubt she would have coped, the way Darina always did, but it wasn't right for her, any more than Surrey was for me.

As I set out for Haslemere I was in a sanguine mood, thinking of the plans I'd made. Roadworks plunged me into gloom, adding ages to the journey. Looking out at other drivers, I could see my own road rage reflected in their glowing faces. I told myself I was escaping, that soon, next week, I would be free, no longer trapped and impotent and breathing in noxious gases.

But I couldn't visualise it. What had made me want to see Darina? I thought furiously. We're not that close, for heaven's sake. By half past twelve, stuck, seemingly forever, on the London side of

Guildford, I'd transferred my wrath to her. I started to add up her faults. She was bossy and self-righteous. She always tried to put me down and while, in theory, I understood why I was a threat to her (she was six when I was born, established as an only child and much put out by my arrival), in practice her resentment threatened *me*. But we didn't *hate* each other... When the traffic flowed more freely, my indignation with her faded. I thought, Darina's loyal and kind at heart. She's so practical and honest. Why was I being mean about her when I know she'd stand by me even if I murdered someone?

By then, I was close to Haslemere. I consulted the directions which Robert, my brother-in-law, had faxed through to me from his office, turned off just before the town and drove up a country lane. The family had recently moved from a Charles Church neo-Geo to a rambling paradise, the core of which was Jacobean. Extensions added to it later, so Darina had informed me, had produced a maze of rooms, cubbyholes and awkward corners. Although the council had objected (paradise was Grade II listed and permission was essential before commencing alternations), Darina swept aside their doubts. Now the house had five big bedrooms, each one with a bathroom en suite. The problems that had come with it – subsidence, wet rot, no back drainage – had been tackled by my sister with the same ferocity she had shown towards the council.

There was an oak tree by the gate and others dotted round the garden. The trees were looking rather woolly – the one beside the house was old, gnarled and balding, out of Grimms – but their broad, rounded, dense crowns cast welcome shade around the grounds.

I parked at the side of the house and dragged myself into the heat. There was no one to be seen but the heavy, oak-panelled front door was open and I went inside, intrigued to see what had been done in the way of decorating.

The hall was painted fuschia pink. Two gilt chairs, upholstered purple, stood beside a gilded table. Typical Darina décor. A bit ornate, in my opinion, but our tastes were very different.

The drawing room was papered coral, toned to match the floral curtains. Darina was on duty there, on her knees in a sea of bubblewrap, unpacking pottery and glasses.

'Oh, *there* you are,' she said. 'You're late.'

You'd never think that we were sisters. Darina was tall and willowy, with ash-blonde hair and dark blue eyes. Her face was long without being horsey. She had high cheekbones and a slender nose and skin as fine as Belek china. The sort of looks I'd have killed for. Joe's looks.

'Sorry. The traffic's awful out of Guildford. Where are Robert and the children?'

'He took them out for riding lessons. Here, hold this.' Darina handed me an ironstone bowl and delved in the box again.

I recognised the ironstone bowl. It was mine. I'd left it at Darina's house before going abroad, along with other goods and chattels. When I took them back again, I found the bowl had been extracted. I looked at it now, thinking again how pretty it was. The colours, blue and orange, had been painted on by children employed by Mason's. Transfer patterns were put on and kids as young as nine or ten years shown how to fill them in.

'I love the colours in that bowl,' Darina said, rising from her knees and wading through the bubblewrap to retrieve the bowl from me. 'I've used them in the dining room. The bowl looks marvellous in there.' So lay off it, said her face.

It wasn't worth an argument.

'Dar,' I said. 'I've got some news. I'm going to Ireland for the summer.'

'Going to Ireland? But what for?'

'To research an article. On the arts scene over there. For the *Independent on Sunday*.'

'How much will you get paid for that?'

I told her what the paper said.

'You can't live on that,' she said.

'No. But I'm going to let my flat. That will cover my expenses.'

'Are you going to stay with Mammy?'

'For the time I'll be in Dublin. But I'm going to move around. Catch the mood of the country-side. It's all happening over there – music, films, art, theatre.' I developed this theme, explaining about the success of the five-year government plan to upgrade the arts in Ireland.

'Are you going to take the car?'

'No,' I said, having just decided that. 'I won't need a car in Dublin.'

'But you'll be moving round the country.'

'I'll catch a train. Or go by bus.'

Before she could comment further, Robert

came in with the children, the twins, Clare and Noeline, who were eight, and Mikey, who had just turned five.

'Hello, Aunty Brit,' they chorused.

'Good to see you,' Robert said.

'Brigit's going to Ireland, Robert.'

'Off on holidays again?'

'It's an article I'm writing. For the–'

'Come through to the dining room,' Darina interrupted us. 'You three, go and tidy up. Don't forget to brush your hair. Robert, get a drink for Brigit.'

I found it quite remarkable the way Darina bossed her husband. Robert was MD of a large aviation company employing several thousand people, all of whom looked up to him. At home, Darina was the big controller. Still, the marriage worked for them. I think he was amused by her.

The children, having tidied up, joined us at the luncheon table. Mikey looked rather worried. There was nothing new in that. He was a nervous child by nature and made more so by his sisters who were an assertive pair. I liked him best of all the children. Looking at his anxious face, I wondered what was bugging him. Later on, we'd have a talk and maybe I could reassure him.

'How was riding?' I asked now.

Clare and Noeline pulled a face.

'Pan-*do*-monium,' said Clare. 'Mrs Jackson had hysterics.'

'Why?'

'Her husband has walked out on her,' Noeline announced.

I caught Darina's eye and grimaced. In that

moment we *were* close, our thoughts reverting back to Joe. I was six when he left home. My memory of his face was hazy, but his voice I could remember.

'A gorgeous voice. The voice of a storyteller. The voice of Joe the magic maker who searched inside his treasure chest for wonders that would flabbergast me. The chest was only in his mind but it had seemed real to me. A black tin chest, I'd thought it was, with his full name, John Joseph Flood, printed in gold letters on it. Inside the chest were jewels and silks, voiles and scent and tasselled sashes, and bottles made of coloured glass, the things that Joe had bought for me on the journeys he had taken. There were shells in there as well, big conch shells from India, and pansy shells from Mozambique, flat with little faces on them, and once a flock of red flamingos which had flown across the bay to mingle with the local seagulls...

'Never mind,' Darina said briskly. 'I'm sure he hasn't gone for ever.'

'But he has,' insisted Clare. 'He's gone off with another woman.'

That was not why Joe left home, not for a specific woman. In a way, that made it worse. It made Mammy face the fact that he left because of *her*. She could have blamed another woman. Said she was a ruthless bitch, or that her youth and beauty lured him. As it was, she had two choices, to blame herself or censure Joe. Naturally she hit on Joe.

I always thought of him as Joe. Daddy was that dreadful man who walked out on all of us. Joe was, well, the magic maker. Joe was – Harlequin.

He told me once he'd gone to Rome, so that he could see a play.

'A play?'

'A pantomime for grown-ups, Brigit. Let me show you.'

He leapt up, grabbed a cushion, Mammy's un-completed tapestry, a skein of wool, a silver bowl, and took me to the pantomime. In our sitting room in Dalkey I was introduced by Joe to the comic routines of *commedia dell'arte*.

I met them all through him that day. Pantoline, the merchant in his ill-fitting clothes. The mis-shapen rascal, Pucinella. The Captain, the Doctor and Columbine. Agile Harlequin the acrobat.

Harlequin as played by Joe was, for me, the superstar.

'You didn't have to act *that* part,' I said when the curtain had come down and Joe had joined me on the sofa.

'I didn't?'

'No. Harlequin is just like you.' Exciting. Funny. Fascinating. Bewitching. Charming. Full of life.

Darina's eyes were still on me. She smiled at me across the table. She said, 'Forget about Mrs Jackson. It's not our business, what has hap-pened.'

'But it is,' Noeline persisted. 'They're going to close the stables down. Then Mrs Jackson's going away. She says she's going to live in Norfolk.'

Joe did not move far away – or not in miles, at any rate. The four of us still lived in Dublin, three in Dalkey, one in Howth. I never saw the house in Howth. After the break-up, Joe agreed he wouldn't see us until we had finished school. Darina took him up on that the year she did her Leaving Cert. He died before I reached that stage.

'We'll find another riding school.'

Darina started serving lunch. As usual, it was delicious – salmon with a cous-cous crust, followed by a rhubarb pie.

Having done justice to this feast, I'd planned to have a chat with Mikey, but I didn't get the chance. After coffee, Darina shooed the others out and asked if I would come upstairs. To see what else she'd done, I thought, and marvel at her renovations.

Instead, she ushered me into the master bedroom (quite dramatic, black and lemon) and said that she had something for me.

'You have?'

'Yes.'

She hesitated, then added, 'I've been bad about it, Brigit.'

'Bad about what?' I said, mystified by her behaviour.

'It's something that was meant for you, but I kept it for myself. I was jealous, I suppose.'

'Jealous? Of me?'

None of this was making sense.

'Of what Daddy felt about you. And then – downstairs – when I saw the way you looked, I realised what he meant to you.'

What is going on? I thought. Darina talking about feelings?

'All through lunch I kept on thinking that I had

to hand it over.'

'You can keep that bowl, Darina.'

'It's not a bowl I'm giving you.'

'It's not?'

'No.'

'What is it then?'

She handed me a little box. 'Go on. Open it,' she said.

I did, and found a signet ring. A man's ring, by the look of it.

'What's this?'

'It's Daddy's ring,' Darina said. 'You used to say how much you liked it when you were a little girl.'

'Did I? I'd forgotten about that.'

'When I saw him that first time he said that I should give it to you. I'm really, really sorry, Brigit.'

'Oh, God,' I said. 'I'm going to cry.'

Actually, we both shed tears. When we'd pulled ourselves together, I put on the signet ring. Although it was too big for me, I said I'd never take it off.

'And you *can* keep the Mason's bowl.'

All that put Mikey right out of my head. By the time I did remember, I was on the motorway, wedged in yet another jam.

The following week I left for Ireland. I went to Heathrow on the Tube, thinking I was travelling light, with just my laptop and one case. After I left the flat, the case appeared to put on weight. As I lugged it up the steps from the Underground, three men turned and smirked at me, enjoying my discomfiture.

Inside Terminal One I joined an Aer Lingus queue stretched back to the Body Shop. In front of me was a beautiful black woman dressed in an elegant grey shift with a baby in her arms. The child, a boy, had dimples in his rosy cheeks and folds of skin round his wrists. I smiled at him and he smiled back, showing off his brand new teeth. He really was adorable.

I met them later on the plane. The baby boy sat next to me. His mother, having settled him, sank into the aisle seat and smoothed the creases from her dress. Don't disturb me, said her face.

The 'fasten seat belts' sign came on. Here we go again, I thought. I was terrified of planes. It's not that crashing bothered me – not in theory, anyway. I just feared the floor would open and that I'd fall through the crack. Only Liquorice Allsorts helped. I had brought a packet with me. I popped a sweet into my mouth, closed my eyes and tried to visualise those paintings. Pounding waves on shore and rocks … I was on my way to Ireland. Within the month I'd head off west. Go to Galway. Have a look around the Taibhdhearc, the theatre of the *Fíor Gaeilgoiri*, the true Irish speakers, where all productions, even opera, were through the medium of Irish. After that–

A hand reached out and touched my knee. Opening my eyes, I saw that the baby boy was trying to take the sweets from me. I let him have a beady one. He ate the sweet with greedy relish and put out his hand again. His eyes were huge and black and liquid. He was irresistible. I let him have another one.

His mother disregarded us. I wondered if she

41

was a model – she looked as if she could be one. What a snooty cow, I thought, feeling crushed by her aloofness.

Her son and I ate all the sweets. He gurgled and beamed delightedly when I made funny faces at him.

The plane dipped, prior to landing, and as it did so, the baby without any warning, vomited all over me.

'Oh, my God!' exclaimed his mother, suddenly becoming human. 'I'm sorry. Has he ruined your shirt?'

'It's not his fault. I gave him sweets.'

'You poor thing,' his mother said, producing wads of tissue paper and trying to mop up the damage.

Later, when we'd disembarked, she came up to me again, by which time I'd sponged myself in the ladies' room and, though damp, was clean again.

'That's a silk shirt you have on. I must pay for your dry cleaning.'

'It's not necessary,' I said. 'I promise you it's washable.'

Still protesting, she walked beside me through the blue EU channel and into the arrivals hall. I saw my mother waiting there, holding a copy of *Homes and Gardens*. Spotting me, she held it up.

'Brigit!'

The magazine disgorged its contents, ads for other magazines and subscription slips for them. Instantly, as if summoned by a wand, a burly hunk of a man appeared and picked the leaflets up for her.

'Thank you,' I could see her mouthing. 'That's really very kind of you.'

The man went red and lumbered off.

'Hello, Mammy.'

'Hello, Brigit.'

We didn't hug, we just touched cheeks; that way I wouldn't muss her clothes.

'Who were they that you were with?'

The other two had disappeared.

'I sat beside them on the plane.'

'You're just like your father, Brigit, always picking up strangers. Your shirt's all wet. What happened to it?'

'I'll tell you later on.' I said. Already, I was getting peevish. It didn't take me very long to get cranky with my mother. My irritation permeated from a sense of isolation. Add a pinch of guilt to this. No, not a pinch, a whole big heap, because I couldn't be the person Mammy wished I was, which would be the clone of her, not Brigit the iconoclast.

I told myself to act composed, to take my mother in good part. Hadn't I misjudged Darina? I mustn't make the same mistake in dealing with my mother now.

Trailing my case along behind me, I followed her to where she had parked her car and off-loaded my luggage into the boot. We set off in silence for Dalkey. Mammy never talking in cars. She said that it distracted the driver. I was grateful for the silence, the chance to ease back into Dublin.

We drove past the docks and across the east link toll bridge until we reached the southern

43

suburbs. Sandymount. Monkstown. Blackrock. Dun Laoghaire. For me, each had its own association which came from my father's stories. Foxhunts, shipwrecks, highwaymen. Ancient crosses. Melon feasts.

Mammy's house – what had been our family home – was in a quiet cul-de-sac. It was one of those pretty Georgian cottages which was much larger than it looked, fronting directly on to the street with the garden in the back. I noticed that it had been re-painted and was now a delicate peach with the door, the fanlight and the sash windows picked out in frosty white.

Inside, it was peach as well. As soon as we were in the door, three large balls of white wool hurtled down the stairs at us. Maltese poodles are supposed to be sociable by nature but they also tend to snap at strangers. Mammy's dogs, Bo, Vi and Godiva, were no exceptions to this rule. Godiva bared her teeth at me.

'Don't upset her,' Mammy said. 'She's having problems with her ears.'

'Is she?'

'You never took to dogs and cats.'

'That's not true. I love them, Mammy. I just can't have a pet in London.'

'If you still worked for RTE you could.'

This was Mammy's favourite subject: why did I leave RTE? To extend myself, I'd say. To explore what might be out there. Exploration was dangerous ground. It always got us back to Joe.

So, this time round, I didn't react. I was dying to phone Lorcan, but I'd only just arrived and if I called him now, Mammy would feel pushed

44

aside. Making contact with my friends wasn't on the first night home. And Lorcan fell into the same category – the Danger File – as my need for exploration. After all, Lorcan used to be *Joe's* friend. The man who still stayed close to Joe after he deserted Mammy.

I wasn't close to Lorcan Burke until I worked at RTE. I had a job on *Live at Three*, an afternoon magazine programme for mass audience that ran through the working week. The programme was very popular, covering a wide range of subjects – music, fashion, cookery, antiques, weddings, farming news – in a lively, chatty manner.

One afternoon, we had a slot about memory recall which linked up to another story about child abuse that had been running in the papers all that week. Just how valid were our memories? To examine that, the presenters, Derek Davies and Thelma Mansfield, interviewed a range of experts, amongst whom was Lorcan Burke.

Lorcan worked from memory and painted in a naive style. Naive painting puzzled people. It was not something that was taught, and it wasn't logical. As Lorcan Burke explained that day, it comes through from the subconscious. Something gets a hold of you, he said, and the artist that's possessed is forced to realise his vision. He spoke honestly and simply, sounding neither mad nor precious.

Afterwards, he asked for me.

'You're Joe Flood's daughter, Brigit, aren't you? Your father was friend of mine.'

We went across to Madigan's.

'How did you meet Joe?' I asked.

My father was a barrister. Not that this would stop them meeting. Dublin is a melting pot, Gossip City, where professions intermingle not only to exchange ideas but to pry and analyse. In Joe, talking was an aptitude, one which would have sought expression in a crowded smoky pub with Anaglypta on the walls.

'In my studio,' said Lorcan.

'He went there to buy a painting?' If so, I had never seen it.

'He was interested in art.'

In *everything*, I might have said. But I was intrigued by the idea of Joe turning up on Lorcan's doorstep, seemingly out of the blue, and saying, look, I'm curious. Someone told me that you paint.

'He came without an introduction?'

'His car broke down in Benburb Street. He asked if he could make a phone call. Then he saw what I was doing...'

Well, that was much more like our Joe. According to Darina's stories, he was un-mechanical. His cars were always giving trouble.

'When would this have been?' I asked.

'Twenty years or more ago.'

'Did he bring you to our house?'

'I went there once or twice,' said Lorcan. 'You were just a baby then.'

We ordered up another round. I felt that I could grow fond of Lorcan, not as a man, you understand – to me he was asexual – but as someone I could trust. And then there was all that talent. He'd already made his name. Despite the national conviction that all artists should feel

46

pain and reflect it in their work, Lorcan painted happy pictures, ones in which religious themes were allied to the pastoral. A little puzzled by them at first, the establishment in Ireland afterwards accepted them and it was fashionable now to possess a Lorcan Burke.

I wondered if my father owned one – he must have done, if they were friends – and if so what had happened to it. I asked Lorcan about that. But he said he didn't know, and then that he had to go.

We arranged to meet again and after that we kept in touch. As we got to know each other, Lorcan told me more of Joe. How stimulating, passionate and well-informed my father was. The gift he had for reaching people and bringing out the best in them. His wit that had no malice in it. How often he had mentioned me.

There was a void in me for Joe, and Lorcan didn't fill it. In fact, he made it grow. I was insatiable for stories and any scrap of information made Joe live again for me.

Lorcan's value in my life intensified as time went by. His vast knowledge of the arts, passed on so willingly to me, helped my career at RTE and got me to the BBC. And it could help again, I thought. Before I started my research, I had to talk to Lorcan Burke.

'You're back in your old room,' said Mammy.

My former bedroom was transformed from the tip it used to be. It looked lovely – blue and white, with a Descamps duvet cover, floral pictures on the walls and fresh pink roses in a stoneware jug.

'Thank you for the roses, Mammy,' I said, moved by the gesture.

'I got them from the garden, Brigit. This year has been good for roses They need a lot of looking after.' She went on talking about roses – the planting mixture that they need, how much watering they like, how they last until November. I know nothing about gardening. Conversations about soil preparation, planting and aftercare act on me like sleeping pills. I stifled a yawn, glancing slyly at my watch.

It was only half past three and here I was, already bored, wanting to get on with things instead of chatting to my mother. A sense of shame came over me.

'I want to hear about Darina,' she said.

I told her all about Darina, about the children and the house. By then it was ten to four. Six more hours before I could decently excuse myself on the basis of being weary...

'Can I do some shopping for you?'

'We've got everything we need.'

I ironed my clothes and hung them up. That got us through to five o'clock. Mammy checked the TV programmes.

'*EastEnders* is on at half past seven.'

I wondered what intrigued my mother about the people in *EastEnders*. *The Commitments* horrified her. She carried on about 'those accents' as if they had a smell to them. I swear the vowel sounds shocked her more than the use of the expletives. If RTE produced a soap set in Finglas or Baldoyle, Mammy wouldn't deign to watch it. But England had a cachet for her. She might regret I no longer worked for RTE but she was proud that I was with the BBC.

'We'll have our suppers on a tray,' she said.

I sat down next to her, resigned to half an hour with Ian and his trials and tribulations. Godiva bared her teeth at me.

'Pass that napkin, Brigit, please.'

I passed the napkin and Mammy's eyes lit on the ring. There was a disapproving silence. Then she said in a hollow voice, 'That's your father's ring you're wearing.'

'Yes.' I couldn't very well deny it.

'And how did you get hold of it?'

I hesitated, wondering what I should say. If I told the truth, it would make trouble for Darina.

'Lorcan gave the ring to me. The last time I came to Dublin.'

'I could never stand that man. He's homosexual, of course.'

'Mammy–'

'I know a lot of artists are. No wonder we have AIDS in Ireland.'

I groaned, and Godiva turned her head and growled at me.

'He was mad about your father. The two of them were strange together.'

'You're telling me that Joe was gay?'

'Of course not. The thought of it! But still, he gave that ring to Lorcan. There may be other things as well. Other things he gave away. Things his daughters should have had. Has that ever crossed your mind?'

The only thing that crossed my mind was how to stop this conversation. But just then the phone

49

rang in the hall and Mammy went to answer it. I took advantage of her absence to take the plates through to the kitchen.

She's going to drive me wild, I thought. She's even worse than she used to be. There was no way I could phone Lorcan from the house. I'd have to go to town to call him.

The next morning I got up at six and caught the DART to Pearse Street station. Mr Mehta had been wrong. Not a drop of rain was falling and Dublin was as hot as London. But the train was not crowded and at this early hour not many people were about.

I walked the short distance to Grafton Street. It wasn't so long since I'd been back. The year before we'd all been over for Mammy's sixtieth birthday party, celebrated in style at the Shelbourne Hotel, and the year before that I'd been in Dublin on my own to set up an interview.

Those visits were on different levels. They were other people's journeys. This was mine. My own peculiar quest. Again, I thought about the paintings and how they had called out to me.

It was too early for the street musicians but the flower stalls were already stacked with vibrant early summer flowers and Bewley's café never closed. Lured in by the smell of coffee, bread and scones and cherry buns, I went up to the mezzanine floor and found a table by the window. Within the year, there'd been a change. The waitresses had gone contemporary and in place of their old-fashioned black dresses, white aprons and traditional lace-trimmed caps, they now wore black trousers, white shirts and

50

fashionable waistcoats.

This is more like it, I said to myself, ordering a sizzling breakfast and guzzling coffee topped with cream.

It was still too early to phone Lorcan so when I'd finished feeding my face, I went across to Temple Bar and wandered round the cobbled streets. The violin makers had long gone from the district, along with the hatters, the dye sellers and the feather merchants, and some of the old street names – Blind Quay, Fish Street, Scarlet Abbey – had been replaced with modern ones. But the new developers had worked well and sensitively and the area had become a successful, upmarket home for young designers and the film crowd.

At ten, I made my way to Angelsea Street and called Lorcan from Bloom's Hotel.

'Come on over,' Lorcan said.

'You mean over to Benburb Street?' This was something new. I'd never been to Lorcan's home. I'd always met him in a pub, or sometimes in a restaurant.

'Yes, why not?' said Lorcan.

Why not indeed? I went on foot to Benburb Street, crossing the river by the Halfpenny Bridge and walking along Ormond Quay. Mammy would have had a fit if she'd known where I was going. Benburb Street isn't far from Collins' Barracks, so the hookers hang out there, and the dossers and the winos. The area is sparsely populated with a few commercial units and a sprinkling of pubs and shops.

There was no one in the street. I walked past a green post office, Bargain Town and Benburn

Motors until I reached a red-brick house. Like the street, it looked rundown. There was no knocker on the door and the door itself was badly in need of a coat of paint.

I was about to bang on it when it was suddenly wrenched open.

'It's good to see you,' Lorcan said.

He hadn't changed. He never did. He was in his fifties, one of those people who, it seems, start out life as middle-aged and remain middle-aged for ever, a short, small-boned, wiry man with sandy, slightly greying hair.

We didn't kiss. We never touched. He stepped aside to let me in. The hall was tiny, more a cupboard than a room, completely bare of furniture.

'In here,' Lorcan said.

'Here' was a bed-sitting room. Once, it would have been two rooms but a wall had been knocked out and now there was only one, with a sofa bed in it, a few chairs that didn't match and a wobbly coffee table. I was surprised, I must admit. I'd expected more of Lorcan – if not style or luxury, at least comfort in his life. This was truly Spartan living. And the room was in a mess, with clothes and books on the floor and unwashed crockery in the sink.

He watched me take this in and said, 'Mrs Mac's been sick this week. She normally looks after me. I don't know what I'd do without her.'

'Don't worry. You should see my flat. Is your studio upstairs?'

'Yes. Another room the size of this. I had to build a bathroom on.' He gestured towards another doorway. 'It's through there if you should need it. Will you be in Dublin long?'

'That depends.' I told him why I had come over and about my article. 'I hoped that you might help me with it. I'm out of touch. I need updating.'

He was a fount of information. I jotted down the names he gave me, not just those of other artists but of writers and musicians and contacts in the Film Centre.

'That's Dublin in a nutshell for you,' he said at last. 'Now let's do the provinces.'

That brought us round to Conor Byrne.

'I saw his show the other day.'

'I hear he's made a killing with it. You know he's opening Young EVA, do you?' EVA – the annual Exhibition of Visual Art – was a major art event. Young EVA was the junior section.

'So where is that being staged?' I asked.

'In Limerick. At the Belltable Arts Centre.'

Built to be an opera house so the daughter of the owner could demonstrate her talent there, the Belltable in the nineties was primarily a theatre, with an exhibition gallery. It was a hive of cultural life in Limerick and the surrounding countryside, whose aim was to expand access not only to the performing arts but also to the visual.

Lorcan said, 'I have an invitation somewhere.' He rooted round until he found it, buried underneath some books. 'It's on the seventeenth.' That was just ten days away. 'That's important for you, Brigit. Young EVA can be controversial.'

'I know.'

Young EVA showed the best work of students

53

from Limerick city centre schools who had participated in a series of weekend workshops with the adult EVA artists. The purpose of the workshops was to bring the student into contact with a wide variety of contemporary art styles and practices. Central to the show's success was its ability to help young people familiar with literal and figurative painting come to terms with that of contemporary artists who often produced abstract work.

'Why choose Conor Byrne?' I asked. 'He's not an abstract artist, Lorcan.'

'True, but he's a brilliant speaker.'

'Fair enough, I guess. Are you going down yourself?'

'I can't afford the time,' said Lorcan. 'Why don't you go instead of me?'

'Oh, yes. That's a great idea.'

'Good.' He handed me the invitation. 'Let me know how you get on.'

Limerick isn't on the coast. I didn't hear the pounding sea. But I had the strange conviction that a route had been mapped out and that I must follow it. Not that I told Lorcan that. I thanked him for the help he'd given, stowed away the notes I'd taken, pocketed the invitation and asked him if he fancied lunch.

Walking back along the quays, I realised I was off the hook as far as Mammy was concerned. The next nine days I would be busy, following up on Lorcan's contacts. Then I would be Limerick-bound.

THREE

The next nine days were quite productive. The contacts Lorcan had provided proved invaluable to me. Everybody had a view, and not just about the arts scene. Three days into my research I could have written a gossip column as well as the commissioned feature. As I soon found out, the visual arts in particular was a rich field for picking up the latest scandal. It was divided into two major groups – the forces of modernism and the academic standard bearers, both of whom detested each other. As I listened, fascinated, reputations were destroyed, sexual proclivities were revealed and artists and gallery owners dismissed as 'street bandits', 'ya hoos' and 'so sharp' they stood in danger of cutting themselves.

Along the line, I also learnt a little more about the painter Conor Byrne. A major talent he might have been but he wasn't popular in Dublin. The success of his London show made his fellow artists feel that he should be trashed at home, to contain his arrogance.

'That fellow got it all too easy,' the director of a gallery told me within minutes of our meeting.

'He comes from a wealthy family?'

'No, but he married into money, not to mention the connections.'

'Is her father a politician?'

'Don't tell me that you didn't know! Her father's Seamus Talbot-Kelly.'

'Is that so? I never heard.'

Mammy would have been impressed. Seamus Talbot-Kelly was a famous film star, an Abbey actor who had cracked it when he went to Hollywood. Although he was no longer young, he was still a potent symbol. I thought, wait until I tell Louise. How come she slipped up on that one?

We were in the Shelbourne bar when I got this information. Socialising was essential for the work that I was doing. A lot of dinners were consumed – the people who were helping me were often busy in the daytime, which meant meeting them at night. My mother was upset by this.

'You mightn't be at home at all for all the while you spend with me.'

'I know,' I said. 'I'm sorry, Mammy.' What a hypocrite I was.

'You're the image of your father. He was always going out, making friends in bars and pubs. Peculiar friends like Lorcan Burke. No doubt you're spending time with him.'

'You've got loads of friends as well,' said I, edging round this snaggy question.

'My friends have husbands with them, Brigit. Husbands that stay home at night instead of roaming round the city, the way your father used to do.'

'When I've finished my research...' It would be no different then. I knew that, and so did she. It was becoming increasingly obvious that I couldn't stay in Dublin. Once I'd finished my research, I'd have to make another plan and find a quiet place to write.

Meanwhile, there were five more days – five more nights holed up in Dalkey. We survived without a row, though we got very close to it the night before I left for Limerick. Godiva was the cause of it. I'd got quite used to Vi and Bo, and they were tolerant of me. Godiva was a different matter. She was very highly strung, neurotically hyperactive, incapable of staying still when I was around the house.

That last evening I decided to pour oil on troubled waters by spending it at home with Mammy. But, carrying in our supper tray, I trod on Godiva's paw. She promptly nipped me on the ankle and, naturally, I swore at her.

Mammy said, 'Brigit, just watch your language.'

'Mammy!'

'I hope you haven't hurt her paw. Come here and let me see it, pet.'

Pet! I left the two of them alone and went upstairs to pack a bag. The roses in the vase were wilting. I dumped them, and felt better for it. Later, when I went downstairs, I found Mammy had dozed off, with Godiva on her knee. We did not meet up again before I fled the house at dawn.

I went to Limerick on the train, intending to stay overnight. The paper coughed up for expenses, so I'd made a hotel booking. No more traffic jams for me. The proximity of the Royal George Hotel to the Belltable Arts Centre would entail merely a short stroll across and up O'Connell Street.

The dawn departure left me with a free

afternoon in Limerick which I should have spent at EVA, checking out the adult work. I spent it at the shops instead, emerging triumphantly from Todds with an apple-green Escada jacket, in the full knowledge that if I'd waited a few weeks more I could have bought it in the sales. This made the jacket seem more precious. I took it back to the hotel and tried it on a second time. Success! I'll wear it at the show, I thought. Except I hadn't brought a skirt or trousers that would go with it.

Determined now to wear the jacket, I went back to Todds again. Escada had a matching skirt hanging up on the rail. A size 10. I took it to the changing room. It was too tight across the hips. They didn't have the next size up. A navy skirt? No, not this season. Oh, well, never mind, I thought. I'll try one of the other labels. There's bound to be a navy skirt, perhaps in Windsmoor or in Planet.

But all the other skirts looked wrong when I tried them with that jacket. Then I got lucky. The shop assistant from Escada ran towards me with a skirt.

'Someone's just returned a twelve!'

'Brilliant!'

I didn't even try it on. This wasn't such a good idea because, back at the hotel again, the skirt turned out to be too small. I had to pull my stomach in in order to do up the zip. I cursed myself for going out and pigging it in restaurants.

Too late now. The skirt would have to do and who would notice anyway in the crush that there would be?

I was right about the crush. I arrived to find the foyer of the Belltable packed with artists, students and lecturers from the School of Art and Design, people from the Limerick arts community, priests and members of the public, all of whom were talking loudly in an effort to be heard.

I couldn't see the pictures but the crowd that had assembled might well have been an abstract painting, what with all the colours and the range of clothes on show. There were men in tweeds and leather with their hair in pony tails, youths in jeans and denim jackets, pre-Raphaelites with flowing locks, and a marvellous black-haired woman in a scarlet velvet dress, a nose-ring and Doc Marten boots with silver chains tied onto them. Girls in navy sweatshirts embossed with the Belltable logo circulating, carrying drinks.

'I've not seen you in years!' yelled someone. 'Tell me, are you still in town!'

'I am!'

'We'll have to get together then.'

I fought my way through to where a group of anxious parents were scrutinising student work.

'But it's all brown and tan and black,' I heard a puzzled mother say.

'Quiet, please!'

Gradually, the noise abated. A woman in a silky sweater took her place upon a dais.

'Ladies and gentlemen, you are really welcome here.'

There was a little more of this, an allusion to the high quality of work by young people over the last three months as they explored the field of contemporary art and tried to make a meaning of

59

it, and an announcement that Conor Byrne – 'maybe our most prestigious modern artist' was about to make a speech. The woman stepped down from her pedestal, to be replaced by Conor Byrne.

A clique of students started clapping. A photographer rushed forward. Burning with curiosity, I squeezed between a pair of parents to get a better look.

Frankly, I was disappointed. Conor Byrne was not good-looking. He was tall and strongly well-built but his face was pale and craggy and his nose overshadowed lips that were much too thin. His hair was mousy brown and curly, long and tied back in a knot. I put him down as forty-ish. Despite the hair, he looked un-arty. He was wearing dark blue cords and a blue and green Gant shirt that I had seen on sale in Harrods.

He smiled, waiting for the noise to die down again. When it did, he started talking. At once, I was captivated. His voice was just like Frank Delaney's, so much so that, for a moment, I thought my eyes were playing tricks and that it *was* Frank up there, speaking to us in that splendid, mellow, honeyed voice that made *Bookshelf* what it was.

With such a gorgeous voice, it was appropriate that Conor Byrne should begin his speech by talking to us about music, informing us that Kandinsky had confessed a debt to Wagner. It was *Lohengrin*, he said, that showed the artist an 'unsuspected power' in art. 'As a result, for him, a work of art came into being "in the same way as the cosmos, through a series of cataclysms which, finally, out of the chaotic roar of the instruments, form a symphony called the music of the spheres." This is the man whose first abstract painting – *the* first abstract work – was actually a watercolour.'

He spoke at length about Kandinsky before moving on to Kupka, Delaunay, Picabia and Mondrian. Then, making a connection between purity and discipline on the one hand and artificial mystique on the other, he changed tack. Anger crept into the voice. He talked disdainfully of a movement designed, so he said, to make the mythical man in the street feel alienated from painting and cut off from artists, whom he was encouraged to see as precious, weedy and pathetic.

'The instigators of this movement converse in a dialect that is known to us as "arts speak". People think this is a language spoken by the cognoscenti, by the arbiters of taste. It's not. It's just an affectation. A few long words that were invented by the founders of a club that's no different from the Freemasons. We're talking now about the need for elitist codes and signs…'

They were loving it, eating it up. Spontaneous applause broke out, to be quenched by cries of 'Ssh!'

'This isn't only arrogance. It's false, a lie that denies the very essence of the arts. A technique that is designed to keep people at a distance – except the members of the club. The true artist has no need for such devices. His prerequisites are talent, honesty and courage, and a taste for anarchy.'

It wasn't just the voice, I thought. It was the delivery – the gestures and the confidence. And, of course, the speech itself. I wasn't quibbling with the words which seemed true enough to me. 'Matisse used to tell his students, if you want to be a painter, you must first cut out your tongue. In his words, you, as artists, only have the right to use your brush to express yourself. So don't let arts speak get to you. And don't think you need to use it. You don't need to join a club. You only need to use your brushes...'

Afterwards, they lionised him. In seconds, much to my dismay, the crowd closed in and swallowed him up. It was a bad moment. I couldn't let him disappear. I needed a few words from him – more, no doubt, than I would use when I wrote my article but that was beside the point, not something that he'd know about until he read it in the paper. Apart from that, it was important for my own state of mind to meet the man whose paintings had cast that spell on me.

Muttering 'Sorry' and 'Excuse me, please' I managed to get out of there. From the doorway, I got a better view of where the action seemed to be. And, yes, there was Conor Byrne, wedged between three young men, Silky Sweater and the black-haired woman in the scarlet dress.

Silky Sweater was all over him. I saw him shake his head at her. She shrugged her shoulders, looking wistful. He turned to talk to other people and he shook his head again. It struck me that he was making his apologies; that he was on the brink of leaving, opting for an early night. That would disappoint all those who had organised the evening but it suited me quite well. Instead of fighting my way back in, queuing up to interview him, I could nab him as he left.

What if he nipped out the back and I missed him in the process? But it didn't seem likely. Though celebrities complain that the press intrudes on them, most of them – artists in particular – enjoy their fame enormously and like basking in the limelight. They're not by nature back-door people. I took a bet that Conor Byrne would be the same as all the rest. Doubtless Seamus Talbot-Kelly had taught him how to make an exit.

Whether that was true or not, he did head in my direction but not for nearly fifteen minutes. I waited by the door for him, feeling quite relaxed about it. Since I'd listened to that speech, I'd cheered up enormously. The tension I'd endured in Dublin and before that back in London had gone out of me completely. I've disentangled myself, I thought. I'm free. I'm out on the open road again. The sense of release was exhilarating, affecting not only my mind but my limbs and muscles too, all of which had loosened up. It even struck me that my skirt had settled down around my hips and no longer felt so tight.

Funny how a state of mind, irritation and ennui, could affect the body also, so it could become quite bloated. Whereas now–

Conor Byrne was coming towards me. He looked like a king, I thought, surrounded by his courtiers. They were hanging on his words – a nuisance, from my point of view. I'd have to prise him away from them. While the two of us were talking we wouldn't need an audience, however adulatory.

As the idol reached the door, I stepped out in front of him.

'Excuse me,' I said, giving his hangers-on the kind of look that said 'Get Lost', 'I'm Brigit Flood from the *Independent on Sunday*. I've just seen your show in London and I'd like to interview you.'

'Do you mean now?' said Conor Byrne.

'Yes, if you've the time for it.'

The courtiers, despite my look, continued to surround their king. They were mostly very young, students seeking words of wisdom. I wondered how the king had shaken off the VIPs who must have wanted him to stay and share whatever festivities had been planned to bring the evening to a close. That he had done so encouraged me. If he was ruthless enough to get out of their well-meaning clutches, he could escape the students too – especially for publicity.

'I can make the time,' he said, 'if you're who you say you are.'

The students laughed at this remark.

I said, 'Of course I am. I'm Brigit Flood.'

'I know that name. But the *Indo* sent you here? It's odd that they'd send two reporters.'

Light dawned.

'I'm not from the Irish *Indo*. This is an assignment for the London *Independent*.'

'Sorry. My mistake. You'd like to see me now, you say? That's not a problem. Here I am.'

'Can we go somewhere quiet then?' I said, casting a meaningful glance at the assembled courtiers and then back to Conor Byrne.

He responded positively. He turned to his audience and said, regretfully, 'Looks like we must break it up. Don't forget what I told you now.'

Having no alternative, the students acquiesced.

'We won't, for sure,' said one of them.

Their resentment of me showed but they dragged themselves away and I was left alone with him.

'Where do you suggest we go?' he asked.

'Over to the George perhaps?'

'Why not?' he said. 'I'm staying there.'

I didn't tell him I was too.

'Brigit Flood,' he said again as we walked along the street. 'Why does that name seem familiar?'

'I'm working freelance for the summer. A break from the BBC...' I explained my background.

'That's it. I've seen your name come up on credits. Brigit Flood. You're a producer.'

'Yes. Good to hear you watch the show.'

That got us back to the hotel. I led the way into the lounge and found a quiet corner table.

'Would you like a drink?' I asked.

'A beer. That is, if it's on the paper.'

'It is.'

The drinks came. I sipped mine and waited for him to ask me more about the feature I was writing. He didn't. He gulped a quarter of his beer, leant back in his chair, took a deep breath and then expelled it.

'It takes it out of you,' he said. 'That speech, it was a performance really.'

'Do you always bring it off?'

'Usually.' He drank again and smiled at me.

No false modesty, I thought. I wondered what response I'd get if I told him what had happened. If I were to say to him, your paintings lured me back to Ireland. Naturally, I never would.

'But afterwards I pay for it. I couldn't have stayed on tonight. I couldn't cope with all those people.'

'But you came back here with me.'

'Yes.' He looked at me expectantly. 'What do you want to talk about?'

I thought, about your work, but not that much. Enough to make ten lines or so. But I could hardly tell him that. If I spelt out what space he'd get, he might hump off to bed on me. All the same, I owed him something.

I said, tentatively, 'I should explain that this interview is to form part of a long feature on the arts scene over here.'

'Quite a lot of research for you.'

'Yes,' I said, relieved that we'd got over that one without an interrogation into how much space I was planning to devote to Conor Byrne. 'To get back to yourself, can I check some facts with you?'

These were biographical details. Before coming down to Limerick, I'd got cuttings about him, taken out of other papers, but they needed confirmation. You cannot rely on cuttings. Mistakes made by someone else can get set in concrete that way.

He was born in Connemara, then the family moved to Galway. His talent had been recognised by a teacher at his school who'd helped him with his college fees. He'd graduated from the Dublin School of Art and Design, won a bursary to the Slade, returned to Ireland as a teacher. The cuttings didn't give his age. He was younger than he looked – thirty-eight last month, he said.

'When did your career take off?'

'It didn't happen overnight. I moved out of education to establish a new school of art based on exploratory thought rather than on stylistic imitation. That was my first success. It led to an exhibition. Five years later I closed the school to concentrate on creative painting.'

We touched briefly on the school.

'It caused a furore when it opened. The die-hards were upset by it. But it was based on simple thinking.'

'Go on.'

'We are individuals. What we offer, as people, as artists, is unique because of that. Each creative person therefore should draw on his or her subconscious for the premise of a painting, rather than attempting to feed off the crumbs that a master painter's dropped. It's elementary – fundamental to the whole creative process.'

'It must have been rewarding for you, drawing out a unique talent from every student you taught.'

'It was. It still is.'

'I thought you said you'd closed the school.'

'As a full-time enterprise. I still have a summer school. At my home in Kilnaboy.'

Kilnaboy is in County Clare, a mile or so from Corofin, close to stony Burren land, that strange, entrancing limestone region, once a Celtic settlement and now a botanist's delight. A perfect spot for outdoor painting. I could imagine Conor Byrne making speeches on the rocks, talking about the *aes dana*, that elitist Celtic group, the poets, artists, historians and priests who'd paid allegiance to the high king, the *ri ruirech*, long ago. Food for the imagination. Foreign students would devour it.

'Who goes to your summer school?'

'Anyone and everyone. I don't have an age restriction. The students there don't take exams. The school is more of a meeting place for people drawn from all walks of life – as well as from the arts of course.'

'How long are these summer courses?'

'They vary. I accommodate the students. Some people come for a couple of weeks. Others for a month or more. One of my students, a marvellous woman in her sixties, spends the entire summer there.'

I put her down as being lonely, a widow who had time to kill. Some students must be dilettantes, dabblers who would get their kicks mixing with the master minds. Who else would go to Kilnaboy? Doctors, dentists, scientists? Shop assistants? Lorry drivers? I was getting curious. I had all the facts I needed but I didn't want to leave. Not yet. Leaving meant going up one floor or having dinner on my own. I didn't want to go to bed. I didn't fancy food just yet.

The man that I was interviewing wasn't in a hurry either – at least, he didn't seem to be. Perhaps he felt the same as I did, reluctant to go up to bed or to eat alone downstairs.

Before I could ask more questions, he said thoughtfully, 'About that woman I mentioned, the one who spends the summers with me. *She's* what I would call rewarding.'

'She's a gifted artist, is she?'

He shook his head. 'Not really. She'll never have a one-man show but that doesn't bother her.'

'In what sense is she rewarding?'

'I'll buy *you* a drink,' he said. 'Then I'll tell you all about her.'

I snuggled down into my chair and waited for my drink to come, feeling rather like my nephew waiting for a *Kipper* story. I wondered what had upset Mikey but I wasn't that concerned. By now Darina would have dealt with it, the way she did with everything.

Conor Byrne returned with drinks and I told him to go on. 'I want to hear about that woman.'

It was a rather moving story. The woman, Sheila Ferguson, had lost her husband in a car crash six or seven years before. Afterwards, she wouldn't speak, though she seemed normal otherwise.

'I mean, she wouldn't say a word. She might as well have lost her tongue. The family put it down to shock. They thought she would get over it.'

But Sheila Ferguson stayed mute. A month, then two went by in silence. The family started panicking.

'So how did you get into it?'

'Her eldest daughter lives near me. She came up to the house one night and said her mother used to paint. They'd all been talking to her doctor. She needed therapy, he said. He thought that she should come to me. Take some lessons at the school.'

'And you were sure that you could cure her?'

'I was no such thing,' said Conor. 'But I said I'd take her on. I was rather apprehensive. I thought that she might be aggressive. Angry. The way people sometimes are when a person dies on them. But she was the opposite. Very gentle. Very sweet. And as silent as the grave.'

'How long did that silence last?'

'She never spoke at all that summer and I thought I'd failed with her. I told her daughter that I had. I didn't see her all year round. But there she was again next summer, signing on – and mute as ever.'

'My God. You mean she's like that still?'

'No. I told you that I was rewarded. On this occasion she'd brought her work along with her, the paintings she'd been doing in winter. Something was emerging in them. Something of herself, of the person she had been before the car crash took her husband. And that summer I could see she was progressing. Her spirits gradually improved. Then, in August, as if there was nothing wrong, she started speaking normally. It happened just like that. I came up to her one day in the studio and I said, "I like the way you've mixed that pink and taken it across the paper," and she said, "I was going to add some blue. I thought the shadow needed it." At first I thought I must be dreaming. Hearing things, at any rate. But after that she never looked back. So there it was, she'd cured herself.'

'Or maybe you did that for her.'

I was taken aback by the simplicity of the way he'd told the story, as well as what he'd had to say. Had someone asked what I'd expected out of this tale, I'd have said a huge breakthrough for Conor Byrne. An egotistical reward. Honours showered on him and Sheila whom he'd found to be a genius. But this was a human story, an emotional success, without honours being conferred. And he seemed to be sincere when he said he thought Sheila had cured herself.

While I was mulling that one over, the mind of the man I was with had moved on to other matters.

He said, 'Are you hungry? I'm starving.'

For me, eating is to do with people. A meal alone has no appeal but add another person to it and, suddenly, I'm ravenous. Before Conor mentioned food, I was sure I wasn't hungry. Now I realised that I was.

When I said, 'I am indeed,' he suggested that we eat on the spot, in the hotel.

I followed him into the restaurant and sat opposite him again while we consumed enormous T-bones, a jug of wine and loads of chips. That was when we swapped roles and he became the questioner. In response to what he asked, I told him more about my background, about growing up in Dalkey and a bit about Darina.

'You went to school in Dublin, did you? And to university?'

'I went to UCD,' I said.

'You studied art?'

71

I shook my head. 'English was my major subject.'

In relating all those details, I didn't mention Joe of course. But, somehow, we got on to Mammy and I told him about her and about her Maltese poodles. 'You won't believe the names they have...'

On being told about Godiva, he laughed, took a sketchbook from his pocket and drew a few lines on it.

'Would you say she looks like this?' He passed the sketchpad across to me. I looked at it and burst out laughing. Caricature can be cruel, even with a dog as a model, but his drawing of Godiva had no spite or venom in it, even though she looked so snappy and her coat was sticking out as if she'd been electrified.

'That's exactly what she's like!'

'It must be hard to work when you're staying in that house.'

'It is,' I said. 'Impossible.'

But it was good to laugh about it. We laughed a lot that night at dinner, at that drawing and the others that he made as the meal progressed – the ones of people in the restaurant, and the one he did of me as I fended off the students.

'They didn't stand a chance with you!'

'They weren't intended to,' I said.

By then, the barriers were down and I felt at ease with him. Leaving out his sense of humour, what I liked about the man was his lack of affectation. I thought the speech that he had made when he was condemning 'arts speak' reflected what he really felt: 'The true artist has no need for such devices. His prerequisites are talent, honesty and courage.' Oh yes, I thought, and anarchy.

It was a statement that touched a chord within the very heart of me. Halfway through the meal, I felt a change inside myself. I wasn't restless anymore. The ennui was gone from me. Where, earlier on, I'd been feeling quite relaxed, now I'd gone beyond that stage and reached an unfamiliar spot. It was a better place to be. A fine place. There, I felt at ease with myself. As if I'd come home at last. As if I'd taken a long journey into a land where the person I was with spoke my language for a change. Peace enveloped me. I might have lain down on a water bed, or lowered myself into the Adriatic on a summer night in June, as I'd done one holiday when I went to Montenegro.

I'd been with the wrong man then. With Tom Reddan, I recalled, with whom I'd worked at RTE and who, dazzled by the sun and sea, had thought himself in love with me. Whereas now...

This is not to say that I fancied Conor Byrne enough to go to bed with him. Bed did not come into it. I wasn't thinking sexually. If I'd been thinking along those lines, I might have thought of Janice Seton, or of Hannah for that matter, and seen a warning signal flash. But, as I said, it was not like that. It was more important than attraction, and so simple it needed no analysis. That's what I thought, anyway.

So there I was, enjoying myself in the way that people do when life seems free of complications. But I knew well what I was like, the fear I had of being trapped, the way I tended to back off when anyone got close to me. I should have known – of course I should – that I would complicate the issue.

I did. One minute I was sitting at that table, content to talk to Conor Byrne, and the next I'd taken flight.

He contributed, in that he offered me a lift. He said, 'When are you going back to Dublin?'

'In the morning. After breakfast.'

'You drove down from Dublin, did you?'

'No,' I said. 'I came by train.'

'I have to go to Dublin myself tomorrow. I'll be driving up. You could keep me company.'

I hadn't thought about next day. Hadn't thought ahead at all. I'd been happy in the present, conscious only of the fact that I'd made it to my doorstep and found myself at home again. Now, reality intruded. Panic took hold of me. A voice inside my head said, *run*. You feel at home with Conor Byrne but home can be a danger zone. Can't you see the pitfalls here? The minefield that is lying in wait? Don't get too close to anybody, and don't let them get close to you.

Say sorry, said the voice to me, but you'd prefer to catch the train.

So I apologised to Conor and said the train was better for me. 'I can work on it, you see. I have some catching-up to do. But it was kind of you to offer.'

Conor raised an eyebrow at me. 'It wasn't kind at all,' he said. 'Don't ever think that I am kind.'

That made me backtrack even more. I tried to make my voice sound light. 'You were kind

74

enough tonight. I appreciate the dinner, and the chance to talk to you. But I'd better leave you now.'

'Don't you need a taxi back?'

'Back?'

'Back to your hotel, I mean.'

'Don't worry. I don't need a taxi.' I stood up, hoping that I looked decisive. 'Thanks again for everything.'

'Thanks for having dinner with me.' He got to his feet as well. 'I'll think of you along the road. Working in the train like that.'

Oh, sod off, I nearly said. Knowing that he saw through me.

I forced myself to smile at him. ''Bye.'

'Sleep well, Brigit.'

I left him standing there and fled, egged on by that inner voice which still insisted I was right not to let him close to me. I fetched my key, decided not to use the lift in case Conor caught me waiting, and bolted up the stairs to bed.

Safe inside my room, I re-considered next day's plans. Breakfast wasn't on the cards. In order to avoid meeting Conor, I would catch the early train, the one that left at ten past seven. Another dawn departure then.

I arranged a wake-up call and prepared to go to bed. I took off my new green jacket and tried to unzip my skirt. But the zip was down already. It must have undone itself at the opening of Young EVA when I fought my way inside. Oh God! No wonder I had felt released, convinced the skirt was not so tight. It wouldn't have been noticed there, not with all those people around me. But afterwards, going down the street with Conor, walking out just now…

He must have laughed his head off at me. The humiliation of it. Cringing, I went hot all over. How could I have been so stupid?

The only consolation was that I had done the interview. Conor might be laughing at me but I wouldn't have to face him, not at the breakfast table or in my life again.

Sobered, I got into bed. I drifted off to sleep quite quickly but I dreamt of Conor Byrne. I dreamt of being completely naked, walking down O'Connell Street. He asked me if I wasn't cold, if I never needed clothes. I told him that I never wore them, that they never fitted me. Then I woke up with a jump and started to go hot again.

In the morning I was off as soon as I had paid the bill. The station wasn't far away and the Dublin train was in, though no one else was on the platform. I climbed on board, relieved to have got away without any more ado.

But I'd got into the dining car. Somebody was frying bacon. There was a delicious smell. I could have an Irish breakfast, with eggs and soda bread and coffee…

No more food, I told myself. I'm going on a diet *now*. I'm never going to gorge again.

I dived into the next compartment which also had a table in it. I could write my notes there. But working on the early train had never been an option for me. I knew I couldn't concentrate, not with other passengers sharing the compartment with me.

They were on the platform now. Doors were

opening and slamming. Voices drifted in to me. But no one entered my compartment.

At Nenagh, I discovered why. The compartment I was in had been reserved for little girls travelling up to see the zoo. There were nearly thirty of them. A whole classroom, it turned out. I was swamped by noise and colour. None of them wore uniforms. Leggings seemed to be the norm and most of them had earrings on.

The two teachers who were with them were young enough still to be students. They were looking apprehensive. 'I'll be wrecked when I get back!' I heard one of them remark.

The train pulled out from Nenagh station. As it did, the little girls produced make-up and began to put it on. One of them had earphones on and three were singing lustily. The teachers didn't intervene. I thought again of Conor Byrne who no doubt would be amused if he could see me now, the po-faced woman who'd maintained that she needed space to work.

Two hours later I felt deaf, numbed by the cacophony. The train arrived in Heuston station and the girls and I got out. Surrounded by their energy, I drifted towards the barrier.

Somebody was waiting there. Someone I recognised. Someone I had been avoiding. But I hadn't been successful. Conor had caught up with me.

FOUR

I was amazed. Unable to believe my eyes. He must have followed me last night when I went to fetch my key. Realised where I was staying. Checked the time I left the George. It took the breath away from me.

I was caught off guard. I had no time to build defences. Already he had spotted me, emerging from that sea of children.

'Brigit!'

'What are you doing here?' I said.

'I had an idea,' said Conor, 'and I want to put it to you. Where did all those girls come from? And why have they got lipstick on?'

'They're going to the zoo apparently.'

'They way they look, the zoo will keep them. Can I take that bag off you?'

'It's not heavy,' I said weakly, wondering what was coming next.

'The car is parked across the road. Come. We'll talk as we go into town.'

'What is this idea of yours?'

'I'll tell you when we're in the car.' He strode ahead, out of the station and across the road towards a bright red Jaguar.

'This is your car?'

'I've given it a name,' said Conor. 'Brigit, meet the Shell.'

'The Shell? I'd call it a phallic symbol!'

78

Conor shook his head. 'You've got it wrong, it's not like that. You see, cynics go for artists, Brigit, especially the successful ones. We need our defences. This happens to be mine.' He unlocked the door for me. 'I promise you it's comfortable.'

It was. The leather seats were red as well.

'Are you going straight to Dalkey?' he asked.

'I have things to do in town.' I had more cuttings to collect. I'd planned to go to Hodges-Figgis to buy a book. Then I would have headed home, back to Mammy and the dogs. Now I'd changed my mind. I didn't fancy taking Conor to meet Mammy out in Dalkey. I thought, they're poles apart, the two of them. Everything an artist is – inventive, dreamy and anarchic – is anathema to Mammy. And her conventional approach would turn Conor Byrne right off.

'Can you fit in lunch with me?'

'It's barely ten o'clock, you know.'

'We'll call it breakfast then,' said Conor.

'About this idea of yours...'

'Let's discuss it over coffee.'

He took me to the Westbury, bribed the porter on the steps and got himself a parking space as if he was a hotel guest.

I've always liked the Westbury, the view it gives of Grafton Street and of my favourite church, St Ann's, with its Romanesque façade. I like the way that people gossip over coffee on the Terrace, the glossy décor, the Polo Bar and the gourmet foreign food. Not that I was going to eat.

I thought of Hannah who was thin. Hannah painting on the rocks. Until then, I hadn't thought of her as real but as part of a com-

79

position, less animated than the sea, and much less so than the childish shadows who cavorted all around her. But she existed. She was real. She was Mrs Conor Byrne.

The waiter had come up to us. Conor ordered everything. 'Rashers, sausage and black pudding. Two fried eggs and soda bread. You *are* hungry, Brigit, aren't you?'

I should have been ashamed of myself but I nodded my acquiescence, adding, 'And, please, could we have coffee now, before you bring the rest of it?'

The coffee came. Pouring it, I said to Conor, 'Tell me about your idea.'

'Right. It's this. Would you like to come to Clare and help me in the next few months?'

'To Kilnaboy? What help could I be to you?'

'There's the studio to run. The classes to co-ordinate. There's a lot that I can't handle. But it wouldn't be full-time. You'd be free to write as well.'

'Well—'

'You'd learn a lot about the arts scene. There'd be free accommodation. There's a car that you could use.'

'Sounds like I'd get more from you than you could hope to get from me.'

'I don't think so,' Conor said.

What an offer, I thought. But I didn't jump at it. I could hear that voice again, telling me I should beware. It wasn't shouting at me, though; it was only whispering.

Beware of what? I said to it. What harm could I do in going? I can only profit from it. And I'd be

going to Conor's home. It's not as if I'd be
exposed to any real temptation there. It's not as
if I fancy him...

Don't you?

Well, ye-es, I do, I must admit. More so than I
did last night but that doesn't have to matter.
Because Hannah will be there. Their home could
never be the setting for a raging love affair. Conor
will be – just my friend. As Hannah probably will
be. In fact Hannah will be helpful. The role she
has as Conor's wife will neutralise the intimacy
which is building up between us. I really can't
envisage trouble. It seems safe enough to me.

The voice said, don't rush into it.

Oh, all right, I won't, I conceded.

'Can I think your offer over?'

'By all means,' responded Conor. 'There's no
hurry anyway. I wasn't going to suggest that you
came down with me today. In any case, I'm going
to London. I have to leave this afternoon.'

'You're going over on the boat? Driving down
from Holyhead?'

'No, I'm not. I'm flying over. I thought I'd leave
the car for you.'

'Come on,' I said. 'You must be joking.' This
was all a dream, I thought. That silly business
with my zip. The little girls with make-up on.
Conor waiting at the station.

Breakfast, though, looked real enough. I took a
bite of soda bread.

'You are joking, aren't you, Conor?'

'No, I'm not, and this is why. If you decide to
come to Clare you can take the car back for me.
In that case, I could catch a London-Dublin-

Galway flight. There's someone I should see in Galway – someone who can drop me home. It would suit the two of us. That way, I can cut Dublin out. I've nothing that I need to do here.'

It struck me that he never had. He didn't have to come to Dublin just to catch a flight to London. It would have been more sensible if he had flown out of Shannon. Dublin was to do with me. When he offered me a lift, the idea he'd put to me was already in his mind.

'Amazing. And you'd trust me with your car?'

'You strike me as being competent. I'm prepared to take a risk.'

'How long will you be away?'

'I'm going to London for three days. I've got some things to wrap up there.'

Janice Seton, for one, I thought, and wondered what he felt for her, whether it was love or lust, or whether she was just a change from his life with Hannah Byrne.

Not my business anyway.

'Are three days long enough for you? Can you decide while I'm away?'

'Yes, they are. I can,' I said. 'I'll make up my mind by tomorrow. Can I phone you over there and tell you what I have decided?'

He pulled the sketchpad out again, tore a strip of paper from it and scribbled down a number for me. 'Here,' he said. 'That's where I'm staying. At the Basil Street Hotel. Take the car keys in the meantime. Drive the car while I'm away. Don't protest. You'd be doing me a favour. It would solve the parking problem. You could drop me at the airport and drive back to Dalkey, Brigit.'

That was going to freak out Mammy, seeing me in that bright red Jag.

'And if I don't go to Clare?'

He shrugged. 'Simple. Let me know and I'll fly here and retrieve the car from you.'

'What time is your flight to London?'

'I haven't booked it yet,' he said. 'I'd better go and do that now.'

He got on a six thirty flight. For someone with no chores in Dublin, he'd left himself with time to kill – or maybe time to spend with me.

It turned out to be the latter. When he'd made his booking, he said, 'Those things you had to do yourself, do you have to do them now?'

'I suppose they're not that urgent.'

'Great. Because I thought we'd go to Howth. Take a walk across the hill.'

The hill, the Ben of Howth, rises some six hundred feet or so above the little town. It towers over Dublin Bay and contemplates the Wicklow coast. I'd been there often on my own. I felt that it belonged to Joe, that his spirit lived up there, enveloped in the silver mist that wraps itself round the hill. Walking there, I'd talk to Joe, convinced that he was by my side, that we were sharing the wind and the sea, the gulls that soared above our heads, the freedom and exhilaration. Essential to this pilgrimage was being on my own up there. And now Conor was suggesting that we go to Howth together.

I was going to tell him, no, I don't want to go to Howth. Not with you, or anyone. I only go there on my own. But before I found the words, Conor cut into my thoughts.

'I love that hill. I used to walk for hours up there when I was a student here. It saved my life, it really did, on more than one occasion, Brigit. It's the sense of freedom up there. Life seems somehow undefiled. You think you can escape the crap. The hell that's waiting down below. It's illusionary of course. A delusion. But it's a necessary respite.'

His craggy face was serious. Despite the fact he'd used my name, I thought he had forgotten me; that he was talking to himself, remembering his student days. I knew I shouldn't interrupt. And in that moment I knew, too, that there was pain in Conor Byrne.

But surely I'd know that before. That painting I had seen of his. That house. The shadow of a crucifix… A surge of pity coursed through me. I wanted to comfort him.

I waited for him to speak again. Before he did, he looked at me as if I was a total stranger. Then, realising where he was, he suddenly re-registered. 'Sorry, Brigit, I was thinking.'

By then, I'd changed my mind about the hill. It was important for him too – more so, maybe, than for me.

'I love the hill as well,' I said. 'I haven't been up there for ages.'

'Then we'll go.'

Driving out of the city, taking the Finglas and Santry road towards Clontarf and Dollymount, I thought of Joe. The tide was very nearly out and dogs cavorted on the strand, unleashed by their watchful owners. With North Bull Island on our right, like an arrow pointing northwards, we

84

wove on, through Raheny and Sutton. The hill loomed up ahead of us.

I thought we'd make for it at once. But when we reached the town, Conor pulled in to the left, parked by the harbour, unclipped his safety belt and leant back in the driver's seat. He closed his eyes.

'Put up with me awhile,' he said.

I did, staring at the glorious panorama stretching out on my right-hand side – yachts galore and, beyond their red and yellow sails, the two islands, Lambay and Ireland's Eye, in a sea of cornflower blue. Joe's house – two up, two-down, unmodernised – was only yards away from us.

I'd never been inside his house, not even after he died. Darina hadn't been there either. She and Joe had met elsewhere – gone to films, eaten out. But she'd driven past the house and we were curious about it, wondering how it looked inside and why Joe had chosen it when he could have lived in style. Perhaps, I thought, he didn't care too much for style and, after living with our mother, he needed to be free, like me, instead of letting possessions impinge upon his liberty.

It was a little sad, sitting there and thinking of him and the years that had been wasted when we could have been together. It was a relief to me when Conor came to life again.

'Let's move on.'

'That's fine by me.'

Conor, having drifted off on some private expedition, was slow in coming back from it but you could see that he'd set out. Then he back-tracked once again.

I'd been thinking that if I decided to go to Clare I must tell Lorcan that I was going. Then I mentioned Lorcan's name.

'Have you come across him, Conor?'

Conor frowned. 'I was his pupil for a while.'

'Really? Lorcan never told me that.'

'Why should he? We were never close.'

'All the same, he should have said. Lorcan's one of my best friends.'

'Is he?'

'You must meet up with him again. Maybe we'll go out together.'

'I don't think that's necessary.'

Talk about Siberia. For heaven's sake, I thought, perplexed, why is Conor being so cold? What's gone on between those two? How odd that Lorcan never said that Conor was his pupil once. What precisely *did* he say when he spoke of Conor Byrne? That Conor was a brilliant speaker. Nothing else I could remember. Nothing hostile, certainly.

But they must have fallen out, I thought. A pity, from my point of view, but it was nothing that I could resolve until I knew Conor better. Still, I should have a word with Lorcan, ask him if they'd had a row. I might pop round to see him later, after I'd dropped Conor off.

Meanwhile, there was Conor sulking. Then the ice began to thaw. We reached the summit of the hill, left the car and stood together, paying homage to the vista. The view that day was every bit as wonderful as Maud Gonne used to rave about. The sea as deep a blue again as her mother's turquoises, and the Welsh mountains as clear as they would ever be.

'It's marvellous!' Conor began to laugh, perhaps partly at himself but mostly in delight, I think. 'I've never seen it quite like this. I've never been up here in summer. Have you?'

'A few times. Never when it's been so warm.'

The hill had been transformed by heat. Its shawl of mist and cloud was missing. All it wore that day was green. I couldn't see a sign of Joe. Perhaps he didn't like the heat, or maybe he had moved away so Conor Byrne could take his place.

We walked there for an hour or more. Nothing notable occurred. No confidences were exchanged that flash across my memory. It was, simply, a respite.

Later, we had tea in Howth. Then I took Conor to the airport.

'Don't forget to ring me now.'

'Would I forget to ring?' I said.

It was only half past five. I could go to Benburb Street and still be home by half past seven.

The street was not deserted this time. A group of winos had assembled. They were sitting on the pavement; getting stuck into the booze. Further down, at Lorcan's end, two young women in tight skirts were leaning up against a wall. As the car approached, they edged forward expectantly. Seeing me, their faces fell.

As I banged on Lorcan's door I could feel them scowling at me. I didn't have to wait for long. The door was opened within seconds.

'Hi,' I said. 'Oh, sorry, I expected Lorcan.'

There was a woman at the door, a small, grey-haired woman wearing an old-fashioned blue shirtwaister with an apron over it.

'Mr Burke is out,' she said.

'I might have known. I should have phoned.'

'Come in and wait for him,' she said. 'Though there's no knowing when he'll come. You know the way it is with him.'

I didn't really know the way but I agreed with what she said. It suited me to wait for him, at least until the rush hour ended.

'I'm Mrs Mac,' the woman said. 'I'd say he's mentioned me to you. This place has been a right disgrace. I've been here since the morning, cleaning.'

'It looks much better now,' I said.

'It does indeed,' said Mrs Mac. 'You can't trust men to clean a house. Mind you, Mr Burke doesn't even try to keep the place the way he should, which I'd say is just as well, he'd only make a bags of it.'

Remembering what it was like the last time I'd been at the house, I heartily agreed with her.

'I was going to make some tea if you'd like some.'

'I'd love some.'

She presented me with a cup of tea so strong, I could have stood on it, and took a seat across from me.

'You saw them scrubbers in the street?'

'Those two women near the car?'

'That's then. Benburb Street's destroyed with them!'

'Do you live in this street as well?'

'Indeed I don't! The thought of it! And Mr

88

Burke should move away.' She leant forward confidingly. 'They work on shift, did you know that? Those two hussies out there now, they came on at four o'clock.'

'They don't wait till it gets dark.'

'They don't have to wait,' she said. 'I'll tell you how it works round here. The clients come here after work.'

'The clients?'

'Politicians. Businessmen. Solicitors and barristers. The Law Society is near. It's further up in Blackhall Place. You get them coming out of there.'

'They're not frightened of the guards?'

Garda headquarters wasn't very far away, in Phoenix Park, past Collins Barracks.

At the mention of the guards, Mrs Mac rolled up her eyes. 'The guards go easy on the scrubbers. Unless there's violence they don't care. The thing is, you don't have crime along this street. Not what they would rate as crime. There's nothing round here you could rob.'

'That sounds fair enough to me, to leave the prostitutes alone.'

'And what about morality?'

Oh God, I thought, morality. I peered discreetly at my watch. It wasn't even seven yet.

Mrs Mac, to my relief, wasn't waiting for an answer. She plunged on indignantly. 'The guards feel sorry for those sluts. Then again, there's one or two you might feel sorry for yourself. Mr Burke had one of them coming in to model for him. She came from Cork at the weekends. Her husband lost his job down there. She needed money for the kids.'

'Her husband knew what she was doing?'

Mrs Mac shook her head vigorously. 'He did not! He'd have a fit. She told him she came up to Dublin so she could be with her sister. She was raking in a packet. They get fifteen pounds a time.'

'It doesn't sound much fun to me. The winters must be hell for them.'

'There was one that froze to death...'

Lorcan, where *are* you? Mrs Mac, like many worthy citizens, seemed to me to be obsessed with the hookers and their clients. She was something of an expert on the life in Benburb Street. Listening to her diatribe, I learnt, much against my will, how the hookers operated.

'They dress in a mini skirt and put a coat on top of it. They walk up and down the street. When a client comes along they open up their coats for him. They say that some of them are students, studying at UCD.'

'Surely not?' I said to her.

'And some of them are over sixty. A lot of them are alcoholics.'

'Yes,' I said. 'I'm sure they are.' Nearly seven. Come home, Lorcan.

'They think they own the street, you know. There's one that has a patch up there,' she gestured to the left of me. 'She wouldn't let you walk near her.'

I was getting sick of hookers. Maybe she realised that because she switched from them to clients.

'They're nervous of being recognised. They

90

have a trick they always play, as if they're looking for directions...'

I thought, I'll wait another fifteen minutes. That's as much as I can take. If Lorcan isn't home by then I'll write a note and leave it for him.

'A lot of them are family men,' Mrs Mac was droning on. 'They come round here on their way home.'

'Has Benburb Street been that way long?' I didn't really want to know. The hookers were a fact of life. The ones outside looked quite down-market but there were others, stunning women, in the city, operating out of Ballsbridge, putting cards on people's windscreens. At RTE we knew about them. Those women carried mobile phones and had apartments leased for them. And then there were the relief parlours, the magazines and porno films. Dublin wasn't innocent.

'It's been going on for years. You'd not believe the half of it. Married men, the most of them. The kind that others would call decent. The worst of them was Mr Flood. A friend of Mr Burke's, he was. That was how he got the house. 'Twas that Joe Flood put up the money.'

My stomach did a cartwheel on me. I thought I was going to vomit. 'Joe Flood?' But I don't think I spoke out loud. I thought – it wasn't – it could not be true.

Unaware, Mrs Mac continued blithely. 'Mr Burke, he kept a room and Joe Flood brought his women here. Scrubbers off the street out there. You'd not believe the cut of them.'

Someone interrupted her. A voice that sounded

like my own asked her when those things occurred.

She remembered and she told me. It was after I was born. Just after. When my parents were still married.

I was stunned. Devastated. Joe, my father, carrying on with prostitutes. And Lorcan – he was just as bad. I couldn't stand to see him now. I couldn't bear to wait for him.

I stood up, feeling shaky on my feet. 'I must go,' I said abruptly. 'Tell Mr Burke I couldn't stay. There's something that I have to do.'

'That's a pity. He'll be raging that he missed you.'

Raging... Somehow I got out of there before screaming out with pain. In the street, the two women were slumped against the wall again. I hated them. And I hated Lorcan too. Lorcan who had been my friend and was now beyond contempt. Who had been my father's friend.

I got into the car and sat there, trembling, holding onto the steering wheel, aware that the women were staring at me.

After a while, I started to cry. Leaning forward, my eyes fell on the signet ring given to me by Darina – ages ago, it seemed now – and which I'd been so proud to wear.

Not any more. I should take it off, I thought. But I couldn't bear to do so.

Rush hour was well over. I told myself that I should go home, that if I stayed in Benburb Street, Lorcan might well find me there. That was a meeting I had to avoid. And Mammy would be waiting for me. Mammy, who had been betrayed. I'd been hard on her, I knew. I'd compared her to Joe and found she didn't measure up. I'd put him up on a pedestal and turned him into a deity. Fool that I was.

But despite my suspect judgement – or perhaps because of it – I knew I couldn't cope with my mother on any substantial basis. Not at this stage, I thought, I have to think this whole thing out and I can't do that in Dublin. I must get away from Mammy. From the bustle of the city.

And then I thought not so much of Conor's offer that I join him down in Clare, but about the paintings. Those images of sea and rocks, the purple clouds and ancient ruins that had put a spell on me. They were still enticing me. Saying, come to Kilnaboy.

And why not? I thought. Why not? I only need to make a phone call. Then I can be off.

FIVE

Driving to Clare, I continued to brood on what Mrs Mac had said. Was her story really true? Maybe she just made it up. Lorcan said she was a blabber. Maybe she'd been showing off, pretending she was in the know but only telling lies to shock.

The miles put distance between Mrs Mac and me and I was diverted by the blatant signs of summer that the land was flashing at me. In the city, seasonal changes are demarcated by what the window dressers show us; the latest fashion shades or the length of skirts or jackets tell us if it's May or June. Now, it was the fields and hedges, the hawthorn and the mountain ash, the lush green grass, the lambs and calves that registered the time of year. Near Tyrrellspass, I saw a cat with a litter of new kittens curled up by an iron gate. I stopped to have a look at them, and got spat at for my pains.

All along, at the back of my mind, was the thought of Kilnaboy. I'd kept it there for safety's sake, like a child taking possession of a new toy and storing it away until it becomes more familiar and acceptable. Every so often, it defied me and pressed forward. When it did, I imagined Conor teaching, maybe in a rundown cottage (my vision of the studio was a rather blurry one) while his students sat and listened, mesmerised

94

by what he said and the timbre of his voice.

Hang on, I thought. It's too soon to think about the studio. I may be going to Kilnaboy but I haven't got there yet. I forced the thought of it back in my mind where it belonged and tried to think of other things.

But I'd put a banning order on so many other subjects. Following the N6 through Kilbeggan and Moate, counting the miles along the way, I refused point-blank to consider Mrs Mac or think of Lorcan or Joe.

I sought, somewhat desperately, for something else to focus on and found it unexpectedly. It's odd how something in your past which isn't even personal, a story someone told you one time, or possibly a news report, can bring about a change of mood when you subconsciously respond to an outside influence. Just before Athlone, I felt a cloud descend on me and wondered why I felt unhappy. Seconds later, I recalled a history lesson long ago and the story of the siege started coming back to me in the words of the nun who had read it out to us. She'd spoken of the Irish heroes who had given up their lives to fight against the Williamites and said the name of only one – Sergeant Custance, I remembered – had been handed down to us.

Someone else came from Athlone... Of course, I thought, it was that boy, Darina's friend, the owner of that wretched rat. From there, my mind meandered back again to contemplate the other Rat. Well, at least I'd solved that problem. Life might have had its ups and downs in the time that I'd been back but I had evaded him.

After Loughrea, the direct route to Kilnaboy would have taken me south-west, along the road that led to Gort. But I had something else to do before I reached the studio. The Merriman Summer School for Writers is held every year in Clare. That year, Ballyvaughan, a small fishing and trading port facing onto Galway Bay, had been selected as the venue, a fact I knew I had to mention in the feature I was writing. The article would be in print before the school commenced its programme but I could describe the setting if I paid the town a visit. It wouldn't be a huge diversion. The distance between Ballyvaughan and Kilnaboy is only fifteen miles or so.

I swung due west, towards Clarinbridge. The landscape was quite different now. Drystone walls ran round the fields and barns were closer to the road. A farmhouse nestled in the ruins of what had been a castle keep. Gulls flew low above the car. I smelt the sea before I saw it. Soon, I was in writers' country. Driving round Kinvara Bay, I discovered Duras House where the Abbey Theatre was conceived by Lady Gregory and Yeats, and after it Dungaire Castle, once owned by the poet and wit Oliver St John Gogarty. All good stuff to write about.

I'd done another dawn departure. It was only half past ten when Ballyvaughan came into view and with it the rocky island of Illaunloe, sitting squatly in the bay. The town was neat and very pretty. There was a fair-sized hotel, Hylands, which was painted red and yellow, where I thought I'd stop for coffee. I turned the corner, looked for parking, saw a cottage on my left.

It was a white cottage with a red door and windows and a gate to match. That's not unusual, of course. In Ballyvaughan, there are enough thatched cottages to put up a fair-sized army. But this one, set well back from the road, had the most amazing garden. The flowers were all quite delicate. Pansies, violets and aubretia mingled in a rocky settings with pinks, stonecrop, wild strawberries and fairy foxgloves, and up against the cottage wall, roses had come into bloom.

It took me a few minutes to work out that the cottage was a teashop. *'An Fear Gorta'* said a sign which had been carved above the door.

I followed a flagged pavement and went inside, trying not to drool at the array of homemade cakes – chocolate, lemon, coffee, carrot – displayed on a table covered by a crisp white cloth. Giving way to wickedness, I said I'd have the coffee cake.

Beside me was a little stand for holding leaflets and brochures. One explained the real meaning of the sign above the door. *'An Fear Gorta'*, literally 'The Hungry Man', also meant 'The Hungry Grass'. This mythical grass, the leaflet declared, had origins in famine days. It grew in the area and gave off a magic scent which incited pangs of hunger.

'Can you smell it?' someone asked.

The speaker was a silver-haired woman sitting at a nearby table. She wasn't young, in her middle sixties, but her face was so serene that I thought her beautiful.

I smiled and said I thought I could.

'It's very powerful,' said the woman. 'I can smell it miles away if I think about those cakes!'

'Do you live in Ballyvaughan?'

'No. I live in Lisdoonvarna. It's not far away of course.'

'Do you come here for the cakes?'

The woman laughed. 'They'd be worth it on their own but I usually drive through Ballyvaughan on my way to Kilnaboy. I was going to classes there.'

She said she'd been one of Conor's students for several years. When I explained where I was going, she moved over to my table.

'You must tell me all about it.'

I did, without mentioning the spell that the paintings cast on me.

'How long do you envisage staying?' she asked.

'I don't know. A month or two.'

'I hope it all works out for you.' She sounded rather dubious.

'I'm sure it will. I'll let you know. We're bound to run across each other.'

'Maybe not,' the woman said. 'I've decided to give up.'

'Your classes, or to give up painting?'

'Both. I've just come to that conclusion. You see, I know I haven't got the talent. I've enjoyed myself all right but I've had enough of it. I went on for far too long. And I've got something else to do, something that is more rewarding.'

'What is that?' I asked, intrigued.

'Have you seen the garden here?'

'At the front? It's very pretty.'

'Not just the front, the back as well. There's

another garden there. Come and have a look at it.'

I did. It was a sunken, walled rock garden, much larger than the one in front and even more astonishing. Stepping down into it out of the teashop, I felt that I'd been snatched from Clare and repositioned in the tropics. Strange, unfamiliar plants, exquisite and luxurious, grew everywhere amongst the rocks, as well as ones I recognised, lilacs, brooms and candytuft. White clematis crawled up the walls. I smelt but couldn't spot the fennel, though I did see more aubretia.

'This is what I want to do,' my new companion said to me. 'To create a pretty garden. Not the same as this of course but something of my own. Something I'll enjoy creating.'

I told her, insincerely, that her project sounded fun and said I hoped we'd meet again. 'In the teashop possibly.'

'Yes, indeed, I hope we will.'

'Pity, though, about your painting. You don't think you'll change your mind.'

'No, I won't,' the woman said emphatically. 'It took me time to work it out but this morning – at the studio, in fact – I realised what I was doing.'

'Taking time off from your garden?'

'Paying off a debt,' she said. 'I owed a lot to Conor Byrne but I've settled that account. Goodbye and, as I said, I hope we meet.'

'It would be nice. I'm Brigit Flood.'

'I'm Sheila Ferguson,' she said.

At first, the name just rang a bell. I was in the car again before I realised who she was. Sheila

Ferguson. Sheila, who had lost her voice. She left me feeling disappointed after Conor's big build-up. What a let-down, I decided. But it was Conor she'd let down. That remark about a debt – it seemed rather cheap to me.

I shrugged it off, backtracked, edging round the bay. There were paintings all around me. A Mondrian in blue and red (the turquoise sea, a crimson sail). A brown and green relief by Tapies (seaweed strewn across the shingle). A great Cezanne (the limestone hills).

I should have driven up those hills and set off for Kilnaboy but the sea delayed my going, urging me to wait awhile, not to be in such a hurry. Impulsively, I turned off by an empty house and headed for the shore again along a road bordered by untidy hedgerows. A scattering of scarlet poppies cheered the car as it went past and, in an adjacent field, someone had set up a tent and installed a barbecue.

But the terrain by the shoreline was stony-hearted, cold, despite the summer heat; more austere than I'd bargained for. Smooth, round, black pumice stones with holes in them were piled upon the silver sand. There was no one else in sight, no children playing with spades and buckets.

Ahead was the stark outline of a martello tower. On the strand, the pumice stones had been replaced by shiny, flat, black limestone shelves that stretched out to meet the sea. I shivered without knowing why and wished I'd left the shore alone.

I swung left, away from the tower and the

limestone slabs. The winding grey road led me back towards the scree that is part of the Burren formation. I drove along one side of it, catching sight of a hilltop lake. Then the road dipped and plunged and, to my immense relief, I descended into a green valley and saw a sign for Kilnaboy.

I found the house without a problem. Conor had told me that the gates were new, that they had been painted blue and that there was a small lodge just inside them, on the left. The lodge was newly painted too – creamy yellow, with the doors and windows white.

I drove along a winding avenue through wooded grassland until the house leapt out at me from behind a belt of trees. It was Victorian, solid and slightly pompous, shaped like a fore-shortened E, with a heavy arched stone doorway and great big windows in Gothic surrounds. It was freshly painted also, creamy yellow, like the lodge, which helped relieve its stodgy look. But there was no getting away from the fact that it wasn't well-proportioned, built not to an architect's design but to suit the specifications of a businessman or banker. A family man…

With a start, I realised I didn't know if Conor Byrne had any children, whether or not those shadows cavorting on the rocks were his and Hannah's sons. Any minute now, I might find out. A trio of small impertinent boys might come sprinting round the corner, demanding to know what I was doing, driving around in Daddy's car.

This didn't happen. There was no sign of life at all as I pulled into the pebblestoned driveway.

But then, as I was hauling my suitcase out, I caught a fleeting glimpse of someone peering at me from a window. A pale-faced woman with red hair. It must be Hannah Byrne, I thought, anticipating that she would open the door for me.

Someone else came out to meet me, a portly woman in an old grey suit. She was anything but friendly.

'Yes?'

'I'm Brigit Flood,' I said. 'Mr Byrne's expecting me.'

'Is that so? He didn't say.' She stood in the doorway, blocking my entrance.

'Well, he is,' I said, determined to stand up to her. 'Can you tell me where he is?'

'At the back,' the woman said, about to close the door on me.

'You mean in his studio?'

'In the barn. He's giving lessons.'

I suppose I should have asked to speak to Mrs Byrne instead but I was too irritated. 'Thank you for your help,' I said sarcastically. 'I daresay I can find the barn.'

I exited, towing my case as best I could over the pebblestones. Stalking round the back of the house, I found myself in a stable yard. Here, what had once been a coachhouse, harness room and looseboxes for at least a dozen mounts had been turned into a series of modern apartments, also painted creamy-yellow, and far more attractive in their restored state than the house they used to serve. Running between them was an open corridor which led, I guessed, towards the barn.

It did, but the barn itself was some distance

away. Between it and me were more apartments converted from existing sheds. It was all extremely smart and must, I thought, have cost a bomb.

I trundled my case towards the barn. It was large and very long. Probably part of it in the past had been additional stabling added onto an older barn. Now it looked like one big building. To one side of it was a generous parking space which seemed to be full of cars.

There was no sound from within. I banged on the door but nobody came. I was about to bang again when I heard a woman's voice. 'Hold on, please. We've lost the key.' There was a long pause, a giggle from inside the barn and a triumphant, 'Here it is!' Then at last the door was opened. A tall, pear-shaped woman looked at me expectantly.

'Are you Brigit?' she said, sounding more welcoming than the woman at the house. 'Conor told us you'd arrive.'

'Conor isn't here himself?'

'He is,' she said, 'but he's upstairs. Come on in and wait for him.'

Inside the barn, some thirty or so students were ensconced behind a series of whitewashed trestle tables that ran down either side of the room. I'd obviously interrupted a life class. The model, a nondescript, mousy-haired girl, was sitting on a mat in the middle of the floor, with a gown wrapped loosely round her.

'We always lock the door during a life class,' the pear-shaped woman was explaining. 'Sorry we kept you waiting.'

'That's OK. I understand.'

Inside the door, a rickety set of wooden steps ran up to the upper floor. At the other end of the room was an enormous Victorian wardrobe with a full-length mirror sandwiched between two long doors. Like the tables, it was white. Beside it was a long-legged window dummy, bereft of hair and naked except for her high-heeled shoes. Somebody had sprayed her white.

The students, having taken stock of me, were talking now amongst themselves. I cast an eye around the group. Conor had said that the school was a meeting place for anyone and everyone, that there was no age restriction. That was evidently true. Some were white-haired, many not. One had shaved off all her hair. Another wore a nose-ring. Most were wearing jeans and T-shirts but some had summer dresses on and one rather voluptuous woman was squeezed into a pair of shorts and a revealing halter-neck.

'I'll tell Conor that you're here,' the pear-shaped woman said. 'Em will make you a cup of coffee, won't you, Em?'

'If she wants it,' said the model.

'No. Don't worry. I've just had some.'

The pear-shaped woman went upstairs. Then, 'Is that so?' said Conor's voice.

He came down immediately. He was wearing the same clothes that he'd worn to open EVA, along with the kind of smile that I had been hoping for.

'You got here finally,' he said. 'I was looking out for you. I thought you might come earlier.'

'I dawdled on the road a bit.'

'You had no trouble with the car?'

'Not a scrap. I left it round the front for you.'

'You went to the house, did you? Did Hannah tell you where I was?'

It was the first time that he'd mentioned Hannah's name. He seemed a bit uneasy with it, as if the subject of his wife was a rather tricky one. I thought of the face at the window again.

'No. It was an older woman.'

'Clodagh Moran,' Conor said. 'I hope she wasn't rude to you.'

'Well...'

'She's a bloody pain,' said Conor, 'but she's good around the house. Good with Hannah. I can trust her. I see you've got your case with you. Let's go up to where you're staying so you can get settled in. The class is nearly finished here. When it's over we'll come back.'

He took me to the second set of apartments, the ones converted from the sheds.

'Here you are.'

'Here' was a neat bed-sitting room, creamy yellow like the outside, with a shower room attached. A sofa bed had been made up and yellow towels laid out for me. There was a table at which I could work and a bookcase in a corner. On the table was a torch.

'For emergencies,' said Conor.

'That was thoughtful. It's a lovely room. Thank you very much.'

'Settle in and then come back.'

It didn't take me long to settle but even so the class was over when I got back to the barn. Em had disappeared as well. Conor was sitting alone

105

at one of the tables. He jumped up as I came in.

'I should have introduced you to the class,' he said, 'but we can do all that tomorrow. In the meantime, I must show that car to you – the one I said you could use.'

'How many cars have you got here?'

'Myself? I only have the one. This was one that Hannah used but she doesn't drive it now.'

'She won't mind my taking it?'

'Why should she mind? She doesn't use it. You'll meet her later on tonight. I take it that you'll eat with us? I said we'd be up there at seven.'

'Will I meet your children then?'

'Children?' Conor laughed. 'I don't have a family, Brigit. What made you think that I had children?'

'I thought... Never mind. It doesn't matter.' Anxious to get off the subject, I added quickly, 'Conor, tell me, what's that wardrobe doing here? Do you keep paint and sketchbooks in it?'

'No. Body parts,' said Conor, smiling. He went over to the wardrobe. 'See here.'

He opened both doors and I went to have a look. Inside the wardrobe was an assortment of papier-mâché limbs – arms, hands, legs and feet, all of which were painted white, and several pairs of moulded breasts. On one shelf was a curious collection of glass eyes, blue and green and brown and grey, and on another at least a dozen wigs in a variety of shades ranging from ash-blonde to black and brown and golden-red.

Conor said, 'I use them on her ladyship,' nodding at the manikin.

'But you could do that with the live model. You don't have to use a dummy.'

'Yes. But it's fun to use the dummy, and anyway Em wouldn't like it if I dressed her up like that. She's rather sensitive, is Em. She spent her life in a children's home in Dublin and turned up here in search of work. She's a strange girl in lots of ways but she fits in well and she's very loyal to me.'

'She's your only model then?'

'No, but she's the one that's lasted longest. She came here at the beginning of last summer and at the end of it I didn't have the heart to let her go without a job so I suggested she stay on and do some work around the place. She turned out to be surprisingly versatile, ready to turn her hand to anything. I've taught her how to frame my paintings. Until then, I'd done it myself. I don't use canvas, only boards. The process isn't complicated and it's given her a skill.'

'She must be very grateful to you.'

'So she tells me,' Conor said.

'And upstairs, what goes on up there?' I asked.

'Nothing much. It's mainly storage. Come on up, though, if you like.'

I followed him up the rickety staircase. The room upstairs was as he said, used for storing art materials, untreated boards, rolls of bubblewrap, rocks, shells, dried flowers and several rather pretty vases. The far end of the room was given over to half-finished pictures, mostly on board. There were tons of them stacked up haphazardly against the wall.

'None of them are mine,' said Conor. 'My

studio is in the house. I'll show it to you later on.'
He checked his watch. 'A bit too early yet to eat.'
He hesitated. I got the impression that he wasn't
that keen to go up to the house. I wasn't either.
Going to the house entailed meeting Hannah,
the prospect of which grew less appealing by the
minute. The conviction I'd had before, that, in
being with Conor, I had finally come home, was
even stronger now. Meeting Hannah would
sabotage that. Resenting her, I'd also feel a
hypocrite, eating the meal that she had cooked.

I cast around for an excuse to put off the evil
moment.

'What about that car?' I said. 'The one you said
I could use.'

'Ah, the car. Just as well you mentioned that.
I've had it serviced for you, Brigit. Em said that
she'd get it back. It should be out there in the car
park.'

The car park was no longer full. Conor
explained that, though several of his students
lived nearby and commuted to their classes,
others stayed in the apartments, and some of
them had come by car.

The car he had reserved for me was a BMW.

'But it's almost new,' I said. 'And Hannah
doesn't want to use it?'

All this money, I was thinking. The house. The
grounds. Apartments. Cars. Conor must be
making packets. From private clients, I supposed, along with profits from his shows. All the
same...

'Do you want to try it out?'

I did, to postpone that dreaded meeting. At

Conor's suggestion, I went back onto the main road and around the country lanes. We stopped to inspect the medieval church at Kilnaboy with its unique stone cross on the western gable and, above the door, the ancient carving of *Sile Ni Gig*, the pagan symbol of fertility. Then we saw the dog.

Conor was the first to see him.

'For Christ's sake, look at that!' he said.

'What? Where?'

But then I spotted him as well. He was limping very slowly along the road ahead of us. He was pathetic, emaciated, no more than a skeleton, with bones protruding through his fur.

'What is he?'

'It doesn't matter what he is. He's *hungry*, Brigit, that's the point. We've got to get some food to him.'

'I've got some biscuits in my bag.'

I stopped the car and rummaged for them. The dog, I saw, had stopped as well and was looking back at us. I rolled the window down and threw the biscuits out at him. The dog jerked convulsively then, ignoring the biscuits, sloped off to the right and crawled underneath a gate.

'Christ!' said Conor angrily.

He thrust open his door and jumped out, picking up the scattered biscuits. He turned round once to glare at me then, with the biscuits in his hand, he climbed the gate and disappeared.

Upset myself and uncertain what to do, I stayed behind the steering wheel, half apprehensive, half resentful at the anger I'd aroused. I thought, I did try to feed the dog. I didn't mean to frighten it.

I waited for what seemed an age but was only a few minutes. After a while, a tractor drew up and the driver shouted at me.

'Can you pull in? You're blocking me.'

'Sorry.' I was annoying everyone. But then the driver grinned at me.

'Thanks,' he said and raised a hand.

Conor did not come back. I got out myself and went in search of him. The gate gave access to a field surrounded by a drystone wall. At the other end was Conor, striding back in my direction. He didn't have the dog with him. I rested on the gate and waited, wondering if he'd still be cross or if he'd be apologetic.

He was neither. He reached the gate, his eyes downcast.

'Did you get to him?' I said.

'Yes.'

'And?'

'He has a huge big growth on him. He's dying, Brigit. It was hopeless.'

Tears were streaming down his cheeks. Nothing could have moved me more, and nothing else he could have done could have made me want him more. My resentment died away and my apprehension went. I longed to put my arms round him, cursed the social inhibitions that prevented me from doing so, that made me get into the car and turn the key in the ignition.

'Shall we go home?' I said.

'We may as well.'

Despite this curt reply, something had happened between us, I knew. A barrier had been removed.

Conor felt it too, I thought. He was quiet, driving back. I parked the car where we had found it and, without saying any more, we made our way towards the house.

Once there he broke the silence, saying, 'We'll go in the back way, Brigit.'

We trailed through an old-fashioned scullery with pots and pans stuck up on shelves into a big kitchen where Clodagh Moran was washing dishes in the sink. She gave me the kind of look that said, 'So, *you're* back again, are you?' but I totally ignored her.

'Where's Hannah?' Conor asked.

'She's upstairs. She's getting dressed.'

Dressed? I thought. Don't tell me they dress up for dinner? Was Conor going to dump me here and go upstairs to change his clothes? If so, I hoped I wouldn't be left to the charms of Clodagh Moran.

But he didn't change for dinner. He swept me out of the kitchen, through a dark and gloomy back hall, into the dining room where a table had been set. I don't know what I was expecting; not that décor, anyway, not the furniture and fittings, not in Conor Byrne's abode. But Mrs Beeton would have liked it. The room was dominated by an enormous bow-fronted mahogany sideboard. On it were a silver tea and coffee set and two hideously over-ornate vases. The table, covered by a damask cloth, was oval-shaped. Surrounding it were twelve ugly balloon-type chairs, also in mahogany.

In the centre of the table was a large silver and cut-glass cruet stand. The crystal glasses and the

111

blue and white Staffordshire china were complemented by snow-white napkins starched, no doubt, by Clodagh Moran.

I've stepped back in time, I thought, into an era I've always detested. Was this really Conor's taste? I couldn't credit that it was. Despite its authenticity, the room had the contrived look of a film set. But that is what it is, I thought. This house was purchased by an actor. He must have bought the contents too, and it stayed the way it was when he gave it to his daughter.

'Conor?'

Hannah Byrne was standing there. When I think of Hannah now, I see her as she was that day – a blazing fire in the room. It wasn't just her red-gold hair or the fact that she wore orange, a full-length orange floral dress with a sixties look to it, and a pair of old gold earrings. The fire was an energy that emanated from her. She was burning, all of her – her eyes, her face, her too-thin body. I automatically drew back, the way you do from too much heat.

'Is this Brigit Flood?' she said. 'Brigit, you came down today from Dublin? Conor told me all about you. You met at EVA, didn't you? Conor, ring the bell for Clodagh, please. Brigit must be fed, you know. I've been cooking all day long. I made some olive bread for us. And a pot roast – I did lamb. Do you like aubergines and garlic? I hope you do. I put them in…' She went on, speaking very fast, so it was hard to follow her. I thought that she was exquisite, small and dainty with a heart-shaped face, a porcelain figure come alive and then set alight by someone.

'Lamb sounds lovely,' I began, but Hannah was still chattering, talking now about the weather and how hot the summer was.

From this she leapt on to several unrelated topics – the morning news, an accident, someone who had phoned for Conor. I thought at first that she was nervous and, remembering Louise saying that she had a drinking problem, wondered if she was hungover. But she seemed quite confident. Her energy was bubbling over.

'Ring the bell,' she said again. 'Poor Brigit's going to die of hunger.'

Inevitably, this remark made me recollect the dog and that made me look at Conor. But he didn't look at me. He wasn't present any more – not in spirit, anyway. Physically, he loomed above us, but mentally he had withdrawn again.

My heart sank. I felt lonely, standing there. I wasn't in the least bit hungry. I didn't fancy aubergines. I hate them at the best of times, that slightly smoky taste they have, and the fact that Hannah had cooked them made them even less appealing.

She was confusing me, was Hannah. I'd expected – I had hoped – to dislike the sight of her but I didn't, not at all. On the contrary, she touched a little chord in me, something muted, very soft, that I didn't want to hear.

Conor hadn't pressed the bell. Hannah didn't do it either. Still talking – about what I don't remember – she opened a hatch door in the wall, shouted, 'Bring the food in, Clodagh,' and resumed her monologue.

We took our places at the table, Conor sitting in

113

the middle. Clodagh carried in a tray and set the food in front of us. The menu was incongruous, I thought, too contemporary for the setting. But Hannah Byrne could cook all right. The lamb, preceded by a Caesar salad and served with homemade olive bread, was up to Darina's standard.

Not that I ate much of it. As the meal progressed, I grew more and more uneasy. For a start, Conor remained distant, concentrating on his food, eating it like a condemned prisoner who's only too aware that this will be his final meal.

Hannah, on the other hand, didn't eat a single bite. And when Conor poured the wine he didn't give a glass to her. She's given up the booze, I thought. It must be difficult for her. I could hear that chord again. I tried to shut my ears to it. But I couldn't block my ears to the sound of Hannah's voice. It went on and on and on. She was becoming more and more manic, her words like bullets splaying us.

Conor said nothing. He helped himself to more lamb, munched a lot of olive bread, consumed a plate of pureed plums. I willed him to say something, anything, that would stop the flow of words. But he had switched off.

I should have seen it from the start, should have understood the problem. I was not an innocent and the signs were visible. But I was tired out by then and distracted by my feelings – the ones I had for both the Byrnes – and the meal was nearly over when I finally wised up.

Hannah was addressing me, saying, 'How long

are you staying, Brigit? Are you going to paint yourself? I went to art school too, you know. I gave it up when we got married. My father said it didn't matter and he...'

I looked more closely at her. Her big deep eyes looked into mine. In those eyes I read the truth. She was drugged up to the eyeballs. I guessed that she was high on speed. She had all the classic symptoms of being on amphetamines – the energy, the confidence, the tendency to talk a lot. And the loss of appetite. No wonder she was so thin. The drug had that effect as well, if you took a lot of it.

She must have taken it upstairs. The effect would last for hours, maybe up to four, I thought. Later on, she would be a different person – anxious, edgy, paranoid.

I leant back in my chair and took a sideways peep at Conor. I could see that he was weary. But other signs were obvious. The signs of boredom, exasperation and loss of interest in his wife. Despite the meal that she had cooked, it was evident that Conor was sick to death of Hannah Byrne.

SIX

Though it was nearly eleven, it wasn't that dark when I got away. That's the west for you, in the summer anyway; the evenings stretch out so much you think they're going to reach the dawn.

Conor came to the door with me.

'Thanks for being here,' he said bleakly.

I couldn't say I'd enjoyed myself but I did praise Hannah's cooking. 'It was fabulous,' I said.

'See you in the morning, Brigit.'

I set off, retracing my steps across the yard. But now I was too wide awake, as jumpy as Hannah was going to be later, to consider going to bed, or to read or to watch TV. It was a perfect night, the air balmy and a tinge of red still to be seen in a sky as reluctant to sleep as I was myself. Being out of doors was a relief; above all, it felt safe. It occurred to me that, while I'd inspected the back of the house, I'd had only a cursory glimpse of the parkland at the front as I drove in from the road. What I'd seen had looked attractive.

I turned back, went round the side of the house – the lights downstairs were all switched off; the Byrnes, I thought, had gone to bed – and headed for the wide expanse of grass bordered by towering beeches and oaks that must have been planted long before the house was built.

Perhaps there had been another house once, a less, self-conscious, more idiosyncratic, happier house. A house that was destroyed not by design but by accident, burnt down, perhaps, after a riotous party got out of control – something one knew could never have happened in the ostentatious monstrosity which had been built as a replacement.

Concocting my story, envisaging that other house (Georgian? Palladian?) and the family who might have lived and partied in it, I wandered on until I strayed into a grove of oaks. Villages and then towns must have grown up from settings like this, sylvan shelters where people met and felt protected. I thought again how safe I felt and how the trees, with their longevity, their thick, rough trunks and rugged branches, underlined the conviction.

Beyond the trees the grass looked bleached, striated with daisies and Lady's Fingers which, growing not far from the sea, had turned out white instead of yellow. I love wild flowers – I always have – much more than any others. Wandering round the park that night, I remembered a fight I'd had as a child over what Mammy termed Pincushion Flowers and I'd insisted were Gypsy Roses – those blueish-mauve wild flowers with flat, cushiony heads and hairy stalks that we came across on walks. Both of us were right of course but, to her, my choice of name was fanciful and too exotic, while to me hers was dull and snug and–

Someone was watching me. I knew it, even before I caught sight of the person. The sense – the knowledge – that I was being stalked came from the realisation that it had become unnaturally quiet in the park, that all around me the barely audible sounds of the night had stopped as if myriads of tiny, unseen creatures had paused in fear and caught their breath. I was frightened too. I thought, it isn't, it can't be happening to me again. It couldn't be the Rat of course, but–

I saw a shadow move. As I watched in terror, it detached itself from the tree behind which it had been hiding and fused with the shadow of another one.

My stomach heaved. My courage waned. As I had done before with the Rat, I tried telling myself that my pursuer was just a bully; that he got his kicks from observing my reactions; that, in himself, he was not a threat to me.

I didn't believe a word of it. I knew – I was convinced – that he, whoever he might be, was a psychopath. That he meant to murder me.

I didn't stand and brood on that. I did what I always did when the Rat appeared in my life. I fled. I ran across the white daisy carpet and round the grove of oaks towards the house which was now in complete darkness.

As I ran, I heard *him* run after me. I reached the driveway and heard my footsteps, and his, crunching on the pebblestones. I didn't dare look over my shoulder. If I did, I knew I'd fall, give up, lie beaten and doomed at the feet of a killer, waiting for his blows to flay me.

Panting, hearing myself gasp and moan, I rushed round the side of the house and back into the yard. If I'd hoped for signs of life I was promptly disappointed. Wherever the students were that night, they were not out there for me.

Maybe they were in their rooms. If I screamed, would they come out? But my old inhibition, the one that had stopped me speaking out when the Rat was after me, took control of me again and I didn't shout for help.

But perhaps there was no need. I couldn't hear the footsteps now. My pursuer had given up.

Or was he hiding, waiting for me? Reaching my doorway, I feared he'd be there, having dodged round the back; that he was lurking in the shadows, waiting for the chance to pounce.

But there were no shadows near my doorway. The light above it had been thoughtfully switched on, illuminating the façades of the converted outbuildings and the space around them.

I flung myself inside the room and double-locked the door. My throat was dry and I was panting. I checked the windows. They were shut. There was no one peeping through them. No one waiting to break in. Only my cowardly self, soaked in sweat and steeped in terror. I was ashamed, degraded by what had happened to me.

Disgusted, I showered, but not before pushing my bed against the door as another precaution against invasion. The windows were an obvious risk. My pursuer might break the glass, re-creating *Psycho*. I didn't close the bathroom door or draw the shower curtain either, as if these wholly inadequate actions could prevent his intrusion once he had made up his mind.

But no one tried to break in. Nothing happened. I finished showering and, still quaking, got into bed, cowering like a small child terrorised by tales of witches. I was sure I wouldn't sleep, but I was wrong. Almost at once, I fell asleep and only woke at half past seven. Going over what happened, I blushed scarlet with the shame.

But it was pointless dwelling on that. My first thought was that something positive had to be done to ensure that the events of the night before would not be repeated. That meant enlisting outside help. Like it or not, I had to admit that I was powerless on my own. Logic dictated I had to confess and tell someone about my pursuer.

But who? Conor was the obvious answer. But wouldn't he think that I was the nut? And who could blame him if he did? The Rat in Chiswick was bad enough, his behaviour barely credible. A Rat in Clare defied belief.

Who could it be? For a moment, I toyed with the crazy idea that it *was* the Chiswick Rat. That he had followed me to Dublin on the same flight, observed Mammy meeting me, pursued us in another car, been behind me ever since...

Honestly, Brigit, I said to myself. Of course it isn't the Chiswick Rat.

Trying my best to feel sanguine, I showered again and put my clothes on. It was early still for classes but I didn't feel like waiting. Thinking Conor might be there, I went to the studio. This time round, the door was open.

'Conor?'

'He's not here,' a voice called out.

'Em?'

'Who's that down there?' said the voice. Em

120

was on the upper floor.

'It's Brigit Flood. We've met already.'

'Oh, yeah?'

'I'm going to sit in on a life class.'

There was no reply to this but there was movement up above. Seconds later, legs appeared, coming down the ladder staircase.

'Hi,' I said when all of Em was in my sights.

She nodded at me without smiling.

'Are you going to model for it?'

She nodded again, her lips apparently glued together. It seemed I wasn't doing well in the making friends department, between Em and Clodagh Moran. Em, however, was half the size of Mrs Moran and as thin as Hannah anytime. Not another one, I thought. But Em, for all that she was skinny, didn't strike me as addictive. And hadn't Conor praised her efforts, said how useful she'd become, something he'd have hardly said if she was into Hannah's game.

Why was she being grumpy with me? Light dawned. Of course, I thought. Em's upset because I'm here. She's been Conor's right-hand woman. Naturally, she'd be resentful, thinking I'm a threat to her.

I hate being unpopular. Clodagh Moran's hostility had got under my skin last night. True, I didn't know the woman and her bad mood might just as easily have been due to an abscess in her tooth or a problem with her husband rather than with my presence. My sister would have told me off ('Stop being so subjective, Brigit') if I'd talked to her about it. Nonetheless, it was depressing and the thought of Em sulking in my presence all

121

through my stay in County Clare was deeply discouraging. I'd just have to reassure her that we weren't competitors, that her role was not affected by my advent. There should be room for both of us...

I suspected that there wasn't but I didn't dwell on that.

I said brightly, 'Did Conor tell you why I'm here?'

Em shrugged. 'He might have done. I don't remember.'

'I'm going to write an article. It's about the arts in Ireland. The studio will feature in it. Conor felt it was important that I see the work that the two of you are doing.'

This was wicked flattery, linking Conor's work with Em. A voice – not Darina's, my own – told me I should be ashamed. I was but it didn't stop me talking.

'So I'm staying down here awhile.'

This elicited a grunt.

'You do Conor's framing, don't you? I saw your work on show in London. The idea for my feature came as a result of that. Those paintings were extraordinary. I saw them and I was bewitched.'

That bit, anyway, was truthful. I realised I'd got Em's attention.

She said, 'They're shocking marvellous, so they are.'

'It must be brilliant working here.'

'It is, especially after–' She stopped, and let the words hang in the air.

I thought, she came from an orphanage, or was it a children's home? Either way, it must have been a complete contrast to life at the studio. I wondered what had brought her here, whether it was simply chance or if she'd heard about the school and thought it sounded interesting, or read an article on Conor and decided to approach him in the hope he'd give her work. I wondered how old she was. Seventeen? Eighteen? Not much more. But her eyes were much older. The eyes of a woman who has seen too much.

Remaining disconcertingly silent, she slipped a hand into her pocket and pulled out a packet of chewing gum. As she did so, her sleeve rolled up and I noticed that she had a small butterfly tattoo on her right wrist. She unwrapped a piece of gum, popped it into her mouth and chewed audibly on it.

I returned to the subject of Conor's exhibition. 'How long was he preparing for it?'

Em could not resist the question. She said, reverently, 'It took him a year, it did.'

'And did you go to London too?'

Em puffed out one cheek and cracked the gum she had been chewing. Mammy would have walloped her.

'Only Conor went to London.' She sounded wistful. Poor kid, I thought. She framed the pictures, after all. She would have liked to see them hung. Conor should have taken her.

'Anyways,' said Em with dignity, 'I was busy here.'

'Lots more paintings to be framed?'

She nodded. 'Conor works that hard,' she said. 'Always painting *her*, he is.' Painting Hannah, I presumed.

'She must be his muse.'

Em snorted. 'A queer kind of muse *she* is!'

I let that pass.

'There's a new one over there.' Em jerked her thumb towards the wardrobe. Propped against it was a picture which was turned the wrong way round.

'Can I have a look at it?'

'I can't stop you doing that.'

I went over and turned the picture right side round. It was a nude of Hannah, sitting on a kitchen chair. The light fell on her breasts and hair. The rest of her was all in shadow. The initial effect was sensuous but melancholy. There was anger there as well. I thought again about last night. The way Hannah had behaved. The way Conor had looked at her. Not surprisingly there was anger in the portrait.

Em was watching me, noting my reactions. 'He's made her beautiful,' she said.

'But she is, she's lovely looking.'

'He doesn't love her, though,' said Em.

The statement took me by surprise. I said, tentatively, 'Well, I suppose it's difficult–'

'He's destroyed by her!' said Em. 'The way she carries on is fearful. You know she lost her licence, don't you? That's why he's given you her car.'

The conversation was getting out of hand. I said briskly, 'I'm grateful for the loan of it. I left my car behind in England.'

'I thought you were down from Dublin?'

'I was up there with my mother. But I live in London now.' Was that true any more? I wondered. It didn't feel like it.

Before I could work that out, the door burst open and three people came in.

'Hiya, Em!' said one of them, a stocky girl wearing a magenta T-shirt the same colour as her hair.

Em smiled, grudgingly. I obviously wasn't the only one who had to coax a response from her.

The other two students I recognised from the day before – Miss Voluptuous, clad today in an outfit that the Spice Girls would have chosen had they felt adventurous, and a white-haired man in clean blue jeans.

'You're Brigit Flood, aren't you?' inquired the stocky girl. 'Orla Hickey is my name. This is Patrick Henderson and that's Celia Corrigan.'

'Nice to meet you,' I managed to say before another crowd came in.

Further introductions followed. I tried, and failed, to catch the names as one after the other greeted me. Then, talking and laughing, opening portfolios, unravelling rolled up paintings and unpacking paints and brushes, they began to take their places, spreading their pictures and sketches out on the white tables and exchanging views about them.

The result was a mixed bag, the efforts of professional or talented amateur work combined with that of real beginners. To my surprise, Celia Corrigan produced two superb watercolours, delicately executed on a small format, that placed her firmly in category one, while Patrick Henderson, who looked more in control of his life, was obviously still struggling with the semblance of a drawing. I remembered what Conor had said, that the studio was mixed, that it was designed for people from all walks of life and, clearly, of varied ability.

The door swung open again and Conor came in backwards, lugging something after him. The talk and laughter died down and people leant forward curiously, peering to see what he had brought with him. It proved to be a trolley. On it was a projector, a screen, and a box of slides.

What interested me more than the contents of the trolley was the effect that Conor's presence in the room had upon the assembled students. Some people have it, most people don't: that mesmeric combination of charm, internal energy and power that sun kings and their queens possess.

Before Conor entered the room, the students had been cheerful enough. But his arrival was a dart that, seemingly, injected them with radiance. He hadn't said a single word and yet they were suddenly motivated in a way they hadn't been until he was in their midst. You could see it in their eyes, in the way they held themselves, like horses quivering to be off at the onset of a race.

Something happened to me, too. An idea was conceived in me. It was embryonic still, but I was aware that it was there and I was excited by it.

Meanwhile, Conor had made his way between the tables and was facing us. He didn't say hello to me or good morning to the others. He wasn't wasting any time. He just said, 'We're talking landscape today,' set the projector up, unrolled the screen, and opened up the box of slides.

No one spoke. No one dared to speak. Everybody sat and waited. I had found an empty chair and perched on the edge of it. Em had crept forward and taken up a cross-legged position on her mat, her eyes shining brighter than anyone else's.

For a moment, I felt uneasy. It was a little too charismatic. Had people chanted and clapped their hands, I wouldn't have been that surprised.

But the moment passed and Conor spoke again.

'There are people, so-called artists, who have come to terms with the medium they're using. They can handle oils. Or they're comfortable with watercolour. But they cannot paint a landscape. They look at a view of a wood or lake and reproduce it as it is. This is not painting.

'You paint when you see something that appeals to you and you can alter its components *until they harmonise*. Nature's not an artist. Do not expect her to create ready-made pictures which you only have to copy. As Gauguin said, "Art is an abstraction. Draw it out of nature. Dream about it. And think more of the resulting creation."

'Great landscape artists move trees, hack down bushes, reduce the size of islands and build bigger, better boats than the ones they may see moored alongside a charming harbour. I'm going to show you what I mean.'

He pressed a button. An image came up on the screen – a photograph of a country lane, a gateway leading to a field and gently undulating hills. It might have been a pleasing view. But it was completely spoilt by the presence of a tree intruding in the middle of it.

I thought, now what has this to do with Gauguin? And I wondered if Conor, too, secretly wished to live a primitive life and find new strength far away from any human being.

But he had someone else in mind, another artist altogether. He said, 'That was how the landscape was until Cezanne walked up that lane. Now have a look at what he did.'

He projected a second imagine on to the screen. The tree had moved a few feet right. The gateway was less prominent. A scattering of chunky rocks had been reduced to just a couple.

'Structure mattered to Cezanne,' Conor went on. 'He was fond of solid objects – rocks, houses, tree trunks, hills – stable elements which he could rearrange in geometric, harmonious lines. He was not in love with nature in the intuitive way that, for instance, Monet was. He responded to it sensitively but he applied order to it. In other words, he used his brain.'

He talked to us about Cezanne, explaining that only after he'd left Paris and settled in the south of France did his work become exciting.

Then, employing the same technique as before, he showed us several other slides depicting nature's landscapes and how those landscapes changed for the better after various artists, from the Neo-Impressionists to the Fauves and the Hyper-Realists, had redesigned them on the canvas.

I wondered where he'd got the photos; out of art books, I supposed. I watched the class react to him in the same mesmerised way as I and the EVA students had. I listened to the golden voice and marvelled at the pitch of it.

But it wasn't just the voice, it was the overall production. The way that Conor smiled and laughed and how he used his hands and eyes. I thought, this man isn't just a teacher and a fine artist. He's a performer.

My idea was growing. I could feel it stirring in me.

'That's it.' Conor switched the projector off and rolled up the screen again. I watched him do so, fascinated by these mimetics. He didn't have to tidy up. The screen wasn't getting in anyone's way. But Conor, I realised, was still on stage, still playing to the gallery. In front of an audience who didn't want his performance to end, he was putting his props away. He had an innate sense of the dramatic and yet he gave the impression of being completely natural. I thought he should exploit that gift.

My idea gained more strength. I was mad about it. It's got to work, I said to myself. Conor's living proof it can. I must talk to him about it, and see if he'll co-operate.

SEVEN

I had to wait until the evening to catch Conor on his own. Between times, he moved from landscape into life. Em stripped off and got to work. She was stoical about it, holding a poise for so long that she appeared anaesthetised, not a woman any more but a statue Conor had sculpted out of living flesh and bone. I felt quite concerned about her. How could she bear it, standing on her mat for such an age?

But she didn't seem to mind. Not that I could read her face. She was entirely enigmatic, her thoughts apparently miles away and all of them reserved for Em.

The students sketched her earnestly, producing several dozen Ems. None of them resembled her but this was not their intention. To them, she was just a skeleton who happened to have flesh on her, a basic, bony female form; the fundamental underpinning upon which each student superimposed his or her own specific vision of a woman.

Again, the work was very varied, ranging from tentative beginners' sketches to ideas for major paintings. At Conor's suggestion, I wandered quietly round the room, peering over people's shoulders.

I was surprised by Orla's drawing, an abstraction of the breasts which was powerful and erotic. Celia Corrigan, on the other hand, had produced another of her dainty sketches showing a maternal Em with a baby in her arms. Someone else, a youngish man with ginger hair, had a realistic Em cowering in an alleyway, while a woman I'd not noticed before depicted her more sensuously, contained inside a tulip head which had phallic overtones.

Conor strolled between the tables, inspecting everybody's work, commenting on the results and, in some cases, sitting down beside a student and embellishing a drawing.

'Let yourself go,' I heard him say. 'Inhibition only cripples.'

As the afternoon progressed, Conor's liberation process included drawing with the left hand.

'All sorts of things come out of this,' he said to me when our paths crossed again. 'It doesn't just release the hand. It frees the mind as well, you'll see.'

I did, and though technically there were some problems for the students, new ideas developed.

'Is it always like this here?'

'The life class, do you mean?' asked Conor.

I nodded and he shook his head.

'The fundamental purpose of a life class is to understand the body. You can't escape anatomy. You must not forget how the limbs and bones relate. Lines must always have a function. Otherwise, it's just a nonsense. Most days, we just slog away, concentrating on the form. Then we have a day like this. Yes? Hold on there a minute, will you?'

The woman who had drawn the tulip had

attracted his attention. He crossed the room to deal with her. I had nothing else to do but sit and wait for his return. It had been that way all day. What had been in Conor's mind when he'd invited me to Clare? He'd said there would be work for me. But no work had been produced. And what was there for me to do? Between them, Conor and Em had it all sewn up as far as I could see.

Out of this thought came a dangerous one, that he'd asked me down to Clare for reasons other than my work. But that wasn't something I wanted to face. Not yet. Maybe not at any stage. I thought, I mustn't contemplate the dangers. Or concede that they exist. If I do, they'll multiply. And after all, it doesn't matter that when Conor asked me down there was no role for me to play, because now there *is* a role. The one that goes with my idea.

Nearly five o'clock. The class would end soon.

When it did, I stayed behind. All the others ebbed away. All the others except Em.

She put on her clothes and switched parts, from playing model at the life class to being Conor's picture framer.

'I've done that new one for you, Conor.'

'Have you? Great. Where is it, Em?'

Her back to me, she gave it to him.

'Good girl!' he said. 'Mind you, I've more than that for you to do. There's something that's dried out already.'

'For Inishbofin, or for here?'

'For Inishbofin,' Conor said.

He had an Inishbofin buyer? That seemed

unlikely. Despite its beauty, Inishbofin was not the sort of place that attracted wealthy people interested in buying art. But I didn't dwell on that, having more to think about.

If only Em would just piss off!

'I'll bring it down to you,' said Conor. 'Will you be around this evening?'

'I will so. I'll wait for you.'

'Half past seven, I'll be there.' With this statement he dismissed her. But she didn't look displeased.

'I'll see you then,' she said, and smiled, the way she didn't smile at me.

You can't win them all, I thought.

She was almost at the door.

''Bye for now,' I said to her.

'Oh, yeah. 'Night,' she said, and left.

Now I had the chance to talk to Conor on his own. I was concerned about the timing. He was tired, worn out by his big performance. His eyes had smudges underneath them and when Em went out the door, he sank into the nearest chair.

'God! I could kill a drink!' he said.

'Is there something here you could drink?'

'No. And there's nothing at the house. We'll go into Corofin.'

He was taking it for granted that I'd go along with him. I didn't make a fuss about it. I'd do that another time if I thought it necessary. Right now, I had something else in mind.

'Which car do you want to take?' I asked.

'Yours. Mine is parked up at the house. Anyway, I'm knackered. I'd prefer it if you'd drive.'

We went to the Anglers' Arms, an apt name for a hotel set in brown trout fishing country. Being teatime, the bar was more or less deserted. All the better for my purpose.

I waited till the drinks were brought and let Conor take a gulp, followed by another one. He stretched his arms, clasped his hands behind his neck and eased lower in his chair. He was certainly relaxing. The tiredness was going out of him. I seized my opportunity.

'Conor,' I said, 'there's something that I want to tell you.'

He looked up and feigned alarm. 'What is it? Is it something bad?'

'Something that could do you good.'

'Get on with it and tell me then!'

'I was watching you this morning. You'd be brilliant on the box.'

'You see me as a Gay Byrne clone?'

For nearly thirty years, the incredibly popular Gay Byrne had directed, produced and presented *The Late Late Show* at RTE. People used to say that he'd be President of Ireland when he retired from the station.

'Don't joke, Conor. I'm not teasing. You're a natural for it. You could be big. You really could.'

'On RTE? Aw, come on, Brigit.'

'I meant UK television. Maybe a co-production with RTE. That way you'd get the money, Conor, and the audience you need.'

'That's very flattering but–'

'Wait a minute. Listen to me. You've got the presence – honestly. The charisma. The voice. The lot. And you're classless – that's important.'

'Ireland is classless. What's new about that?'

'I mean classless in the sense of getting through to everybody – the man and woman in the street *and* your intellectual viewer. No bullshit. No arts speak. Isn't what you're about – what the studio's about?'

'Of course, what else?'

'Well, *that* is new. And there's a market for it. One that's growing all the time.'

'There is?'

'Yes. Think about it, Conor. Fine arts was the last refuge of the Establishment in the media in Britain. In the days when Lord Clark presented *Civilisation*, people weren't that put off by his public school persona. It was a fantastic programme and viewers had been brainwashed into the belief that no one else but Lord Clark and his ilk had the gravitas to present it. But that was back in the eighties, before we had satellite.'

I continued in this vein, emphasising how multi-channel television had influenced viewers' thinking and made people realise that there was more to television than traditional public service broadcasting and the baggage that it carried.

'We've learnt lessons from the States where there are all sorts of channels, including one just for the arts.'

'That's America,' said Conor, sounding maddeningly dismissive.

'It could be Europe in the future. UK television even. There's a major interest in painting. Check the turn-out at the Tate. At any major exhibition. It isn't just the tourists, Conor. It's the British public too. The people who'd respond to you if

135

they saw you on the box.'

'So?'

'So, I have contacts in the business. Someone in particular. I'd like to talk to her about you. That is, if you're interested.'

I didn't need a verbal answer. He was interested all right. I could see it in his eyes. Great, I thought. I've got him now. I know he's going to run with this.

I waited till he spoke again before expanding on my theme. As soon as Conor said, 'I could be,' I told him about Natalie.

'Natalie is a New Yorker but she lives in London now. She works for an American agency specialising in the arts. The States have been promoting artists for as long as I remember. London has been way behind. But recently there's been a change. These days, big companies build artists up. Businessmen back up the arts. Take Charles Saatchi, for example.'

I went on about Charles Saatchi and what he did to promote artists.

'He watches out for real talent. He goes to all the degree shows and buys the best of what he sees. He never sells those paintings, Conor. He's got one of the biggest private collections in the world, but he does exhibit them. That way the artists' names get known. Damien Hirst is the most famous but he's not the only one.'

'What's all that to do with me? Are you telling me Charles Saatchi needs an artist-as-presenter?'

'No. I'm only talking of the interest – the growing interest – in the artists as a breed. Take the Internet, for instance. Christie's and

Sotheby's and some of the major galleries use it these days to sell pictures. People want a flower painting or perhaps a Mary Feddan, so they check it out on their computer. But let's get back to you. You need somebody specific. Someone who'll promote your image and get you into television.'

In passing, it struck me that Janice Seton might well have thought along these lines and found such a person for him. Silly cow. She should have done.

Conor cut into my thoughts. 'This somebody is Natalie?'

'I think so, yes. I'm sure it is. I know we could work with her. I know what she could do for you.' I bubbled with enthusiasm. Tucked away in County Clare, everything seemed possible, including the elevation of an Irish artist to a mega TV star.

Conor gave me a quizzical look. 'I may have sold well in London but I'm not that famous, Brigit. I wonder if there'd be that interest.'

'That's where Natalie could help. Let me talk to her about it.'

He laughed. 'Why not? Go ahead. Do what you like.'

'I'll call Natalie tomorrow.'

The idea was buzzing round me. Conor would make a great presenter. Of course, he'd need a good producer. That would be where I'd come in, later in the scheme of things. After Natalie signed him. I had to sell him to her first.

'Tell me what this woman's like.'

'Natalie? Jewish. From the Bronx. And clever.

Not to mention energetic.'

We sat there talking about her until nearly eight o'clock. Conor had forgotten Em. I never thought of her myself.

'You hungry?' he said at last.

I nodded, and we were just about to rectify that when Celia Corrigan came in. Patrick Henderson was with her.

'Hello, Conor,' Celia said, rather shyly for a woman wearing such a low-cut T-shirt. 'Could I ask a favour of you?'

'Sure. What is it?' Conor asked.

I noticed Patrick looking at me and then taking note of Conor, wondering why we were together.

'I need a picture framed,' said Celia. 'Would you mind if I asked Em?'

'Not at all. She'd be delighted.'

'I thought she might be all tied up doing all *your* framing, Conor.'

That did it.

'Jesus, I'm a bloody fool! Sorry, Celia, I'd forgotten. I told Em to wait for me because I had a painting for her. It won't affect you using her. Sorry about dinner, Brigit.' He was on his feet already.

'Never mind. It doesn't matter.'

It did, a bit, for I was starving. I hadn't shopped for food that day and I'd run right out of biscuits.

Conor took the car and I stayed on at the Anglers' Arms to have a meal on the understanding that Patrick and Celia would give me a lift back later. They were going to eat as well.

'Come and sit with us,' they said.

The bar, which had been slowly filling up,

became crowded and quite jolly. Other students turned up and in the end there were eleven at our table. It didn't take me long to feel at home with everyone. Before I noticed, it was midnight, which meant that it was pretty dark when we drove back into the car park.

'I'll leave you here, if that's all right,' Patrick said.

'Thanks. And thank you for the dinner, Patrick. 'Night, Celia.'

''Night, Brigit.'

They shot off in the car again and, buoyed up by my idea, I wandered towards my room.

Elation soon gave way to terror. I sensed, and then I knew for sure that *he* was watching me again. I could see him lurking behind a car.

It was too much for me. I burst into a flood of tears and just stood there transfixed, even though I was convinced that the figure would attack me.

I'm not sure how long I was there. To me, it seemed like several hours but it was probably just minutes. Then another car pulled in and shone its light across the car park. The figure was illuminated. It was small and very thin. I saw that it was wearing black, and that it had a black cap on.

Then the car lights dazzled me. I raised my hand instinctively to shield my eyes and stepped aside to let it pass. Its driver took no notice of me. She (I soon saw it was a woman) found a parking space and, unaware of the drama that was taking place around her, got out, opened the boot and hauled out several plastic bags, probably with groceries in them.

It was the pear-shaped woman who'd let me in the day before – a nice, friendly kind of person. A person you could confide in if you felt the way I did.

But that was the trouble, I couldn't let on, couldn't bring myself to say that someone vile was stalking me. I was like the kind of victim who is beaten by her lover and keeps going back for more, and I was aware of it and ashamed. Rooted in my fear and shame, I couldn't seek the help I needed. Couldn't tell the pear-shaped woman that my pursuer was somewhere near and ask if she'd walk to my room with me. And so off she went without even knowing I was there.

But her arrival got me going. I didn't waste another minute. I made a dash for it, listening, looking for *him*, certain he was watching me with cruel eyes.

I reached my room unscathed. I slipped inside, locked the door, and checked the windows. Then I cried again. Shivering, I crept into bed and sank into heavy sleep.

Next morning, I pushed the memory away, wondering if it really happened.

I phoned Natalie.

'Hi, honey, how are you?' she said.

I lied and said that I was fine, then put my proposition to her.

'You sleeping with the guy?' she asked.

'No, I'm not! It's not like that.'

'No? OK. I take your word. So tell me more about him. What major prizes has he won? The Turner Prize? The Biennale?'

I had been prepared for this and countered it

immediately. 'Prizes aren't the point with Conor. He *has* it. Trust me. Honestly.' I described his presence for her, his voice, his classless quality, and added in an urgent voice, 'You should see the whole performance, Natalie.'

'If you say so, I believe you. But I can't come over now. There's too much happening this month. If I had a video... Can you get one made in Clare? A video of Conor Byrne? I want him in the studio. I want his work as well, of course. I'd need a treatment to go with it. You can do that, Brigit, can't you?'

'A treatment's not a problem.'

'What about the video?'

'We-ell...'

'Wait. The massive brain is working, Brigit. Parky's cousin's back in town. David, the photographer. Remember, he was at our party?'

I tore my mind back to the party, one of many that Natalie and her husband, Peter Parker, had hosted at their home in Hampstead. Above the crowd loomed up a figure, a fair-haired man whom I had liked. With him was a gorgeous woman who just had to be a model.

'I remember him,' I said.

'He's had a problem with his foot. He hurt it filming in New York. He's had to rest but now he's bored, dying to get back to work, except the doctors say he can't. But he could make a video. That wouldn't be too strenuous.'

'You think he'll want to come to Ireland?'

'Why not? He needs the stimulus. I'll ask him now. I'll call you back.'

She called me back in fifteen minutes.

'OK. He's on. He'll be with you. But only in a week or two. When the doctors say he can. You get in touch with him yourself and let me know what's going on.'

As usual with Natalie, action followed quick decision. I took down David Parker's number and said I'd have a word with Conor about his accommodation.

I was glowing with achievement. It was only one small step but Natalie was interested. And we'd got David Parker coming. The rest was really up to Conor, about whom I had no doubts. Wonderful, I told myself. I know we're going to pull it off.

I set off to look for Conor and found him in the studio. Classes hadn't started yet. Natalie being Natalie, she was at her desk by eight and, knowing that, I'd phoned her early.

Conor was engrossed, sorting out the students' drawings, work that had been left for him to comment upon at his leisure.

'I've had these sketches here for weeks,' he said, shaking his head in near despair. 'I've had no time to sort them out and now there is a mountain of them.'

I was about to break the news and tell him about my achievements. But I'd spotted a signature on one of the paintings – a watercolour, quite proficient, not outstanding, of a fiddler and a dancer – and I was diverted by it.

'Sheila Ferguson,' I said. 'The woman who was so withdrawn. I meant to tell you that I met her.'

Silence fell. I felt that I'd said something wrong. Then Conor said, 'You met Sheila Ferguson?'

'Mm. When I stopped in Ballyvaughan. In the restaurant. *An Fear Gorta.* We got into conversation.'

'What did she say to you?' said Conor.

'She talked mostly about gardening. Oh, and she said she lacked the talent to continue with her painting.'

But there had been more than that. She'd said, 'I hope it all works out for you,' sounding rather dubious. And, 'I was paying off a debt. I owed a lot to Conor Byrne but I've settled that account.' A cheap remark, I had declared. Not one to repeat to Conor.

'And that was all she had to say? She didn't mention me at all?'

'Just in passing,' I said lightly.

Conor looked relieved. 'Thank goodness,' he said. 'I was concerned about her. You see, I had to ask her to leave here.'

'What happened? Was she hard to get along with?'

'Not exactly *hard*. In a way, she was too easy.'

I guess I looked mystified because Conor added quickly, 'I suppose I should explain. Sheila fell in love with me. In an environment like this, people can get stimulated. And I suppose it was inevitable that she would transpose her feelings for her dead husband onto me for saving her. I made a big mistake. I should have seen it coming, but,' he shrugged ruefully. 'In the end I had no choice. The students were aware of it. It became embarrassing. I had to get her out of here.'

'That must have been distressing for you.'

'It was. It screwed me up. I hated it. I tried to

do it tactfully. But these things are never easy. She was furious with me. Screamed and yelled and called me names.'

'God. Did anybody hear her yelling?'

'I hope not. But you never know. I couldn't wait for her to go.' He paused and asked in a worried voice, 'How was she when you came across her?'

'She wasn't in a state,' I said. 'She actually seemed quite normal.'

'She takes tranquillisers all the time. It's a wretched business, Brigit. I just hope she won't relapse. Go back to where she was before.'

'Maybe not. She was talking about her garden. She seemed quite enthusiastic.'

'Good. She desperately needs a project. But I feel awful about her.'

'Let me cheer you up,' I said. 'I've got news about our project. Natalie is interested. She wants a video of you. She knows someone who can make one. A photographer connection. David Parker is his name. I'll phone him later on today to confirm when he'll come over but it seems he's keen enough.'

Conor brightened. 'You set all that up this morning?'

'It wasn't very difficult.'

'No?' He grinned, obviously pleased as Punch. I smiled back, luxuriating in approval. 'You'll phone this fellow Parker now?'

'I thought I'd wait until eleven. For all I know, he's still in bed. He's hurt his foot. He's resting it.'

'You seem to know a lot about him. You've come across the fellow, have you?'

144

'I've met him briefly. He seems pleasant.'

'Is he gay?'

'I shouldn't think so,' I retorted, thinking of the gorgeous woman who'd been at the party with him and wondering why it was important whether he was gay or not.

'OK,' Conor said thoughtfully. 'When will he come over then?'

'He can't come for a week or so.'

'Make it two weeks if you can. We're going to Inishbofin around that time. All of us. The entire school. That should be on the video.'

'Brilliant. It will all tie in. That way, too, we can show the island pictures, and then where you painted them. Natalie will love that, Conor.' But then I realised that most, if not all, of those paintings must have been sold. 'Maybe we can ask the purchasers if David can take photos of them. Would Janice Seton co-operate?'

'No doubt she would,' said Conor slowly. 'But we needn't take that route. There are other island paintings – the ones I don't intend to sell.'

'That's great. They're here? At the house?'

'They're in Inishbofin. I have a house up there as well. I use it as a gallery. I'll take you there when we go up.'

'All right.' But then I thought, it's not all right. We've left my favourite painting out. 'Conor,' I said, 'about that picture, "Hannah Painting". Janice sold it I suppose?'

'She did. But there's another one. The same theme but it's slightly different. I think you might prefer it, Brigit.'

'As long as it's still "Hannah Painting".'

'It is. It's her. You needn't worry. Incidentally, that reminds me. She hasn't been a nuisance, has she?'

'A nuisance? Hannah? But I've only met her once. How could she be a nuisance, Conor?'

He laughed wryly. 'She could be. Just believe it, Brigit. You saw her for yourself that night. That's what I would call a nuisance.'

'She didn't bother me, I promise.'

'At the house she didn't maybe. But later, when you left us, did she? Upstairs, you see, it's sub-divided. I have my rooms away from hers – my studio and bedroom. I tend to lock myself away. Hannah doesn't always know if I'm in the house or not. That can cause a problem sometimes. It might have done with you, for instance. What I mean is, did she, well, check up on you? Has she been wandering round the grounds? Hanging round your room perhaps?'

I gaped at him, too surprised to answer. *Hannah* checking up on me? *Hannah* wandering round the grounds?

Conor saw my face and swooped. 'Ah-ha, she *has* been bothering you! I might have known she'd be a nuisance. You should have mentioned it to me. I'm sorry if you've been embarrassed. I should have talked to you about it. It's typical of Hannah, Brigit. Every time a woman comes here – an attractive woman, that is – Hannah does her stalker act, thinking that she'll catch me out.'

I was still struck dumb. It was Hannah, I thought, not a man. There's no need to feel afraid. It was only Hannah out there. Hannah doing her stalker act. She wasn't a threat to me...

'Brigit,' Conor said, 'you're not saying anything but you're looking very happy. What is it that I've said to you to make your face light up like that?'

Eventually, I found my voice.

'It's complicated. Leave it there. But you're right, I am happy. And Hannah's not a nuisance, Conor. She's not going to bother me.'

EIGHT

Filled with goodwill towards mankind (it was Hannah – not an unidentified nutter) I dialled David Parker's number. A recorded voice informed me that David Parker wasn't free but that he'd return my call. I'd only just put down the phone when it rang again.

The same voice on the line.

'Hi, Brigit, this is David Parker. I was hoping that you'd phone. It's about the video?'

'I gather that you're interested.'

'More than that. I'd love to do it. A good excuse to go to Ireland.' He sounded warm and optimistic. We talked about the video and how much it would cost Conor. Quite expensive, it worked out, but I had expected that.

'I'll have to check this out with Conor and come back to you again.'

'Of course. Come back when it suits you, Brigit. What's the weather like in Ireland?'

'It's cooled down a lot,' I said. 'What's it up to over there?'

'It's boiling hot and London's hell. You lot have got the right idea.'

He was obviously on for a chat, the way people often are when illness binds them to the house.

'How's your injured foot?' I asked.

'On the mend. I've had a skin graft.'

'What happened to it?'

148

David plunged into a long but cheerful explanation about filming in New York, a commercial he was making, and a house with railings round it. 'The railings had these spikes on top. You know the kind of thing I mean. Sharp as icepicks. Wretched things. I was climbing over them so I could get a better shot. Somehow I lost my balance and a spike went through my foot. They stitched it up but it wouldn't heal, or not until they did the graft. But now it's looking rather good. I have a butterfly down there! I had a tattoo on my hip. Years ago. A big mistake. Anyway, they've used that skin and now it's on my foot instead!'

'Butterflies are all the rage,' I said. 'Our model has one on her wrist.'

'Does she? Listen, about yourself. I remember meeting you at one of Nat and Peter's parties. You're dark-haired and you have brown eyes and your father's name was Joe.'

'You remember that about me?' I was amazed, especially that he knew Joe's name.

'Oh, I remember more than that. You'd just come back from Africa. You said you had a travel bug and that you caught it from your father. He'd been an inspiration to you. You were very close to him. It stuck in my mind, you see, because my father had just died.'

A knife – a spike – went through my heart. An inspiration. You were very close... Well, that was a joke, I thought.

The conversation was becoming too intimate for me to handle. I changed the subject and went back to the video.

'Could you come here in two weeks' time?' I explained about the trip. He said the dates were fine by him. Said it sounded quite exciting. Where was this island, Inishbofin?

By the time we'd finished talking, I felt I knew him rather well. What a tonic to chat to someone so spontaneous. Conor would be bound to like him.

Conor had a life class going. Better let him finish it before the two of us talked money.

The goodwill feeling was still on me, so I thought I'd phone the family, starting with Mammy.

That was a mistake. It immediately threw a damper on my spirits.

'That's you, Brigit, is it then?' she said, acting all remote and cool. 'And what have you been doing lately?' It might have been years since I'd been in touch and was phoning now from Mars.

'I'm still settling down,' I said.

She laughed at this. It sounded brittle. 'Settling down? That's not like you.'

'Settling in then,' I amended. 'There's quite a lot of work to do. That article I have to finish, and a treatment I must write.'

The word 'treatment' meant nothing to her. It was an incomprehensible word, part of the vernacular I spoke way out there in foreign parts.

I kept my temper and said I'd phone her in a week.

'If you find the time,' she said. 'I wouldn't like to pressurise you.'

Determined to extract some reciprocal good feeling from a member of my family, I called Darina next.

'It's all right for some!' she said. 'I hear you've taken off for Clare.'

'For Kilnaboy, to be precise.'

'I thought you didn't like the country.'

I wouldn't be provoked. 'The country here is looking gorgeous. How's everything with you?' I asked. 'The house is finished, is it now?'

Darina spoke about the house. The lampshades weren't delivered yet, the ones she'd ordered for the bedrooms. She'd found an antique butcher's table and some lovely gold silk napkins. There was trouble with the Aga. I felt as if I was being taken on a conducted tour around Balmoral or Buck House, with the Queen as guide.

'And the children, how are they?'

'The girls are great. They always are. They think the house is wonderful. Mikey's not adjusted still. He's always been a funny child. You know the way it is with him.'

'He's unhappy? Why is that?'

'I told you, it's adjustment problems. He'll get over it in time.'

'But what's he doing? Is he crying?'

'Not crying. Only having nightmares, Bridge. Afterwards he wets the bed. And I thought we were over that. It really is an awful bore.'

'But that's serious,' I said.

'No, it's not. You don't know children. They go through these passing phases and they soon grow out of them.'

'If you say so.'

'Yes. I do,' Darina said. 'After all, I've three of them.'

Chastened by her, I rang off.

151

The life class was nearly over. I got to the studio as Celia Corrigan emerged, followed by the other students.

'What's the news?' demanded Conor.

When I told him, he looked green. 'It's going to cost that much?' he said.

'I know it sounds expensive, but–'

'*Expensive?* It's a rip-off, Brigit! Photographers are all the same. Tea boys dressed in velvet suits.'

'Come on, Conor. That's not fair.'

'Fucking narcissistic poseurs…'

I let him rant and rave about it. When he had run out of insults, I switched tack and tried again.

'I'd say it is the going rate. But if you like I'll check it out.'

'Will you then, and let me know?'

I phoned around and got some quotes. David Parker's was the lowest. I reported this to Conor.

'What a bunch of crooks,' he said. But I could see that he'd calmed down; that he was resigned to David.

Two weeks … I realised I had been coasting. I had that article to finish, and then the treatment after that. I'd better get a move on fast; complete the article this week and then get down to work with Conor.

I'd almost finished my research on the background for the feature. In my room, reams of typed notes hung like snakes across the chair. But before I started writing I felt that I should see the Taibhdhearc theatre. I might lead my article with the Irish language question and pinpoint where it stood precisely in the arts scene in the nineties.

Speaking Irish fluently, once regarded as a chore, was now a fashionable pastime, something Irish yuppies did to show their pride in Gaelic culture. But while the smart set spoke the language, interest in it was decreasing amongst the people in the west because of tourist infiltration. The swing might well affect the Taibhdhearc. I wondered what the crowd up there felt about the tourists' presence, a question that I'd have to ask them.

The theatre was in Galway. Having lined up an appointment, I set off in Hannah's car. For me, it was a perfect day, not too warm to be in town, but sunny, balmy, nicely lazy. The road ran sweetly past the lakes, Lough Atedaun and several others, as well as Ballyportry Tower House and Fiddaun Castle, near Lough Bunny.

I drove, concocting sentences in my head, planning the feature that I would write. Yes, the Taibhdhearc was the lead. Then I could take in the Abbey. Perhaps I'd link the two theatres with the plays of Sean O'Casey.

A figure stepped from the grass verge onto the road and put a hand up for a lift. A slender figure with red hair... My God, I thought, it's Hannah Byrne.

I pulled in, conscious of the irony of being in her car. Seeing who the driver was, Hannah seemed to be relieved. To my surprise, she smiled at me. Because of the clothes she wore – a black and white flared mini skirt, a T-shirt and black high-heeled sandals – she was looking very young. She was carrying a cumbersome black satchel and her hair – her lovely hair, I thought again – was hanging loose around her shoulders. The feeling that I'd had before, the compulsion to protect her, came upon me once again.

I reminded myself that she didn't deserve it. Hadn't she been stalking me, scaring me to death at night? Why should I bother about her now?

All the same, I was concerned and, at the same time, irritated. I sensed that I was in for trouble, that she would muck up my day. Still, I knew I had no choice but to take her in the car.

'What a coincidence,' I said, opening the passenger door for her.

Hannah obviously thought so too. 'Brigit Flood!' she said. 'That's funny!'

I tried, and failed, to agree with her.

'How did you get this far?' I asked. 'Did someone drop you off, or what?'

'A farmer brought me here,' she said.

I wondered whether Conor knew, or Clodagh Moran for that matter. Maybe they were looking for Hannah. Maybe I should take her home. But going back would make me late and, anyway, if I turned round, Hannah would protest.

'Where are you heading for?'

She shrugged. 'I'm on my way to town,' she said.

That left several options open. The little market town of Gort was just a mile or two away. But, once there, the road bisected: right to Ennis and Limerick; left through the town to Galway.

'Which town, Hannah?' I demanded.

'It doesn't bother me,' she said. 'I only want to go to town.' She didn't ask where I was going.

Nonplussed, I drove on. There was a strange smell in the car, something vaguely chemical. I prayed it was not the engine overheating.

'Do you like my outfit, Brigit?'

'Yes,' I said. 'It's very pretty,' wondering what was coming next.

'Conor says that it looks tarty. Am I looking like a hooker?'

'Not at all,' I said, surprised. What was Conor thinking of? Hookers didn't dress like that.

Hannah sighed, relaxed and stretched her legs. Glancing fleetingly at her, I noticed she was wearing stockings. Black stockings. Rather odd, in this warm weather. They didn't really go with sandals.

'The trouble is,' Hannah said, 'Conor's jealous of my father. You do know who my father is?'

'I do. He's Seamus Talbot-Kelly.'

'Good.' Her voice told me I'd passed a test and that she was pleased about it. I waited for her to say more but she stayed quiet for a while, her eyes upon me – I could feel them.

She seemed different today from the woman I'd met my first night at Kilnaboy. Not so talkative and jumpy. Not high on drugs, as she'd been then. But there was something odd about her, apart from the stockings and the high-heeled shoes. The fact that she was being so friendly after she'd been stalking me – that was surely strange behaviour.

I realised that the chemical smell in the car came from her. What the hell was it?

As we were approaching Gort, I told her I was going to Galway.

'That will do me fine,' she said. 'It's every bit as good as Limerick.'

Good for what? I wondered. Good for buying amphetamines?

Gort loomed up in front of us. I was going to drive straight through but Hannah asked if I would stop.

'I've run out of cigarettes.'

'I didn't know you were a smoker.' She'd not smoked the night we met.

'Not when Conor is around. I won't keep you long,' she said.

I parked illegally on a yellow line and Hannah jumped out. As I watched, she crossed the street and went into a supermarket. She came back smiling to herself and snuggling back into her seat.

'I don't mind if you smoke.' After all, it was her car.

'I don't want to smoke right now. Only later, over coffee.'

If that was the case, I thought, you could have waited until then to stop and buy your cigarettes.

We drove on in silence for a while.

Then she said, 'You've seen my father's films, have you?'

'I've seen some of them,' I said, not wanting to admit that I'd only seen one.

There was another pause. Then she began to talk, not as she had done before at the house, but slowly and confidently. She spoke at length about her father, about his looks, his fame and money. The life they'd lived in Hollywood.

'Have you been to LA, Brigit?'

156

'Only once, and not for long.' I didn't say I'd hated it – the toothpaste smiles, the money values.

'We went there when I was four. My mother was an actress too. She was American, you know.'

'Was she? Whereabouts did she come from?'

'She's not important,' Hannah said. 'My father is the one that counts.'

Hannah sounded like a little girl. Was I as bad as that, I thought, when I told people about Joe? When I'd talked about him to David, that night at the Parkers' party, had I seemed so young and silly? Did I often tell strangers about my father? If so, I had better watch it. But maybe I was cured for good, now I knew how vile he'd been.

'She left,' said Hannah suddenly, 'when I was six. She bolted, Brigit.'

'Your mother left you when you were six?'

'She ran off with another man.'

'Did she leave you with your father?'

'Yes. And that was wonderful for me because I had him to myself.'

'You didn't miss your mother then?'

'Why should I miss her?' Hannah said. 'I told you, she got in the way.'

She expanded on this theme, explaining that she had been happy as Daddy's little darling. But her happiness was threatened when other girls came on the scene. Older girls, long-legged blondes, whom Daddy took to bed with him. The other girls squeezed her out. Although they never lasted long and Daddy soon grew tired of them, their presence was a distraction, so Daddy didn't have so much time to pay attention to his

157

daughter. They were never on their own, the way they'd been when she was six.

It was sad to listen to her. Everything that Hannah was came from her father. She saw herself as a princess and her father was a king, ruling over Tinseltown, but despite their power and money it was pretty obvious that she was deeply insecure. And fixated on herself. So much so, it sickened me. And yet there was a sweetness in her. Poor little rich girl, I couldn't help thinking. Peter Pan with long red hair.

'Where did you and Conor meet?'

'At the Dublin School of Art. I only went there for a term. *Kitty's Lover* brought us over. That was Daddy's fourteenth film. Daddy was Parnell, of course. Some of it was shot in Ireland. It was lovely being here. Daddy bought the house for us. But then he got involved again, with a make-up artist this time, so I needed a diversion.'

'But why just a term?' I asked.

'I told you, I met Conor there. He was finishing that year and we wanted to get married.'

'I see,' I said. I thought I did.

I'd had enough of her story. But Hannah the fugitive was still on my mind. I thought I should hang on to her.

Minutes later, we reached Galway.

'Look,' I said, 'I have to do an interview. Will you wait while I do that and then we'll go and grab some lunch?'

Surprisingly, she said she would.

Hannah followed me inside the Taibhdhearc. The person I was going to meet, the director, Patrick Hogan, was in the rehearsal room.

158

'I'll wait over there,' said Hannah when they had been introduced. 'I brought a flask of coffee with me.' She pointed to her bag and smiled. 'But first, is there a ladies' room?'

'It's over there,' said Patrick Hogan.

He and I sat down and spent a pleasant hour talking. He told me about staff and budgets, audiences and productions. Seven plays went on a year, all of which were newly written, one a children's show at Christmas and the opera in the spring. We discussed the Irish question and Patrick showed me some of O'Casey's correspondence on the subject of the language.

All this while, Hannah waited patiently with her flask of coffee. I noticed that she wasn't smoking. She was being polite, I thought.

When we were through, I went across to Hannah. 'Are you starving? I am, Hannah.'

Now that I was close to her, that smell was in the air again. Could Patrick smell it too? He was looking rather puzzled, frowning when he glanced at Hannah.

'Thank you for your time,' I said to him.

'Not at all. It was a pleasure.'

I'd parked the car round the back.

'I'll wait here for you,' said Hannah. 'This bag is such a bind to carry.'

'See you in a minute then.'

I trotted off and fetched the car. But when I drove back round the front, there was no sign of Hannah.

At first I thought she'd slipped back inside to the ladies' room. Five minutes passed, ten, then fifteen. She'd given me the slip.

All the same, I went inside, hoping that I had misjudged her. Just inside the foyer door, I ran into Patrick Hogan.

'I'm looking for my friend,' I said.

'She went over to the pub. The one that's on your right-hand side after leaving the theatre.'

I suspected this spelt trouble. Who else could be in that pub? A dealer Hannah knew about?

Returning to the car again, I found I had a parking ticket. By the time I reached the pub, I was set to murder Hannah. The pub was stuffed with noisy drinkers, nearly all of whom were men. A hurling match was on the box. Galway versus Clare, I gathered. I pushed my way through to the bar, from where I hoped I might catch sight of Hannah if she was still here.

Thankfully, I saw her. She was sitting on a bar stool, with a group of men around her. I elbowed through to where she was. She had a glass that was half full, of vodka, possibly, or gin. One man had his arm round her. The sight of him gave me a turn. He had narrow lips and cold blue eyes – a killer's face, I thought.

'Hannah!' I said. 'I've been looking for you.'

The other men inspected me.

'What ails you?' said one of them.

'We've got to go,' I said to Hannah.

She downed the contents of her glass. 'I'll have another one,' she said.

'Good on you,' said Killer Face.

'Hannah, please, we should be going. Conor will be looking for you.'

She stared at me with vacant eyes. Was she drunk already? She'd not been missing very long.

160

'A double vodka for my friend. She wants it neat and not with ice.'

'She doesn't want another drink.'

'I do. I want a double vodka.'

'You do not,' I said, incensed. 'We've got to leave. I must go home.'

'What home?' Hannah said, and laughed. 'Do you mean home to Kilnaboy? Is that your home now, Brigit Flood?'

A goal was scored. The drinkers groaned. 'Come on, Galway!' they shouted.

'Hannah–'

'Leave her be,' said Killer Face.

'Ah, Miceal, tog go bog e!' Patrick Hogan was beside us, mediating on my behalf. A saint sent down to me from Heaven. I blessed him for his intervention.

He and Killer Face talked in Irish for a while. Then they turned to Hannah.

'Come on, girl, you should be going,' said Killer Face.

'Why should I go? It's nice here.'

'Now then, pet,' said Patrick Hogan. 'You just come along with me.'

He coaxed her gently off the bar stool. As she stepped off, her skirt slid up. She was wearing hold-up stockings but she wasn't wearing panties. The others didn't seem to notice. No wonder Conor had protested at the way she was dressed.

Once on her feet, she was steady enough. Patrick linked his arm through hers and we got her to the car.

As I was thanking him for that, Hannah said

161

she'd lost her bag. 'I must have left it in the bar.'

'I'll get it for you,' I said quickly, before she could escape again.

'Go on, and I'll stay here,' said Patrick.

The bag was underneath the stool. It opened as I picked it up. Inside was the flask and mug, make-up, tissues, lots of junk – and an empty vodka bottle.

I sniffed the flask. She must have put the vodka in it in the ladies' room at Taibhdhearc. And there were no cigarettes. The vodka had been what she'd purchased when she'd made me stop in Gort. How stupid I had been!

I strode back to the car. Just to get her home, I said to myself. That's all that matters.

'Are you sure you'll be all right?' asked Patrick Hogan.

'Yes, I think I'll manage now.'

The prospects appeared reasonably hopeful. Hannah seemed content enough. A mile or two along the road, she hummed the music from *Titanic*.

'Did you like that film, Brigit?'

'Mm – it was rather sentimental.'

'But it was so sad!' said Hannah. All of a sudden, she started to cry. She fumbled in her bag for a tissue, I assumed. *'Life's* so sad,' she said. 'I want to die!' and then I heard her choke and cough.

I stopped the car and turned to her. A phial was lying on her lap. 'Aspirin' the label said.

'How many did you take?' I asked.

She shook her head and coughed again. She demonstrated with her fingers.

'Twenty? Thirty? Jesus, Hannah!'

We had passed a hospital as we were coming out of Galway. Unnerved, I turned the car round.

Hours later, at the hospital, after her stomach had been pumped, I learnt that she had lied to me and that the phial was almost empty. She'd only swallowed five or six aspirin.

'A call for help,' the doctor said.

By then, Conor had arrived. I'd phoned him from the hospital. I thought he might be cross with Hannah, as I was at that stage. She had run me out of patience and I half expected Conor to explode all over her.

He didn't. He was compassionate. Not personally tender towards her but dismayed at her condition. She was very pale and her hands were shaking.

Outside the hospital, in the car park, she begged him to bring her vodka. 'I only need the one,' she said. 'It's hurting me to go without.'

'You know that I won't give you drink.'

'Please,' she said. 'I need it, Conor.'

'You don't.' He looked at her as if she was a broken creature. A wounded animal. A dog...

I thought of the dog that we had seen my first day at Kilnaboy. The compassion Conor showed when he realised it was dying. His anger at its suffering. The tears that had been in his eyes.

Hannah was the one in tears that day at the hospital.

'*Please*, Conor. *Please...*'

'For the last time, no,' he said. And then he put her in his car and we all set off for Clare in convoy. Perhaps I should have wept for her – she

163

was pitiable. But I'd no more patience where Hannah was concerned. My compassion was for Conor.

No wonder he got terse at times. No wonder he could be moody. The marvel was that he could paint like that, and teach us as well, while having Hannah as his wife. What concentration – and what talent. And yet he felt and cared so deeply.

Following his car that night, I put him on a pedestal.

NINE

Two weeks later David rang and said he'd booked a flight to Shannon. When I said I'd go and fetch him, Conor wanted to come with me.

'The flight's due in at half past two. You've got a class that afternoon.'

Conor frowned. 'In that case take Em with you.'

'What for?' I said. 'It isn't far.' I would not have chosen Em as a travelling companion.

Conor temporised. 'The country roads are full of potholes. Supposing that you get a puncture?'

'Come on. The roads are not so bad. And surely I can cope with punctures.'

'If you prefer it that way then.'

'I do, and I'll be fine,' I said.

I was feeling fine already. My feature on the arts was finished, accepted by the newspaper; I'd moved on to the treatment of Conor, who read the draft and declared he was delighted with it.

It was a perfect July day. The countryside was at its best, the fields and verges rich with flowers. Honeysuckle in the hedgerows. Harebells growing in the pastures. Daisies in the meadow grass. The sky had been mopped clean of clouds. The road was almost pothole free.

I thought I might write a book on Conor. Once we'd launched him on TV, there'd be a market for a book. Buoyed up by this new idea, I planned the introduction to it, sketching a brief outline of Conor's insight and vocabulary, a precis of his development as a major Irish artist and a sympathetic analysis of his unique approach to teaching.

Between Corofin and Ennis I finished working on the prologue inside my head. We'd talked so much about his work, the sentences just wrote themselves. That was the cushy part. Chapter one was not so easy. It meant going back in time, to capture Conor as a child.

At that point I ran into trouble. I realised then that I knew hardly anything about Conor's early life. He was born in Connemara. Then his family moved to Galway. I'd discovered that much from cuttings and Conor had confirmed these facts when I first met him. But he'd not embellished them, and since then he'd never mentioned his family to me. He'd only talked about his work. I didn't know what his father did, or where his mother's people came from. I had no idea if he had siblings or if he was an only child. I knew that a teacher at his school had recognised his talent and helped him with his college fees but I didn't know who that teacher was or whether he was alive or dead. For all Conor had said, he might have started life as a student at the art school.

I gave up on chapter one. The book would have to wait awhile, until the video was made. Work on that was scheduled to begin the following day when David would film Conor in the studio at a life class. The day after, we were going to Inishbofin. Hannah would be coming with us.

Hannah... At the thought of her I groaned. I'd only seen her in the distance since the day we'd been to Galway. I thought she was avoiding me, embarrassed by her antics there. I hoped to God that she'd behave when we were all in Inishbofin. We had to have her on the trip, had to have a shot of her – of her back, anyhow – painting on the rocks, to tie in with the picture of her. I'd been adamant about it. 'Show the picture, then the source. The viewers will be fascinated,' and Conor had agreed with me.

But what if Hannah gave us trouble? What if she got drunk again? Or, just as bad, took pills with her? What a menace she could be. Something should be done about her when the video was made. She should be straightened out, put into a hospital that specialised in booze and drugs.

But would she agree to go? If she refused, could Conor maybe section her? And even if he could, would he want to do something so drastic?

I groaned again, depressed for Conor. Poor fellow, tied to Hannah Byrne. No wonder he took off and slept with Janice Seton in London. What did *she* mean to him? He never spoke of her to me, but then why would he? He hadn't been to London lately so maybe she was not important.

I was approaching Ennis. I glanced quickly at my watch. It was only ten past one. Time to go into town and have a look around the shops? Orla, who'd grown up in Ennis, had said that it was worth a visit. But parking might be problematic. David's flight might come in early. I resisted the temptation and virtuously headed south.

167

Shannon is a chilly spot. A nippy south-west wind was blowing, a fact that only dawned on me after I had parked the car and exposed myself to it. Wishing that I'd brought a jacket, I legged it over to arrivals. The terminal was packed with people of all ages, standing round with bored expressions or slumped resignedly on seats.

I checked the indicator board and realised why. Several flights were running late – the ones due in from Heathrow.

'What's happening?' I asked a man who was standing next to me.

'They say there's been a fire in London.'

'A fire at Heathrow, you mean?'

'In the chip shop,' said a woman.

'Have they said how bad it is?'

The woman shrugged. 'People were evacuated.'

David's flight was two hours late. I could have driven back to Ennis. Instead, I hung around the airport. A chip shop fire, I thought. I rather fancied fish and chips.

I found a restaurant by the check-in counters. It was jammed with other hungry people. The alternative – the bar – was every bit as over-crowded. The smell of food was titillating. I probed inside my bag for sweets. I'd nearly half a Tiffin bar and one whole packet of Maltesers. It didn't take me long to eat them.

I was still hungry. I bought myself a chocolate ice cream. Half past three. An hour to kill. More, till David got his luggage. I thought of going into Limerick. It was less than fifteen miles. I'd be there in twenty minutes. Or I could stop and have a coffee somewhere between here and there. Or I could go to Shannon town. It was only up the road, within easy walking distance if I'd been feeling energetic.

But somehow I could not be bothered. I wandered across to the newsagent's stall and flipped through several magazines.

'Send in the gowns,' said *Woman's Journal.* 'Dressing up is glamorous.'

The same magazine informed me that 'starved supermodels in slip dresses' aren't that attractive to the opposite sex, a theme to which I instantly warmed. The ice cream settled in my stomach. I read on and learnt that 'glossy' was The Look: 'Glossy suggests self-possession.'

In the ladies' cloakroom later, I decided I was glossy, though not in the way that the writer had meant. My nose was shining but not my hair.

Less than half an hour to go, unless there was another hold-up. I hurried to the board again. 'Expected 1645.'

I trailed back to the newsagent's stand and picked up *Woman's Way* this time. Looking at the contents page, I saw Hannah's father listed under the strapline, 'Celebrities. Whatever happened to our own Seamus Talbot-Kelly?'

Curious, I turned the pages until I reached the article on him. There was a photo in the middle, showing Seamus to advantage. He was a gorgeous-looking fellow but he wasn't much like Hannah.

'That was then,' the caption read. The feature took the story up: 'Dublin-born Seamus Talbot-Kelly was an icon of the sixties, linked to many leading ladies. The son of a builder from

Baldoyle, Seamus was an Abbey actor...'

His rise to stardom was outlined. The films that he'd made were listed. There was a reference to his fortune and the houses that he owned. Then the news became more gloomy.

'This week Seamus checked into the Cedars-Sinai Medical Center in Beverly Hills,' the feature continued. 'Early last year he was treated for prostate cancer. His doctors have refused to confirm or deny that the cancer may have spread...'

There was no mention of relations in attendance at his bedside, or of recent leading ladies. And no reference to his daughter. I wondered if they kept in touch – if Hannah knew that he was ill.

A young woman tapped my arm. 'Excuse me.'

'Yes?'

'Are you buying that magazine?'

'I suppose I should,' I said. 'I've got the value out of it.' It occurred to me, too, that Conor might be interested in the feature on his father-in-law.

'It's the last one left, you see. I'm following the serial.'

I took pity on her. Unlike me, she was carrying hand luggage and was bound for foreign parts.

'You have it,' I said. 'I don't mind. I can get another one.'

'Aw, thanks,' she said. 'That's kind of you.'

I handed over the magazine and wandered back to the board again. The flight from London had just landed.

'About time!' a woman said.

170

The small girl who was by her side declared that she was sick of waiting.

'Will you hush up, for goodness sake!'

'It's *boring* here,' the small girl whined.

I squeezed in next to them, risking the wrath of an elderly man who'd found himself a prime position, and leant on the barrier. After a few minutes, the passengers came trickling through, relieved to have arrived at last.

'Daddy, Daddy!' the small girl yelled. She hurled herself into the arms of a dark-haired fellow with a chain round his neck.

'Hello, angel,' said the man.

'Angel, is it!' said the woman.

Then I spotted David Parker with a trolley full of cameras.

'David?'

'Brigit! God, it's taken ages. Sorry you had to wait.' He looked behind him. 'Hang on a minute, here she is.'

Another trolley came towards us. Pushing it was a young woman of skeletal thinness, glossy hair in a pony tail. What made me eat those sweets, I thought, and who is *she*, for goodness sake?

'This is Jorie Lane,' said David. 'Jorie's short for Marjorie. Jorie, this is Brigit Flood.'

'Hello, Brigit,' Jorie said, baring snow-white teeth at me.

I grunted something in return. I was furious with David. Why did he have a woman with him? He was meant to be here working, not on a vacation break with some model who'd only be getting in his way – in *our* way – at Kilnaboy and

171

Inishbofin. Jorie, indeed.

I took another look at her. She was not the woman he'd had with him at the party. Being a photographer, with ready access to the gorgeous (and the super-thin, I thought), he doubtless played the field with women.

'Jorie's from Meanus, Brigit.' Meanus is a little village on the other side of Limerick.

'Oh yes?' As if I cared where she came from.

'She's going to pick up a car.' a bit heavy!

'A car?'

I lost my voice, I was so cross. I'd driven miles to meet the flight. Resisted going into Ennis. Hung around at Shannon airport. And here was David telling me that they were going to hire a car. He should have said so on the phone – saved me coming all this way. My presence was unnecessary. They could get to Kilnaboy without an escort. Why use me as a tour guide?

'Don't bother waiting,' Jorie said.

She's got a bloody nerve, I thought.

David cut across my thoughts, though it was Jorie he addressed.

'You'll let me know how things work out?' he said gently. 'You promise that you won't forget?'

'I will. I promise.' She turned towards me. 'I must go,' she said – and walked away, her shoulders slumped.

'Poor girl. It's tough,' David said when she was out of earshot. 'Her sister's had an accident. A bad one, on the Dublin road.'

'She isn't coming with us then?'

'Coming with us? Of course not. I only met her on the plane.'

'I see…'

I left him there and fetched the car. Driving out of Shannon later, I inquired about Jorie's sister.

'Is she very badly hurt?'

'She's unconscious,' David said.

I felt myself go hot with shame. For several miles I drove in silence. David remained quiet too, perhaps thinking of Jorie Lane and what had happened to her sister.

We left the major road at Ennis. As we turned off towards Corofin, David came out of his thoughts and asked me about Conor Byrne.

'What kind of fellow is he, Brigit? Is he difficult to work with?'

'He's under lots of strain,' I said.

David sighed. 'Is that code for he's a monster?'

'No. Conor's not the monster.' I told him about Hannah then; her problems with the pills and booze, the way she affected Conor. 'It makes him edgy on occasions.'

'What's the story with her now?'

'She's capable of causing trouble.'

'Looks like we'll be having fun.' He watched the fields as they flashed by. Suddenly he said, 'Brigit, stop! Go back a bit.'

I did as he asked, wondering what he could have seen. We drew up by a rusty gate.

'Could you hang on here for a minute? I promise I won't be long.'

'Was something moving in that field?' I thought he'd maybe seen a fox. I'd spotted one at Kilnaboy, a mean one, on the scent of lambs.

'No, not a fox. A shed,' said David. He delved into his camera bag and pulled a Leica out of it.

'I won't be long,' he said again.

He yanked the gate open and vanished from view. I sat and waited for a while, remembering that other day when I'd first come to Kilnaboy, and Conor, just like David now, had left me sitting in the car. That time it had been a dog. This time it was a shed.

Some shed, I thought as time went by. After ten or fifteen minutes, I got out to look for David. The shed was old and tumbledown with ivy growing over it. A bike was leaning up against it. David, perched perilously on a pile of loose stones, was taking pictures of them both.

'Oh, there you are at last,' he said as if he'd been expecting me. 'The stonework's lovely, isn't it? It's got a touch of gold in it. A pity that the light has gone but I'll get something out of it. The bike was an amazing bonus. It was lying in the shed. Must have been in there for ages. Mind you, it was pretty filthy.'

He was so enthusiastic, I couldn't get annoyed with him, especially as he seemed so keen to share the shed and bike with me.

'Have you finished? Can we go?'

He nodded. He was looking pretty grubby, his clothes striated with mud and dust, and cobwebs clinging to his hair. As he walked ahead of me, I noticed he was limping slightly. Of course, the foot, I thought.

'I'm sorry. Are we in a hurry, Brigit?'

'Not really. I'm not fussed about it.'

'I promise we won't stop again.'

But we did, a mile or two along the road. It wasn't David's fault this time, although he saw

174

the woman first.

'Look, someone's trying to flag us down.'

'Maybe she's run out of petrol.'

Parked on the grass verge up ahead was an aged Mazda, its rear number plate tied on loosely with a piece of string. Naturally, we stopped to help.

'I've got a puncture,' said the woman, 'but I haven't got a jack.' She was on the verge of tears. She'd been waiting there for ages.

David changed the wheel for her. By the time we'd seen her off, the old heap backfiring alarmingly, it was going on for eight. By then my thoughts had turned to food – and so had David's, as it happened.

'We could stop at Corofin.'

That was hold-up number four. We had supper in the bar and talked. David, as I already knew, was a loquacious, friendly person. We chatted about life in London and found that we had friends in common. And we discussed the party where we'd run across each other.

'You were with a gorgeous woman.'

'Lauren Hardy. Yes, I was.'

'Are you still together with her?'

'No. I came to the conclusion later that she was too like my sister.'

'What's your sister like?' I said.

'Loving. Loyal. A power freak.'

'She sounds rather like *my* sister.'

'I didn't know you had a sister,' David said, as if he knew a lot about me. He seemed anxious to know more. 'There are just the two of you then?'

'Yes. And are there any more of you?'

'No. There's a six-year gap between Penny and

myself. After I arrived, the folks decided to give up and get on with their careers.'

His parents were doctors, both GPs, senior partners in a practice they had built up together. As the conversation progressed, I tried to concentrate on them and to veer away from Joe but David's questions were persistent and I didn't get off lightly.

It was almost midnight when we got to Kilnaboy. I knew that one of the bed-sitting rooms had been set aside for David. I drew up in front of it and, conscious of his injury, helped him to offload his luggage.

'Don't worry, Brigit. I can do it.'

'Where the *fuck* have you two been?'

Conor had crept up on us. I had left the car lights on. They were shining on his face. It was obvious that he was in a fearful temper; his eyes were burning, his cheeks flushed. He loomed over the two of us, an apoplectic, red-eyed giant. Both of us were caught off-balance. Conor looked so angry, so self-righteous in his fury that I, who had done nothing wrong, felt like a naughty child caught red-handed in the act of pinching chocolate from a shop.

'Conor,' I said weakly, 'where on earth did you come out of?'

'That's a fucking stupid question!'

I suppose he had a point. Taken aback both by his sudden appearance and his belligerence towards us, I hesitated, wondering why he was upset.

Then I realised he was jealous. His resentful face and his body language said so clearly – he

176

had positioned himself between the two of us.

I was flabbergasted. But then with another flash of insight, I realised he had been jealous of David all along – jealous of the competition. 'Photographers are all the same,' he'd said scathingly. 'Tea boys dressed in velvet suits.' And when I said I'd go and fetch David, Conor had wanted to come with me, and then had suggested Em accompany me. To act as my chaperone.

How ridiculous, I thought. But I was flattered, all the same. Delighted even.

David had recovered his balance and was taking charge of things.

'I'm sorry we're late,' he said, although he had no reason whatsoever to apologise to Conor. 'There was a fire at Heathrow,' but he didn't say we'd stopped to take photographs and have dinner.

Conor didn't melt exactly but he looked a lot less threatening.

'You should have phoned,' he said to me.

I might well have asked him why. I might have told him I was free to do exactly as I liked and why should I check in with him? Instead, I said placatingly, 'I forgot to take my mobile with me.'

'If it's all right with you,' said David, 'I'd like to go straight to bed. I'll see you in the studio. Thank you for the lift here, Brigit. And my apologies again.'

'That's OK. Goodnight,' I said.

He left us standing in the yard. Conor and I stared at each other for a couple of minutes without saying anything. There was a *frisson* between us, a sense of danger and excitement. I

177

acknowledged and welcomed it, and at the same time became aware of how tired I was.

'What a day,' I said to Conor.

Another stupid observation. A pat phrase. A device to put a smokescreen over my thoughts. Because I knew then that our relationship had taken a leap forward; it was gathering momentum.

'*You* seem to have enjoyed yourself,' Conor said in a final effort to regain the moral high ground. But the anger had gone out of his voice.

'I wouldn't put it like that,' I said.

He had the grace to look ashamed. He muttered a phrase as pat as my own about seeing me in the morning. Then he turned and went back to the house he shared with Hannah.

The following day, work began on the video. To see Conor and David together, you would never have suspected that one was jealous of the other. That day in the studio, the two got into double harness. The synergy between them took my breath away.

Em, as usual, was the model for the life class. I noticed that she'd washed her hair and put some make-up on her face.

The students, too, had tarted up. Even the youngest ones had made a determined effort to look their best on camera. The more conservative amongst them had clean jeans and T-shirts on. Those who tended towards the freaky ensured their spikes and tattoos showed.

They were all slightly self-conscious and nervous. But David was prepared for that.

'The rule here is to over-shoot,' he told them, 'and cut and edit afterwards. So this is going to take awhile – until the afternoon, at least. Just ignore me, if you can, and treat this as a normal day.'

They settled down eventually. Our star became his charming self, Em did her compliant bit and David stood on a chair to get a better shot of them. As he had warned, the work was slow and also spasmodic. He prowled and shot and knelt and climbed, searching for the perfect angle, focusing a lot on Conor. The class soon lost its fear of him. After the first hour or so, his presence in the studio seemed, if not exactly normal, certainly acceptable.

We broke for lunch and then resumed. Halfway through the afternoon, there was a loud knocking on the door. As I was sitting down that end, observing what was going on, I got up to answer it, waiting until Em had slipped her gown back on again.

Clodagh Moran was outside with a suitcase in her hand. As usual, she glared at me.

'Is himself in there?' she said.

Conor was at the other end of the studio, checking out the students' drawings.

'He is. He's busy. Is it urgent?'

Clodagh hesitated. 'Has he got Mr Parker with him?'

'Yes. They're working on a video.'

'He told me they'd be doing that.'

'Is it urgent?' I persisted. 'Should I interrupt him for you?'

She bit her lip and thought about it. 'You'd

better tell him that I'm off. I did say that I had to go the weekend you all went away. I was going to leave tomorrow. That's what he thinks, anyways.'

'So are you going tonight instead?'

''Tis better if I go tonight. But I'll be back on Tuesday, tell him.'

'All right,' I said. 'I'll let him know.'

She did not move.

'Was there something else?' I asked.

She dithered. 'Just tell him – tell him that I've done my best and no one could do more than that.'

I waited for her to continue, suspecting there was more to come. There was.

'Anyhows, she's sleeping now,' said Clodagh, somewhat defensively. 'She's been asleep this last half-hour.'

I took it that the 'she' was Hannah. Sleeping? Sleeping off the booze? It boded ill for Inishbofin.

'I'll tell Conor now,' I said, wondering how he would respond.

'Make sure that you do that,' said Clodagh. She stomped off and I locked the door behind her. Then I went across to Conor.

'That was Clodagh Moran.' I passed on the messages. Conor grunted in response and concentrated on the sketches. Oh well, I thought resignedly, I guess he's used to it.

The class continued as before. We'd normally have stopped by six, but just as we were packing up, Conor produced the manikin and its various body parts.

'Brilliant! Em, can you come over here? I want

you with the manikin.'

It was nearly nine o'clock when David wrapped the whole thing up.

'I think we need a jar,' he said.

A cheer went round the studio. Laughing and jostling, the students rushed outside, carrying David in their wake and taking Em along with them. In a surprisingly short time, the studio completely cleared – except for Conor and myself.

'Aren't you going with them, Brigit?'

I shook my head. 'Not this evening. Not tonight. I'll help you tidy up in here.'

'Leave it. Have a drink with me instead. I brought a bottle down with me.'

Perhaps he'd planned it in advance, confident I'd stay with him when all the others had gone off. Maybe so. I didn't care a jot whether it was planned or not.

We sat facing each other across one of the big white tables and Conor poured the wine for us.

'We need to unwind,' he said. 'Thanks for all your efforts, Brigit.'

'I haven't really done that much. Not today, at any rate.'

'You have. You've been here. That's what counts.'

Outside, cars were starting up and leaving. I heard Celia call to David, 'Come on in the car with us.'

'You're sure you don't want to join them?'

'I want to stay with you,' I said.

Outside, the noise soon died away. We drank the wine, discussed the day, accepting what

181

would follow later. When Conor reached out for my hand, I wasn't thinking about Hannah – not consciously, at any rate. But Hannah was the kind of person who pervaded everything. When you were sure you'd had enough, that you'd have no more truck with her, she crept up on you again and found a place inside your head. So I suppose she was there, the night I made love with Conor, because of the question I put to him then.

'How much harm can we do?' I asked.

Conor looked surprised and touched. His reaction was to say how compassionate I was, how other women wouldn't care about doing harm to Hannah.

Other women? Janice Seton being one of them? I pushed the thought of her away. It was bad enough being three – four would be unbearable.

After that, we didn't talk much. Em had left her mat rolled out. It wasn't quite a waterbed but making love in the studio with the drawings strewn all around and the smell of paint seemed apt and sexy and yes, romantic.

'Well?' Louise asked many months later. 'Was he good in bed or not? Tell me all the details! Was it great the first time with him?'

'Lou, you know, I can't remember.'

'You can't *remember*? Aw, come off it!'

'Do you remember being with Tom?' I asked her. 'I'm talking of the first time now.'

Louise bridled. 'Of course I do. I still remember what I felt.'

'But what about the sex?' I said. Because you do forget the sex, unless it's extraordinary, and even in great love affairs it's seldom great when you do it first.

But, like Louise, I still remember what I *felt* about that night. That sense of being where I belonged, which making love intensified. The conviction that it was right, permissible for us to be together. A blind belief that it was pre-planned.

I think – I *hope* that Hannah had gone by the time we took off our clothes. Certainly the thought of the harm that we might do was eclipsed by the pleasure we shared on the mat.

TEN

Conor left me and went to check on Hannah, or so I imagined. Getting into bed alone, I was missing him already. He was so absurdly near, and yet, in terms of his other life, the ghastly one he led with Hannah, so hideously far away.

I rolled myself inside the duvet, convinced that I would dream of him. Instead, my dreams were all of Joe. In one of them he came to meet me from a photo in a frame. This seemed quite normal at the time.

'Oh, there you are,' he said to me. 'I see that you escaped the fire.'

'I was the only one that did.'

The fact that all the rest had died did not appear to worry Joe. 'We'll have to get the bike,' he said. 'I left it lying in the shed.'

Embarking on a rural idyll, driving down a country lane so we could find the shed and bike, I was somewhat disillusioned when I suddenly woke up. No Joe. No car. No rural idyll.

The duvet was still wrapped round me. I unravelled myself and sat up, switched on the bedside light, reached out for a glass of water, noticed that my ring was missing. Joe's ring. I must have lost it in the bed.

Another person would have thought, I guess I'll find it in the morning, and gone back to sleep again. But I couldn't go to sleep, not until I found the ring.

I turned on the overhead light and began to search for it. It wasn't lying in the bed. It hadn't fallen to the floor. It hadn't slipped inside the duvet.

I rummaged round a second time. The ring was not inside my room.

I thought, it must be in the studio. I suppose it slipped off when I was making love with Conor.

Muttering to myself – I knew I'd have to look for it or I'd get no sleep – I put on my dressing gown, grabbed the torch and set off for the studio. I'd no idea what time it was – 2 or 3 a.m. perhaps. The revellers had long since returned from the pub and were all tucked in bed. Lucky for some, I said to myself.

The studio, naturally, was in darkness. I knew the door would not be locked. A life class was the only reason that we ever bolted it.

Inside, I didn't bother with the lights. I just relied on the torch, convinced I'd find the ring at once, that it would be beside the mat.

But it wasn't. I extended my search to encompass the whole floor. I couldn't see it any-where. Maybe underneath a table? I got down on hands and knees. No luck.

It's gone, I thought. I've lost Joe's ring. And then, Come on, it *must* be here. Perhaps if I turned on the lights?

I'd no sooner had that thought when someone switched them on for me. Surprised, I froze beneath the table.

The someone started moving around. I heard the sound of steps going up the ladder staircase and soon afterwards, a plop, as if something light had been thrown down from above.

The footsteps came back down again. Feeling that it would be rather silly to announce my presence now, I stayed underneath the table. From my curious position, I could see something of the person who was moving round the room. Feet in trainers. Legs in jeans.

I heard the wardrobe door being opened. Nothing happened for a moment. Then I heard a squeaky sound followed by a funny 'pop'.

Curiosity got the better of me. I eased myself onto my tummy to get a better view of whoever was doing what at this ungodly hour of the morning.

Now I could see half a body. It was a woman. She was heading for the door. A little more manoeuvring and I could see the whole of her.

She had her back to me but I could tell that it was Em. She seemed to have her arms round something.

What was it? Intrigued, I poked my head right out. But all I saw was Em's back view.

Suddenly, the lights went off. I might have expected that but all the same I got a shock.

When I had recovered from it, I crawled out from under the table and turned on the lights again. It was pointless speculating about Em and her behaviour. I'd come to find my missing ring. I should resume my search for it.

I found the ring eventually. It had rolled into a corner. Finding it was wonderful. I put it on delightedly, turned the lights off and went back to my room again where I fell asleep at once, without further thoughts of Em or anything except my ring.

I was woken by the phone. I answered it and then remembered that it was my wake-up call. Of course, we were going to Inishbofin.

I put my jeans and T-shirt on, found my Nikes, stuffed a sweater in a bag, turned to go – and saw a note lying just inside the door.

Conor's writing. I unfolded it and read, 'Brigit, Hannah's being difficult. Em is going to help me with her. We're going to catch the early ferry and get Hannah settled in before the rest of you arrive. Can you co-ordinate the others? See you later on the island.'

I was absurdly disappointed. Not only did the note seem curt, but I felt sidelined by the contents, left to organise the students while Em went on ahead with Conor.

But that was silly, and I knew it. Silly, petty and self-seeking. I told myself to cut it out. On this of all days, I should be putting Conor first. Poor man. It was not his fault that Hannah chose to give him trouble. My own experience with her had taught me what she could be like. And I'd just had that one day with her; Conor had her all the time. No wonder his note seemed curt and that it wasn't signed with love. And as for taking Em to help him, I should not be so possessive. Em was not a threat to Hannah so she might behave with her. And Em was not a threat to me, so did it matter if she went ahead with Conor in the car as long as they got Hannah settled?

No, of course it didn't matter. Instead of being envious, piqued because I was left out, I should be out there, in the yard, getting people into cars and heading north for Inishbofin. Get on with it, I told myself.

As there were nearly sixty of us, carrying out my own instructions proved an excellent distraction from the onset of self-pity. I'd marked out David to travel with me, but Celia, who seemed to have her eye on him, offered him a lift with her. Outmanoeuvred, I settled for Patrick, Orla and Jimmy Mullen from Crosshaven, who'd joined the group the week before.

We set off in convoy, with Celia acting as our leader. The route we took bypassed Galway, taking us close to the shore of Lough Corrib, into Oughterard and through the enchanted lakelands of Connemara. Each turn in the road made you want to stop awhile and marvel at the gentle landscape. I curtailed the other three as they sighed and ooh-ed and ah-ed, and told them that there would be trouble if we missed the midday ferry.

'Ah now, Brigit,' Orla pleaded. 'Would it matter all that much? There'll be another ferry later. That lake over on the right is crying out for me to sketch it! Can't you stop for half an hour.'

'We're going to shoot this afternoon. I can't afford to miss the ferry.'

'Can't they go ahead without you?'

'No, they can't,' I said abruptly.

Orla must have got the message because she shut up at that point and we reached the port of Creggan without more demands from her.

Once in Creggan, all of us became impatient, finding parking for our cars, yanking bags and knapsacks out, slamming doors and locking up, anxious to be off the mainland and push on to Inishbofin.

Our ferry, the *Island Discovery*, was waiting for us in the harbour. The vessel was pristine white, a contrast to the umbra seascape and the opaque quality of the morning. The perfect weather of the last few days had decided to move on, leaving uncertainty in its wake. The sky was smudgy, ink on ash, and the sea reflected its charred appearance.

The islands continued the tenebrous theme. I broke away from the others and walked a short way down the jetty to get a better look at the islands. I'd known about the bigger islands but not about the little ones, Inis Goirt, Inis Scine Beag and Inis Scine Mor, nestling round the rocky shorelines of their intimate relations. Later, when the *Island Discovery* brought us nearer, I was able to see just how close they were to each other and wondered if, in another age, they'd been an amalgam, a fusion of islands, conjugated with the mainland.

But something about the islands said that they'd always been cut off. From the harbour, they appeared not only alienated, but dark and intimidating. Their taciturn nature rebuffed and yet attracted me. I said to myself that this was how I felt they should be, that Conor's paintings of the islands never told me they were sunny. Gazing over the water at them, I thought how honest those pictures were. The islands *were* harsh and bleak but from those qualities came their beauty. Had Conor used a brighter palette, he'd have cheapened their appearance.

'Brigit?'

'Oh, hi, David.'

'I've been thinking,' David began.

'Thinking about what?' I said.

'Um, this shot you want of Hannah painting. Is it scheduled for today?'

'Yes, I'm almost sure it is – if Her Ladyship behaves. And if it's OK with you. Are you concerned about the light?'

'I am a bit. I listened to the weather forecast. It's cheering up this afternoon. We may even get some sunshine. On the other hand...'

'The afternoons *are* often better in the west. The wind seems to come up then and blow the clouds away.'

'Hold thumbs. The location for that painting – Cromwell's Fort, isn't it?'

'The rocks beneath the fort,' I said.

'Whatever. Do we hire a car to get there?'

'We won't need a car,' I said. 'The fort's across from our hotel. The island's only three miles long. You don't hire cars on Inishbofin. I gather people get around on ponies or on bicycles.'

'Sounds fun. My foot should be able to cope with that.'

'Oh, I'm sure it will.'

We strolled back and joined the queue jostling to board the boat. The *Island Discovery* was much larger than I had expected, capable of carrying up to 130 passengers, and it was fully booked that day. We mingled with a crowd of holiday-makers, mostly from the Continent, seeking out good positions and settling ourselves down for the short journey over to Inishbofin.

As we got out to sea, I noticed wryly that Celia's would-be romance with David wasn't progressing as she had planned. He sat near her initially but after a few minutes he wandered over to talk to us.

The sea was rough enough that day to make us conscious of its power. We were barely under way when Orla said that she felt sick. David handed her a pill.

'That should sort you out,' he said.

It did – though David told me afterwards that it was only aspirin. *Mind over matter.*

Anticipation of arrival sent a tremor through the students. The atmosphere was very lively. Even Orla acted skittish. I felt isolated from them, sundered from their levity by a need for privacy, an unusual emotion for me, which was all to do with Conor.

It became unbearable, being with so many people while I was in such a state. The closer to Inishbofin I got, the more I wanted to be alone, to savour the proximity of it without comments from my companions. I felt that the island was Conor's and mine, a presumption that would have driven the islanders wild if they'd had access to my mind. I had an image of the harbour, of Conor waiting there for me, pacing up and down the pier. As we sailed in I'd wave to him. His face would light up when he saw me. He'd have sorted Hannah out. We'd make plans to be together.

I took these thoughts on deck with me and leant over the rails, breathing in the salty air, sucking it back into my lungs, holding it while I closed my eyes and let the wind tear at my hair. I reached back to the night before, trying to recapture the feeling of Conor, his power and taste and the smell of him. But the power that I felt was the strength of the wind, and the taste and the smell were to do with the sea.

Opening my eyes, I saw with a shock that we were nearly in the harbour – we were passing Cromwell's Fort. The fort, well over three hundred years old, was star-shaped and well-preserved. Built as a barracks to house members of the Catholic clergy whom Cromwell had condemned to exile, later on it changed its function and was used by Irish forces fighting off the Williamites.

To the east of the barracks was a crescent-shaped medieval harbour, almost totally silted up now and, according to what Patrick had said in the car, only visible at spring tide. Today, there was no trace of it. What you could see were the rocks – Conor's rocks, as black as sin, some of which had pools in them.

I thought again how true he'd been to the seascape in his paintings. Then I scanned the pier for him. Already, we were in the harbour. I could see the jetty clearly. But there was no sign of Conor. I groaned inwardly, hoping that his non-appearance wasn't due to Hannah's drinking. But maybe he was running late and would turn up in a minute.

We disembarked. He didn't show.

Orla said, 'Funny Conor isn't here. You'd think that he'd be meeting us.'

'Why would he be meeting us?' I said, trying to

keep my spirits up. 'He'll have masses else to do.'

'Brigit?' Patrick plonked his knapsack down. 'Where exactly are we staying? Is it here, or further up?'

There were two hotels nearby – Day's, which was right beside the harbour, and the Doonmore Hotel, up the road on the right-hand side.

I knew who was staying where. Patrick was down for the Doonmore Hotel. So was I, and so was David.

'Patrick, Orla, you're with us. But you're in Day's,' I said to Celia.

She pulled a face, casting wistful eyes at David who did not respond to her.

We sorted ourselves out and the two groups split. The Doonmore Hotel looked directly at the fort, separated by the sea. A half hope that Conor might be in the foyer was immediately dashed. I went to the reception desk.

'You're the students?' the receptionist asked.

I nodded. 'I'm Brigit Flood.'

'Ah, we have a message for you, Brigit.'

Another bulletin from Conor. Like the first, it was direct. 'Brigit, I'm taking Hannah to the fort. Can you and David follow us? Tell the others not to come in case Hannah gets upset. If they want to paint, they can, but not near where we'll be shooting. Send them to Cnoc Mor instead. I think they'll find it interesting.'

He had signed it 'Love from Conor' which did much to raise my spirits.

I told the group about Cnoc Mor, where field systems and house sites, believed to date from the Bronze Age, pointed to intensive farming.

193

Orla said that they were famished and that it was time for lunch.

For once, I wasn't hungry. I was eager to be off, to be with Conor at the fort.

'Let's skip lunch,' I said to David.

Fortuitously, the sun was peering through the clouds, prompting David to depart, to take advantage of the light.

We trotted back along the road in the direction of the pier. The fort looked near, perched at the far end of the small headland which, curving out from the harbour, doubled back to form the bay. David must have thought the same because he cheerfully remarked that it would make a pleasant walk. Despite his limp, he didn't grumble. His Sony camera wasn't heavy and he had a shoulder bag.

'Can you see a path?' he said when we got to Day's Hotel.

'I think it must be further on.'

But further on the road veered left, moving inland from the sea.

'We must have missed it,' I said. 'Let's take a short cut through that field. That should take us to the path.'

David looked dubious. 'You think so? The field is a quagmire, Brigit.'

All the same, he followed me. He was right about the field, which soaked our feet and sagged beneath them.

The field was bordered at the far end with a nasty barbed-wire fence. We climbed over it and found ourselves on a rough track that led towards a craggy hillock. After only a few yards, the track completely petered out, abandoning us in a heather bed. Ahead of us, shaggy sheep with coal-black faces stared at us through sooty eyes.

We soldiered upwards through the heather until we could climb no further. I realised we were on a cliff. Far below the water lapped.

'Look!' David said, distracting me from vertigo.

I hadn't noticed it before but there was a tiny island in the middle of the harbour. Geese had made it their habitat. Several of them were at home, standing in a solemn line, their bills turned out to face the sea.

'Fascinating,' David said. 'Is that because of rain, or sunshine?'

But I couldn't answer him. Maybe Conor could, I thought, relishing the prospect of seeing him again.

From where we stood, we had a clear view of the rocky terrain at the water's edge. It struck us then that there was no path, that the only way to Cromwell's Fort was through the heather and the rocks.

We caught each other's eyes and giggled.

'A pleasant walk, I think you said?'

David grinned. 'Come on, let's continue the martyrdom.'

We walked in silence after that because the going was so rough. The heather was replaced by rocks, with wild flowers growing between them, hogweed and forget-me-nots, cuckooflowers and spotted orchids.

Then the landmass veered left and descended to lower ground. We came upon two sandy coves, deserted places, quite delightful. I took my shoes off and walked barefoot. It was delicious to feel the sand beneath my feet.

But the relief was short-lived and soon we were back to warily stepping from rock to rock. The fort which earlier had appeared to be so close had disappeared from view entirely. But then we crossed a sandy inlet and caught sight of it.

The last leg was the easiest. As we drew nearer to the ruins, I saw the figure of a man waiting in the entrance to them.

'Conor!'

He was still too far from us to tune in to my delight. I sensed David looking at me but pretended not to notice. A sea of emotions was flooding through me. The same feelings that had come upon me when I first saw Conor's paintings; when the sea called out to me and I ached to be in Ireland. A curious out-of-body sensation that I had fused with the sea and rocks. An enormous urge to love. A compulsion to give myself without any reservations. Unfamiliar inclinations...

'Hurry up,' I said to David – as if either of us could.

At his end, Conor stuck limpet-like to the ruins of the fort – guarding Hannah, I imagined. Pressing on, we got to him, panting like two eager puppies. The gush was knocked right out of me the minute I saw Conor's face. He looked frightful, pale and haggard, as if he'd heard appalling news and hadn't slept for weeks and weeks. His eyes were dull and discontented, with smoky shadows underneath them. That bloody woman, I thought. She'll be the death of him.

His voice however seemed quite normal and he even made us laugh, referring to the walk we'd had, promising that, next time round, he'd provide a helicopter.

Then he said, 'I've set the shot up for you, David, and got Hannah organised. You can film from the fort. I've found the ideal spot for you. Come on. I'll show you what I mean.'

He strode inside ahead of us. I took stock of my surroundings. The fort had lost its roof but all its walls were intact. Inside was one enormous open space, with what would once have been separate quarters to the right and left of us. At the far end of this space was a tiny anteroom with a window in one wall that overlooked the sea and rocks.

Conor beckoned me towards it. 'Brigit, come and have a look out here.'

I looked out of the narrow window. I saw Hannah down there painting, sitting on a rock outcrop. It was the picture re-enacted. Hannah with her back to us, her red hair floating past her shoulders, teased and tangled by the wind, wearing green again – the same gown, I was almost sure, that she'd worn the time she posed for the painting that I'd loved.

'That's terrific. What a shot.'

Drawn and yet repelled by it, I stared down at the scene below. What was missing were the shadows of the children playing games. But now I saw the real location, I was rather shocked by it. This, I thought, was not a place for anyone to take a child. The rocks looked slippery, spiked with shells. The reef itself did not allow much room for movement. Boisterous children playing there could easily fall into the sea. I wondered why Conor had envisaged children when he put those shadows in. It was not a playground down there, it was too beset with perils. Mikey flashed into my mind. I shuddered at the thought of him somersaulting on those rocks.

My old fear of heights returned and I quickly backed away.

'You OK?' asked David kindly.

'Now I am. It's just the drop.'

'Let me see.'

At the window, David whistled.

'As you say, it's quite a drop. Well, I can do some shots from here. The height will add intrigue to them. But I'll do better down below.'

Conor said, 'I told you, that's not necessary.'

'Let me be the judge of that.'

'But it's dangerous,' said Conor.

'Didn't you take Hannah down there?'

'Dangerous for you, I meant. You might hurt your foot again. You're doing a job for me, remember, and I'd be responsible.'

'If it bothers you that much…'

'Yes, it does,' said Conor firmly.

But David didn't look happy. As he unpacked his camera bag, I found a wall on which to sit and Conor came and sat beside me.

'You look all in,' I said to him.

'I am. Hannah – last night was a nightmare, Brigit. You've no idea what hell it was.' He grimaced, added, less to me than to himself, 'But it's going to be worth it. After all, it has to be,' and then asked about the students. 'Have they settled in?'

'Yes. They were going to grab some lunch and then go over to Cnoc Mor.'

'Good. Look, Brigit, things will be much easier once this exercise is over. Em is taking Hannah home. I've booked them on the evening ferry.' He smiled conspiratorially. 'We'll have the whole weekend together.'

I was delighted – then concerned. 'You're not on my hotel list. And I think they're pretty full.'

'We'll get around the hotel later.'

'If Hannah needs to freshen up after you've finished here, she can always use my room.' I wondered vaguely where Em was while all of this was going on. I hadn't once laid eyes on her.

'That's not a problem,' Conor said. 'There's a B and B on Low Road, within walking distance of the harbour. I took a room there for the girls. It's quiet there. Good for Hannah. And it doesn't have a bar.' His eyes wandered back to David who was checking out the light. 'I'll just go back and talk to him.'

The whole weekend, I thought again. Peace at last. Even if we have to share it with another sixty people.

'Look, I *do* know what I'm doing, Conor.'

I was jerked from my reverie by the sound of David's voice. Its tone was exasperated.

'And *I* know what I want from you.'

Quarrelling was all we needed. I got up and joined the men. They were glaring at each other.

Conor said, 'We don't need a close-up shot. What we require is an impression, to compare it with the painting.'

'You don't understand,' said David in a level

199

voice. 'Photography is not like painting and one shot is not enough. I have to try all sorts of angles. The film is not set in concrete after I've finished shooting. We do edit it, you know, and if the close-up doesn't work, we can always cut it out.'

I intervened. 'Let me see once more,' I said, and steeled myself to look again at the scene below the fort.

The south-west wind was whipping up, just as I'd anticipated. It played with Hannah's long green dress and blew her hair back from her face. She put her hand behind her head and clutched the lustrous red-gold tresses. I said to Conor, 'I've explained to David. He does know what we want, I promise.'

'Does he?'

'Yes, he does,' I told him firmly.

He was as jumpy as a cat when it sees a dog approaching but I managed to restrain him until David had finished.

'You've wrapped it up then?' Conor demanded.

David nodded rather coolly.

Conor checked his watch and said, 'Fine. I'm concerned about the tide, but if you're ready to leave now–'

'The tide?'

'The fort is on an island, Brigit. You may not have realised that, but on the way you crossed an inlet between here and Braud. That's the spot where you'll have seen two attractive little coves. Braud is co-joined to Closhkeem, the high ground up above the Pool. There's no problem there with tides but here on Port Island, it's another story. The inlet, Beal na Brad, fills up when the tide comes in and cuts this island off from Braud. Bearing in mind what time it is now, we can't hang about for long. You two should be making tracks.'

'Aren't we going to wait for you?'

'I don't think so,' Conor said. 'For one thing, there's David's foot. That might slow you down, so you should get moving right away. And there's Hannah to consider. She feels awkward about you after all that Galway shit. I think she'd rather dodge you, Brigit – for the moment, anyway.'

'There's no need for her to worry.' But I was feeling awkward too, and just as anxious to dodge Hannah as she was to avoid me. 'Perhaps you're right. We'll go ahead.'

The minute Conor was out of earshot, David said furiously, 'What's the matter with that guy?'

'He's just stressed. It's Hannah, David.'

'She's not giving trouble now. And that's not stress. That's control, Brigit. The man's a bloody power freak.'

'You should be more compassionate.'

'He was mucking up my work. Interfering all the time. And he doesn't have a clue. His direction is appalling.'

'I think you're being insensitive.'

'Insensitive?'

We had a blazing row about it. Conor, David kept insisting, wasn't all he seemed to be. I told David he was jealous of the talent Conor had.

'You must be joking,' David said.

We walked on in angry silence. I was still without my shoes – I'd got used to being barefoot.

201

We crossed the inlet, got to Braud, found the pretty coves again. Walking on the sand this time, I remembered strolling on the beach as a child with Joe – at Sandycove, I think it was.

Water is a healing power; the waves dissolving on the sand broke down my anger with my father. What I'd learnt in Lorcan's house seemed unimportant on the beach. Crossing Braud again that day, the old Joe was restored to me. Joe, the maker of enchantment, the king of my imagination.

'You still mad with me?' said David.

I might not have been cross with Joe but I'd not forgiven David.

'I think you've been ridiculous.'

'OK. If that's how you see it, Brigit.'

We reached Closhkeem and saw a ram standing on a rock and glowering.

'Fuck on out of there!' yelled a young man who was walking towards us. He was a gorgeous-looking fellow, like an actor off a film set, tall and thin with long black hair tied back in a pony tail.

As he approached us, I said, 'Hi.'

'You fucking cunt! Get out of here!'

He was shouting at the ram but I didn't realise that. Shocked by his response, I failed to see the clump of thistles right in front of me. I put a bare foot down on it, shrieked, reacted, lost my balance – and brought David down with me.

It was his turn to swear – and to groan with pain. He'd damaged his foot again.

ELEVEN

'Don't try to move,' I said, getting to my feet. 'That will only make it worse.'

We obviously needed help. I looked back the way we'd come. Where was Conor? Where was Hannah? Scanning the horizon for them, I saw, not those two familiar figures but the black-haired fellow with the pony tail. I raised my arms and yelled at him, expecting him to swear again or ignore me altogether.

'My friend is hurt. He can't get up.'

He didn't answer or acknowledge my shout with a wave but he came to our assistance. As we struggled home, we met Celia. I guessed that she'd been lying in wait for David. Before she could ask us questions, I told her what the problem was.

'Come up to my room,' she said. 'I brought Neurofen with me. That will help reduce the pain. And we'll inquire about a doctor.'

It didn't take us long to learn that there was no doctor on the island.

'We'll have to take him to the mainland. We can catch the evening ferry,' Celia said, looking tenderly at David.

He was lying on the bed nearest to the window. The Neurofen had worked quite quickly – I could tell from his expression that the pain was not so bad.

'It might be best,' Celia went on, 'if he went to Kilnaboy, instead of messing about trying to find the Creggan doctor. If he goes to Kilnaboy, he can go to Conor's doctor. We could phone him from here.'

'David can't go on his own. Not all the way to Kilnaboy.'

'Don't worry about me,' said David.

'I can probably hire a driver,' Celia cut in. 'I'll go with him if you like. Unless you feel that you should, Brigit?'

'I'd love it if you'd go,' I said, happy to get shot of David now that we had fallen out. 'But it will ruin your whole weekend.'

'No, it won't,' said Celia sweetly.

There were still two hours to go before the evening ferry left.

I said, 'I should go and look for Conor so he knows what's going on. I'll come back here afterwards.'

I had second thoughts about going to the B and B. Hannah wouldn't want to meet me and I felt the same about her. To phone would be less complicated. I could do that from the Doonmore.

I set off in that direction. The tide was fully in, I noticed. The rocks and sand had drowned in it. I stopped to look at Cromwell's Fort. Maybe Conor wasn't back. Maybe he was out there still.

'Brigit?'

With relief, I saw Conor coming towards me.

'Where the hell have you been, Brigit? I thought you'd be at the hotel but they said you weren't back yet.'

'We had a mishap,' I told him. 'David's hurt his

204

foot again. Celia's looking after him. They're leaving on the evening ferry.'

'They're *what?*'

'Going to catch the evening ferry.'

'They'll do no such thing!' said Conor angrily. 'He's stacks of work to do here yet. I wanted him to film my pictures in the gallery.'

'He can come back and do that.' Now I had the shot I wanted, I wasn't fussed about the pictures on Inishbofin. The paintings that I'd seen in London, particularly 'Hannah Painting', were what mattered to me, not what Conor had in his little cottage gallery.

'Where is the eejit at this moment?'

'David? He's in Day's Hotel. Lying down in Celia's room.'

Conor swung around and, muttering darkly about David, headed off for the hotel. I followed apprehensively. But once he got to Celia's room, Conor was a different person.

'I hear you've crocked your foot again,' he said to David, all concern.

'Bloody nuisance,' David said. 'I'm sorry it's messed up the shoot. I'd hoped to finish it to-morrow.'

'Your foot is more important, David. It's pretty swollen, isn't it?'

'It is rather, I'm afraid.'

'Well,' said Conor, taking charge, 'this plan of leaving here this evening, that would be a crazy move. You need to rest that foot tonight. I have some Mogadon with me. I'll give you one so you can sleep. And I'll get hold of Dr Moylan, so he'll see you in the morning. You can catch the early ferry and get back to Kilnaboy just as surgery is starting.'

'Oh, but Conor–' began Celia.

'No buts,' said Conor firmly. 'David needs a decent rest. Travelling down tonight would kill him. You've got the two beds here, I see. Will you sleep in the other one, Celia, or should I book another room?'

'No,' said Celia. 'Not at all. I'll be happy to sleep here.'

'I'll bring you back the Mogadon when I've got Hannah on the ferry. Brigit, I want you to help me plan tomorrow's projects. I'll meet you later at the Doonmore.'

We went our separate ways. At the Doonmore, I changed and went downstairs to wait for Conor. The bar was busy with our students.

'Where's David?' Jimmy asked.

I told him, and he told the others. They said it was awful news. Was David coming back tomorrow? No? But he'd miss out on all the *craic*.

David, it appeared, had become quite popular.

'I'm sorry, Brigit,' Conor said when he joined me later. 'I shouldn't have got angry like that. But I'm responsible for David. It all got too much for me. Getting Hannah there and back, and then David on the top of it.'

'Don't apologise,' I said. 'I know what you're going through. Did you get Em and Hannah off?'

Conor nodded. 'The ferry's packed but they got on.'

'And Em will be all right with Hannah?'

'Em's a wonder,' Conor said. 'I don't know what I'd do without her. Anyway, it's sorted out.

Come on, let's talk about tomorrow.' He had brought a map with him. 'This is Inishbofin, Brigit.' The map depicted townland boundaries, turf bogs, lakes and ruined buildings. 'I've selected painting sites for the students in the morning.'

There were four sites: Closhkeem, Braud – but not Port Island, because of the tide, said Conor – St Colman's Abbey and the Hill.

'I'll commute between the sites but it won't keep me all the while. I'll take time off in the morning. There's something I want to show you.'

'The gallery?'

'The paintings in it. I think you'll be knocked out by them. They must be on the video.'

'They will be, in a week or so.'

Conor didn't stay late. He'd got a room at Day's Hotel because, he said, he wanted to be close to David. Celia might need his help to get David on the ferry.

When he had left the bar I lost interest in it too and opted for an early night. But I stayed awake for ages. There was so much going on, I couldn't clear my mind for sleep. I would have liked to think of Conor, to doze off anticipating the weekend with him, or what was still left of it. Instead, I got stuck with Hannah. She stepped into my mind and stubbornly refused to leave it.

Hannah. I tossed and turned and thought of her. I closed my eyes and saw her down there, painting on the rock outcrop. Why had Conor painted shadows of those children dancing round her? Because she had longed for children? Because she'd tried and failed to have one? Were those shadows Hannah's sorrows, babies that she might have lost? Did that explain the pills and booze?

When at last I fell asleep, Hannah tiptoed through my dreams, holding babies in her arms.

I went down to breakfast bleary-eyed, to find Conor already there, buttering a piece of toast.

'You're here early,' I said, yawning.

'I've been up for hours,' he said.

'You saw the others off, did you?'

'Yes. The swelling's not so bad this morning but David must see Dr Moylan and perhaps a specialist. I wouldn't want it on my conscience if complications did develop and we had neglected David.'

David should hear this, I thought. Then he wouldn't say that Conor wasn't all he seemed to be.

'Did you bring your mobile, Brigit?'

'No, I didn't. I forgot it. Did you want to borrow it?'

'Yes. You never know with Hannah, Brigit. I'll be wandering round this morning. I'd like to stay in touch with Em.'

'Jimmy Mullen has a mobile. I just hope you get a signal.'

'So do I,' said Conor, sighing.

Jimmy said the mobile worked. 'It's not great but it will do. Keep it with you. I don't need it.'

By then, we'd rounded up the students, split them into groups, allocated destinations and provided them with maps. They went off, gratified to see the sun sneaking glimpses of the island.

'Where's the cottage?' I asked Conor. 'Can I walk to it from here?'

'You'd do better on a bike. I have one here that I use. Or you could hire a pony.'

'I'm no good on horseback, Conor.'

'You don't have to be on 'Bofin. The ponies here are tame as kittens.'

I laughed. 'All right so. It might be fun. And where would I hire this pony?'

'On Low Road. I'll show you where.'

Low Road went past Day's Hotel. It was, in fact, the same road I'd been on the day before, looking for a pathway that didn't exist.

Conor left me by the field where the ponies could be hired. Before he went, he said he'd meet me at a place called East End Bay. 'Then I'll take you to the cottage and you'll see the paintings.'

I stopped in the road for a little while, looking at the ponies grazing. Although I wasn't good with horses, I'd had a pony once myself – one of Joe's creations, not a real one. Looking back, I think Chagall had a hand in his design. Like the animals he painted, my pony, with his silver coat and his pale blue mane, was as happy in the air as riding on more solid ground. Astride him, I could fly as well. We roamed the clouds on the days that Joe decided to cast spells for me.

Those flights of fancy would be cancelled if there was a row at home. Joe and Mammy used to argue about almost everything. An angry Joe was terrifying, though Mammy could get just as mad when she cast off her inhibitions. If words were knives they would have died, the way they used to carry on.

But when Joe left I missed those rows. They gave an edge to life, I thought. When Joe was there you didn't know what was going to happen next. When he had gone, the house was dead and our existence stripped of colour.

'You want a pony, do you then?'

The man in the field was calling to me. I returned to Inishbofin, to the place where real ponies could be hired for a day. If you didn't count the grass, there wasn't that much variation in the scene in front of me. The silver clouds. The low stone wall. The ponies either white or dappled. The man was grey all over too, and coming down the field to meet me.

I hired a fat, white Connemara pony from him. It had an elongated mane and a tail so long that it touched the ground.

The man told me more about the island and the legends that surround it. What we call Inishbofin used to be known as *Inis Bo Finne*, the Island of the White Cow. There's a lake called *Loch Bo Finne* over in West Quarter village. In it lives a red-haired woman, so the man I spoke to said. She has a cow down there with her. They're only seen every seven years, unless there's a disaster pending, in which case both of them come out to warn the islanders about it. Another version of this story has the woman kill the cow, whose roar when dying can be heard throughout the length and breadth of Ireland.

I thanked the man who told these stories and set off astride my pony. Nervous at first, I soon relaxed. Just as Conor had predicted, the pony was a placid creature. I knew that it would take me safely all the way to East End Bay without much effort on my part.

We meandered down the road without seeing a soul. I grinned, thinking of the crowds in London. The heat. The noise. The traffic jams. This is more like it, I said to myself – and saw three donkeys coming towards me.

Walking slowly side by side, they blocked the road ahead. It didn't bother me at first. When we met up, I thought naively, one of the donkeys would step back, clearing a space for me to pass.

The donkeys didn't see it that way. Within minutes we were nose to nose but, far from parting company to facilitate my passage, all three remained glued together.

'Push off,' I said. 'Go on. Get moving.'

The donkeys took no notice of me. I raised my voice and shouted at them. They looked at me disdainfully, the way people do in London if you try to jump a queue.

Exasperated, I dismounted and looked in the ditch for a stick or twig. There was only grass and creepy-crawlies. I twirled my arms around like windmills, hoping that would do the trick. The donkeys, unimpressed by these gyrations, didn't budge from their positions.

Just beyond them was a house. I told my pony to stay put. I wasn't sure that he'd obey but I had to take the chance. Muttering to myself, I squeezed past the nearest obdurate donkey and found myself beside a gate. A short path led to the house. In the garden was a sign saying it was a B and B. Conor's B and B, I thought.

A helpful woman came to the door – she knew

211

what to do to unblock the road. She fetched a dog lead and an apple and half led, half coaxed the smallest donkey off the road until he was inside the gateway.

'Go on while there's space,' she said.

'Thanks a million. You've been brilliant.'

My pony was still waiting for me. The minute we'd passed the house, the woman got the donkey out and firmly shut the gate behind him.

I came to St Colman's Abbey. A group of students were sketching in the entrance but there was no sign of Conor. I rode on, thankful there were no more donkeys. The road turned sharply to the left. Following it, I came to a cluster of five or six cottages, most of which appeared deserted. On the wall of one of them somebody had pinned a notice. 'NOT for sale or rent,' it said. A clear statement that tourists were welcomed but not encouraged to stay overlong in this close-knit community.

I knew before I saw the sea that it would be round the corner. Gulls of several different species soared and dipped above my head. I heard their high-pitched yelping call and then the strangest gargling sound as a colony of guillemots announced its presence on the island. I saw a dozen taking flight, their sharp black bills stuck out like daggers.

Until then, I had been unaware of island noise. But now my ears opened and I heard the unmistakable sound of terns as well, their harsh 'k-reeagh' and grating 'kro-ick' clashing with the raucous notes emitted by black-headed gulls.

Veering to the left again, I arrived in East End

Bay. To my right, a slender quay pushed its way into the sea. There were buildings at the end of it and what must have been a curing station, like the one in Bofin Harbour that I'd vaguely registered. I recalled that Inishbofin had been an important fishing centre, known for herrings, cod and ling, in the days when locally made currachs first supplemented the basic rowboats used by island fishermen.

To my left, the bay made an impressive arc, curling round a sandy beach – a would-be paradise for children. But there were none in evidence, and no adults either. The only sign of habitation was a few more cottages, some of which were newly painted, their doors and windows red or yellow, while others had a forlorn air, as if abandoned by their owners who'd forgotten all about them.

A hundred years ago, I knew, nearly two hundred families had lived and worked on Inishbofin. Then, there were five villages on the island, a spinning wheel in every house and local craftsmen to provide everything the people needed. Now, there were hardly any shops and less than eighty families left. People with names like Burke and Darcy. Norman names, though no one knew quite how and when those Normans went to Inishbofin.

All the families might have gone the day I went to East End Bay. The only form of life I saw were all those colonies of birds. The lack of any human contact left me with a basic problem. I was concerned about the pony, thinking that he must be thirsty. I couldn't see an outdoor tap. I didn't like to bang on doors, in case I wasn't well received. We'd have to wait till Conor came. He'd said we'd meet at half past ten. It was only ten past now.

I rode on a little further. Then, at last, I saw a child wandering along the beach. A boy or girl? I couldn't tell. The figure was too far away.

I was distracted by the sight of a cottage. Isolated on a slope, at first sight it was just another cottage, a replica of those I'd seen when I'd located East End Bay. It conformed to the norm in having the customary thatched roof with a chimney at one end, as is usual in the west, and the inevitable small windows, designed to keep the weather out rather than admit the light. But, unlike the others that I'd seen, with their contrasting doors and windows, this cottage was entirely white. A white cloud hung down low behind it, so the thatch came into focus and the walls and doors and windows seemed to melt into the sky. It was longer too; wider than the other houses – stretched out a bit on either side as if someone had decided to add on two tiny rooms, or maybe byres for animals, once the building was erected.

My memory was coming back, comparing the reality with Conor's picture in the gallery. It was the same cottage. The same location. But without a tree in it.

And why would there be a tree by a house beside the sea? The soil round here was much too sandy for a tree to put down roots. What made Conor put a tree into this unlikely setting? And why did he make that tree look so like a crucifix?

Because he liked the shape of it? Probably. Artists thought in visual terms. They made paintings in their minds, as if they were erecting buildings. If they were happy with the framework, symbols could be less important. Never mind about the tree. Concentrate on the cottage.

The more I scrutinised the setting, the more I realised how exactly it conformed to Conor's painting. The capricious sun had tired and gone to have a vapour bath. Without its sheen, the bay was pale, as if the sun had scoured it out before it went behind the clouds. The beach was grey as wych-elm trunks, the sky like silver birches peeling, the rocks as black as alder leaves when autumn strips them of their colour.

The magnet acted in reverse. In London, Conor's vision of the scene had drawn me to this pallid bay. Now, I was being suctioned back and put inside the picture frame, as if I was an element in Conor's painting of the cottage.

I must have stared at it for ages. I didn't see the child approaching. It was only when he said, 'What are *you* doing, waiting here?' that I realised he was near me.

He was maybe eight years old, tousle-haired and wearing jeans with two patches on the knees.

'Hello,' I said. 'I didn't see you.'

He didn't smile – he scowled at me. 'What is it you're wanting here?'

'I'm meeting somebody,' I said, and added sarcastically, 'That is, if you've no objections.'

'That's *our* house you're looking at.'

'Your house?'

'That house is ours by right,' he said.

'Your daddy owned it once, did he?'

'Me daddy's father's brother had it.'

'I see.' I thought about the sign I'd seen. 'NOT for rent or sale.' What the small boy said to me summed up what the islanders felt. Everything is ours by right. But time had moved on. Some people *had* sold off their homes. And more would do so in the future.

Without saying another word, the small boy turned and ran away. Watching him depart, I saw Conor on the beach. I forgot about the boy. The picture came to life at once, but only for the two of us. The seclusion of the bay, its isolated atmosphere, helped sustain this fantasy. It's possible that people were inside those simple cottages; that they were peering out at us, resentful of our presence there. But, if so, they hid themselves away from view and I was left with the illusion that we were on our own that day.

'So, did you enjoy the ride?' inquired Conor, reminding me we weren't alone, or not entirely – we had a pony with us.

'It was fine. A lot of fun.' I was still astride the pony.

Conor patted him and asked if I'd had any problems with him.

'No. But I'd say he's thirsty now.'

'There's a bucket at the house.'

I didn't ask which house he meant. I didn't have to question him. He took the reins and led the pony to the cottage on the slope. Close up, it looked in good condition, pristine clean and newly painted. Tins of whitewash and emulsion were lined up beside the door.

'Stay here a minute,' Conor said when I'd finally dismounted.

He went inside the cottage and returned carrying a length of rope and a bucket of cold water which the pony promptly guzzled.

'Wait until I tether him.' He slipped the rope between the reins and tied a paint tin to it.

'Will that be secure enough?'

'It will be in the pony's mind. I promise you, he won't go off.' Conor groped behind the pot and produced a bunch of keys. 'What are you waiting for?' he asked.

I couldn't answer. Didn't know. But, now that we were going inside, I was nervous.

'The pony's fine,' insisted Conor.

'Yes. He is. He's fine,' I said.

I was the one who wasn't fine, wondering what it was I'd find when we went inside the house.

Conor had the door wide open. 'What's up, Brigit? What is wrong?'

'Nothing's wrong at all,' I said.

Conor raised an eyebrow at me.

'Nothing's wrong,' I said again hastily and followed him inside the door.

The shock was in there, on the walls. The house itself was not a shock. The room we entered was quite large, for a cottage anyway. I'd say that once it was two rooms; that Conor had knocked down a wall to create the space he needed. This space had been painted white, walls, woodwork – everything. Conor seemed obsessed with white. It was clean, he told me later; easier than colour was when it needed touching up.

All the colour in that room radiated from the

paintings. As with Conor's other pictures, those that I had seen in London, these paintings mirrored island shades, the colours of the sea and sky, of rocks and sand and boats at anchor. Subtle shades of island flowers, blue and mauve and milky-pink, and the gaudier tone of the emerald grass.

The pictures had a lot in common with the ones I had seen in London. The subject matter was the same. A sturdy, austere, stonework house. A currach and a sailing boat. A seated figure dressed in green, painting on a rock out-crop, red hair streaked with golden lights flowing down a slender back. A cottage – this one – painted white, standing on a grassy slope.

The same pictures, you might say. But if you did, you would be wrong. These pictures were quite different from the ones I'd seen in London. As the scene outside had changed when the sun grew weary of it, so these paintings had been altered by the use of light and shade, their mood and meaning modified by what Conor did with shadows.

In the paintings I'd seen first, his shadows were of unseen people and of objects just outside the picture frame. The shadows touched upon the action that was going on inside it, but they'd been inanimate, unable to affect the outcome. You felt that they were ghosts and symbols, that the people in the pictures didn't know that they were there. In the paintings I saw now, Conor's shadows alchemised and played a part in what went on.

In the picture 'Hannah Painting' that I had

seen in London, the shadows, although enigmatic, had been those of little people playing games upon the rocks. I'd suspected they were boys. Looking at the second version, that suspicion was confirmed. The shadows-come-to-life *were* boys – little boys with naughty faces, wicked grins and freckled noses. You knew at once that they were villains. Handfuls. Boisterous. Innocent and unaware of the dangers they were facing playing on that rock outcrop.

In other paintings the shadows brought to life by Conor had been objects at the onset. Take the painting of the cottage, with the tree in front of it that might have been a crucifix. In this depiction of the scene, the ambiguity was gone. The shadow cast across the grass was clearly shown to be a cross. Jesus wasn't hanging from it. Mary wasn't present, weeping. Conor had got rid of them and made the crucifix his victim. For him, it was a living cross, condemned to die in agony, and bleeding just as Jesus did.

An image of three cheerful children. Another one of agony. Those were the extremes; the other paintings fitted somewhere between the ecstasy and pain.

But that was not the end of it. Another shadow now replaced the ones that Conor brought to life. It appeared in every painting, a single shadow compensating for a dozen diverse ones. It was the shadow of a man. He might have been of any age. He could have been extremely tall. He might have been emaciated, six feet tall and overweight, or short and fat, or small and lean. I couldn't tell the shape of him because the sun, and Conor, too, had played tricks with him, pulling out his arms and legs to make him line up with the cross over which his shadow fell.

He was there in all the pictures, that evasive shadowed figure. I couldn't ascertain his shape but I could tell that he was evil – repressed, destructive and corrupt. His intrusion made a mockery of the suffering of the cross. In 'Hannah Painting', he stretched right across the picture towards the rocks where she was sitting, too engrossed to be aware that his presence threatened her and the naked children playing.

But, though he was sinister, grey in shadow, black in intent, he was an intrinsic adjunct to what Conor had to say. Without him, the paintings, though remarkable, wouldn't have been masterpieces. Staring at them, mesmerised, I thought about the other pictures, those that I had seen in London.

Louise's words came back to me: 'The paintings are unfinished, Brigit.' At the time I'd challenged that, thinking she was talking nonsense. Now I realised she'd been right. The London pictures were rough sketches. *These* were the finished paintings.

A critic would have pointed out the link between them and the romantic Expressionist movement which had impressed de Chirico. But, while his uneasy works of art echoed the feelings of a war-torn world, that movement had reflected many different states of mind, much of it too personal to be of interest to the viewer. Those Expressionists who did succeed had pulled the suffering out of their souls, relating to humanity through universal desperation. As Conor did, in these paintings.

He'd pulled off a master stroke. But they were disturbing pictures. I was both transfixed and troubled. I felt as if I'd fallen into a melting pot of mixed emotions. Shock, distress, delight and awe bubbled up and overflowed.

Until then, I'd thought that I was close to Conor. That as well as our being lovers, we'd been soul mates from the start. The paintings split my feelings open, forcing me to reassess us.

I realised that I'd conned myself in believing that, for me at that time, fulfilment could come out of a coalescence with a man who was intelligent, funny, sensitive – and strong enough to be a challenge. Conor was all these things. But I'd wanted more than that. Add to the list of my needs venture, jeopardy, the possibility that, in loving a man, I might lose myself.

The paintings rattled me. I was frightened by their source, by what was in Conor's head when he set out to paint like that. With the fear came excitement. And with excitement, recognition.

I knew I was where I'd longed to be. At risk. On the edge. That was what it was all about.

TWELVE

This time we had a bed. There was a small bedroom and shower room on one side of the galley, a tiny kitchen on the other. The bedroom had been sparsely furnished – a trunk, a chair, the double bed.

This time the love we made was too intense to be forgotten. The paintings set the mood for it. I had a different slant on Conor, and a new perception of myself and of what it was I needed. For me, all pretence was stripped away. What remained was fundamental, artless, primitive and sexy.

The austerity of our surroundings contributed to my desire. The sounds from outside the cottage – the sea pounding in the distance, the cacophony of calls as gulls and terns flew overhead – heightened what I felt already. Nature fusing with her lovers as they coupled. Eden in a cell-like room.

But Eden didn't have a phone. As we made love a second time, Jimmy Mullen's mobile rang.

Conor pulled away from me. The phone was lying on the trunk, beside the clothes he had discarded. Still erect, he answered it.

'Yes?'

He listened, his face turned towards the open doorway. The person he was talking to seemed to have a lot to say. The call went on and on and on while I lay thwarted on the bed.

At last, Conor got a word in. 'Why don't you call *them?*' he said.

The other person spoke again. Conor didn't interrupt, responding just with grunts and sighs.

Finally he said, 'Tuesday. But I *told* you that,' and rang off impatiently.

'What's going on?' I said to him. 'Is Hannah in a state or what?'

'Hannah's always in a state.' He looked sullen and frustrated. He did not come back to bed. I cursed Hannah silently and wished she hadn't phoned just then.

'Why don't you relax?' I said. 'Hannah is OK for now. Em is looking after her.'

'Yes. I *know,*' said Conor crossly.

Hannah being a touchy subject, I decided I would drop it. Casting round for a diversion, the donkeys flashed into my mind. Thinking that he'd be amused, I told Conor what had happened.

But Conor didn't laugh. He stared at me, his body tense. 'This happened at the B and B?'

'Mm. The woman there is really sweet.'

'You mentioned me to her?' said Conor.

'No. I never thought of mentioning you. We just talked about the donkeys.'

'Just the donkeys?' Conor said.

'Yes.'

The tension went, but the call had ruined the atmosphere. It was getting late, said Conor. He had to think about the students.

Leaving me in bed, he showered. I fell asleep while he was gone and woke to find myself alone.

Initially, I was uncertain where it was I'd landed up, conscious of how white things were. I felt the way Darina did when she was in hospital, having her tonsils out. Emerging from the anaesthetic, she'd thought she must be up in Heaven, the operation having killed her. 'The whole place was so *white,* you see,' she told me. 'Then I heard the nurses talking. I didn't know it was the nurses. I still thought I was Up There. I remember being relieved. I thought I wouldn't have to worry – the angels all had Irish accents!'

When I'd established where I was, I also went to have a shower. Both the towels I found were damp but not so moist I couldn't use them.

Dressed again, I wondered what I might do all afternoon. Look for Conor? Join the students? Ride further along East End Bay or even right around the island? But it was nearly five o'clock. *Five?* I'd been asleep for hours and hours! I panicked, thinking of the pony, standing tethered, waiting for me.

Someone – Conor, I supposed – had refilled the bucket for him but he hadn't drunk it all.

Well, I hadn't worn him out, riding him around all day. When I returned him to his owner, he'd be as fresh as when we started.

The two of us set off again, back the way that we had come. We didn't see the donkeys again but the group of students were still painting in the entrance to the abbey. Conor wasn't with them though. I presumed that he'd gone on to supervise another group.

When I had returned the pony to the man from whom I'd hired him I went into Day's Hotel and bought myself a glass of shandy.

The man behind the counter said Mr Byrne was looking for me.

'He was?'

'I take it that you're Brigit Flood? He described your looks to us. Told us that you had long hair. He'd been inquiring at the Doonmore and he left a message there.'

'Do you know where he is now?'

'I think he went to buy a ticket.'

'But he already has a ticket.'

The man shrugged. 'He said that he was going back. That he would catch the evening ferry.'

'*Tonight?*'

'That was what I thought he said.'

'Tell me where he'd buy the ticket.'

'Up the road. You'll see a shop.'

I was on the verge of tears. Why was Conor leaving now? I'd thought we'd spend the night together. Having made love so intensely, I felt horribly let down.

Outside the shop, I spotted Conor, paying for something at the counter. I nearly didn't go inside. I had a sudden urge to flee – to run away as he was doing.

Then the door swung open and Conor came out.

'Ah, Brigit,' he said, and he looked relieved. 'I was in a state about you. I couldn't find you anywhere. I thought you'd fallen off the pony. I was just about to go back to East End Bay to find you.'

'I hear you're leaving this evening.'

Conor nodded. 'Seamus Talbot-Kelly's dead –

Hannah's father. I just got the news about him. I must go back to Kilnaboy. Hannah will be devastated. She was nuts about her father.'

'That's sad,' I said. 'I'm really sorry. I knew that he was in a clinic. It was cancer, wasn't it?'

'Yes. It was sudden, in the end. He was in remission. We were sure that he'd pull through. The signs were good. He was a fighter. Hannah wasn't worrying. It will kill her, Brigit. They were close, the two of them. Her mother left them long ago.'

'Hannah told me that,' I said.

'Did she? It's always on her mind. The root of everything in her. That woman was a real bitch.' He shook his head. 'The things that people do to children. Anyway, I have to go. I'm leaving on the evening ferry. I thought it might be overbooked but it turns out there's room for me.' He added vehemently, 'I wish I didn't have to go.'

He was looking miserable. My heart went out to him. What a selfish bitch I am, I thought, giving in to my emotions while Conor was involved with this. Poor Hannah, too. All the problems that she has and now her father dies on her.

Guilt, which hadn't bothered me before, promptly stuck its knife in me. Until Conor broke the news about Hannah's father's death, I'd separated man and wife by interposing Hannah's drinking. Their marriage was a sham, I'd thought. There was no love in it at all. Conor only stayed with Hannah so he could look after her. But wasn't that a kind of love? A love that, if you were in Hannah's state, was an essential prophylactic?

Take that medicine away and Hannah would be dead without it. Threatening to remove it was bad enough.

Another woman was a threat. *Bitch, bitch, bitch,* said guilt to me as it drove the knife in further.

'I'll have to take your car,' said Conor, oblivious of all this angst. 'Em took Hannah in the Shell. I'd meant to travel back with you. You'll have to re-arrange the transport.'

'I know.'

'And take charge of things up here. The weekend's been screwed up already, with that other bloody business. Will Parker be at Kilnaboy?'

'I suppose he will,' I said. 'Unless he had to go to England to let his doctor see his foot.'

'And Celia? Would she go with him?'

'If she got the chance she would.'

'Anyway,' said Conor, letting this go, 'I can't deal with all of that. Here,' he groped in his pocket and pulled out the phone. 'Give this back to Jimmy, will you?'

There wasn't that much left to say. The ferry would be leaving shortly. Conor didn't want to linger. I said goodbye and he went off.

I joined the gang of students later but I didn't have the heart to stay partying with them. I went outside alone instead and, leaning over the low stone wall that ran between the road and shore, I watched the sun bow off the scene. Cromwell's Fort was grey and gloomy, as downcast as myself, I thought.

I wondered if Conor was home yet and, if so, what was facing him. Em might well have thought it prudent to keep the news from Hannah. At this very minute, Conor might be breaking it, dreading how she would react. Hannah might be in hysterics, trying to grab the pills off him, reaching for the nearest bottle. He's the one that counts, she'd said of her father the day I'd taken her to Galway. And now he was dead.

I went back indoors where I encountered Jimmy Mullen.

'Oh, I forgot your phone,' I said. 'Conor left it with me for you.'

'Thanks.'

Having pocketed the phone, Jimmy added thoughtfully, 'Brigit, about getting home. Do we have enough cars with us? I hear that Conor's taken yours.'

'Yes, he has, but we'll squash in.'

'I wish now that I'd driven up. But that car of mine is new. It's an Audi – have you seen it? I didn't fancy leaving it parked at Creggan all weekend.'

'Just as well you didn't bring it. You'd only have been worried, Jimmy. At Kilnaboy you know it's safe.'

I left him and went up to bed.

Taking charge of things didn't involve doing anything really. The students wanted to go sketching again next day so I left them to their own devices and went exploring on my own. I hired a bicycle this time. I cycled up High Road to Cloonamore, which had been an ancient village, and through the bogs of Middlequarter. I stopped for lunch and rode to Fawnmore. I wandered up to Loch Bo Finne over in West Quarter village without seeing the red-haired woman who resides inside the lake or the cow she keeps with her. I didn't go to East End Bay.

I thought incessantly of Conor and of how he would be coping. The gulls that screamed above my head evoked sounds of Hannah weeping.

We caught the evening ferry back. I watched the islands recede, wondering when I would come back. When David's foot permitted it, to see the video completed. But would there be another time, a time when I'd return with Conor and no other person present? Would we move into the cottage and stay there without feeling guilty? Or was the death of Hannah's father the lethal weapon that would kill off our affair?

The boat pulled into Creggan Harbour and we took our leave of it. The transport wasn't problematic. In less than half an hour, the convoy headed south again.

It was Jimmy who suggested we should go to Ballyvaughan. The car that he was travelling in was at the front of the procession. Jimmy stopped and got out. The convoy ground to a halt.

'Have you been to Monk's,' he called.

'Do you mean Monk's Bar?' said Orla.

'I think so. I just heard about it. They say the seafood's very good.'

His idea went up the line. The cry went out, to eat at Monk's. I wasn't one bit pleased about it. I was keen to get home to Conor quickly but I couldn't tell the others in case I aroused suspicions.

'Brigit, will we go?' said Patrick who was in the

car with me.

'All right so. If you're so keen.'

Monk's Bar looks out at the bay, and at Finavara Point with the Martello tower on it. The sea that night was chilly grey, as grim as Cromwell's Fort had been. But it was warm inside the bar, and cosy round the great big fireplace. The comfy chairs that stood before it, the woven red and emerald curtains, the tables made from slabs of wood gave the place a homely look. And the choice of seafood was impressive – crab, smoked salmon, oysters, mussels, prawns, trout. 'And there's lobster,' Orla marvelled.

The bar was already crowded and while we were placing orders, two more men came in the door. The waitress stopped to talk to them.

'Did you find who did it yet?' she asked.

'No, we didn't, more's the pity. But that's not the half of it. They took nothing out of it.'

'Ah, you're joking,' said the waitress.

'No, I swear to you I'm not.' The speaker was a black-haired man, with a gingery moustache.

'So what was the point of it?'

'Ask me!' said the black-haired man. His eyes fell upon our group. 'No chance of a seat tonight.'

'They're going in the restaurant. We'll have their dinners ready soon.'

'We can double up,' said Orla. 'Take my chair. I'll share with him.' She went to sit on Patrick's knee.

The two men joined our group. They were guards, it transpired, off duty and in casual clothes. We got into conversation. They told us that there'd been a break-in last night at the boathouse.

The boathouse, said the black-haired guard, wasn't ever used for boats. 'People who have boats round here store their oars and engines there. No one tries to take a boat if there's no way they can move it.'

'But someone had a go last night?'

'Not at trying to steal a boat. They broke the padlock on the boathouse door and I think they went inside. But, like I said to Maureen now, they took nothing out of it.'

'Really,' I said. 'Maybe someone else surprised them.'

'If they did, they're saying nothing. We've talked to stacks of people here but no one knows a thing about it.'

'I suppose that they were vandals.'

'I suppose they must have been.'

'We've not had trouble here before,' said the other guard. 'Not with vandals, anyway. Tourists come to Ballyvaughan. Quiet people, most of them. They tour the west and see the flowers and stop off here to have the seafood.'

'It's our turn for trouble, Brian,' Maureen had come back again. She added darkly, 'What else do you expect, I ask you? Ireland's full of crime these days. It's crack cocaine and ecstasy. Your food is ready now for you.'

We left the two guards sitting there and filed into the restaurant.

'That was odd, about the break-in,' Patrick said as we tucked in.

'Kids playing silly games,' said Orla.

'Kids with powerful wrists on them. The guards said it was one big padlock.'

231

'We breed them tough here in the west!' a student down from Galway remarked.

The chat descended into banter. I couldn't join in it myself. My thoughts were at Kilnaboy. It would be late when we got back. Conor would have gone to bed. He could be asleep already, worn out by last night's events. Or maybe he was wide awake, too wound up to think of sleep. Should I phone him now, I wondered, to let him know our whereabouts? I might get through to Hannah. Better leave it. Wait till morning.

It felt like morning when we left but it wasn't all that late when we finally got home. The stream of cars went up the drive and parked, as usual, at the back. I registered that Celia's car wasn't in its normal spot.

When I went into my room, I found two letters on the mat, one of which had come from her.

Dear Brigit,

David has to go to England and I said I'd go with him. I hope the weekend went off well. Not sure when we will be back. Please tell Conor that I'll phone.

Love,
Celia.

The other letter was from David.

Dr Moylan's sent me packing so my man can see the foot. Very sorry about this. Won't take long, I promise you. Phone you in a day or two.

Love from your repentant
David.

Repentant over what? His insensitivity or because his injured foot was holding up the video? Still, nice that he apologised. Forgetting that the injured foot was all my doing and not his, I decided I'd forgive him. We'd be friends again when he came back to Kilnaboy.

There was a knock at the door. Thinking it must be Conor, that he'd waited up for me, I rushed across to open it, beaming in anticipation.

But it was Jimmy Mullen.

'Sorry, Brigit,' he began. Everyone was saying sorry. 'My car's not in the car park.' He was on the verge of tears. A new Audi, I remembered.

'It must be, Jimmy.'

'No, it's not.' He was adamant.

'I'll come and help you look,' I said. 'The car park's all full up again. They've parked around you, that's what's happened.'

'I don't think so,' Jimmy said.

'Let's look anyway.' Jimmy's overtired, I thought, and he's drunk a lot of wine, that's why he can't see the Audi.

But the Audi wasn't there.

'And there's something else,' said Jimmy. 'I thought I had the keys with me when we went to Inishbofin but I can't find them either, Brigit.'

'Have you searched your room for them?'

'Yes. I must have left them in the car. Jesus, what a fool I am.'

'We'd better tell the guards about it.'

'Will they bother at this hour?'

'Hardly for a car,' I said. 'We should tell Conor first.'

'Now?'

'Better wait until the morning.' But then I had another thought. 'Look, before we go to bed, let's check the front of Conor's house. Who knows, Conor might have moved the car.'

'I can't imagine why, can you?'

'No. But let's try, in case.'

We tried. The Audi wasn't in the front. The Shell was there, as I'd expected. And there was another car. It was marked *'Garda'*.

'How weird,' I said. 'It's going on for one. What can the guards be doing here?'

All the downstairs lights were on. The front door had been left ajar. I went into the hall and called, 'Conor?'

He didn't answer. I called to him a second time.

Suddenly, the door leading from the front hall into the back was jerked open and a woman came in.

'Em!' I said.

'Oh, it's you. You're back,' she said. Her face had a question on it. What are you doing here? it said.

I answered automatically. 'We're here because of Jimmy's car. It seems to have been stolen. But you've already got the guards.'

'That's not to do with Jimmy's car.' Her voice was hard. It sounded odd.

'Where's Conor?' I demanded.

'Through there with them, in the kitchen.' She nodded towards the open door. By then, I'd had enough of her. With Jimmy trailing in my wake, I strode into the other hall and stopped outside the kitchen door.

Conor and two more guards, both of them in uniform, were seated at the kitchen table. They all looked up as I appeared.

'Brigit!' Conor said and added, 'This is Brigit Flood. She's working with us on a project.'

I said, 'Jimmy Mullen's with me, Conor. His car's been taken from the car park.'

'Has it? I'm sorry, Jimmy.' Conor sounded odd as well.

The guards were nodding to each other. The older of the two took over.

'A car's been taken, did you say?'

Jimmy answered, sounding rueful. 'I think I left the keys in it. It's an Audi. It's brand new.'

'We'd better take a statement from you. Sit down here, the two of you.'

Like two good children we obeyed as Em returned and joined the group, sitting on the right of Conor. What was going on?

'Conor?'

He looked me in the face, his own full of misery. 'Brigit, I'm afraid that Hannah's missing. That's why the guards are here tonight.'

'How long has she been gone?' I said.

'Too long. She was gone when I got back. She gave Em the slip last evening. She said that she was going to bed. Em checked, and thought she was asleep. When Em went to have a bath, Hannah must have crept downstairs.'

'How long before she was missed?'

'Not long. Half an hour at most. Em looked everywhere for her. Phoned the pubs and the hotels. She didn't want to leave the house until I came back, you see.'

'And then?'

'Then we looked for her together. We were sure that we would find her. She's done this before but each time she's turned up again. Or we've had news of where she is. But this time she's completely vanished.' He ran his fingers through his hair. His face was pale.

'Had she heard about her father?'

'She had. She got a phone call from the States. Em says that she started screaming. Em had trouble calming her. She wanted drink. She always does.'

'Did Em give her drink?' I asked.

'Of course I didn't!' Em retorted.

'Now, miss,' said the older guard. 'There's no call to get excited. About this car you say you've lost...?'

Jimmy told the story once again and the younger guard took notes. When they'd finished, Em got up and made us tea. As she was handing Conor his, I saw engraved upon her face the identical expression – apprehensive and unhappy – that he was already wearing. When they frowned, they looked alike, neither of them handsome people, both of them distressed and jaded.

I thought of Hannah, saw her in that pub again – remembered the get-up she wore. Wherever she was now, she was in jeopardy.

'Your wife has a licence, does she?' the older guard inquired of Conor.

Conor licked his lips. 'No. She lost it. She was drinking.'

'It looks as if that didn't stop her.'

Jimmy gave a little moan.

'I'm afraid it does,' said Conor.

The older guard got to his feet. 'There's no more we can do tonight – or rather this morning. We'll leave it there until tomorrow. We'll come back about eleven. We'll need to take more statements then. From your students, Mr Byrne.'

'They were all at Inishbofin. They wouldn't know where Hannah was.'

'Even so. We'll see you at eleven then.'

They left, and Jimmy and I, our faces itchy with fatigue, said we'd better go as well. Conor didn't try to stop us. Em was doing the washing up. She barely said goodnight to us.

The lights downstairs had been turned off. There was one still on upstairs but as I watched, it went off, too.

As a cloud obscured the moon, I stumbled wearily to bed.

THIRTEEN

Next day's classes were all cancelled. Students turning up for them were confronted with the news that Hannah Byrne had disappeared. Conor warned them that the guards would be taking statements from them.

The senior guard was John McMahon. Along with the younger one – Gerald Brennan was his name – he set up a makeshift office in what had been the studio. I gave him a list of students.

'A lot of people,' he observed.

'Nearly sixty.'

'Yes, I see. Now, Miss Flood, about last night. You were with the gentleman who stated that his car is missing.'

'Jimmy Mullen. Yes, I was. After we got home last night, he came over to my room to say he couldn't find the Audi.'

'We know enough about the Audi. It's Mrs Byrne that interests us. She went to Inishbofin, did she, on this painting expedition?'

'Yes,' I said. 'She was with us.'

'And was she drinking, would you say?'

'She wasn't at the time I saw her.'

'And that was?'

'When we were at Cromwell's Fort.'

He looked at me above his glasses. 'Cromwell's Fort?'

I drew my breath and explained. It wasn't easy,

238

telling him. He found it hard to understand what we'd all been doing with Hannah, re-enacting a painting. I could tell that Guard McMahon thought that we were most peculiar.

When he was through with me, Jimmy took my place and I went off to look for Conor whom I hadn't seen since very early that morning. Being lunchtime, I presumed I would find him at the house.

Again, the doors downstairs were open but he wasn't in the kitchen or either of the living rooms. I decided that he must be in his private studio, which I knew was upstairs. It had been a bedroom once but Conor had converted it, he told me, replacing the existing windows with two others twice the size, to allow more light inside.

At the foot of the stairs I hesitated. Conor might be up there painting. I was reluctant to disturb him. But he'd been disturbed already, by Guard McMahon and Guard Brennan. It wasn't likely he'd be working, not on this disrupted morning.

I climbed the stairs, calling out to Conor as I went up. He didn't answer but as I reached the landing I heard him talking to somebody.

Another voice chipped in. ''Twill be over by the weekend.'

Em's voice.

'I hope so.' I heard Conor say.

'It has to be. It stands to reason.'

I called again. 'It's Brigit, Conor. Can I come in?'

A brief silence. Then, 'Of course. We're here in my studio.'

I followed the voice into a large room that must have been the master bedroom once. There were no beds in it now but through a doorway leading off it I could see a bed made up. That must be where Conor slept.

Conor was sitting in a white cane chair and Em was perched on a high stool that might have started its working life doing duty by a bar. Like all the shelves that lined the room, the stool was painted snowy-white. The shelves contained assorted objects. Pots and plates and earthenware. China from the 1930s. Wooden boxes and ceramics. A shelf clock in mahogany with a painted glass front panel – it had stopped at seven twenty. The only other furniture was a huge table covered by a white oilcloth. There were tubes of paint on it, along with white spirits, brushes, cleaning rags – everything an artist needs for work.

The room was tidy to the point of obsession. Not a cobweb to be seen. Not even one unsharpened pencil. The tubes of paint were all lined up, like soldiers on a parade. The brushes had been newly wiped. The cleaning rags were neatly folded. Conor's private studio would have baffled those outsiders who think artists can't create without chaos all around them. His schematic working place was in stark contrast to his paintings of the windswept west.

'What's going on with Guard McMahon?' said Conor. 'You were in with him for ages.'

'I know. He couldn't comprehend what we were trying to do with Hannah.' I was willing Em to leave. But she didn't, she just sat. She was like a nanny put there to protect her charge, the way she hovered over Conor. Irritating, stodgy girl...

'Who's in there being questioned now?' Conor asked.

'Jimmy went in as I left. I don't think they'll keep him long. And no one else has much to say.'

'They're putting posters up,' said Conor.

'Posters?'

'Missing Persons posters. I gave them a photograph. I don't know if it will help.'

'Someone must have seen her, Conor.'

'Maybe.' He sounded pessimistic.

'There was a piece on Hannah's father in this morning's *Independent*.'

'I know. And something in the *Irish Times*.'

'They had it on television,' said Em, breaking out of her silence. 'On the news.'

'Did they?'

'They never mentioned Hannah on it.'

'That's odd,' I said. 'You'd think they would have known.'

'She didn't like it known,' said Conor. 'She wanted to be independent of her father. You know how stupid people are about celebrity connections. Hannah hated all that stuff. She wanted to be herself, not Seamus Talbot-Kelly's daughter.'

'Really?' I'd had the opposite impression. The way that I'd read Hannah Byrne, she'd been shackled to her father. But I didn't like to say so.

It dawned on me that we were all using the past tense each time we referred to Hannah.

I said, as much to convince myself as the other two, 'Perhaps she's dashed off to LA. To attend

241

the funeral. Left Jimmy's car at Shannon and–'

'Her passport's here. We checked,' said Em.

'Did she take her bag with her?'

'Her handbag? Yes, she took her handbag.'

'If she went to London she wouldn't need a passport.'

'She didn't leave the country, Brigit.' Conor sounded definite. He went on, 'She had hardly any money and she had no credit cards.'

'Didn't she? But–'

'You're going to say that she was rich. We had to take the cards away. Confiscate her money, Brigit. You know what she used it on.'

'But she managed to get booze.' Not to mention drugs, I thought.

'She stole money all the time. From me. From Em. From Clodagh Moran.'

'From Em?'

'Yes,' Em said. 'She stole from me. My room is downstairs, you know.'

'Is it?' I'd never wondered where Em slept, never thought that much about her.

'Next to Clodagh Moran's room. The people working in this house would have slept there long ago.' There was something rather grand in the way that Em said this, as if to tell me that 'those people' were beneath the likes of her.

'Is there money missing now?'

'We don't know for sure,' said Em. 'Clodagh Moran's not back yet. Hannah could have stolen from her. She might not have noticed it before she went off last week.'

'Clodagh's coming back today,' I said.

'Yes. We can ask her then,' said Conor. 'But she

wouldn't have much on her, not enough to pay for air fares.'

We weren't getting anywhere. And I felt as if I was intruding. Everything was upside down, the whole day in disarray. Unlike Conor's studio.

I let my eyes run round the shelves. All those objects lying on them. I especially liked the boxes. They were marvellous, each one different: a tiny silver-mounted box, lying open to reveal rather aged green silk lining; a box with a mosaic picture made from strips of coloured wood; a mukwa box from Africa, with vivacious tribal carvings; a larger box from India, made from sandalwood and brass, with lotus blossoms on the lid in the shape of tear drops.

'Where did you get all those boxes?'

'Hannah used to give them to me. She was crazy about boxes.'

The past tense was being used again.

'And all the other bits and pieces?'

'The pots and earthenware are mine. All the rest belonged to Hannah. When we first moved here, this was her studio. In those days I didn't have the summer school, so I painted in the barn. Hannah had the shelves put up. Collecting things to put on them became her project for a while. You can see how she arranged the objects.'

I looked again and realised that all the objects on the shelves were unified through colour, shape and pattern. From a distance, each compartment might have been an abstract painting.

'But they're lovely,' I said, taking in the way a bowl, a box, a jug and a pot had been positioned on the shelf. 'Hannah's very talented.'

'She could have made something of herself all right.'

'I'm glad that you've preserved her shelves.'

'They're worth preserving. Mind you, they are dust collectors.'

'Not so one would notice, Conor.'

Conor smiled, the first time that he'd smiled in days. 'I can't stand muck around me, Brigit. I do the dusting here myself. Clodagh Moran does the house, but this studio is my preserve and she never comes in here.'

Em had been listening to this in silence. Perhaps she'd had too much of it because she suddenly leapt off the chair. I thought how like a cat she was. Not a Persian or Burmese, nothing so sophisticated. Em was an alley cat, the kind of cat that spits at you if you get too close to it. Her eyes were like a cat's as well, their expression fathomless.

'I'll be off. I'll see you later,' she said.

'The guards may want to talk to you.' Conor gave her an anxious look.

She shrugged. 'They can come and find me then.'

I mightn't have been in the room, the way she behaved towards me. Funny girl, I thought again. I thought I'd made a breakthrough with her but she'd gone all uppity.

'She's a bit upset,' said Conor when Em had finally departed. 'She was very fond of Hannah.'

This was news to me. Conor, I thought, had some strange ideas, both about how Hannah saw herself in relation to her father and about Em's feelings for his missing wife.

Once again, I let it go.

'Let's go down and get a sandwich,' Conor said. 'I haven't had a bite to eat.'

There wasn't much in the fridge. Just as I was asking Conor if he fancied scrambled eggs, Clodagh Moran came through the door. Her eyes were red. She had been crying.

'Oh, Mr Byrne, I'm fearful sorry. I saw a poster on the way here.'

'Ah. They have them up,' said Conor.

'The photograph of her is lovely. It shows off all her gorgeous hair.'

'It is a good one,' Conor agreed.

'Mr Byrne, when did she go? I thought she went to Inishbofin.' Clodagh's voice was all choked up. The tears were pouring down her face. 'I can't believe that this has happened. I hoped that she was getting better. I said to her a week ago...'

Conor couldn't handle it. He started edging towards the door. 'I have to go and make a phone call.'

He sidled out and left me there. Clodagh collapsed onto the nearest chair and fumbled for a handkerchief. Her grief was so genuine, I couldn't but be touched by it.

'Don't cry,' I said. 'They're looking for her. I'm sure the guards are going to find her.' I wasn't in the least bit sure but I hoped this was true.

Clodagh gave me a watery smile. 'Aw, Brigit, but she's very sweet.'

She'd never smiled at me before, never called me by my name. The day was standing on its head. Em reverted to being hostile. Clodagh

245

Moran smiling at me.

'I'm going to make some tea for you.' I didn't ask if she took sugar, I put two lumps in the cup. Clodagh didn't seem to notice. Perhaps she always drank it that way.

'She does no harm to anybody.'

I thought about our trip to Galway. The trouble that I'd had with Hannah. But it wasn't *that* much trouble.

'No, you're right. She doesn't, Clodagh.'

I'd forgotten Conor's hunger. I left the eggs lying there, unscrambled.

'Did the guards come round?' said Clodagh. 'Guard McMahon's very kind. He helped me when my brother died. His wife gave me a lift to Ennis.'

'There's someone at the door,' I said, having heard a bang on it.

Clodagh pulled herself together. 'You stay here. I'll answer it.'

She came back looking hot and bothered. 'There's someone out there from the papers. A man. He wants to speak to Mr Byrne.'

'Let me have a word with him.'

She'd left him waiting on the doorstep. He was young, only in his middle twenties, with sallow skin and light-brown hair. Mammy would have sized him up and said he was a Protestant.

'Hello,' he said. 'I'm Tony Lyons. I'm from the *Examiner*. Is Mr Conor Byrne at home?'

'Will you come in and wait a minute?'

I took him into the sitting room. Like the dining room, its décor was Victorian, the dainty chairs around the walls contrasting with a large settee. The wallpaper was dusty pink. Persian rugs almost hid the Wilton carpet and a crystal chandelier hung from the middle of the ornate ceiling. It was quite a pretty room, much nicer than the dining room, but it was designed for people from a bygone era. It was hard to believe that the woman who'd arranged the shelves upstairs was the mistress of this house.

Tony Lyons eyed the room. 'Interesting,' he observed.

'Sit down. I'll get Conor here for you.'

Conor had gone back upstairs. He was in his studio, trying to look occupied, doodling on a sketching pad.

He glanced up, frowning, then seemed relieved. 'Sorry, but I'm dodging Clodagh.'

'I think I had worked that out. There's a journalist downstairs. Tony Lyons. He's from the *Examiner*.' The *Examiner* is one of Ireland's leading papers.

Conor frowned again. 'Is the fellow after me?'

'Yes. You'd better come and talk to him.'

'This is all I need,' Conor said irritably. But he came downstairs with me.

'Where is he?'

'In the sitting room.'

Tony Lyons was scribbling notes, possibly about the room which appeared to fascinate him.

'Conor Byrne? I'm Tony Lyons.'

'I know. What exactly are you after?'

Tony Lyons blinked. 'It's in connection with your wife.'

'Have you seen her?' Conor said.

'No. I wish I had,' said Tony.

247

'So, what is it then?' asked Conor, standing over by the door, glowering at the visitor.

'She's Seamus Talbot-Kelly's daughter.'

'How the hell do you know that?' Conor's face went red with temper.

Tony Lyons was surprised, but he stood his ground. 'I interviewed him in LA. He told me that he had a daughter. He showed me photographs of her. I've just come from Ballyvaughan – I'm on holiday, in fact – and I came across a poster. Naturally I recognised her and I made a few inquiries.'

'And you think by coming here you'll get a story out of me?'

'I hoped that you would talk to me.'

'Fuck off!' Conor said. 'Get out!'

'But Mr Byrne, if we run a story on her, it might help you find your wife.'

'You heard me,' Conor said. 'Get out!'

'Conor?'

'Brigit, you keep out of this.'

I backed off reluctantly, hoping Conor wouldn't pay for the stance that he was taking.

'OK,' Tony Lyons said. 'I'm going.'

He left the room with dignity. We followed him into the hall. Conor held the front door open.

'Don't come snooping here again. You reporters, you're just scum.'

Tony looked him in the eye. 'The old man was right about you.'

'What bullshit are you talking now?'

'Seamus Talbot-Kelly told me that you were a real shit. I thought he was exaggerating. Now I realise he was right.'

248

Having got the last word in, our visitor strode out the door. Conor slammed it after him.

'Bastard!'

I sighed, only too aware that Conor had mishandled things. Then I remembered he was hungry.

'You need to eat. You're in a state.'

'Don't tell me! It's uncertainty.'

'I know.'

His temper was like Joe's, I thought. A sudden flare. A huge eruption.

'Not knowing kills me,' Conor said. 'I don't feel in control of things.'

'It's miserable.' I was at a loss for words, conscious that my love for Conor couldn't help him one iota.

'I can't stand sitting here and waiting. What's happening down there with the guards? They haven't finished yet, have they?'

He fussed and fretted, paced and growled. Eventually, Clodagh Moran, sizing up the situation, set some food down on the table. She'd unfrozen sausages, heated up a tin of beans and fried the eggs that I'd forgotten.

After Conor had been fed, he took himself upstairs again and I helped Clodagh with the dishes. She was still all over me. I wondered what I could have done to make her change her mind about me.

Then, as we were putting the plates away, she started talking about Hannah.

'The poor pet, 'twas hard on her. All those women coming here and chasing after Mr Byrne.'

I swallowed. All those women. I was one of them...

'That used to bother her a lot?'

'It *lambasted* her,' said Clodagh. 'Every time a new one came, she used to think about her father taking up with fancy women. She told me how it was with them after they had lost their mother. Her father was the world to her. She'd just be feeling close to him, thinking he'd look after her, and then his eyes went straying. The minute he saw a woman, off he'd go, neglecting her.'

'Poor little girl, to be so insecure.' I thought, yes, that's Hannah, poor little rich girl who never grew up. Who needs so much looking after.

'It affected her for life.'

'And the women who came here – you said they were a threat to her?'

'The ones that had the looks,' said Clodagh. 'She'd say she could pick them out the minute they came up the drive and know they'd be a worry for her.'

I thought of the time when I'd arrived at Kilnaboy and realised that I was being watched from behind a twitching curtain. And then Hannah followed me. Did she suspect I was after Conor? What other reason would she have for stalking me around the grounds?

Clodagh passed a plate to me. 'She wasn't always right, mind you. The drink had made her paranoiac. She was upset when you came, Brigit. Then she changed her mind about you.'

'Did she? Did she tell you that herself?'

'Yes. The last time I laid eyes on her. Just before I went away. I was going down the drive and she

250

came running after me. She was strange, I grant you that.'

'Strange?'

'Hot and bothered. All wound up.'

'Yes. I saw her in that state myself.'

Clodagh frowned. 'She never used to be like that. Only this last year or so. I don't know what got into her.'

Amphetamines, that's what, I thought. But I kept that to myself and went off on another tack.

'When she ran after you that time, have you told the guards about it?'

'There's no call to tell the guards?'

'No? But why did she run after you?'

'She felt bad about you, Brigit.'

'About *me?*'

Clodagh nodded. 'You see, she'd been suspicious of you. Thinking you were like the others. But she changed her mind about you. She would have been brooding on it, sitting up there in her room. Then she saw me going off and decided she must tell me.

'What exactly did she say?'

'That she had been wrong about you. And that you'd been good to her the day you went to Galway with her. "Brigit's on my side," she said. "I want to tell you I can trust her".'

Guilt was back again. It stuck another knife in me.

As I was wincing from the impact, Conor reappeared and said, 'I must talk to Guard McMahon. Maybe he has news for me.'

'I'll walk back that way with you,' I said, anxious to escape from guilt.

251

Guard McMahon had no news apart from being fed up with students, none of whom knew anything about Hannah's disappearance.

'I told you that,' said Conor smugly. 'My wife seldom met my students. I didn't encourage contact with them. With the problem she had, it was better that way round. Of course there were a few occasions, usually disastrous, when they came across each other, in a pub or hotel. That time with Brigit here, for instance. She had her own run-in with Hannah.'

'What run-in was that, Miss Flood? You didn't mention this before.'

'I never thought of it,' I said. 'It was when we went to Galway...'

While I was getting out of that one, Conor rounded up the students. Since the guards were through with them – for the moment, anyway – he organised another trip, this time to the Kerry coast to see Cill Rialaig.

Dubbed the Irish St Ives, Cill Rialaig is a pre-famine village set upon a slate-grey cliff which, thanks to the effort of a Dublin publisher, Mrs Noelle Campbell-Sharpe, has become an artists' haven instead of a motorway. I wrote about it in my feature. Lorcan was involved in it and in the two other projects – the arts complex in Dun Geagan and the international art gallery in Waterville – that are linked to the same scheme. To be an artist in Cill Rialaig is to live ascetically, as the monks did long ago on the nearby Skellig rocks, in the bay off Bolus Head. It was just the place to send a team of restless students on a Celtic exploration.

252

If it hadn't been for Conor, I'd have gone with them myself. I was feeling just as restless, which was why, the next day, I volunteered for shopping duty, so Clodagh would be spared the trouble.

Instead of going to Corofin, I drove alone to Ballyvaughan. The weather had the sulks that week. The coast was all togged out in grey and there was rain on the horizon.

I'd already bought the groceries when I felt a pang of hunger and remembered *An Fear Gorta* and all those delicious cakes. It was bordering on midday, which justified a stop for lunch.

But I was not the only one who'd come upon the hungry grass. The place was packed with people and I was forced to share a table with an elderly couple. The smell of cakes made up for that. Thinking that I'd have some later – chocolate or maybe the lemon – I ordered sandwiches and coffee.

'Hello, and how are you?' said someone.

It was Sheila Ferguson. She had another woman with her – her daughter, by the looks of her, with the same serene expression.

'I'm fine,' I said although I wasn't – I kept thinking about Hannah.

'It's very crowded here today. I can't see a table, Mammy.'

'No, I can't either,' Sheila said.

'We've finished,' said the woman who was sitting at the table with me. 'You can sit here if you like.'

Sheila looked at me. 'Could we, Brigit? Would you mind?'

'Of course I wouldn't,' I replied.

253

'This is Nuala,' Sheila said when the other two had left. 'She's my eldest daughter.'

Nuala smiled engagingly. 'Mammy told me about you. She met you here some time ago.'

I was flattered that Sheila would remember me. I warmed again to her.

For someone who once lost her voice, she was very talkative, wanting to hear all my news.

'Brigit, tell me,' she began. 'Are you still at Kilnaboy? You are? So you'll know all about poor Hannah. We saw the posters up this morning. But Nuala knew before today.'

'I live in Corofin,' said Nuala.

'Conor mentioned that, I think – that you were living near to him.'

'I am. In fact my husband is his doctor.'

'Are you Dr Moylan's wife?'

Nuala nodded. 'Yes, I am.'

'Brigit,' Sheila interrupted. 'We want to hear your views on Hannah. What happened that she went away?'

'I don't have a clue,' I said. 'We all went up to Inishbofin but Hannah didn't stay there long. By the time we got back, she'd already upped and gone.'

'Was she distressed about her father?'

'I'm sure she was but I don't know. I didn't see her when the news came. I never saw that much of her.'

'Conor would make sure you didn't. Did you see this morning's paper? The *Examiner,* I mean?'

My heart sank. 'No, I haven't seen it.'

'I have a copy here,' said Sheila. 'I brought it with me to show Nuala.' She dug the paper out of her bag and handed it across to me. 'The story's on page four,' she said.

The headline said, 'A Distressed Daughter Disappears'. There was a photograph of Hannah and another one of Seamus. Hannah's photo had been lifted from the one used in the posters. The one of Seamus wasn't recent. In it, he looked very handsome, every bit the movie star.

I read the piece with trepidation, half expecting Tony Lyons to show Conor as a monster after what he'd said to him. But Tony had done no such thing. The story told the facts, no more.

'Has Conor talked to you about it?' Sheila was as bad as Tony, out to get the real story.

'Just to say he's worried sick.'

'And so he should be,' Sheila said. 'Potentially, it could be tragic. Seamus would be up the walls if he was alive. Hannah troubled him no end.'

'Did you know him?' I inquired.

'Yes, I did. He bought the house at Kilnaboy from people we used to know. I came across him several times. A gorgeous man, but very selfish, the way actors tend to be. But he cared about his daughter. Gave her everything she wanted. Far too much, in my opinion, but she was the only one.'

'Yes. I know. She told me that.'

'So you *did* have contact with her?'

'A few times, not a lot,' I said. 'So Seamus was a loving father?'

'A careful one in many ways. He did his best to protect Hannah.'

'And was he...?' I thought again, and then plunged in, 'Was he pleased about her marriage?'

255

'*Pleased?*'

'Mammy,' Nuala intervened. 'We need to get our order in. Are you going to have a sandwich?'

'Ham with salad,' Sheila said. '*Of course* he wasn't pleased about it. Conor didn't have a penny. Just that house at Inishbofin and we know how he got that!'

'Mammy!' Nuala said again. 'God, you are a fearful gossip!'

'Am I?'

'Yes, you are. You should be careful. Brigit, are you having cake? I'm not going to have a sandwich, just a piece of chocolate cake and to hell with calories! Mammy, will you have a slice?'

'Maybe later,' Sheila said.

I'd backed off from her again. She was bitchy, I decided, trying to stick her knife in Conor. Nuala was the nicer person.

I ate my sandwich and then left, without stopping for the cake. I didn't want to stay with Sheila who was so disloyal to Conor.

'I hope we'll meet in here again,' Sheila said as I was leaving.

I lied and said I hoped so too. The way I felt, I really hoped we would never meet again.

Outside, the rain was drizzling down. I couldn't find my keys at first and by the time I dredged them up from the bottom of my bag, the moisture had gone through my clothes.

Driving home, I asked myself why were people so revolting? Sheila owed Conor a lot. He restored her power of speech. You'd think she would remember that when she was discussing him, instead of going for his throat because he rejected her. *Cow*...

Driving back across the scree, I thought about the cake I'd missed because of Sheila Ferguson. The drizzle hid the hilltop lake. Hannah, where are you? I thought. Are you wandering in the rain or are you snug inside a bar?

Halfway home, I heard the wail of the Garda car. The car itself soon flashed by me, splashing water as it did so. That did not improve my mood.

I drove faster, eager to get back to Conor and away from irritations. Clodagh would be eager too, to get her hands on the groceries.

I turned in by the white lodge and wove my way up the winding avenue to the house.

The guards' car was parked beside the Jaguar. More guards, I remember thinking. Don't we have enough of them?

Then the front door opened and people came out. Two strange guards and Clodagh Moran.

Clodagh was in tears again. I left the groceries in the car and ran over to the group.

'What's going on? Has there been news?'

The two guards only stared at me.

'Clodagh, is there news of Hannah?'

'Not the kind of news we want.'

'But what is it?' I persisted.

Clodagh told me tearfully. 'They've found Jimmy Mullen's car. It was by the Flaggy Shore. Hannah's bag was in it, Brigit. Mr Byrne is devastated. He's in there crying like a baby, sure that harm has come to her.'

Conor said he feared the worst and secretly I felt the same. When Clodagh returned to the kitchen,

Conor disappeared upstairs to his studio.

'Did she leave a note?' asked Clodagh. 'Did they find one in the car?'

But they hadn't found a note, only Hannah's big black satchel. In it was a make-up pouch, a comb, a few pound coins, and two empty vodka bottles.

'Oh, and a photo of her father apparently,' I added.

'And that was all there was in it?' asked Clodagh.

'That's what the guards told Conor. There wasn't room for more, I guess.'

'Still, it doesn't sound like her.'

'What do you mean?'

Clodagh said, 'She always had her letters with her. She'd carry them around with her. They'd be ones her father sent her.'

'He wrote her lots of letters, did he?' I asked.

'Not so much these last few months. Hardly anything in fact. But before that they could come maybe once or twice a month.'

'Did she get other post as well?'

'From America, she did. They'd have "Confidential" on them. She didn't tell me what they said.'

'No letters from her friends?'

But Hannah had no friends, said Clodagh, not in Ireland, anyway. 'Unless you counted those yahoos she'd join up with in the pubs. The sort that would be waiting for her in the hope she'd buy them drinks. Parasites, the lot of them.'

The phone went and it was David. He'd heard of Hannah's disappearance. Celia had called up her mother who'd read about it in the papers.

For a while, we talked about Hannah. Then I asked about the foot.

'The foot is doing well,' said David. 'A week or two and I'll be back. That is, if I'm wanted there.'

'I'll let you know how things develop.'

The situation got more gloomy as the afternoon wore on. Conor said it was the waiting, convinced that the worst had happened but unable to confirm it. 'It tears the heart from you,' he said.

He looked quite haggard, older than he really was. I couldn't get to him at all. He'd shut himself away from me. I thought if I reached out to him, hugged or kissed or cuddled him, that I'd be insulting Hannah. So I, too, withdrew and turned for company to Clodagh.

That evening, Conor didn't come for supper. Em, who had popped up to see him, announced that he would eat upstairs. She waited pointedly for Clodagh to prepare a tray for him and then took it up herself. I knew I was being edged aside, that she was playing games with me, mutely sending out signals that she was in control, not me.

The evening passed without further news of Hannah. I began to feel that it would always be this way, that all of us at Kilnaboy would stay inside the vacuum; that life would not move on again.

But of course it did. And when that happened, less than twenty-four hours later, I wished devoutly that we could return to yesterday's vacuum.

I was with Conor in the kitchen when the guards banged on the door. Guard McMahon was amongst them.

'Mr Byrne, we have bad news. A woman's body has been found and we think it is your wife's.'

Conor tensed and closed his eyes. For a moment no one spoke. Guard Brennan gave a discreet cough. The rest of us just held our breath.

Then Conor said, 'Where was the body found?'

'At Aughinish Point. That's near the Martello tower.'

'I know Aughinish Point. Who discovered it?'

'Two young boys,' said Guard McMahon. 'One of them is only nine. They had no business being there. Their parents should be watching them.' He spoke as if the point harboured bodies all the time and parents should watch out in case their offspring stumbled over them.

'Two young boys,' repeated Conor. 'Are they from the area?'

I saw the guards exchanging glances. Their eyes were saying, he's in shock. He can't focus on the body. Just on the circumstances of its discovery.

'Where's the body now?' said Conor.

'It's been taken through to Ennis.'

'So it's in the hospital. What else has been done about it?'

'Certain procedures are being carried out. The coroner has been contacted. The pathologist from Limerick will be holding an autopsy this evening to determine the cause of death. You understand, Mr Byrne, we need to be satisfied that no foul play has been involved.'

'Of course, I understand,' said Conor. 'But what can I be doing to assist in your inquiries?'

'I'm afraid we have to ask you to identify the body.'

'I was expecting that,' said Conor. He had switched to automatic. His voice was mechanical, as if it had been pre-recorded. It made me think of the Underground, of the distinctive voice that, as you're stepping from the Tube, warns that you must 'Mind the gap!'

'The sooner the better, from our point of view.'

'Then we'll do it now,' said Conor.

He seemed to have forgotten me. Without saying another word, he went out to the Garda car. I watched him getting into it. To me, he didn't look like Conor. He'd become an automaton, about to carry out a task from which a person would have shrunk.

Clodagh, entering the hall just then, said she got the same impression. I had to break the news to her and tell her a body had been found and the guards thought it was Hannah's.

Clodagh didn't weep this time. She said that she'd used up her tears, that this was only confirmation of what we'd already known and that, instead of crying buckets, we should pray for Hannah's soul.

'But we're not certain that it is Hannah,' I said. 'It might be someone else's body.'

'In the same vicinity?' Aughinish Point was opposite the Flaggy Shore, a distance you could swim across.

I gave up arguing with Clodagh who promptly rang up Father Roche, at the church in Corofin,

261

to arrange a Mass for Hannah.

She'd barely finished with this call when another one came in and she picked up the receiver.

'Yes? Ah, Mr Byrne, it's Clodagh here.'

I leant forward, watching her, trying to gauge the news from the look upon her face. But her expression told me nothing.

'Yes,' she said, and, 'Yes.'

Clodagh, what's going on? I mouthed.

She didn't answer, not directly. Instead, she spoke those words that are used by country people to try and give comfort when there is a funeral.

'I'm sorry for your trouble.'

And that was when I knew for certain that they had found Hannah's body.

FOURTEEN

We got the verdict in the morning. Foul play was ruled out, which Clodagh said was a relief. There were no suspicious factors. But Hannah hadn't died by drowning. Her death was due to other reasons – the alcohol she had consumed, combined with temazepam and a mix of other drugs. The pathologist decreed that she was already dead before immersion in the water.

I guessed that she'd wanted to numb her grief, collapsed and died upon the shore as the tide was coming in. The pull of it would have borne her out to sea.

'When's the funeral?' I asked Conor.

To my surprise he told me Hannah was to be buried in Los Angeles next to Seamus Talbot-Kelly. 'Hannah wanted it,' he said. 'She told her father long ago and he made arrangements for it.'

To me, it seemed a strange request, somebody of Hannah's age planning where she would be buried. But Conor had no quarrel with it. And when I gave more thought to it, it seemed logical to me that Hannah who'd adored her father and suffered when she was displaced by the women he had taken should return to him in death. The loving daughter reinstated.

I assumed Conor would go to LA to attend the funeral but he said he couldn't bear it. 'I had to identify her. I've been through enough already.'

'Yes...' Identifying Hannah's body must have been horrendous for him. To think of it was bad enough. As an antidote, I conjured up her living image. Hannah Byrne the way she'd been when I first laid eyes on her. The energy that came from her. Those burning eyes. The too-thin body. The lovely, flaming red-gold hair. Auburn

The remedy proved ineffective. It made me feel sick at heart.

Conor said, 'Don't look so sad.'

'I was thinking of her hair. What the sea would do to it...'

'You can think but I have seen it.'

'Sorry. Yes. I know you have.'

He pulled me to him. Held me closely. 'Don't think about her hair,' he said. 'When I look at you, I will know what you are thinking. It will bring it back to me. Seeing her was hell for me. *Please* don't think about her hair.'

But of course we thought of Hannah, all of us at Kilnaboy. When the body was flown out, it freed us, in a way. It was as if the night had ended and those dark satanic demons that we feared when we were children had retreated from our lives into the forest of the night.

That new-found freedom was reflected in the look on Clodagh's face.

'Poor pet,' she said. 'But all the same I don't feel bad about her, Brigit. Her troubles are all over now. And they'll look after her Up There.'

I knew Conor was relieved. Anxiety was gone from him. Within a week of Hannah's death, he was back at work again. And the studio re-opened, for Conor said there was no point in carrying on the mourning process and could I bring the students back.

Some returned and some did not. Jimmy Mullen didn't come, being overly concerned for the welfare of his Audi, and two of the older people said that they'd stay down in Kerry. And there was another drop-out, one I wouldn't have expected and which I only learnt about when I spoke by phone to David.

'We're back to normal, more or less. Are you two ready to come back?'

'I am. I'll book a flight to Shannon now.'

'Isn't Celia coming with you?'

'No, she's not,' said David shortly.

It sounded like a touchy subject. I shelved it for the time being and moved onto other ground.

'You'll bring the video with you? I don't suppose you've cut it yet.'

'I'll show it to you,' David said. 'And no, I haven't done the cuts. I'll do them after it's finished. When we've been back to Inishbofin.'

'Right. Call me when you've done your booking and I'll pick you up at Shannon.'

The broken romance was intriguing. I wondered who had severed it. It must be David, I decided. And Celia must be too upset to go on with her summer class.

My own reaction to this news was a little disconcerting. Part of me was sympathetic to Celia but the other part was pleased to hear that David would be free again.

Having recognised my feelings, I began to query them. I didn't fancy David, did I? I already had a lover. I didn't need another one. Was I greedy? Power mad? Maybe I was just unsettled. By then, it was already August and soon, in less than a month, I'd be going back to London.

I could sleep with Conor now without feeling culpable. We still preserved the secrecy. He never visited my room but he left the front door open when he went to bed at night so I could slip inside and join him. Tucked up in their downstairs bedrooms, Em and Clodagh never knew of the hours I spent with him, for I was always gone by dawn. We talked about the book that I would write on Conor's life, though when I'd find the time to do it, with my programme back on air, was not a question I could answer.

When David and his cameras returned alone to Kilnaboy, I was absurdly pleased to see him, which, when I recalled how he'd upset me when we were in Inishbofin, seemed disloyal to Conor.

This was all rather complicated and I quickly turned my thoughts to Celia.

'What happened that you two broke up?'

'Oh, well – you know,' said David vaguely.

'No. I don't. So what went wrong?'

'Coke and ecstasy, for starters.'

'Cocaine?'

'Anything she can get. I hate the drug thing!' David said. 'I've seen too much of it. Fashion fairly feeds off it. That heroin chic thing got to me. Glamorising fucking poison! I couldn't take those kind of pictures. Those kids – the models are so young today, only in their middle teens, and they're got at by bastards who move in on them. I had a girlfriend in the States who died of an overdose. I couldn't go through that again.'

The angry words poured out of him.

I digested them and said, 'But didn't you suspect before?'

'About Celia? Yes, I did. I thought it was occasional. That she was experimenting. That it wasn't serious. Then she stayed with me in London and I realised that it was.'

'She's not the only one,' I said.

'Too right she's not the only one! The studio is riddled with it.'

'At Kilnaboy we have a problem?'

'Brigit, don't be so naïve.'

But this is Kilnaboy, I thought rather sadly, not London. But that *was* naïve, of course – or wishful thinking. We were dealing with an art school and art schools were experimental. It sometimes seemed to me that students played around with drugs as if they were obliged to do so, to extend their learning prowess.

I became more practical. 'Did Celia tell you who's supplying them?'

'The thing is,' David said, rather vaguely, 'I guess I didn't want to know. I just felt up to here with it.'

More fool Celia, I decided.

That evening, we watched the uncut video, Conor, David, Em and I. Being so intent on seeing the film, I hadn't thought how we might feel when Hannah's back appeared in it.

When the film reached that point, I glanced instinctively at Conor to determine his reactions. But Conor didn't see me looking. He was leaning forward, staring wide-eyed at the screen. I noticed Em was doing the same, that both of

267

them were closely scrutinising what was taking place on film.

David said, 'It's repetitious, naturally. Uncut film always is. But there's good stuff there all right. This bit definitely works.'

The wind was whipping round the fort. The woman seated on the rocks put up a hand to catch her hair.

There was something not quite right with that but I couldn't work out what it was.

'You can *see* the wind!' said David. 'It's wonderfully atmospheric.'

The film ran to half an hour.

'You'll run it that way round?' said Conor. 'Myself, the studio, and Hannah, followed by the gallery?'

'Which I've yet to see. Yes, I think so,' David said. 'It's a logical progression. Unless we use that last shot first. It's excellent dramatic stuff.'

They bounced ideas around between them. They seemed to be on better terms than they had been the last time they met.

But this, I found, was an illusion. Within another day or two, I noticed things were cooling off.

David was all set to go back to Inishbofin. Conor wasn't ready yet. He had business to attend to – that was what he said to David.

David moaned to me about it. '*He* was the one who wanted me back to finish off the video. But now I'm hanging round all day waiting for His Majesty to tell his subjects what to do.'

'It's not like that. You know it's not.'

'It *is*. It always was,' said David. 'Conor Byrne

268

is a dictator. This thing about Inishbofin – is he scared of going back?'

'*Scared?* What would make him scared, David?'

'There's a problem with that cottage. You don't know about it, do you?'

I shook my head and he went on.

'I heard about it coming back. We met a fellow on the ferry and gave him a lift to Galway. He told us that the islanders have it in for Conor Byrne.'

'They do tend to be insular.'

'It's more than insularity. They don't like the circumstances under which he got that cottage.'

'Oh, is that all?' I told him that I'd met a little boy who said his family owned the cottage. 'Insularity, just as I said. They're behind the times. They don't like strangers moving in. That's all there is to it, I promise.'

'I think there may be more,' said David.

'And I think you're being ridiculous!'

'Listen to me, Brigit. Please–'

My mobile rang. I glared at David. Answered curtly. 'Yes?'

'Brigit, it's Darina here.'

'Oh, hi, and how are you?' I said as David walked away from me.

Darina didn't answer that. She said, 'Look, you'll have to go to Dublin, Brigit. Mammy's had an accident.'

The poodles had tripped Mammy up. She'd fallen and her hip was broken. She'd crawled over to the phone and called a neighbour for assistance. She was in the Blackrock Clinic, thanks to BUPA, said Darina. 'You'll go to Dublin now, will you?' she went on briskly.

'Not *now,*' I said, digesting this. 'I could maybe go tomorrow.'

'*Maybe?*' Darina lost her temper with me. She told me I was spoilt and selfish. All the problems in the family always fell upon her shoulders. 'I can't go to Dublin, Brigit. I've the children to look after. You're the one who isn't married. You make me sick. You really do. When I think how I treated you. Protecting you from everything. All that awful stuff with Daddy... And the minute that you're needed... Oh, I don't want to talk about it. I've just had enough of it!' She rang off.

I put the phone back in my bag and contemplated what to do. It was five o'clock. Rather late to go to Dublin. But I could drive up there tomorrow...

I called Darina back. 'I'm sorry if I sounded selfish.'

'I'm sorry that I lost my temper. This weekend was diabolic. Children drive you round the bend.'

'I know. I understand,' I said.

'You don't. How can you? You're not married. If you knew what I've been through...' She launched into a long story involving Mikey, Noeline and a window. Mikey was peculiar lately. He had refused to go to bed. Ordered to obey or else, he'd fled into the dining room, slammed and locked the door behind him. When, after much coaxing, he'd said, yes, he would come out, the lock refused to turn for him.

'He was screaming,' said Darina. 'So Noeline said she'd get him out, she'd climb through the burglar bars. But she didn't. She got stuck. Robert was playing golf – of course. I had to call the fire brigade. And then Moira Riordan phoned...' Moira Riordan was the neighbour who had come to Mammy's rescue.

'No wonder you were all wound up.'

'Yes. And I can't go to Dublin, Brigit.'

'Not to worry. I'll go up tomorrow morning. I'll let you know how Mammy is once I've seen her at the clinic.'

'You do that,' Darina said.

She rang off again before I had the chance to ask her what she had been getting at when she lost her temper with me. I'd been protected, she'd insisted. Protected? Had I somehow been endangered without any knowledge of it? And 'that awful stuff with Daddy'. What was she insinuating?

I nearly phoned her back again but then I thought better of it. She was jumpy as a kitten. I wasn't up to listening to her on the subject of her life and how it compared with mine.

Instead, I tracked Conor down, told him I'd be going away for a day or two, packed the minimum requirements and steeled myself to visit Mammy.

I left the car at Mammy's house and took the DART to Blackrock station. On the train I saw a woman carrying a bunch of flowers. She was around my age and I wondered if, like me, she was going to visit someone who was sick in hospital. She was looking rather pensive. Was she feeling guilty too, wishing that she needn't go, or

271

did she only have a headache?

It was one of those grey mornings that hadn't quite made up its mind which direction it should take. While I was on the train, it drizzled. When I got out, it spat at me. I had to wait to cross Rock Road and by the time I managed it, my hair and clothes were sopping wet.

The last time that I had been rained on, I had been in Ballyvaughan, after being at *An Fear Gorta*. Afterwards I'd heard the news that Jimmy Mullen's car was found. And, all the while, without my knowing, Hannah had been in the sea.

Hannah… Didn't I escape from her? I thought. Surely she can't touch me now?

Trying to get away from her, I scampered towards the clinic gates, clutching Mammy's get-well goodies. The trees that lined the avenue shook more raindrops down on me.

The clinic was an attractive, glass-fronted modern building. Hastening inside, I might have entered a hotel. There were murals on the walls, green settees around a fountain, a gift shop and a restaurant. Mammy wasn't short of money. Joe, no matter what his sins, had looked after her finances. And Mammy was a prudent woman. She had saved, invested wisely. Paid her medical insurance.

Reception directed me to Mammy's room. A doorway on the left would lead me to the lift. Doing as I had been told, I could hear more water splashing. Beyond the doorway was another spacious room pleasingly designed to look like a verdant indoor garden. Palms and potted plants blended with more green settees. A simulated waterfall with an all-glass lift behind it formed a backdrop to a pool. There were rocks inside the pool. Sculpted figures on the rocks. Figures of three naked children, fishing, playing with the water...

'Hello, Brigit!' someone called.

'Mr Sheehan,' I said, turning.

Ivor Sheehan was a senior specialist affiliated to the clinic. I'd been at school with his two daughters. Now, he was a widower. He told me that he'd repaired Mammy's hip.

'How's she getting on?' I asked, trying to avert my eyes from the figures in the pool.

'She's doing brilliantly,' he said, radiating optimism. As we waited for the lift, he spoke at length of Mammy's progress.

'Isn't she in pain?' I said, doing my best to think of Mammy instead of the memories evoked by the sculpted figures.

'A little, but your Mammy's brave. A great woman altogether.' He explained about the break, assuming I had knowledge of the ilium and ala. I didn't disillusion him. Mammy would translate his meaning.

'So it's not too bad?' I said.

'Not too bad at all, at all. She'll be out of here in no time.' He reached out to pat my shoulder, noticed that it had been rained on and withdrew his hand again. 'She'll be grand, you'll see,' he said.

We travelled to the second floor, then we parted company.

Mammy, located in a private room with a generous bathroom en suite, didn't look that

273

grand to me. But she had her make-up on and a pale pink nightie with a gown to match.

She let me kiss her cheek and said, rather disapprovingly, 'Ah, Brigit, but you're soaking wet.'

'I got rained on coming here.' I deposited her gifts – *Hello!* and her favourite chocolates – on the table by her bed.

'You didn't bring the other nighties?'

'Nighties?'

'Darina said you'd get them to me.'

'She never mentioned them to me.'

'What got into her? It's not like her to forget. But anyway, I need them, Brigit. I've only got the one I've on. I don't like asking Moira Riordan. Having strangers in your bedroom…'

'How many do you want?' I said.

'There's a yellow and a peach. And a white one, with a frill. All of them have gowns to match. You'll find them in my chest of drawers. I keep them in the third drawer down.'

'Is that all that you'll be needing?'

'For the moment, anyway. How long are you staying this time?'

I didn't want to answer that. Pretending that I didn't hear, I wandered over to the window, thinking I would see the harbour, sea and yachts, the mail boat coming. But Mammy's room didn't face Dun Laoire Harbour. Instead, I saw a rugby pitch. Blackrock College was next door. The lads were wearing college colours – horizontal blue and white.

Mammy said, 'An invitation came for you. It was to an exhibition.'

274

'Do you remember who it's from?'

'Of course.' She sniffed. 'That Lorcan Burke is holding it.'

'Lorcan…' I'd forgotten Lorcan's show.

'And there was something in the paper.'

'Oh, yes?'

'The *Irish Times*. It's over there.'

Under the headline 'Not Quite a Naïve', there was half a page on Lorcan. I immersed myself in it.

The Origin Gallery at 83 Harcourt Street, a fine Georgian house complete with a tented Napoleonic library, will provide a perfect setting for Lorcan Burke's finely executed work.

His warmth, lyricism and inventiveness are reminiscent of French naïve painting. But Burke's pastoral experience is essentially Irish. To look at his paintings is to step into the looking-glass and find yourself again in childhood.

There is no place for such work in contemporary exhibitions, such as the annual Glen Dimplex Award. On the other hand, Burke does not need the recognition earned by the winners of such awards. A long-time member of the RHA, the memory of his previous exhibitions at Iontas, his involvement with the rebirth of Cill Rialaig and his residencies at the Tyrone Guthrie Centre at Annaghmakerrig…

The Tyrone Guthrie Centre – the fine house and vast acreage of forest, farm, lake and wilderness bequeathed to the Irish people by the theatre producer and director Sir Tyrone Guthrie – is a creative workplace for accomplished artists seeking to develop their ideas in a peaceful, pastoral setting. Conor, I suspected, had Annaghmakerrig in his mind when he created his summer school. But he hadn't gone as far as the Tyrone Guthrie Centre which opens up its residencies to all aspects of the arts.

'Naturally, I didn't read it,' said Mammy. 'But I knew 'twould interest you.' She managed to sound both martyred and disdainful at the same time.

'Mm. Thank you. Yes, it does.' I went on reading.

Like the Swedish artist Hallstrom, Burke's oeuvre falls between naïve and 'high' art. But Hallstrom was a 'hobby' painter. Burke's is a far greater talent.

Amongst the collection will be earlier paintings dating from the onset of Burke's career. These paintings will not be for sale, but are being included to add insight into his vision...

'Well now, isn't that intriguing?' I said, speaking to myself. I'd never seen those early paintings. Didn't know they existed. I wondered idly what they were like.

'What's intriguing?' Mammy asked.

'Never mind. It doesn't matter. Should I get the nighties now?'

'Do, so. If you wouldn't mind.'

'Not a bit. I'll be back soon.'

I'd intended going to town after I had been with Mammy. That was why I'd dumped the car, so I

276

wouldn't have to park it in the crowded city centre. But I could go another time. Mammy's nighties were important.

It was strange being in the house without Mammy and the poodles. All of them had left their smells lingering inside the hall. Doggy odour and shampoo. Calvin Klein's 'Eternity'. Mammy's bedroom smelt the same. It was a room I seldom entered. Even as children, Darina and I were not encouraged to invade it.

I felt intrusive, going in. I didn't mean to stay there long, only while I got the nighties. But then I had to find a bag into which they could be packed. I couldn't see one anywhere so I had to poke around. Opposite Mammy's double bed – the one she used to share with Joe – was a line of built-in cupboards.

The first one contained Mammy's clothes, the ones she wore throughout the summer. Pastel suits and silky dresses hanging up on padded hangers. There were two cases on the shelf that ran above the dressing rail but they were larger than was needed.

Mammy's entire winter wardrobe occupied the second cupboard. Jaeger suits and toning blouses. Some nifty navy Jean Muir numbers that had cost a pretty packet. Two of Paul Costelloe's dresses.

The rail above had shoes in it, all of which had 'Shu-maids' in them so they would retain their shape. But no bag or little case.

I could use a plastic bag or the hold-all I had brought, which I hadn't yet unpacked. Having those alternatives, I very nearly didn't bother checking the remaining cupboard. But then I thought – I might as well.

Opening the cupboard door, I was sure I would find yet another season's wardrobe – autumn possibly, or spring. Or maybe there'd be hats in there, stuffed with tissue paper and deposited in boxes. I was certainly not expecting to come face to face with Joe.

A colour photograph of Joe, blown up virtually to life size, was stapled to the cupboard door, protected by a sheet of glass. Startled, I reeled back from it. The effect was too real, too poignant in its implications. It was as if Joe had stepped into Mammy's bedroom, though whoever took the picture hadn't caught him as he moved but perched cross-legged on the bonnet of a jaunty red sports car.

I had heard about that car. It was a TR3, the car that smart young men in Dublin owned in the Bill Haley era. Joe had been a smart young man and, for a student, affluent, indulged by his doting parents, delighted to produce a son after having several daughters.

Joe was driving that same car on the day he kidnapped Mammy. That had happened after Ireland won the triple crown for rugby. I snuffled, choking back the tears, recalling what I had been told, first by Mammy, then by Joe, in his pre-decampment days.

Grafton Street was one way then and Joe, accompanied by friends, was celebrating the result in the time-honoured style of rugby fans, contravening the regulations by driving up instead of down.

Mammy, clad in the pink uniform worn by the pretty girls who sold cosmetics in Brown Thomas, was standing just outside the store, smiling at the students' antics. The sight of her made Joe pull up, leap out of the TR3 and carry Mammy off with him.

He didn't take her very far, only to the nearest pub, which meant driving round the block and ending up at Davy Byrnes' where Mammy had a Babycham and recognised she was in love.

At six, I had adored that story. Now, twenty-six years afterwards, I realised that it had never ended – not for Mammy, anyway; neither Joe's desertion of her nor his death so long ago had destroyed her love for him.

Whatever made me think it had? Everything that Mammy said, all her rage and condemnation, only pointed to the fact that she was still in love with Joe.

Poor Mammy. Did she lie in bed at night with the cupboard door wide open, worshipping that handsome face and trying to re-live the past? The handsome face in the photograph was rather blurred and had acquired a yellow hue, but that wouldn't worry her, no more than it worried me. It struck me that we were alike; both of us adored Joe.

This was a disturbing thought, to bow down to the idea that Mammy, whom I'd secretly despised and thought inferior to Joe, should share anything with me. It made me turn my eyes away from the photo on the door and hastily re-focus them on the contents of the cupboard. These consisted not of clothes but of rows of coloured files, blue and yellow, red and orange. They all had labels on their spines with Mammy's small neat writing on them.

The blue files were concerned with finance and the red with legal matters. Nothing of much interest there – not to me, at any rate. The yellow files said 'personal'. The orange were marked 'Joe and Family'.

'Personal' was Mammy's province, not for my inspection. But 'Joe and Family' – that was different. Wasn't that to do with me?

I decided that it was. I removed the orange files and laid them out on Mammy's bed. 'Joe and Family' started in the early sixties and ended in the fearful year when we were told that Joe was dead.

I began leafing through the files. Soon, I had lost track of time. I found some cuttings which related to my father rather than to 'Joe and Family'. I read them very, very slowly, taking in their implications. As I did so, I discovered what was in Darina's head when she lost her temper with me.

The story of the 'awful stuff' from which she had protected me – the 'awful stuff' involving Joe – had been reported in the press.

FIFTEEN

I knew that Joe had specialised in planning law and applications. I didn't know he'd been accused of taking part in shady dealings.

The 'awful stuff' concerned a scam centred on a piece of farmland. As well as Joe, three other men had been involved in what went on.

The facts were outlined in the cuttings. Tom Foley, a solicitor, had sent a client called Fergal Dillon to discuss a scheme with Joe. Mr Dillon, a Dublin property developer, had ambitions to turn designated farmland on the outskirts of the city into a shopping centre. When application for re-zoning was rejected by the council, Joe decided to appeal on behalf of Fergal Dillon and the company he'd formed to the Planning Appeals Board.

That was where the rot set in. According to what came out later, Fergal Dillon felt they needed a contact on the appeals board, someone they could bribe to see that their appeal succeeded. The someone's name was George O'Hanlon. In debt and with big commitments, O'Hanlon was an easy target and he soon capitulated. All this Dillon said in court after they'd been prosecuted. Before that, the *Independent* had got onto George O'Hanlon, whose background was exposed as dodgy. Prompted by the press reports, the guards investigated further, learnt about the company that Fergal Dillon had set up, checked the names of those with shares and prosecuted for corruption.

In court, Fergal Dillon crumbled and admitted everything. Joe and Foley, he insisted, had been with him all the way. In lieu of legal fees, they had taken shares in the new development.

The guards had seen Tom Foley's name listed on the register, so they knew that he owned shares. Joe's name, though, had not been there. This – so Fergal Dillon claimed – was because of Joe's proviso that his shares were to be held in trust. A declaration of that trust was issued to him afterwards.

The other two said this was true but Joe denied he was involved. He said that he'd made no proviso, there'd been no declaration.

The guards had searched his home and practice. They hadn't found a declaration. Since there was no evidence to incriminate my father, the charge against him for corruption couldn't be substantiated and Joe had been acquitted while Foley, Dillon and O'Hanlon were found guilty and sent to gaol.

The fate of the other men didn't interest me that much. They were obviously guilty and they'd got what they deserved. All that bothered me was Joe. *He* had not been sent to prison, therefore he was innocent.

Or was he? Reading through those faded cuttings, it was clear that suspicions lingered in the minds of the reporters. Joe, they said, was 'charismatic'. A man with 'a magnetic presence', and the voice to go with it. His charm would 'sway the multitudes, let alone a judge and jury'. The minute you laid eyes on him, the moment he spoke to you, you wanted to believe in him – unless you were a journalist.

Naturally, I felt the way that the masses would for Joe. I needed to believe in him. But I did have reservations. As one columnist had asked, why would Fergal Dillon lie and implicate a blameless man? Why would Foley and O'Hanlon make mendacious accusations? And why had Mammy and Darina felt the need to protect me if Joe was irreproachable?

I tried my best to concoct answers. I thought, rats turn vicious when you trap them. Wasn't Fergal Dillon cornered? He might have acted out of malice, casting stones at my poor father. But that did not explain the fact that Foley and O'Hanlon had supported Dillon. There had to be another reason for their aberrant behaviour.

Perhaps the three of them decided to spread the guilt and smear some over Joe, so less would rest upon their shoulders and they'd get a lighter sentence. All of them seemed ruthless men. They might have wanted to sacrifice my father in a bid to help themselves.

And maybe Mammy and Darina found the case embarrassing, knew that Joe was free from blame but just disliked publicity. Hence the urge to protect me from what, to them, was repugnant. They were both conventional – so orthodox they drove me mad. To close the shutters on a court case would be typical of them.

As for those insinuations that the columnists

283

had made, journalists were cynical. I should know, being one myself. Charm like Joe's aroused suspicion, just as beauty tended to – models were attacked by writers and accused of being brainless in what often seemed to me an unfair conspiracy. It might have been like that with Joe – jealous writers trying to thwack him because he was charismatic. Anyway, why *wouldn't* he be innocent?

But I was still bothered. The columnists had got to me. If only I could talk to someone who had been there at the time. Someone who had understood what was in my father's mind when he answered to the charges.

Mammy might have had some insight but I couldn't speak to her. If I brought the subject up, raised the case with her today, she'd realise that I'd been snooping, opening doors that she kept shut, and she'd feel humiliated.

I couldn't broach Darina either. She'd only ask me awkward questions and I wasn't up to lying.

When I had put back the files and closed the cupboard door on Joe, I went downstairs to check the fridge, hoping that I'd find the makings of a decent toasted sandwich. The invitation Lorcan sent was lying on the kitchen table.

Lorcan! *He* was the person to whom I should talk. That should have been obvious, despite the fact I'd been upset about that business with the hookers. But that didn't matter now – or not as much as it did. The court case cast a longer shadow.

I didn't bother with the sandwich. I got on the phone at once.

'Lorcan? This is Brigit here.'

'I've been wondering about you. Haven't heard from you in ages.'

'Yes, I know,' I said. 'I'm sorry.'

'Did you get my invitation? Are you coming to my show? You do know that it's on this Thursday?'

'Yes, I did. I am. I do. But first I need to talk to you. I'm in Dublin, by the way.'

'This sounds urgent. Am I right?'

'You are, it is. So can we meet?'

'Come over here this afternoon.'

I was going to leave at once, drop the nighties off with Mammy and head on to Lorcan's house, only Conor phoned me first. He said that he was missing me. We chatted about this and that and then I mentioned Lorcan's show and said I would be going to it.

'Why would you do that?' said Conor.

'Lorcan is a friend of mine.'

'Strange taste you've got in friends.'

Jealousy was all I needed. 'Conor,' I said, 'Lorcan used to be your teacher. You know what he's all about. He's a harmless, gentle person.'

'True. There's no substance in his work. He's nothing but a *pompier!*'

This seemed most unfair to me. Lorcan did not paint in a pseudo-naïve manner. I started to stand up for Lorcan, only Conor butted in.

'Lorcan Burke is aeons away from what *I* call naïve painting. Naïve artists suffered, Brigit! What pain has Burke experienced? He knows nothing of real life!'

'I don't want to argue with you. But I'm going

to the opening. It's on Thursday, Lorcan tells me. I'll be leaving here on Friday.'

'Enjoy Thursday,' Conor said. 'If you *can* enjoy the crap that Burke promotes as naïve art!'

What next? I remembered thinking. But I wasn't fussed by Conor, not then. I was thinking about Joe. What would Lorcan say about him when we spoke this afternoon?

I delivered Mammy's nighties. Coming down the corridor, I ran into Ivor Sheehan again, on his way to visit her.

'We can't keep you out of here! Your mother must be pleased with you, the way you dance attendance on her.'

I didn't disillusion him. I told him I'd be back tomorrow and he beamed at me.

This time round, I shared the lift with a mother and two children, one of whom was Mikey's age. It prompted me to look for something I could buy him in the gift shop.

I went inside and found some books – *The River Bank and Other Stories, One Hundred Things for Kids to Make* – and then I saw a clock as well, with leaping frogs all over it and croaks instead of chiming sounds.

I said I would take the lot. The clock had been reduced in price.

'We haven't got the box for it.'

'Don't worry. I'll use bubblewrap.'

I bought a card for Mikey too – more frogs; they were in vogue that year – and took myself to Lorcan's house.

The hookers hadn't surfaced yet. Mrs Mac was not on duty and Lorcan said that I was early.

'I haven't finished yet upstairs. Will you make yourself at home for another little while?'

I told him that was easily done, that I'd find a book to read. Lorcan grinned and scuttled off. I looked round for reading matter.

The room was near to being tidy. The books, which had been on the floor the last time I'd been in the house, had found a home inside a bookcase.

They were art books, most of them – biographies of famous painters. There were books on plays and films. Several books of poetry published in the Irish language – Lorcan was a fluent speaker. Nothing in the way of fiction.

The third shelf down was stacked with hardbacks of a more expensive nature which I guessed would have been presents, possibly from grateful students. *A Century of Modern Art, Naïve Painting* by Jakovsky, *Bonnard,* and *The Nabis Painters.* Six or seven other books on a very different theme were intended as a series. I ran my eyes across the titles. *Irish Georgian Houses, Irish Georgian Silver* and *Irish Georgian Attitudes.* The author, Diarmuid Esmond Darcy, didn't ring a bell with me. Lorcan's interest in the subject wasn't one he'd ever mentioned. The bookcase didn't echo it; it was a rather nasty object and looked as if it had been purchased from a tacky junk shop, or purloined from the nearest skip.

Armed with *Irish Georgian Houses* I sat down on the sofa bed which had lumps and bumps in it and made me wonder whether Lorcan ever got a full night's sleep.

For a while, I lost myself leafing through the book I'd found, looking at the pretty pictures of elegant interiors. I read a little of the text. Mr Darcy knew his subject but his style was rather stuffy. I preferred the illustrations. The ones of Fota House were lovely. I went back to check the contents so I'd find the page again. Then I saw the dedication. It was in the Irish language. 'For My Dear Friend, Lorcan Burke. *Mar. maraionn cach an rud is anfa leis.*'

I was just translating this when Lorcan returned to the room.

'Was I ages? Sorry, Brigit.'

I quickly set the book aside. But I was curious about it, and about the dedication. 'This book on Georgian houses, Lorcan. The author was a friend of yours?'

Lorcan's eyes fell on the book and he gave a little start. Then he pulled himself together. 'Diarmuid Darcy? Yes, he was.'

'I don't think I've heard of him.'

'No? But then he died some years ago.'

Aha, I thought, a mystery here. Lorcan is concealing something. You can see it on his face. And there's sadness in his eyes.

The sadness made me lay off Diarmuid. In any case, I told myself, we have Joe to talk about.

Lorcan helped me out on that. 'You spoke of something urgent, Brigit,' he said. 'I can tell you're worried,' which paved the way to speak of Joe and tell him what I had found out.

The story tumbled out of me. Lorcan didn't interrupt me, only nodded now and then. Eventually, I finished talking and looked expect-

288

antly at Lorcan.

'What's the problem?' Lorcan said.

I shook my head in disbelief that he didn't understand me. 'Was he innocent or guilty?'

'My poor Brigit,' Lorcan said. 'This is what's upsetting you?'

'Of course. I mean, I know he was acquitted, Lorcan. But people thought that he was guilty.'

'"People" being journalists?'

'They were sure he was involved. They said... They made insinuations...' I heard the wobble in my voice and retreated into silence.

Lorcan heard the wobble too. 'My poor Brigit,' he said softly. He sat beside me on the sofa. 'Don't mind the journalists. They were wrong, the lot of them. 'Twas a wonder that your father didn't have them up for libel.'

A ray of hope. I reached for it. 'You really mean that they were wrong? That Joe was not involved in this?'

'I really mean that they were wrong. Joe's sole involvement in the case was representing Fergal Dillon. Appealing to the planning board to have the area re-zoned so it would be a shopping centre. He didn't know that Fergal Dillon had been bribing George O'Hanlon. He was horrified about it when it started coming out. I remember saying to him, "You're sure you're not behind this, Joe?" He denied it absolutely. He looked me in the eyes and said, "Lorcan, would I lie to you?"'

A huge relief washed over me. I said, stupidly, 'He told you that he didn't do it?'

Lorcan laughed. 'When's it going to register?

289

He didn't do it, Brigit, truly. I give you my word on it. Your father wouldn't lie to me. There was perfect trust between us. Joe knew that I'd never fail him and I felt the same for him.'

The ray of hope became a sunbeam. 'Lorcan, that's such good news!'

Lorcan got up from the sofa. 'No more dark thoughts about Joe! Your father wasn't into darkness.'

'No, he definitely wasn't. Thank you, Lorcan. You've been lovely.'

But then I remembered what Mrs Mac had told me went on in Benburb Street. *'You'd not believe the half of it... The worst of them was Mr Flood...'*

More dark thoughts, a blizzard of them.

'Now what's the matter?' Lorcan said.

I hesitated. Muttered something.

'Brigit, come on. I can see you're worried. Have you something else to tell me about the court case?'

'Not about the case,' I whispered.

'But something's on your mind?' said Lorcan.

I rose and paced around the room. Wandered over to the window. Outside, the hookers I had seen before were walking slowly down the street. Both of them were clad in raincoats. I wondered what, if anything, they were wearing underneath them.

'What's on your mind?' said Lorcan.

I told him then. I told him about Mrs Mac and what she'd said about the house. About the money Joe put up. About the room reserved by Lorcan so Joe could have the use of it to screw the scrubbers off the street.

Lorcan swallowed. 'That woman's mind is scurrilous.'

'Mrs Mac is scurrilous?'

'Mrs Mac is sick,' said Lorcan. 'God Almighty, she is crazed. This is all a pack of lies. Your father never went with hookers. Leaving out the moral issue, he was too fastidious, Brigit. And do you really think that I would turn this place into a brothel?'

Since that *was* what I'd been thinking, I decided to keep quiet and let Lorcan carry on.

'Twenty years and more than that I've had her working in this house. You'd think by now she'd understand a bit about an artist's life.'

I stayed silent.

'Beyond belief, that's what she is! I swear that I'd get rid of her if she didn't kill herself trying to keep this place in order. I'll have to have it out with her. Tell her if she ever says one more word about my friends...' he ranted on. I thought he had forgotten me. So when he said, 'Now listen, Brigit,' I was startled into life. 'I want you to understand that I don't condemn the hookers. Some of them have tragic lives. I often use them in a life class if I'm giving painting lessons.'

At that point I did speak out. 'Mrs Mac said you did that. She told me about one of them – the one that came up here from Cork. Her husband lost his job, she said.'

'Oh, she told you that?' said Lorcan. 'So she sometimes speaks the truth. But anyway, forget that woman – for the moment, anyway. Let me tell you about Joe. He helped me buy this house

291

all right. But I paid him back for it, even though it took a while. I didn't "keep a room" for him, not as Mrs Mac inferred. But there are two rooms upstairs. I used one for my studio and kept the second one for students.'

'You were giving private lessons?'

'So I could pay off the house. Joe said that he'd like to paint. I was giving him instructions. He would come here after work and we'd get a life class going. But Wednesday nights were out for me. I had my mother in a home and I used to go and see her. I told Joe to use the room if he had Wednesday evening free and arranged a model for him. That was all there was to it. Nothing nasty. Nothing kinky. No one turning tricks for Joe. Am I getting through to you?'

I nodded, conscious of a burden lifted, filled with sudden jubilation. I thought, Joe is still my hero. He wasn't guilty of corruption. And he never went with hookers – he was having painting lessons. *Painting lessons!*

'Lorcan, tell me. Had he talent?'

'Mm. He enjoyed himself,' said Lorcan. 'It relaxed him, after work. Joe worked very hard, you know. He was a brilliant barrister.'

'I don't suppose you kept his drawings.'

'No. He took them all away.'

'It doesn't matter.' It did. I mourned the drawings for a minute. If only Lorcan had them. Even if they weren't that great, I'd have put a value on them. But Lorcan had been marvellous.

'Lorcan, what would I have done without you! This has been a brilliant evening. Can't we celebrate together? Can I take you out to dinner?'

'No, you can't,' said Lorcan firmly. 'You don't have to feel so grateful.'

'But I am. You've done so much.'

'And you want to pay me back? Well, there *is* one thing that you can do.'

'Yes? What is it? Anything.'

'You be at my opening, Brigit. And, remember, don't be late!'

That was how it was on Monday. I spent the next three days in Dublin, much of them in Blackrock Clinic. I had several calls from Conor, asking me on each occasion when I would be coming back.

'What about the book?' he said. 'We should be starting work on it.'

'We should complete the video.'

'You're right. We should, Parker's getting bloody restless. We'll go up to Inishbofin after you've finished there.'

I thought that he would mention Lorcan. Have another crack at him. Say the show would be pathetic. But, to my relief, he didn't.

I set off early for the opening. Sure there'd be a problem parking, I left the car and took the DART which dropped me off at Pearse Street station.

The rain had cleared and a temperate sun was shining, just enough to warm the body. Ambling up along Kildare Street, I was thinking that my birthplace was a city to be proud of with so many splendid buildings.

I turned into the Green and paused. The opening was at six o'clock. I had half an hour to kill.

Mind you, I had Joe with me and he kept me company, the way he did when I was young and we'd visited the Green – and fed the ducks, as I recalled. Now we could do that again. I had a mental chat with Joe who said, 'But Brigit, we need bread.'

I walked partly round the Green until I came to Leeson Street. A corner shop supplied the bread.

'Come on,' said Joe. 'Let's feed those ducks!'

Inside the Green, other fathers and their offspring were about to do the same. Heading for the Traitors' Arch, I found again my favourite spot, underneath the little bridge, where ducks in dozens congregated.

What is it about dabbling ducks that gets to people like myself who should be into dogs and cats? The males are rather stylish but the females are a dowdy lot. They're not affectionate or friendly. They take from you and don't give back.

But that, I guess, is the attraction – the fact that ducks don't care two hoots. And when they've had enough of you, they spread their wings and fly away.

The ducks in Stephen's Green that day were as greedy as their forebears and impervious to admiration. They gobbled up my load of bread – then they swam away from me.

Joe was going from me too, slipping off into the bushes. I tried to cling on to him and keep his image there with me. But Joe would not co-operate. Having done his duty by me, he had better things to do.

End of my nostalgic outing...

But still I stood there, cogitating. Thinking of

myself as well, vainly trying, like the person in the poem by Robert Louis Stevenson, to find in the garden there the child of air I used to be. So it was something of a shock to find another child beside me. The newcomer bore no resemblance whatsoever to the child that I had been and, anyway, he was a boy.

He was maybe three years old, with fat brown curls and eyes to match. He looked as if he had escaped from one of Mary Cassatt's paintings.

'Hello,' I said.

The child frowned.

'Did you want to feed the ducks?'

Getting no response to that, I looked around, anticipating that his parents would be hovering in the background.

They weren't. There was nobody at all. As the ducks had swum away, the people by the pool had left. The child and I were alone.

'Where's your daddy and your mammy?'

He didn't answer for a minute. He stared intently at the pool. Then he said, *'Goe su patke?'*

I didn't recognise the language.

'Shall we go and look for them?' I said, hoping that he'd understand.

He pointed crossly at the pool. *'Goe su patke?'* he repeated, more aggressively this time.

Things were getting out of hand. I checked my watch and groaned aloud. It was nearly half past six. I'd lost track of time completely. I was late for Lorcan's opening. But I couldn't leave the child. And since he didn't understand me I couldn't suggest that we should wander round the Green together in the hope we'd find his parents.

I put out my arms to him. 'Come, we'll look for Mammy.'

He stamped his foot and yelled at me, *'Goe su patke? Goe su patke?'*

What on earth was I to do? The little boy was crying tears of fury and frustration now.

'Patke! Patke!'

What the hell did *'patke'* mean? Thwarted by a single word, the child and I were waterlogged.

Then, after what seemed hours, someone shouted, *'Milane!'*

The child reacted to the call by running down the path from me. I pursued him, crying, 'Wait!'

'Milane! Milane!'

Two figures, a man and a woman, suddenly appeared, running up the path towards us. The woman was hysterical. She threw her arms round the child and hugged him tightly to her chest.

'Za ime boga goe si bio?' said the man. *'Trazimo te vec pola sata. Mama je skoro dobita infarkt zbog tebe!'*

They were Yugoslavs, they said. Their son had run away from them. They'd been searching everywhere. 'He was looking for the ducks,' said the man in perfect English.

'Goe su patke?' said Milane.

I showed them where the ducks had gone. They thanked me several times and left, Milane smiling like a cherub, perched upon his father's shoulders.

By then, it was after seven. I dashed across the Green again and spurted into Harcourt Street.

The Origin Gallery was a few doors up. The sound of noisy chatter coming from the upstairs windows, audible from the street, told how packed it was. Hoping Lorcan wouldn't notice that I'd not arrived on time, I belted up the Georgian staircase. The gallery was on the right and occupied the whole first floor.

At the door, a smiling woman, thinking I was from the press, handed me a cardboard folder.

'Am I late? I guess I am.'

'Only for the opening speech. But there's a copy in the folder. The drinks are just inside the door.'

'Thanks.'

I slid inside and grabbed a drink. The gallery was very smart, the people in there even smarter. The opening was so well-attended, I could hardly see the paintings, let alone a sign of Lorcan.

At the far end of the room was a lovely stained-glass window. It might be less crowded there. I edged along the wall towards it, with my wine glass in one hand and the folder in the other. People had their backs to me.

I heard a woman ask another, 'Margie, did you buy a painting?'

'Yes, the one with all those shells.'

'I thought that was lovely too but I preferred the horse myself.'

I had almost reached the window when I ran into an object that was standing right beneath it. From the angle I was at, it looked like a leather screen although it was rather chunky. Then I squeezed in front of it and realised what it really was.

It was not a screen. It was a leather steamer trunk which had been opened like a book so you

297

could see the inside of it. It formed a kind of walk-in cupboard, with six drawers down the right-hand side, each with a curved brass handle. On the left-hand side was a hanging space with a shoe box underneath it.

It was a standard cabin trunk, dating from the 1930s. But someone – Lorcan, I presumed – had completely transformed it. The drawers were pulled out in gradation so they formed a set of steps, covered with a length of silk. The shoe box, too, had been left open. Lined with crimson velvet, it became a jewellery box. The hanging space was now a stage, with a tasselled sash round it.

Inside the trunk – on the steps, in the box and between the tasselled curtains – precious objects had been placed. An urn with red flamingoes on it. A gold and seed pearl swallow brooch. An enamelled ivory horse prancing on an onyx base. Several little coloured bottles. A Chinese gold and lacquer fan. A Continental needle case.

And shells. Lots and lots of different shells. Big conch shells from India. Pansy shells from Mozambique, flat with little faces on them...

Despite the clamour all around me, I was sure I was dreaming. That I'd slipped back into childhood. Drifted off to sleep as Joe was telling me another story.

Then I read the press release. 'The paintings you will see tonight were inspired by the artist's father. The steamer trunk belonged to him and all the objects on display were owned by Mr Owen Burke and purchased when he was abroad.'

298

The area around the trunk was not as crowded as the rest of the room. If I shifted slightly right, I could see some of Lorcan's paintings.

In one, a flock of red flamingoes flew across a tranquil bay to mingle with the local seagulls. A second painting showed a pony with a charming pale-blue mane trotting through a clouded sky. Familiar birds. Familiar pony…

I thought, what a bastard Lorcan is! He has stolen Joe's ideas. And now he's trying to con the public that he got them from *his* father, Mr Owen sodding Burke. What some people will resort to just to get publicity! So much for his protest-ations that he was my father's friend. So much for the perfect trust Lorcan said there was between them. *'Joe knew that I'd never fail him…'* But wasn't stealing from him failing? In my eyes it was.

How dare Lorcan steal from Joe? And to think he had the nerve to ask *me* to see this show!

I turned and glowered at the trunk, wondering where Lorcan had got it. Perhaps he'd stolen it from Joe too.

I examined it more closely. And then I saw the name imprinted on the trunk. 'Owen Robert Burke,' I read.

The penny dropped. I understood. Lorcan hadn't been the thief. It was Joe who had stolen from Lorcan.

SIXTEEN

I never did meet up with Lorcan. I didn't wait another minute. Scrunching up that press release, I squeezed my way back through the crowd and, quick as wind, was down the stairs and into Harcourt Street again.

Tears were streaming down my cheeks. Running back towards the Green, I didn't see the lights were red. A lorry nearly knocked me down. The driver stuck two fingers up.

Somewhat sobered, I slowed down as I stumped on towards Grafton Street. The statue of Lord Ardilaun, the chairman of the Guinness brewery, who landscaped Stephen's Green for us and then returned the park to Dublin, looked smugly at me from his chair as I went past the wrought-iron railings.

At the north side of the Green, near the decorative trough and the horses' drinking fountain, several taxis were lined up. But I didn't hail a cab. A taxi ride would mean a chat and I didn't want to talk, not to anyone I knew, let alone a perfect stranger. In any case, I wasn't sure where I was going. But it wasn't Dalkey. Not to that house where Joe had lived – and still resided, on a door.

I was hankering after food, the way I always did in crises. Still, I walked down Grafton Street, straight past Bewley's, which was open, all the way to Trinity and then on to Temple Bar before the urge became too strong.

I had a craving for a pasta, for the comfort of spaghetti, garlic, olives, chilli peppers. The place I went to was Milano, Temple Bar's Italian restaurant. Milano is extremely modern. Marble tables. Lots of glass. Cheerful blue and yellow tiles. I found a table on the pavement and prepared to stuff myself to see if that would cheer me up. But I wasn't only sad, I was furious as well. Angry not so much with Joe but with myself, for being so stupid. So gullible and so naïve.

Hadn't all the signs been there, that my father was a con man? All that artificial charm. The journalists had seen through that. For now I had no doubt at all that Joe was in the scam as well. Lorcan might believe in him – did so touchingly, I thought – but I had no illusions left. Not about my father. A man who would deceive a child, who had robbed his friend's imagination, was nothing but an empty shell.

The waiter handed me a menu. 'Would you like a drink to start with?'

'A carafe of the white,' I said.

Why had I been overtrustful, wanting to believe in Joe? Darina hadn't been so foolish. She had seen right through our father, and she had protected me. And Mammy had protected me. Perhaps she was the best of us. She had not been taken in. She had not been blind like me. But she'd gone on loving Joe, knowing just what he was like. That was real love, I thought. Not the kind that I went in for, which was based on false premises.

What an eejit I had been, trying to hold on to childhood at the age of thirty-two. Pathetic. Stupid. Mortifying...

'Brigit?'

'Huh?' I looked up. David Parker was peering down at me. Struggling with the emotions generated by the opening, trying to come to terms with Joe – Joe the con man as my father instead of Joe the magic maker – I wasn't one bit pleased to see him.

'Are you on your own?' he said. 'Can I join you if you are?'

'What,' I said, 'are *you* doing here?'

'Running into you,' said David.

'I thought you were in Kilnaboy.'

'I got pissed off hanging around so I thought I'd come up here. See if I could track you down.'

'You seem to have managed that all right!'

'Yes,' said David happily. 'Yes, I do. Although I must admit it wasn't just coincidence.' He had been at Lorcan's show. 'I saw you there. I followed you.'

'*You followed me?*' I was mortified. He must have seen me run away. Realised how upset I was. It was all I needed.

'So, can I sit down?' said David.

'I suppose you might as well. What made you go to Lorcan's show?'

'Because I knew that you'd be at it.'

'Here's your wine,' the waiter said. 'Shall I bring another glass?'

David said, 'Yes, please. And a carafe of the red.'

'I don't understand,' I said. 'How could you

302

have known that I'd be going to Lorcan's opening?'

'You told Byrne that you'd be going. I was with him at the time. I went to have a word with him, to ask how long I'd have to wait till we went back to Inishbofin. He shrugged and said he didn't know. And then he made that call to you as if I wasn't in the room.'

'And you stayed there and listened to him?'

'Why not? I think the waiter's coming back. Shall we get our orders in?'

After we had placed our orders – we both chose *spaghetti pollo* and the garlic bread with cheese – David returned to the show and said how much he had enjoyed it.

'I'd say it's going to be a sell-out. The steamer trunk was fun, I thought. And I really liked the paintings. Pure, clean work without being precious. By the way, why is Byrne opposed to it? I hear he has it in for Burke.'

'How did you hear that?' I said.

'He criticised him to the students. Patrick told me afterwards. Byrne said Burke was a poseur and that his work was spurious. Is Burke gay, by any chance?'

'What makes you ask a thing like that?'

'Byrne's uneasy around gays, or so some of the students told me.'

'What *is* it with you about Conor? You're so critical of him. Just because you don't get on...' And then I remembered Conor asking me if David was gay when I first told him David could make the video. I thought it was odd at the time.

'True. I didn't like him to begin with,' David

303

said, sounding maddeningly sane. 'I found his attitude despotic. But now I distrust him too. That funny business with the cottage...'

I glared at him. 'We went through all that already.'

'I know we did. I'm not convinced. The fellow that we spoke to said—'

'That guy was an islander. He's piqued that Conor bought the cottage.'

'Maybe.'

'David, if you've suspicions about Conor, why don't you check up on him? Find out *how* he got the house instead of listening to rumours. Then come back and moan to me.'

'You're right,' David said amiably as our pasta dish arrived. 'This smells terrific, doesn't it? But I will check up, just to satisfy myself. While Byrne's away, I'll check him out.'

While Byrne's away? 'Where is Conor going?'

'LA,' said David. 'In connection with the will. You didn't know that he was going?'

'No, I didn't,' I said crossly. He'd not mentioned that to me. Conor wasn't playing straight – just like Joe.

'What's all this about a will?' I asked.

David told me that Hannah's father had left her millions, and her death meant that Conor had come into her inheritance. But someone else was in the picture. One of Seamus's ex-wives, Miranda James, the movie star. She was contesting the will.

'How do you know about this?' I asked David.

'I got the story out of Em.'

I stabbed my fork in my spaghetti. 'Em? How

did *she* find out about it? Did she read it in the papers?'

'Byrne confides in her, it seems.'

'He does?' I was really raging now though I tried to appear cool.

'They're very close, the two of them.'

'Close? You're telling me that they're *lovers?*' This was inconceivable.

'No,' said David. 'Not at all. But they kind of gel together. Actually, they're quite alike. Hasn't that occurred to you?'

'No, it hasn't,' I said coldly. 'Em is ugly. Unattractive.'

'But reliable, I think.'

Reliable!

'When is Conor going away? Did Em tell you that as well?'

'After the weekend, I think. He won't be away for long. Ten days at the most, she said. He has to find a lawyer who'll represent him over there.'

'I see.' I seethed and raged and fumed and boiled. David didn't seem to notice. He just gobbled his spaghetti.

Beneath the fire that burned inside me, something else was going on. I know now that I was changing. Until that night, before I was forced to face what my father really was, my emotions had been rooted firmly in cloud-cuckoo-land. I had made a lover's image modelled on my father's profile. When men had failed to measure up, I had dropped them instantly. But that image had been false; Joe had been mendacious. In reality, he had been only a shadow of the portrait I'd drawn. Now, I'd had enough of shadows. From this night on, I'd no longer be content with fantasy and make-believe.

Of course, I didn't work that out. Not then. Sitting in the pavement café, I only knew that I was angry because I had been deceived. And that anger engulfed Conor now. I was furious with him because he had not been open with me. Why had he not said that he was going to LA? I couldn't think of any reason why he would conceal this fact from me and yet tell Em so openly that she passed it on to David without any inhibition. It did not make sense.

David cut into my thoughts. 'I hear you're doing a book on Byrne.'

'Yes. Did Em tell you that as well?'

'Actually, she did,' said David.

'Em seems to know a thing or two.'

'But it's not a secret, is it? Has it been commissioned?'

'No, it hasn't. But it will be. As you've finished, shall we go?'

'Must we? I don't feel like going to bed. I thought we might have a drink. Let's go over to the Norseman.'

I hesitated. I didn't want to go to bed either, not if it meant going to Dalkey. But I was mad with David as well, for being the bearer of unwelcome news.

'Brigit,' said David decisively, 'why don't we just cut the crap? I know that you're involved with Byrne – it's pretty obvious. I don't like the man and I won't pretend I do just to press the flesh with you. But I do like you and I can see that you're upset. It's not my business. I won't ask. If you want to leave, then do. Otherwise, I'm here for you.'

His candour acted on my anger and part of it evaporated.

'Thanks,' I said. 'That's good of you.'

'It's not particularly good. Now, do you want that drink or not?'

We went over to the Norseman. Upstairs, in the older section, Tre was playing Irish music. Stained-glass windows in the pub depict scenes from Joyce's novels. The question, 'What is the word known to all men?' is cut into one of them. The answer, 'Love', has not been added.

David returned from the bar with a glass of wine for me.

'Aren't you having one?' I said.

'I can't. Not if I'm going to drive you home. Wherever home may be.'

'My mother's place. It's out in Dalkey. But I can easily catch the DART.'

'That's entirely up to you. The offer stands.'

'Are you booked into a hotel?'

David shook his head. 'I have the use of someone's flat. Patrick's cousin, Emer Brennan. She's just arrived in Kilnaboy to spend a week down there with Patrick and attend a class or two. She lent me her car as well.'

'She sounds like another Celia.'

'No, Emer's not a bit like Celia. By the way, Celia's staying on in London. You know I have a place in Fulham? I told her she could hang out there. It's all I can do for her – at the moment, anyway. She did a lot for me, you know. I haven't quite paid off that debt.' David's talk of repaying debts reminded me of someone else. But I was too tired to remember who it was, although the question bothered me. *She's not like Celia,* David had said, speaking about Patrick's cousin. But my person *was* like Celia – or had some connection with her. Who was it? I tried to dredge the memory up but it wouldn't budge an inch.

Maddening, I thought, and yawned. 'Sorry, but it's getting late.'

'I'm going to take you home,' said David.

'I told you, I can take the DART.'

'Forget the DART. We'll go by car. I've left it parked in Pembroke Road. That's where Emer has her flat. We'll have to take a cab to get it.'

The driver of the cab we caught said the country was being ruined by illegal immigrants. 'It's not the place it used to be. We'll have the Russians in here next.'

I dozed off when the Russians came and woke again in Pembroke Road.

'I've left the keys inside,' said David. 'Come in while I look for them.'

The house where Emer Brennan lived was Victorian red-brick. The flat was on the second floor. It was minimally furnished. A stripped pine cupboard in a corner. An ornate mirror on one wall. No chairs or tables, only cushions. Curtains made of unbleached cotton. A basket with a pot plant in it.

Through an open doorway I could see two mattresses wrapped in Marimekko prints. In such an uncluttered space you would think a set of keys would be difficult to lose, but David lost them all the same.

I heard him talking to himself. 'I left them here. I'm sure I did...' as he tossed aside the cushions.

I joined him in the search for them. We tried the kitchen and the bedroom but we didn't find the keys.

'Did I leave them in the car?' David muttered to himself.

'I'll wait here while you have a look.'

I collapsed on a mattress. The urge to stretch right out on it proved too tempting to resist. As I did so, I wondered again who had reminded me of Celia.

And then I realised it was Sheila. Sheila Ferguson. Of course.

But what did they have in common, Sheila Ferguson and Celia? I yawned again – and then it came. They both took drugs. All kinds of drugs, in Celia's case. In Sheila's it was tranquillisers.

A wretched business, Conor said, when he'd mentioned Sheila's problem and her need to stay on pills. *'She has to take them all the time.'*

It struck me now how strange that was. Both times I had come across her, Sheila had been very perky. Her daughter thought her too outspoken. She had not seemed tranquillised. Quite the opposite, in fact. Conor must have got it wrong. Or Sheila must have told him lies about her need for medication. But why should Sheila tell such lies? Because she wanted his attention? But she'd seemed so balanced.

It was all very complicated. Too difficult to work out now. I smothered an enormous yawn. Decided it was getting cold. Snuggled underneath the covers...

I woke in a tangle of yellow and red, unsure where I was at first. The sun was streaming through the window. I could hear the sound of traffic.

'David?'

There was no reply. Clogged by yesterday's make-up, my skin felt dry and miserable. Disentangled from the covers, I saw that I'd removed my shoes – or maybe David had. Where was he? Showering, shaving in the bathroom? But when I went there to check, only my own eyes outlined by mascara blotches stared dourly at me from the mirror. What a mess I was! Surely Emer Brennan had cleanser.

But there was only soap and water and a box of Kleenex tissues. My face reacted angrily to this unaccustomed treatment. The skin beneath my eyes went red. I looked as if I had been weeping.

Crying made me think of Joe and what I'd seen at Lorcan's show. That nearly set me off again. I was on the verge of tears when I heard David calling for me.

'Where are you? Do you want some breakfast?' He'd returned with takeaway egg and bacon sandwiches. The sight of such indulgent food helped to raise my sinking spirits.

'Marvellous! Sorry I fell asleep.'

'What's the harm in that?' said David.

Peace had been declared between us. Getting stuck into the sandwich, I was sure we could maintain it, provided David laid off Conor.

After we had finished breakfast, David took me back to Dalkey. Within minutes, Conor phoned.

'Where were you last night?' he said. 'I kept

310

phoning. You weren't in. I tried up to midnight, Brigit, and I phoned first thing this morning.'

David hadn't left the house. He was sitting in the kitchen and I knew that he could hear me.

'I went to Lorcan's exhibition.'

'And that kept you out all night?'

I detected jealousy. Decided that I didn't like it. I said coolly, 'Yes it did.'

'You stayed all night at Burke's place, did you?'

'Not at Lorcan's. With a friend.'

'A friend? What friend?' demanded Conor.

I was still wound up inside, brooding darkly about Joe and the way he'd lied to me. Conor sounded quite aggressive. Suddenly, I lost my temper.

'You've no right to ask such questions. You don't own me. No one does. You don't tell me what you're doing. Why should I report to you?'

'Brigit, listen,' Conor began.

But I wouldn't let him speak. 'You're going to LA,' I shouted, 'but you didn't mention it. You didn't level with me, Conor. I thought we'd have next week together. Now I hear you're going away.'

'How did you hear that?' he said.

'From–' I stopped. From my position in the hall, I could see David in the kitchen. Sanity got hold of me. It said, don't bring David into this. If you do, there will be trouble. There's the video to finish. Those two men should not be fighting.

'Who told you I was going away?'

With one eye fixed on David's back, I didn't risk a direct answer. I said instead, 'Em told people you'd be going.'

311

'I see.' I heard a sigh come down the line.

Both of us lapsed into silence. Then we spoke in unison.

'I *always* level with you, Brigit—'

'I can't *stand* being lied to, Conor—'

We stopped, drew breath and thought again. Then Conor took control of things.

'Lies are not on the agenda,' he said. 'Just listen to me, will you, Brigit? Em's been talking out of turn. I'll have to have a word with her. I *may* have to go away. It depends what happens next. I said as much to Em. She asked me for a few days off. I told her she could have them if — note the *if* now, Brigit, please — I'd be going away next week. I never thought of telling you because I hadn't made any plans. That's really all there is to it. No evasion. No omissions. No intention to tell lies.'

This sounded so plausible that I felt silly. I mumbled in response to it and Conor went on to tell me about Miranda James and her efforts to contest the will. It was just as David had said, but still I felt uncomfortable, churned up inside by doubts and qualms. Joe's fault surely, not Conor's. Why should I be blaming him when Joe was at the back of it?

The rage was ebbing out of me as quickly as it had washed in. I made myself apologise. 'I didn't understand. I'm sorry.'

Conor became gentle with me. 'You're obviously all worked up. Has something else upset you, Brigit? Your mother isn't worse, I hope?'

'No,' I said. 'She's fine. Much better.'

'And you? It's not like you to make a fuss.

312

There's something wrong. I know there is.'

'It's nothing. Honestly,' I said, and added, contradictorily, 'I'll tell you when I see you, Conor.'

Conor gave up. He asked me when I would be back and said he couldn't wait to see me.

I told myself I was an eejit to be carrying on like this because I had been hurt by Joe. Storm in a teacup, I said to myself as I went into the kitchen to join David at the table. For goodness sake, cool down, you fool.

Knowing David would have heard me yelling on the phone at Conor, I hoped he wouldn't ask me questions that would make me more embarrassed.

Much to my relief, he didn't. Shortly afterwards, he left, saying he had things to do. I changed, intending to see Mammy later in the afternoon.

David said he'd stay in Dublin until after the weekend and I went back to Kilnaboy.

I found a present in my room. At first I thought it was a woman standing there beside my bed. Then I saw a man behind her, with his arms round her waist.

I gasped with shock, and then with joy. I was looking at a sculpture of a pair of entwined lovers.

Setting down my travel bag, I inspected it more closely. It was life-size, made not from stone which had been chiselled but from a .papier-mâché base which was overlaid with cloth and sealed with an acrylic glaze.

313

It was uncomplicated, semi-abstract, the sex of the figures defined by height rather than by graphic detail. Yet the lovers' forms combined purity with passion and made a striking primal statement. To me, the sculpture represented all my feelings about love. I couldn't take my eyes from it.

I saw an envelope lying near it, on the table. Inside it was a painted card which reproduced the lovers' bodies. Conor had written, 'Brigit, I made this for you.' I'd had gifts from men before. Books and perfume. Pens and watches. Trinkets inside pretty boxes or wrapped up in Christmas paper. But nothing that was specially made by the one who'd given it. Nothing that could measure up to the value of this present.

My reservations about Conor faded in the light of his creation. Surely no one who could make such a truthful work of art would be capable of lies. I wanted to give something back to Conor, to reciprocate such a gift. There wasn't much that I could offer. I didn't have his genius. I couldn't make a work of art along the lines of Conor's sculpture. But I could write that book about him. And launch him as a TV star.

All this I told him later on, when I had thanked him for my present. Afterwards, he told me that he'd be going to LA. 'Only for ten days or so. The minute I get home again we'll go back to Inishbofin and finish off the video.' He'd arranged a deputy to take the classes in his absence.

'Are you letting Em go off?'

'Not till I come back,' said Conor. 'She can take me to the airport. I want her to go on to

314

Limerick. We've run out of drawing boards and some other bits and pieces.'

'OK,' I said resignedly.

It was Tuesday when he left. David was still up in Dublin but sometime in the afternoon he phoned me to apologise.

'I was wrong. I'm sorry, Brigit.'

'Sorry about what?' I said.

'About the Inishbofin cottage. Byrne inherited the place. I've got the documents of transfer.'

'How did you lay hands on them?'

'Easy. I went along to the Land Registry in Chancery Street. It's all in the files. Nothing crooky. All legit. You were right and I was wrong.'

I didn't say 'I told you so' but I was secretly delighted, not only to have scored a point but because this information helped to quell those qualms and doubts. And it made my lovely present just that little bit more precious. But the sculpture jogged my conscience, saying there was another gift I hadn't posted off to Mikey. He was going to love that clock!

That evening, I wrote a message on the card that I had bought for him in Dublin and got out the clock and books. The clock was really very fragile. I'd have to get some bubblewrap before I made the parcel up. There was plenty in the loft.

Inside the studio, I half expected to meet Em, putting drawing boards away. But there was no sign of her – and no bubblewrap. How come it was all used up? We'd had two large rolls of it up there. Maybe Conor had taken them over to his studio to wrap his paintings. I decided to check.

I meandered towards the house. Clodagh

wasn't in that evening but she'd left the door unlocked. Thinking Em might be around, I called out but got no answer.

What a creepy house it was. I had never really liked it, and now that Conor wasn't there I disliked it even more. I wondered if, without Hannah to object, he would change the awful décor when he came back from LA. Throw out her father's furniture and have the entire place refurbished.

How dark Victoriana was. How vulgar, arrogant and muddled. It was strange to think that Conor had made such a lovely sculpture in this ugly, gloomy setting. But his studio was different.

I ran upstairs and reached his door which, as usual, was shut. But he hadn't locked me out. He never bothered much with keys. He knew Clodagh wouldn't venture in. But I had no such inhibitions.

Inside, the studio was as neat as ever. Tubes of paint lined up like soldiers. All those newly sharpened pencils. Brushes looking nearly new. It didn't take me long to see there were no rolls of bubblewrap anywhere inside that room.

Maddening. Well, I'd have to buy some more, or maybe Em would bring some back from her shopping expedition to Limerick.

I didn't want to leave the studio just yet. It made me feel I was with Conor. I plomped down in his cane chair and looked again at Hannah's shelves. All the objects she'd arranged. All those boxes she'd collected. I liked her boxes. I liked them more than Conor's pots. The mukwa box attracted me. On the other hand, the one with strips of coloured wood had that lovely picture on it. And the sandalwood and brass – that was absolutely gorgeous. So typically Indian.

I pottered over to the shelves to re-examine all the boxes. The tiny silver-mounted one was the only one open to reveal its rather aged green silk lining. I wondered what was inside those other boxes.

It was too much, I had to look.

I peeked inside the mukwa box and found some potpourri, rather old and sadly faded. The box with strips of coloured wood had nothing in it but a pin. I reached out for the biggest box, the one that came from India, with lotus blossoms on its lid in the shape of tear drops. Such a pretty thing, I thought. The carving is so delicate.

I raised the lid and peered inside. Saw a layer of tissue paper. Inhaled a funny, pungent smell. A familiar smell. It was vaguely chemical.

I opened out the paper folds and found a real treasure there, coiled inside the layers of tissue. A red-gold, precious, eerie treasure.

I nearly screamed, I was so shocked. Inside the box was Hannah's hair.

SEVENTEEN

I wanted it to be a wig, or a hairpiece worn by Hannah to emulate a sixties look. But from the look and smell of it I knew that it was Hannah's hair, as red-gold and glorious as it had been before she died.

Hannah's hair... It might have given me the shivers, or even filled me with repulsion. Instead, I was seized by fury. Here was proof that Conor was a liar. The conversation that we'd had after he had seen the body came back word by word to me. I had said, 'I was thinking of her hair. What the sea would do to it.' And Conor had replied, 'You can think but I have seen it.' It was hell, he said. *'Please* don't think about her hair.'

Now I had no option but to think about her hair. Conor had implied that the sea had ruined it. But it had not been in the sea. It didn't smell of salty water, just of too much alcohol. And it was in good condition, as lustrous, silky and abundant as the last time I had seen it.

Hannah's hair, unviolated by the sea... Which meant it must have been cut off before the tide took her away.

Without her hair, Hannah would look very different. She'd become another woman. Was that the reason it was done, to change her whole appearance? But why? So she could escape from her ailing, tragic self and assume a new persona?

318

Find a new life for herself? Maybe in another country? That seemed hardly credible. Hannah wasn't up to it. And if she had run away, whose body had the children found? Conor had identified it. Told the guards that it was Hannah's. But Conor was a proven liar. If he'd tell a lie to me, he would lie to anyone. The body he'd identified might have been another woman's.

Yet the woman who'd been in the sea had died from drinking alcohol combined with amphetamines, just as Hannah used to do. The likelihood of someone else who suffered from the same addictions turning up to take her place seemed remote, to say the least. Someone about Hannah's age, give or take a year or so. The post mortem would have shown how old the body was. But if the body had been Hannah's why would Conor lie to me about her hair?

I was going round in circles.

Hannah's hair, I thought again. Everything comes back to that. 'I have seen it,' Conor said. But he hadn't. He had lied.

Suddenly, everything to do with Conor seemed anathema to me. His so-schematic studio. His regiments of tubes and pencils. His freshly-laundered cleaning rags. So ultra-white. So clean. So pure.

The urge to smash the whole place up was almost irresistible. But Hannah had arranged those shelves. The pretty boxes were all hers. And in the one that I was holding was her gorgeous red-gold hair. These treasure must remain intact.

I folded back the tissue paper, closed the lid on Hannah's hair and put the box back on the shelf.

319

Time to leave.

Downstairs, all was quiet as ever. Still no Clodagh. Still no Em.

Passing through the silent kitchen, I could hear a wind come up. The forecast for the week ahead had mentioned that it would be breezy. Summer making way for autumn. I could feel the prickle of it, even here, inside the house, and when I walked across the yard the wind plucked at my ears and hair.

I put my hand up to my face and brushed the tangles back from it. That made me remember Hannah sitting on the rock outcrop. I could see her in my mind as I'd seen her from the fort and later on in the video. Hannah in her long green gown, sitting with her back to us, clutching at those red-gold tresses. Just as I was doing now.

No, not as I was doing now. She'd been doing something different...

I stopped. That's what had bothered me about the image of Hannah sitting on the rocks, something about the way she had clutched at her wind-swept hair.

I gave myself a little shake. I'd have to play the video and see that scene again. It would be in David's room, with his cameras. But David, as ill luck would have it, hadn't yet come back from Dublin.

How exasperating of him, to be stopping up in Dublin. What was he doing there all this time? He didn't have a job to do. He was coasting – chilling out, just when he was needed here.

I knew I was being unfair. I did not own David Parker. He was free to come and go. He didn't owe me anything.

Perhaps he hadn't bothered to lock up before he went.

I rushed over to his room. The door was locked and the windows were shut. I'd have to get him on the phone, ask him to come back to Kilnaboy as soon as possible, but I didn't have the number of the flat in Pembroke Road. What was Patrick's cousin's name? An Irish queen's name. Emer something. I could not recall the surname. It started with a B, I thought. Burke? Byrne? Bruton? No. What *was* the bloody woman's surname?

By the time I'd reached my own room, I had almost given up. Then I remembered it was Brennan. Emer Brennan, that was it. I didn't have the telephone book with the Dublin numbers in it, just the one for Clare and Limerick, so I'd have to call Inquiries.

'She's not listed,' said Inquiries.

'What?'

'Sorry but she's ex-directory.'

Ex-directory? Emer Brennan? Silly cow, I thought. What's so special about her that she would be ex-directory?

But I could reach her, all the same. According to David, she was staying in Patrick's room or possibly at Orla's place. Why had I got so worked up? I really didn't have a problem.

But Patrick wasn't in his room and neither was his cousin, Emer. And they weren't at Orla's either.

The pub, I thought. That's where they'll be. That meant a trip to Corofin.

321

It took an age to track them down. The pubs in Corofin were busy and I missed them in the first one. When I'd searched the second pub and failed to come across them there, a student who was down from Mayo said he'd seen them earlier.

'They're across the road,' he told me. 'Patrick has the two girls with him.'

I retraced my steps and, this time, spotted Patrick surrounded by a crowd of students. I eased my way across to him. Saw that Orla was there with him, and another, younger woman who might well have been a model. She was tall and very skinny with a mane of ash-blonde hair.

I was so relieved to find them that the words rushed out of me. 'Patrick! Orla! Are you Emer?'

The skinny blonde surveyed me coolly. Close up, she looked like a camel.

'Yes,' she said, 'I'm Emer Brennan,' and looked down her nose at me.

Patrick jumped up and embraced me. 'Brigit! Join us. Move up. Emer.'

With reluctance, Emer Brennan moved two inches to her right. I decided I disliked her.

'I'm sorry, I can't stay,' I said. 'Emer, David Parker's staying in your flat. I have to get in touch with him.'

'Oh?' said Emer Brennan coldly. Her eyebrows said, 'And why is that?'

Silly cow, I thought again. Ex-directory. Such self importance.

'Could you let me have the number?'

She reached for a Gucci bag and produced a snakeskin case which contained a little notebook. She wrote the number down for me. Her nails were long and painted silver with a tiny leaf motif embossed in the centre of them. ᵘᵍʰ

'Here,' she said disdainfully. 'And do tell David I sent love.' Her voice was uppity as well.

Back at Kilnaboy, I dialled the number with a shaking hand. A voice that I had heard before said, 'This is Emer Brennan's voice mail.' I could have wept with the frustration. Where was David at this hour? Driving back to Kilnaboy or gallivanting round the city?

I left a message asking him to phone me. Then I made a cup of coffee. Ten, fifteen minutes ticked away. I tried David once again. 'This is Emer Brennan's voice mail...'

'Oh, piss off!' I muttered crossly.

And then it struck me that there must be spare keys for all the rooms at Kilnaboy. Students were a careless lot. Keys must often get mislaid. Conor wouldn't be so stupid not to have had spare sets cut. They'd be up at the house. Clodagh would have access to them. Surely she was back by now.

I trotted over to the house. Shouted, 'Clodagh!' when I got there.

Silence – and the lights weren't on.

I called out a second time. 'Clodagh, this is Brigit here. Clodagh? Em? Are you in there? I need another set of keys.'

Not a squeak from anybody. I was talking to the moon. Where was Clodagh? Where was Em? For that matter, where was David?

Still, I could search the house myself for those keys. Where to look? The hall? The kitchen? There should be a keyboard somewhere, or a drawer full of keys.

I ransacked the scullery first. It was also the laundry room. Apart from Biotex and Bold, I found only a laundry basket stuffed with dirty shirts and socks and a pair of aged trainers which, I thought, belonged to Em. The kitchen yielded nothing either, and the keys weren't in the hall.

Maybe Em looked after them. I tried her door but she had locked it. What about Clodagh's room? That seemed more of an intrusion. And what if Clodagh came back and caught me foraging about?

I didn't let that stop me. But Clodagh, too, had locked her door. How peculiar to do that but leave the other doors unlocked.

I checked all the bedrooms, just in case, the drawing room and the dining room. No keys.

It was after midnight now. Why was Clodagh not back home? It wasn't like her to be so late. Maybe she'd decided to make the most of Conor's absence and take the whole week off. But that wasn't like her either.

I wrote a note saying, 'Clodagh, *please*, never mind about the time, phone when you get back. Important!' I left it on the kitchen table and re-treated to my room, hoping somebody would phone.

No one did till 1 a.m. The minute I heard it ring, I nearly fell on the phone.

'Yes?'

'Brigit, did I wake you up? But you said that I should ring...'

'Clodagh!' I exclaimed. 'Thank goodness. Do you keep spare keys at the house?'

'I do. I have them upstairs in my room. You poor thing. You got locked out? I'll be with you in a jiffy.'

'No. Wait,' I said. 'I have my keys but I need David's – David Parker's. I'll come up and get them from you.'

'It's no bother,' Clodagh said. But if she came down and David wasn't here with me, waiting for the keys she'd brought, she'd want to know why I needed to get into his room.

She put the phone down before I could object, and in the event she didn't ask me questions. She'd had problems of her own and she wanted sympathy.

'Brigit, what a night I've had! I went to Galway with my cousin, thinking I might buy a suit. Coming back, the car broke down. No one helped us. No one stopped. We were on that road for hours. If it wasn't for a woman with two children in the back, we'd have been there until the morning.' She put the keys into my hand. 'David Parker's keys, you said. What happened that he lost them then? They're always losing keys round here. The locksmith makes a fortune from us. We only just got back, you know. Three full hours we waited, Brigit. That woman's husband must be worried, wondering why she isn't home. I told her she should use our phone. But she was sure that he'd be sleeping and she didn't want to wake him...'

'It was kind of her to stop.' I couldn't wait for her to go but she wasn't in a hurry. Her eyes ran round my room until they fell upon the entwined lovers.

325

'So he gave that to you?' she said.

'Yes.' I didn't want to talk about it. Didn't want to talk at all.

But Clodagh did. 'I'm glad it's you that has it, Brigit. That's what Hannah would have wanted.'

'Hannah?'

'She was very fond of you.'

I swallowed, willing Clodagh to go.

'Mind you, it's a bit explicit,' she went on. 'That's what I said, anyway, when I first laid eyes on it. But Hannah told me I was wrong. She said, "But can't you see, it's beautiful. The love that he's put into it…"'

'You and *Hannah* saw the sculpture?'

'Of course she saw it,' Clodagh said. 'She used to have it in her room. That's them, you know – the two of them. He made it after they got married. You'd never think it, would you, Brigit? That it isn't new, I mean. It looks as if it's just been done. He must have cleaned it up for you to make it look acceptable.'

I couldn't speak.

'It's sad,' she said, 'to think of them being in love like that and then to think of that poor girl. The way the drink got hold of her. The fearful ending that she had.' She turned to me and touched my hand. 'I'm glad you have the sculpture, Brigit, so you can remember her. Hannah would have wanted it. She was very fond of you.'

Hannah, I thought, oh, Hannah. I turned away so Clodagh wouldn't see me crying.

When Clodagh at last left, I ran across to David's room. I didn't have to search for long. The video was on a chair, partly covered by a

326

jersey that I'd last seen Celia wearing.

I grabbed it and re-locked the door. Headed for the studio.

My hands were clenched as the video began. Painting lessons. Students emulating students. Em doing her compliant act. Conor playing superstar. I didn't need to see all that. Especially not the sight of Conor...

I fast-forwarded. Went on to the island shots. And there was Hannah on the rocks, sitting with her back to us, wearing her green gown. The wind whipped round the fort and the woman seated on the rocks put up a hand to catch her hair.

That was it. That was the shot I wanted to see.

I pressed the button. Froze the shot. Stared intently at the screen. But I wasn't sure. I couldn't see as clearly as I wished. To make sure that I was right, I'd have to get the shot in close-up.

I couldn't do that here in Clare. But I could, with help, in Dublin. Somebody at RTE could magnify that shot for me. I thought, Finn Fogarty's the perfect person. She'll do it for me as a favour.

I'd been friends with Finn for years, since I'd worked on *Live at Three*. Finn was out of town when I first arrived in Dublin, and what with Mammy's accident and all the other things going on, I hadn't yet renewed our friendship. But Finn was a loyal person. I knew that in an emergency she would always be there for me.

I'll phone her now, I thought, this minute. Check when she'll be going to work. And then I'll shoot up to Dublin and meet her at RTE. I was so eager to move forward, I forgot what time it was. But as I left the studio, I looked at my watch. It was 3 a.m. Not the time to phone Finn! But I could be setting out. If I leave now, I thought, the roads up will be traffic-free and I'll arrive in Dublin before rush hour hits the city. I'll catch Finn at breakfast time.

I rang her up at ten to seven. 'Finn. It's Brigit. I'm in Dublin. What time are you going to work? I have a video with me. Will you do a favour for me and put it onto DVA?'

'Jesus, Brigit!' Finn exclaimed. 'Where the hell have you crawled out of to be phoning at this hour?'

But she didn't sound annoyed and when I said that it was urgent she responded positively.

An hour later, we were sitting side by side in a post-production suite. I'd explained what I was after.

'I'll do my best,' Finn said. 'I can bring it up about thirty-five per cent. That would be the maximum. You understand that the detail must be in the picture. If it's muzzy, I can't get it.'

'Yes, I understand.'

Finn inserted the video into the Digital Video Effects processor and fiddled with the control buttons.

'Forget the early stuff,' I said. 'The studio, the painting lessons. It's the Inishbofin sequence. It was done at Cromwell's Fort. The woman has her back to us. She puts her hand up to her head–'

'You're babbling! Calm down,' said Finn. She

328

fast-forwarded, as I had done.

'That's it! That's her! Stop there!' I said as she got to Cromwell's Fort.

Finn zoomed in on the shot. Three images of Hannah painting came up on the monitors. 'Now, let's see what we can do.' She pressed yet another button. The woman sitting on the rocks came a little closer to us. Finn focused on her head and shoulders. 'Can you see it?' she inquired.

'No, not yet.' I was in agony. What if the detail I was after came up so muzzy in the close-up that I couldn't make it out?

Finn said, reassuringly, 'We're only half the way. I'll bring her up some more for you.'

She did. The images of Hannah painting magnified before my eyes. Hannah Byrne in triplicate. Only–

'Is that any better for you?'

'Yes. It is. *It is!*'

'I can pull her out some more.'

But we were already there. The head and shoulders were so close, they were very nearly life-size. And the hand that clutched the hair was more or less the size of mine. But the detail I had looked for wasn't on the hand or hair. It was on the woman's wrist.

'Look, Finn, look!' I reached out and grabbed her arm. 'See the butterfly tattoo.'

It was clearly visible. David and I had been set up on that trip. It wasn't Hannah we had seen sitting down there on the rocks but someone dressed to look like her and wearing a wig.

Someone with a tattooed wrist. Em.

EIGHTEEN

When I explained, Finn was shocked but curious. 'Jesus! What a story! How did you work it out?'

'It was the wind blowing her hair. Something bothered me about the shot. And then it came to me. The wind was blowing it *off* her face so why would she clutch at it? Especially at that time, when she was trying to hold a pose. I couldn't understand it. Then I thought if she'd had a wig on her, it would be a different matter. The wind might well have blown it off, so naturally she'd grab at it.'

When I'd come to that conclusion, I still believed that it was Hannah, sitting down there on the rocks. I knew her hair had been cut off – I had found it in the box. So in theory she had every reason to put on a wig that day. But, in the normal scheme of things, wouldn't Conor comment on it? Say, 'It's unfortunate, I know, but Hannah's had her hair cut off. So we've had to use a wig.'

I already knew that he'd told lies about her hair, inferring that it wasn't cut when she'd gone into the sea. *'I have seen it. It was hell... Please don't think about her hair.'* So I re-played the video, and something rang a bell. It was such a little thing – an involuntary movement as the woman on the rocks put her hand behind her head. I'd seen Em doing that, posing in the studio, and I must have registered the way she raised her arm.

And when I became suspicious, other things fell into place. Conor's strange behaviour, beginning with his note to me. *'Hannah's being difficult. Em is going to help me with her. We're going to catch the early ferry and get Hannah settled in before the rest of you arrive…'* His other bulletin, warning me to keep the students well away from Cromwell's Fort, *'in case Hannah gets upset.'* And the care he'd taken when we'd joined him at the fort to keep us so far away from the woman on the rocks.

When David wanted to climb down and take further shots below, Conor promptly intervened.

'I told you. That's not necessary.'

'Let me be the judge of that.'

'But it's dangerous,' Conor had said. *'You might hurt your foot again.'*

Conor glaring, saying no, he didn't need a close-up shot.

And afterwards, when we were leaving: *'I'm concerned about the tide… You two should be making tracks.'* He'd wanted to get rid of us before the woman down below revealed herself to us as Em.

On the island, I had wondered why I'd not run into her. Now I knew where she'd been hiding. And she'd come to the studio in the middle of the night, before we went to Inishbofin, not knowing I was hiding there. She'd gone over to the wardrobe. Taken something out of it. It was the wig, I knew now.

Finn said, 'God, Brigit, it's incredible! But where was Hannah all that time?'

'Good question. I wish I knew the answer.'

'We'll talk it over later on. You must stay the night with me. We'll make sense of it, I promise. We can work it out together.'

But I was jumpy as a colt and I couldn't stay in Dublin. I should be making tracks and heading back to Kilnaboy. I needed to work it out alone. I told Finn I'd have to go.

'You're off your head,' was her reply. 'You didn't sleep a wink last night. And now you're heading off again. Crazy, Brigit. Idiotic. You look worn out, you really do. You'll fall asleep on the way back.'

But I was wide awake; as strung up as Hannah was when I first laid eyes on her – though for very different reasons. Leaving Finn at RTE, I got on the road again.

All the way to Clare, I turned it over in my head. Why would Em dress up as Hannah? And where was Hannah? On the island, maybe at the B and B, in an alcoholic coma while we were all at Cromwell's Fort?

But I could dismiss that answer. Hannah wasn't on the island, or if she was, she didn't leave with Em. Conor had been terrified, flown into a shocking rage, when I told him about David leaving on the evening ferry. He had altered those arrangements, persuaded David to stop over so that he could rest his foot. Conor knew that Em would be on the evening ferry and that she'd be on her own. David would have met her on it, wondered about Hannah's absence.

Oh, but Conor had been clever! And cunning and manipulative. What an eejit I had been.

Where had Hannah been while we were at

Inishbofin? Why had Em purloined that wig and pretended to be Hannah?

I'd get the answers out of Em when I got my hands on her. I'd pin her down, bully her if necessary when we were face to face again. Which, hopefully, we would be soon.

Funny she'd stopped out so late after dropping Conor off. But she should be back by now.

I couldn't wait to get to her. I was driving fast, faster than the law permitted. But when I reached Kilcolgan village, I did what I had done before, when the sea distracted me from going straight to Kilnaboy. Deferring to my instinct, I turned right towards Kinvarra, and soon after right again.

The scarlet blossoms of the poppies weren't in bloom to cheer me this time, and the tent and barbecue were no longer in the field.

What drew me to the Flaggy Shore? Guilt? Regret? Or just compassion?

A mixture of all three, I guess.

But something else was driving me. The need to retrace Hannah's steps as she set out on her final, fatal journey.

When I reached that austere shore, I pulled in on the grassy verge that ran above the silver sand and put myself in Hannah's shoes. Did she sit here in the car, thinking of her father's death, feeling sorry for herself, sipping vodka from the bottle and swallowing those lethal pills, until the combination of them forced her to get out for air? I imagined being Hannah. Feeling dizzy. Frightened. Helpless. Stumbling out of Jimmy's Audi. Staggering towards the sea. Collapsing on the beach below as the tide came towards her.

I envisaged all that happening. Saw it clearly, frame by frame, Hannah starting to feel faint. Opening the Audi door. The bottle slipping from her hand…

But then I thought, no, wait a minute. The bottle wasn't abandoned on the ground. It was found in Hannah's bag, tucked in with another one. Funny that she was so tidy, so anxious not to leave a mess even then, when she was dying. But perhaps the bottles in her bag had been there for days and Hannah had another one which she dropped as she got out and left lying on the grass.

If so, it wasn't found. And that seemed a lot of bottles, even for an alcoholic.

Try another tack, I thought. You are Hannah, sitting here, brooding on your father's death. You aren't feeling dizzy yet. It looks pleasant on the shore. You decide to take a walk. You stroll along the silver sand with a bottle in your hands. You find a pleasant spot to sit. You drink your vodka, take your pills and gradually fall victim to them.

But why leave your bag behind? You weren't drunk when you arrived, or not so drunk you couldn't drive. Why would you forget your bag?

Most of us can be forgetful. And Hannah was distraught about her father's death.

She had no need to be on guard. Thieves don't frequent the Flaggy Shore the way they do the streets of London. The chances were that Hannah's bag would have been completely safe in Jimmy's car. And indeed, it had been safe, as the guards discovered later.

Hannah's big black satchel, the same one she'd

had with her the day we went up to Galway. I remembered Clodagh saying Hannah kept her letters in it: '*She always had her letters with her. She'd carry them around with her. They'd be the ones her father sent her.*' Odd that they weren't in the bag when it was found inside the car, especially then, when she was grieving for him.

I decided to walk along the beach, as I thought Hannah must have done. The deserted shore was ominously cold and bleak. And yet those very qualities in Conor's paintings of the west had coaxed me out of stifling London. But the Flaggy Shore did not call out to me as Conor's paintings had so loudly. I felt before – and felt again – that this terrain was stony-hearted. Today, the surly sea and sky were dressed the same, in steely grey. The smooth, round stones were black as lead, and as I walked along the beach, a fresh west wind was blowing up. I was tired and didn't have a jersey on, and it seemed as cold as January.

Ahead, the flat limestone shelves that had disturbed me in the past stretched out to meet the sea. How curious they were, I thought, those huge, black, shiny pigeonholes, designed by nature for a giant but unused by our human hands.

Had Hannah thought them odd as well? Did she walk as far as this before deciding to sit down?

If so, she hadn't found a comfy spot. The only seat that I could see was a heap of pumice stones made slimy by a seaweed topping. She must have huddled on the sand and warmed herself by swallowing vodka. And then the pills, or vice versa. Poor Hannah, who'd had everything in life – talent, beauty, money, charm – but hadn't ever quite grown up.

Which made two of us, I thought. I hadn't quite grown up myself, until the night of Lorcan's show, when I had cut those ties with Joe.

I'd reached the far end of the shore. I turned, intending to go back. And then I spotted something flapping, wedged between a big black stone and a piece of rotting seaweed. It was a piece of bubblewrap.

How incongruous, I thought, and incidentally how ironic. No bubblewrap at Kilnaboy and then I come across some here. I moved the stone and yanked it out.

How bizarre, I thought again.

What I did next was automatic. I only did what we all do when we're holding bubblewrap. I squeezed it and popped a bubble.

And then I thought, but that was it! That was the sound I heard the night I lost the signet ring, the same night Em took that red wig.

I'd heard her going up the stairs. And after that there was a plop, as if something – something light – had been thrown down from the loft. As I hid beneath the table, the footsteps had come down again. Em had gone to get the wig – I'd heard the wardrobe door being opened. Nothing happened for a minute. Then I'd heard a squeaky sound followed by a funny 'pop'. The sound of bubblewrap being popped. And the light 'plop' I'd heard before, that was also bubblewrap. Em must have thrown the first roll down and then followed with the second. So, as well as taking that red wig, Em had also carried off all the bubblewrap in stock which was why there was none left for wrapping Mikey's present.

Why would she take bubblewrap? It was kept in stock so we could wrap paintings in it to prevent them getting scratched. Had Em wanted to wrap paintings in the middle of the night? Lots and lots of paintings? She could have wrapped forty paintings in two rolls of bubblewrap.

No, I thought, it wasn't paintings. Whatever needed to be wrapped was connected with the wig. With Em pretending to be Hannah. It would seem now that Hannah had already vanished when we got to Inishbofin. Hannah's body was washed out from this isolated shore. And in this unlikely place I find a sheet of bubblewrap.

It was all starting to add up to a frightening amount.

The cold was going right through me now. But I couldn't leave the shore, not till I'd made sense of things. I stared out at the steely sea, wondering what could have happened. I told myself to think back to the day before we went on the island trip.

We'd started on the video. And then, in the afternoon, Clodagh said that she was leaving, going off for the weekend. She'd been bothered about Hannah. She'd dithered, standing at the door, then she'd given me a message that I should pass on to Conor. What exactly had she said?

'Tell him that I've done my best and no one could do more than that…' And she'd added something else, about Hannah's situation. *'Anyhows, she's sleeping now. She's been asleep this last half-hour.'*

Inferring Hannah had been drinking and was in a boozy stupor.

Clodagh had gone off and left her, thinking Conor would take over. But he hadn't. He'd stayed in the studio as David continued shooting. We hadn't broken up the session until nearly nine o'clock. David and the others had all rushed off to Corofin and the pub while I had stayed behind with Conor, to begin our love affair. It would have been after ten when Conor went to check on Hannah.

What exactly did he find when he went up to her room? Hannah sleeping in her bed? Or was she already dead when he reached their house that night?

The cause of Hannah's death was alcohol combined with pills. So she might have died that evening instead of two or three days later. Died alone, while I was making love with Conor...

Forget the guilt, I told myself. That will have to wait for later. Right now, you should deal with facts. Take off Hannah's shoes and put Conor's on your feet. Become Conor. Think like him. Act as Conor would have done.

You go into Hannah's room to check if she has woken yet. Instead, you find her dead in bed. Your next step is to call a doctor. But you don't. The person you call is Em.

What makes you take that step? All right, you're shocked. You can't think straight. Or perhaps you can. Perhaps you're shocked but calculating.

Hannah's father died of cancer while we were in Inishbofin. He'd been ailing for some time. In the article I'd read, *Woman's Way* had hinted that

Seamus was extremely ill. But Conor said his death was sudden. That Seamus had been in remission and expected to recover.

When did Conor Byrne ever tell the truth to me? Not then, before or afterwards.

Seamus had a ton of money. He was leaving it all to Hannah. But Sheila Ferguson had said he wasn't pleased about her marriage because Conor wasn't wealthy. *'Conor didn't have a penny. Just that house at Inishbofin and we know how he got that...'*

Maybe that was idle gossip, about the Inishbofin house. The cottage had been left to Conor. David had confirmed that. *'Conor didn't have a penny...'* Yet he knew how to spend. When I'd arrived at Kilnaboy, I'd marvelled at what had been done. I'd thought, it must have cost a fortune to do all these smart conversions. You don't make that much money out of summer schools in Clare. You don't become rich with two successful shows in London, not unless you're very famous. Where did Conor get his money? Answer: out of Hannah's pocket.

There would have been more to come, much more, after Hannah's father's death. As Sheila Ferguson had said, Hannah was an only child. Seamus cared about his daughter. Gave her everything she wanted. But if Hannah predeceased him, what would happen then? Seamus wasn't crazy about Conor and he might have changed his will. Conor had a lot to lose if Hannah died before her father. So if he found her dead in bed what would his reaction be?

Be Conor, Brigit. Act like him.

You know Seamus is near death. You think, all that money I may lose because Hannah has pre-deceased him. But what if I conceal her body so people think she's still alive? Ensure that she appears in public – stage that scene at Inishbofin. Pray that Seamus will die soon...

The scenario repelled me. Who could possibly behave in such a manner? Who would take a risk like that? Not my lover surely. But after Lorcan's exhibition, the world had lost its rosy glow. And people did take fearful risks if a fortune was involved.

Think like Conor, Brigit.

You wrap the body, with Em's help. It will be discovered later, at a time that suits you better. Where will you hide it in the meantime? Not at Kilnaboy for sure. Somewhere near the Flaggy Shore where, in due course, you'll leave Hannah's bag inside the Audi. A cool place, so you can preserve the body. A flagstone shelf perhaps, where it would be safe from prying eyes and scavengers.

Those shelves. They'd always given me the creeps. But now I had to steel myself to take a closer look at them.

Approaching them with trepidation, I was thinking of their size, whether they were long enough, wide enough, for a body to be laid there.

The shelves were black and dark as night. At first I couldn't see inside them. But soon my eyes grew accustomed to the gloom and then, at the back of one of them, I spotted something.

I reached in. It was wet and slimy in there and I could feel how cool it was – as cold as a refrigerator. A perfect place to store a body.

I pulled the something out. Another torn piece of bubblewrap.

I thought again about the Audi on the way to Kilnaboy.

Jimmy said he'd lost the keys. But I guessed that they'd been stolen, that Em had taken them from him while we were still at Inishbofin.

She and Conor had been cunning, they had thought of everything. It really was extraordinary, the way that they had operated. Conor issuing instructions, Em being his compliant helper.

The hilltop lake came into view. The road dipped and plunged and then, as I descended into the green valley and saw the sign for Kilnaboy, I thought about the boathouse break-in. The padlock on the door was broken. But as the guards had told us when we stopped for supper at Monk's Bar, nothing had been taken from it. But someone might have *borrowed* something.

The boathouse wasn't used for boats but for engines and for oars. Suppose Conor helped himself? Borrowed what he would have needed to take a boat from Ballyvaughan over to the Flaggy Shore without making too much noise. Put Hannah's body in it so he could dump it in the bay when it suited him. The date was right. Seamus Talbot-Kelly died the same day as the boathouse break-in.

I remembered Em and Conor talking in his studio after Hannah's disappearance.

''Twill be over by the weekend.' Em's voice.

'I hope so,' Conor had replied.

'It has to be. It stands to reason.'

If you had just dumped a body out in Bally-vaughan Bay, you'd be feeling somewhat anxious, wondering when it would be found. You'd hope that it would turn up soon. 'By the weekend,' Em had said trying to cheer Conor up.

Em wouldn't stand a chance with me. I was going to make her talk, own up to the truth at last, the minute I laid hands on her.

Back at Kilnaboy, I zoomed into the parking lot, leaped out of Hannah's car and ran towards the studio.

I banged my fists on the door. 'It's Brigit. Let me in,' I shouted.

'The door's not locked. You can come in.'

The students all turned round to see why I was making such a fuss.

'I need to speak to Em,' I said.

But Em wasn't there. The person standing in for Conor said he had no news of her. 'I'm afraid she's let us down. We're looking for another model.' He looked at me expectantly, no doubt hoping I could help him.

I told him I was in a hurry and ran across the cobblestones to see if Em was in her room.

Arriving at the house, I shouted, 'Em, I want to talk to you!'

'Em's not here,' said David's voice.

It came from inside Em's room. The door was open. I went in.

The room I entered was chaotic. Drawers were pulled open, Em's possessions strewn around, her bed pulled out from the far wall. The drawer beneath it pulled out too.

'Look what I've found,' David said. He pointed at the drawer which had been underneath the bed. It was stuffed with plastic bags. David lifted out a handful so that I could see the contents.

Pink and white and yellow powder. What I thought were marble chips. Tablets which had doves on them. Boxes of temazepam.

'Em was storing *this* in here?'

'Too right, she was,' said David grimly. 'And now the bitch has disappeared.'

NINETEEN

'Didn't she come back at all?'

I put this to a startled Clodagh who, having joined us in the bedroom, was now surveying the cache of drugs.

'If she did, I never saw her,' she answered in a bemused voice.

'But you were expecting her?'

'Yes. After dropping Mr Byrne, she was going on to Limerick. I asked her if she'd go to Dunne's and get some tea towels for the house. I put the money in her hand. She said that she'd be back for tea.'

'She didn't phone you, I suppose?'

'There's not been a peep from her. Mind you, when you see what's here, those pills with birds stamped onto them. And those little yellow chip things...' She looked inquiringly at David.

'Ecstasy and crack cocaine,' he said. 'The white stuff might be heroin. Though I'm not sure, it could be speed.'

'Speed?'

'Amphetamines. Stimulants. The opposite of tranquillisers. Which Em was also stocking here. Temazepam. The liquid capsules. They've been banned for some time to stop users from injecting, and replaced by a gel, I think. But somehow, Em got hold of them.'

'Temazepam,' repeated Clodagh. 'But didn't

that kill Hannah, David?'

'Not temazepam alone. You'd have to take a lot of it to make a fatal overdose. But Hannah was an alcoholic and it was the combination. Plus she took other drugs as well. Speed being one of them, I'd say.'

'Em was selling her all that?'

'I'm absolutely sure she was. I know she was supplying the students. That's why the door was left unlocked whenever you weren't in the house. So anybody who bought from Em could come and go when you were out. She'd leave the key for her own door underneath a certain stone and tell them where it could be found. And then she'd have their order ready, sitting on her dressing table.'

'But how did you find out about it?'

'All right,' David said. 'Let me level with you. Celia told me. I liked her a lot, but she was a mess. Another victim of the Em's of this world. The whole thing made me furious. I thought I'd search Em's room the minute that I got the chance to see what was in there.'

'Are you going to call the guards?'

'I don't think we have an option.'

'I'll get on to Guard McMahon,' Clodagh said briskly. 'He'll be up here in a jiffy.'

On one level, I was listening in to this and registering what was being said. On another, I was gazing at a photo I'd seen on the dressing table. It was in a silver frame. It was obviously special.

When Clodagh left to phone the guards, I looked more closely at the photo. It was of a man and woman, posed outside a whitewashed cottage. The man's arm was round the woman. She was smiling up at him. Her expression was adoring.

My world, which was already out of sync, rotated and turned upside down. The photo was of Em and Conor.

'What's that you're looking at?' said David.

'Just a photo,' said my voice. A small, bewildered childish voice.

Em and Conor, I was thinking. But they couldn't be an item. Em is lightweight, mediocre. She's tatty. Unattractive. Cheap. She's just peanuts – isn't she? Surely Conor, of all people, couldn't be in love with *her?*

'What is it, Brigit?' asked David gently.

'Nothing much,' the small voice said. But David hadn't seen Em as 'nothing much'. He'd thought she was close to Conor. What was it that he'd said when we'd been eating at Milano?

'They kind of gel. They're quite alike. Hasn't that occurred to you?'

'*No, it hasn't,*' I'd said coldly. '*Em is ugly. Unattractive.*'

But judging by the photo, Conor didn't think so.

Looking at that image of them, with his arm round her shoulder, I forgot what they must have done. How they must have dumped poor Hannah. I forgot the charade they'd staged and all their other machinations. I blanked out on everything except what I was staring at. The selfish child inside me shouted, how *dare* he do this thing to me!

346

'Brigit?' David too, was looking at the photo. 'Is that the Inishbofin cottage?'

'Yes,' I answered.

'I wonder when we'll get to see it and finish off the video. When exactly is Conor coming back?'

Before I had time to answer, Clodagh bustled back again.

'Guard McMahon's coming now. Come on to the kitchen and wait for him. I'll make the two of you some tea.'

She'd barely set it on the table when the Garda car pulled up and Guard McMahon was admitted. The cache of drugs was removed and David gave a lengthy statement.

I noticed that he took good care to leave Celia out of it, insisting that his information came from overhearing students talking up in Inishbofin.

'You tell me that Em went to Shannon,' Guard McMahon was saying. 'What car would she have been driving?'

We were sitting round the table, the three of us and Guard McMahon.

'She took Mr Byrne's Jaguar.'

'We'll have a call put out for that. And we should talk to Mr Byrne. He's in America, you say. You have a number for him, do you?'

But Conor hadn't left a number. Hadn't said where he'd be staying. Just that he'd be in LA.

He's probably with Em, I thought. She must be with him in LA, holed up in some smart hotel. The thought enraged me.

'Maybe Em's left the country,' I said. 'You didn't find her passport, did you?'

'There wasn't one in her room.'

Clodagh said, 'Em wouldn't have a passport, Brigit. Where would *she* be going with one?'

Where but to LA, I thought. And then, odd that Conor left no number. Even if Em was with him, he could have said where he'd be staying. Briefed her not to take his calls in case her voice was recognised but stayed in touch with Kilnaboy. Very odd indeed – unless he lied about that too. Unless he wasn't in LA at all.

I said, 'Excuse me. I'm just going upstairs a minute.'

'Yes, of course,' said Guard McMahon, his mind on more important matters. 'We can check if a passport has ever been issued to her. I'll get on to that this minute...'

I dashed upstairs and shot straight into Conor's bedroom. Where would Conor keep *his* passport if it wasn't on his person?

Conor's room was sparsely furnished. He didn't have a wardrobe for his clothes, just a rail in a corner. There was only a chest of drawers and a little three-drawer unit standing by his bed.

I rifled through the chest first. I found his T-shirts and jeans, neatly folded shirts and jerseys, and a hand-knitted Aran sweater. No paperwork of any kind. No sketch books and no passport either.

Next I tried the bedside unit. The top drawer was locked. I tried the second and third drawers. Neither of them were locked and they contained, predictably enough, hankies, socks and under-pants. No key to open the top drawer had been concealed inside the socks or slipped beneath the underwear. No key in Conor's jackets either, or in any trouser pockets. Still, I had expected that. He would have the key with him.

I glowered at the bedside unit. The clue to Conor's whereabouts might be in that locked top drawer and I couldn't find the key.

It was a functional but relatively flimsy piece of modern furniture. The bottom of the drawers were doubtless only made of plywood. If I removed the other drawers I might break through from the inside. It was worth a try.

I'd lifted out the other drawers and had my hand inside the unit when I heard footsteps on the stairs. I couldn't cover up my tracks. I didn't have time to replace the drawers. I left them lying on the floor and dashed into Conor's bathroom. There, I held my breath, convinced that someone – Clodagh or perhaps the guard – would come into Conor's bedroom and find out what I'd been up to.

The footsteps went the other way – into Clodagh's room. I heard her door being firmly closed and, an instant later, a second door closing. She must have gone into her bathroom.

I returned to the bedroom and slid the drawers back into place. It was as far as I could go, for the moment. I'd have to come back when the house was empty – and bring a hammer with me.

I went downstairs again. Guard McMahon was complaining.

'You'd think he'd be more organised. But I suppose that's artists for you.'

'What's the problem?' I inquired.

David answered. 'No one knows Em's other name. And "Em" might be short for Emma, or it might be the initial M.'

'I never thought of that,' I said. I had taken Em for granted. Hadn't thought about her surname, or her family origins. 'That means you can't check her passport?'

'It does,' said Guard McMahon sourly.

'You can ask the students. One of them might know her surname.'

'We can try,' said Guard McMahon. 'But if the house has no idea, it's unlikely the students will know more. The whole thing is ridiculous. Employing a woman with no name, and then not saying where he'll be staying!'

I thought of the drawer. Perhaps there was a file in there that gave Em's surname. Should I suggest that Guard McMahon force the drawer open? If he did, he might discover Conor's passport.

But I wanted to check that. I'd gone far with my inquiry, and I had to finish it. How could I get rid of Clodagh after Guard McMahon left? I only needed a few minutes. What excuse could I dream up?

Clodagh came back, looking worried. 'I had a peep around upstairs in case there was a file or something Mr Byrne kept on models. I had a good look in his room. There wasn't anything there that might help us.'

My mouth fell open as she spoke. She must have been in Conor's bedroom seconds after I was there. I swallowed, hoping nobody had noticed my reaction.

'You got nothing?' said the guard.

'Not a single thing,' said Clodagh.

But Clodagh must have tried that drawer. Found, like me, that it was locked. Yet she'd said nothing about that.

'Those students,' Guard McMahon said. 'Are they still here with him away?'

'The classes are going on,' said Clodagh. 'He got someone to replace him. They'll all be in the studio.'

'I'd better go and talk to them.'

'Are you going to search their rooms?' I asked.

'We'll have to get a warrant first. The fact that we've found drugs in Em's room doesn't mean that she is guilty. They might have been planted on her. We have to proceed properly. Question all the students first.'

'The students won't let on about her.'

'You'd be surprised what they'll say when we've got them on the spot. The main thing is get the facts and then go after the supplier.'

'If you decide that person's Em and you succeed in finding her, what happens to her afterwards?'

Guard McMahon cleared his throat. 'She'd be detained under the Misuse of Drugs Act and charged under section fifteen of that Act with possession of drugs with intent to supply. They'd try her in a district court.'

'And what then if she's found guilty?'

'She could be sent up for life. That would be the maximum. But if it's a first offence, she would only get nine months. We just don't know about this woman. She might have been charged before. We have to find her proper name and see what there is on file about her. We may call

Ennistymon in, and possibly the guards in Ennis. We'll have to see how things pan out.' He got up. 'I'd like you to come with me, Clodagh. You can help me with the students. Do you have a list of names?'

I was hoping that she'd leave so I could break into Conor's drawer but she sabotaged the idea.

'You'd do better taking Brigit,' she said. 'She knows all the students' names. She's more to do with what goes on. She'd be much more help than me.'

Guard McMahon turned to me. 'So you know all the students' names?'

There was no way out of it. I fixed a smile on my face and went to do as Clodagh said.

Guard McMahon took an age to put his questions to the students. I tried to escape from him but he held on to me. His questions were a waste of time, as it turned out. No one knew what Em's name was. And no one knew about the drugs – or so the students all insisted.

Guard McMahon's disappointment was expressed in irritation. He told the students that he'd get a warrant so the guards could search their rooms – by which time, of course, any incriminating evidence would have been removed, as Guard McMahon well knew. This made him even madder.

'They know all right!' he said to me when we had left the studio. 'They know full well what happened here. They're into it – the lot of them! They're covering up. They're hiding her. But I can tell. It's in their eyes.' He paused, and added angrily, 'But what can you expect from artists?'

At last I got shot of him and turned my thoughts back to the drawer. I had car tools in the boot. Amongst them was a tyre lever. It would be a simple task to prise the top of that drawer open. But how could I get Clodagh out while I was working on the drawer? I couldn't think of an excuse to make her leave for half an hour – unless David helped me out. He could ask Clodagh for a drink, coax her down to Corofin. She wasn't really into pubs but she might go if David asked her.

I put this to David. I said, 'There's something I have to do. Will you take Clodagh for a drink so I can get into the house? She'd have to leave the door unlocked. Do you think you could manage that?'

David, bless him, didn't say, 'Brigit, are you off your head? You want me to take Clodagh out while you do something in the house? What is it that you want to do? Why are you being mysterious?'

Instead, he said, 'Well, I can try. I'll come back if it's not all right so stay here for a few minutes.'

I didn't stick around. I got the lever from the car. Returned to find David waiting.

'Sorry but she isn't there. The house is locked. I checked the doors. Perhaps she's gone with Guard McMahon.'

'I saw him going off alone.'

Everyone was disappearing. Hannah first, then Em and Clodagh. And Clodagh had been looking worried after she searched the bedroom. What was going on with *her?*

David's eyes fell on the lever. He didn't say a

word about it only asked another question.

'Maybe you would like that drink?'

'No, I wouldn't. Not tonight.'

I drifted back towards my room, still thinking about the drawer. I'd have to wait until the morning. Have another go at Clodagh. Get her out on some pretext. It might be easier in daylight.

'Brigit, I've been looking for you. I've been to your room and all. I thought you'd gone to Corofin.'

It was Clodagh. She hadn't vanished after all. I was so relieved, I laughed.

'I've been looking for you too,' I said.

'Brigit, I'm worried. I just don't know what to do.'

'What's worrying you?' I asked her, smiling.

Clodagh frowned. 'I had a good search everywhere.' She stopped and tugged at her grey hair.

'Go on.'

'You know I said that I found nothing?'

'Mm?'

'Well, I was lying,' Clodagh said. 'I know that was wrong of me but I was getting in a froth. I wasn't sure what I should do. I thought I'd have to think it over.'

'Think what over?' I inquired.

'What I found when I went in there. When I tried the bedside unit. The top drawer was locked, you see, so I pulled out the second one. That unit isn't all that strong. Or else I was too hard on it, but anyway it broke on me. The bottom of the top drawer just fell out and all the things that were inside it – lots of notebooks and some cards and something stuffed inside a folder – came tumbling out.'

'Was there something about Em?'

Clodagh shook her head. 'Nothing about Em. The folder had the letters in it. Hannah's letters from her father. And something else was in it too. That was why I was so worried.'

'What else did you find?' I knew what she was going to say. I could have spoken her next lines. I heard them ringing in my head before Clodagh uttered them.

'It's Conor's passport, Brigit. See.' She held it out. I took it from her. It was only six months old, not an old one he'd abandoned.

Clodagh said, 'He can't be in Los Angeles. Why did he lie to us?'

'Good question. Can I keep the passport, Clodagh?'

'Of course.'

It had a little pouch with it. I put the passport in the pouch and slipped it in the rear pocket of the jeans that I was wearing.

'He might have had a breakdown, Brigit,' Clodagh said worriedly. 'After all that he's been through, that would not be so surprising.'

'Maybe he forgot his passport. Thought he'd go another time.'

'It could be that he phoned those lawyers and they're meeting him in London. Then he wouldn't need a passport.'

I said, 'Clodagh, when he goes to London, does he stay in a hotel?'

'He stays with Mrs Seton,' said Clodagh. 'I have her number in my book. Or we can try the gallery. I have that number upstairs too.'

'Could you get them for me now?' I said.

If Conor Byrne had gone to London, I was going to talk to him and show that I had tracked him down.

But Conor wasn't staying in London, or not at Janice Seton's apartment. The phone was answered by her son.

'Conor Byrne's not here,' he said. 'But you can try the gallery in case someone there has seen him.'

But no one there had seen him either.

'He lives in Ireland,' said a voice that sounded rather bored with life. 'We have his address on file. Do you need a number for him?'

'No thanks,' I said. 'I have that number.'

I turned to Clodagh, hardly seeing her. 'Seems like he's in Ireland, Clodagh.'

'You see?' she said. 'He's resting here. The poor man is dead tired, Brigit. He's run away from all of us. I think he's gone to Inishbofin.'

I thought Inishbofin, of course! That's where he's taken Em. They're in the cottage, I just know it. Laughing at the lot of us!

And then the pain came back again, that piercing, selfish, childish pain. I thought, they're in the cottage, in the bed where Conor once made love to me.

'That poor, tired man,' said Clodagh sadly. 'I'd say he needs a bit of peace. I think I had a hunch about it when I came across the passport. So maybe I was right, not mentioning it to Guard McMahon. He'd be up there in a jiffy, plaguing Conor about Em. Asking him about the students.

356

Saying they were taking drugs. It's all that Conor would be needing, after all he's suffered, Brigit.'

'Indeed it would be,' I said drily.

'So don't you think that I was right, not telling that to Guard McMahon?'

Inishbofin haunted me. I hardly slept that night, and when I did drop off, my dreams were all about the island – the sea and rocks and Cromwell's Fort.

Asleep, I heard the terns cry out, their harsh 'k-reeagh' and grating 'kro-ick' clashing with the raucous notes emitted by black-headed gulls. And I heard Hannah crying. She was stranded on the rocks, surrounded by a pounding sea.

'I'm going to drown,' she called to me. 'Oh, please, don't let the sea take me.'

I woke up in a guilty sweat and saw that it was half past one. I knew I wouldn't sleep again. I didn't want to anyway. I couldn't bear to hear those cries. To think of Hannah in the sea.

Instead, I thought of Em and Conor, fast asleep in Inishbofin, curled up together in that bed.

The pain came back so I got up and made myself a cup of coffee.

What am I doing here, I thought. I should be confronting them. Saying to Conor that I know what a lying creep he is. Informing him and Em that I've seen through their cunning, mean charade. Telling them what I suspect they did with Hannah's body. I'll go to Inishbofin now. I'll catch the early-morning ferry. I'll confront them in the cottage. Confront them while they're still in bed. Tell Conor I've seen through his lies.

Make sure he knows the way I feel – that he's disgusting and repellent.

Pain and anger energised me. I didn't bother with clean clothes, I used the ones I'd worn before. Within the hour I was on the open road and shooting towards my destination. I bypassed Galway in the dark, drove into pretty Oughterard and through the Connemara lakelands without registering their glory.

A lazy dawn was slowly breaking just as I pulled in to Creggan. This, I thought, will be the test. If I turn that corner now and find the Shell has been left here, I'll know that Clodagh's hunch was right. That I was right to listen to her.

I entered the parking lot and immediately spotted Conor's red Jaguar.

I don't know if the sea was rough or if it was an even crossing. I didn't notice anything. I was too busy anticipating my confrontation with Conor. I didn't even look at Cromwell's Fort.

Then we were at Inishbofin. It was very early. I couldn't hire a pony yet or try to rent a bicycle. I'd have to walk to Conor's cottage.

I did so automatically, striding off along the road where I had met the donkeys last time. They weren't around on this occasion and I passed the B and B without seeing the helpful woman who'd known what to do with them. I saw the graveyard and the abbey, then turned sharply to the left. The empty cottages loomed up. The sea was just round the corner.

I was back in East End Bay. Soon, I'd be at Conor's cottage. I would meet him at the doorway. I could speak my lines to him...

The dawn had truly broken now. The sun had bled into the sky, forecasting that it would rain soon. In contrast to this hectic flush, the cottage looked as white as frost.

The pots of paint had been removed, but otherwise things looked the same. Still rehearsing what I'd say, I walked up to the cottage and banged on it with both my fists.

No one came. The door stayed shut. I banged again and shouted, 'Conor!'

The only answer came from terns. 'K-reeagh. K-reeagh. Kro-ick. Kro-ick.'

'Conor! Em!'

I tried the door but it was locked. It's early, I told myself. They're asleep. They're in the bedroom, all tucked up. The creep and his pernicious pusher. I knew what I had to do. Go round to the bedroom window. Wake them up by banging on it. Tell them they must let me in. That I was on to what they'd done.

But now I shied away from confrontation. I couldn't face them at the window. The thought of seeing them in that bed was churning up my empty stomach. I couldn't do it.

Yes I could. I had no other option if I wanted to regain my self-respect.

My hands were clenched. My shoulders tense. I might have been a clockwork soldier strutting round towards the window.

The curtains on it were not drawn. I steeled myself to peep inside. But Em and Conor weren't in bed. There was no one in the room. No sign they'd been there at all. No garments on the chair or floor. The bed was made. The birds had flown.

I went back to the front again. Where *were* they? Walking on the beach perhaps? Gone to have an early swim?

'She isn't here,' a voice informed me.

I swung round. The small boy I had seen before had suddenly materialised.

'She's gone,' he said with satisfaction.

'Gone?'

He nodded. 'She went off a while ago. It's no good looking for her here.'

'Wasn't Mr Byrne with her?'

''Twas only her,' the small boy said. 'Her daddy wasn't here at all.'

Her daddy. I very nearly laughed out loud. 'What makes you think that he's her daddy?'

'Because he is,' the small boy said. 'She told me that two days ago. She said, "If you come here and give me cheek, I'll get my daddy to lambaist you." I said, "This house belongs to us by rights. My daddy's father's brother had it. It's not your daddy's place at all." "It is,' she said. "It's Mr Byrne's. And Mr Byrne's my father so if you keep hanging around this house, I'll see he takes a stick to you."'

'That's nonsense,' I said. 'Rubbish. Mr Byrne is not her daddy. She's telling fibs. She has to be.'

The small boy looked at me with scorn. 'She isn't telling fibs,' he said. 'I know that Mr Byrne's her daddy.'

'Because she told you he was.'

His scorn was growing by the minute. 'I'm not an eejit. She didn't have to tell me that. I always knew he was her daddy. You've only got to look at them and then you'll see that they're alike.'

TWENTY

David had said the same to me. *'They're very close. They kind of gel. Actually, they're quite alike...'*

I had seen it differently. Convinced myself that they were lovers. It took a small boy's scorn to make me realise I'd been wrong.

Father and daughter. It did make sense. They *were* alike. I saw it now. But why had they concealed the fact?

The small boy had lost interest in me. He was pushing off again.

'Hang on,' I said. 'Don't leave just yet. You say she's gone. When did she go?'

'A while before you came. So she'd be on the ferry now.'

The ferry! This was awful news.

'Anyways,' the small boy went on, 'she went off along High Road, so I suppose 'twas for the ferry.'

I had walked along Low Road, past the graveyard and the abbey. I didn't know about High Road.

'It goes off that way,' said the boy, pointing to the right of us. 'If you turn off at *Barr na Leacan,* you come out by the pier again. Or you could go by the boreen. 'Twould bring you down to Day's Hotel.'

He was a mine of information, but knowing how I'd missed Em wasn't helping me. My

361

stomach churned and heaved in rage. There was nothing I could do except return the way I'd come.

More despondent by the minute, I trailed off back along Low Road. My misery was soon compounded by a sudden heavy shower. My head down and my shoulders bent, as if I was an aged crone, I scuttled on towards the jetty.

Day's Hotel came into view. I could see the harbour now. The land mass stretching out beyond it. Braud. Closhkeem. The quay itself. And then I saw I was in luck. The ferry hadn't yet departed. What's more, it wasn't even boarding. On the jetty, passengers were lining up, surrounded by their bags and cases. Em was somewhere in that line. I still had time to track her down. Drag her kicking out of there and tell her that she'd been found out.

Arriving, mad-eyed, on the jetty, I must have looked a woeful sight, with soaking clothes and sopping hair. But no one took much notice of me. The people waiting for the ferry were nearly all as wet as I was. Two of them – Americans – were marvelling at the Irish climate, wondering how it was the Irish kept their spirits up.

I went slowly up the line, inspecting all the passengers and thinking that I'd soon find Em. But she was not amongst the crowd. I reached the ferry without seeing her. I walked down the line again, repeated my examination, thinking that I must have missed her, that she must be in that queue. But she wasn't.

The passengers began to board. Eyes on stalks, I stood and watched them, checking every single face in case it was the one I sought.

I looked back, thinking that she might be late, that she'd be running down the jetty to catch the ferry.

She wasn't there. She didn't come. The ferry left. I watched it moving towards the fort until it disappeared from view.

I swore and sighed and swore again. I must go back, I thought, annoyed, all the way along Low Road, and see if I can catch her this time. The rain was pounding on my head. The only, tiny consolation was that it would be falling on Em as well. She'd probably gone to buy some food for a cook-up at the cottage.

I thought, I'm going to have my breakfast too. I'll go into Day's Hotel and order up an Irish feast. Bacon. Sausages. Black pudding. Eggs and toast and strong, hot tea. And, after eating, I'll go back.

My mind was occupied with food. The taste of it was in my mouth. What made me look at Cromwell's Fort? What made me think just then of Hannah? But that's exactly what I did. I only stood there for a minute, staring out across the harbour at Port Island and the land that rose and curved and rose again, and led you on to Cromwell's Fort. And while I looked, I saw a figure in the distance moving slowly towards the fort. I couldn't see it very clearly. The figure was a human one but that was all that I could tell because it was so far away. I knew it wasn't chasing sheep. The sheep did not graze on Port Island where the tide would cut them off. They only strayed as far as Braud before their shepherd brought them home.

So who was that little figure?

It's early still, I thought. And this is the west of Ireland. The shops would not have opened yet. What made me think that Em was shopping? That could be her, that little figure, traipsing towards the fort. It could also be a tourist. But who'd go out on such a day, all the way to Cromwell's Fort? And at this hour of the morning?

Was Em meeting Conor there? He could be painting in the fort, beneath an oilskin, dismissive of the wet conditions. The boy had said they weren't together. But the boy could be wrong.

It was obvious to me that I must go to Cromwell's Fort and check out that tiny figure. I forgot how wet it was. I didn't wait to have my breakfast. The urge to track my quarry down replaced the need I had for comfort.

Setting out determinedly, I soon became discouraged. The last time I'd been at the fort, the weather had been very different. Sunshine and good light for David. The going had been heavy then but this time it was horrible. I couldn't have removed my shoes, not with all the vicious thistles that were growing on the hillocks. The wild flowers I had seen before, the hogweed and forget-me-nots, the cuckooflowers and spotted orchids, had signed off until next year. The land was not in happy mode. And nor was I.

I reached the cove which, last time round, had struck me as being so delightful. It didn't seem that way today, in the wind and rain. I kept my trainers on as I walked on the sand. I trudged across Braud, and the rain turned suddenly to sleet. Sleet! But it was only August! How unfair the weather was. I crossed another sandy inlet. Saw the ruins ahead of me.

The last time they'd loomed up like that, I'd spotted Conor in the entrance. I'd been flooded by emotions. Those feelings that had come upon me when I'd first seen Conor's paintings. When the sea called out to me and made me want to be in Ireland. Then I'd felt I had been fused with all of Nature's marine forces. The urge to love had been so strong. I'd wanted to give all of me to the man that I could see waiting for me in the fort.

Not any more. What I wanted to do now was slap that man across the face. Inform him that he was a scumbag. Tell his doting, darling daughter what I thought about her father.

But Conor wasn't in the ruins. It drove me crazy with frustration. The fort had lost its roof so there was no shelter. But all the same I had expected Conor would be working there, lurking underneath an oilskin, concentrating on his painting, unaware how wet it was.

Why wasn't he at Cromwell's Fort so I could vent my anger on him? Hadn't I come all this way, walked my legs off in the rain, so I could stand up to the creep and wrest my self-respect back? Where could the bastard be? And where was Em? They couldn't both have disappeared.

I'd reached the little ante-room with the window that overlooked the sea and rocks. The last time I'd looked out that window, I'd been tricked by Em and Conor. I'd seen 'Hannah' down there, painting. But Hannah had been dead by then, swathed in rolls of bubblewrap.

The window drew me. I looked out. And then I saw her sitting there, perched on the rock outcrop. Em, her back turned to the fort, just as she had been before except she wasn't wearing Hannah's gown and she didn't have a wig on her. And, this time, rain was drenching her. But it was Em, no doubt about it, staring at the pounding sea as if she was enthralled by it.

A shaft of triumph surged through me. So, I'd been right about that figure. Right to follow it out here but wrong in thinking Conor had come with her to Cromwell's Fort – unless he'd slipped off for a pee and would return in a few minutes.

But I didn't think so. Em was at the fort alone, I was sure. There was something about her, the position she'd assumed, the way she sat with her shoulders slumped, that told me she was on her own.

Why was she sitting on those rocks? For one thing, it was dangerous. The sea was lashing spume at her but she didn't seem to notice it. The rain was pouring on her head. She'd get her death of cold down there. Strange girl. But then I'd always thought her strange and wondered what was in her head.

I stared down at the scene below. The slippery rocks. The pounding sea. And the diminutive figure, sitting on its own down there. Well, I thought, I've got her now. When she comes up, then I'll confront her. Tell her I know what's she's done. Demand to know where Conor is.

But Em did not come up the path that linked

the outcrop to the fort. She didn't move from where she sat. She might have been a piece of sculpture, carved by Conor from those rocks and grafted onto them forever.

I gave up waiting in the end. If I wanted to confront Em, I would have to go to her. I shivered at the very thought. The rocks were far below the fort. I was terrified of heights. The path that would lead down to Em was bound to be too steep for me.

Anger helped to strengthen me. It sent me off to find that path and when I saw how steep it was, it told me not to look below but to keep my eyes on where I was.

That journey was horrendous. The path was damp and perilous. I slipped and lost my balance once. I thought I was going to fall and hurtle to the rocks below. I grabbed at a jagged rock. It cut my hand. I gasped with pain. But I hung on for dear life and managed to regain my balance. Don't look down, I told myself. Concentrate on the path. It won't take long. It's not *that* far. But it seemed several miles to me.

Finally, I reached the rocks, convinced that Em must have been aware of me as I scrambled down to her. But she hadn't moved from her position. She might well have been turned to stone, the way she sat on those rocks. Of course the sea was in her ears. I guess that's all that she could hear as I approached and touched her shoulder.

She nearly jumped out of her clothes. 'Brigit! What are you doing here?'

She looked small, pathetic, childish. She's Conor's daughter, I reminded myself, and no doubt besotted with him. Conor is a manipulative man. He would have got her in his power. Made her help him wrap the body, take it to Flaggy Shore, disguise herself as Hannah later so that he could get that money. Bastard.

It was easy to judge him. Harder to condemn his daughter. The drugs were something else though, and not to do with Conor's actions. Or were they? Was Conor Mr Big in that? Em the agent he had used to sell the drugs to his students? Had he given them to Hannah? Had he planned that she would die after she had lost her father?

Anything was possible. Who knew what he might have planned? He was a hard, ruthless man. But his daughter seemed so childish. So vulnerable, huddling there. Her appearance was peculiar. Her hair was sopping wet, of course, but it wasn't only that. She was speckled with white paint – her hair, her hands, her jeans, her shirt. Later, when I told Louise, I said she looked like a Dalmatian.

'Em,' I said. 'You must come back. You'll get your death of cold out here.'

But Em had turned away from me. A ferry had come into view, heading in towards Bofin Harbour. She was staring at it.

'Em, come back with me,' I said.

She ignored me.

My tiresome walk, my scramble down from Cromwell's Fort were adding up to nothing more than an anti-climax. I thought, it's Conor I should confront, not this small, pathetic child.

I was on the verge of leaving, thinking I'd

abandon Em, trudge back to the quay again, phone the Creggan guards from Day's Hotel, tell them where Em could be found, and then boot back to Kilnaboy. But I wanted to see Conor. And Em, I thought, could lead me to him.

To make her pay attention to me, I decided to surprise her.

'Let's stop messing around,' I said. 'I know all about it, Em. I know Conor is your father. I know that you hid Hannah's body – even where you put it. I know you dressed up as Hannah and pretended to be her.'

At that, she did turn round. She stared at me but didn't speak.

'It's all come out, you know,' I said. 'The guards are onto you as well. They've found the drugs. They're looking for you. I guess they've found the car by now.'

She didn't answer. Her expression was quite blank, I couldn't read her face at all.

Having first felt pity for her, now I was exasperated. 'Did you *hear* me?' I demanded, feeling like a third-year teacher coping with a sulky pupil.

Em got up. She stretched. Wiped the raindrops off her face. Walked round the rocks.

'*Em!*'

'I can hear you,' she replied. 'I'm thinking about what you said.'

'And?'

'How did you find out that Conor is my father? You didn't get it out of him.'

So that was what had got to her, not the rest of what I'd said. My irritation with her grew.

369

I said, 'What makes you so sure of that?'

She laughed. 'Because he didn't know himself!'

It was my turn to be caught off balance.

'Conor doesn't know?' I said.

'He does know now because I told him. A few days ago, that was. He didn't know before at all.'

'He didn't know he had a child?'

She stamped her foot on the rocks. '*No!* He knew full well he had a child. He didn't know that I was her.'

'And now he does because you told him?' But I could get those details later. 'Where is he, Em? I need to see, to talk to him. He's here, I'm sure, on Inishbofin.' But I wasn't sure at all.

'You know where Conor is,' said Em. 'Aren't you the one that's sleeping with him?' She glared at me. Em, the small, resentful daughter.

'Not any more,' I said to her. 'That's all over. That's not why I want to see him. I just want to talk to him. Didn't you come here with him? Is he on the island with you?'

She looked bored. She shrugged her shoulders. 'You know where he's gone,' she said.

I tried another tack with her. 'Stop protecting him! He's manipulating you. You're frightened of him, aren't you, Em?'

'Frightened?' She sounded quite incredulous.

'You've been through a lot – too much. What Conor made you do was dreadful. Using you the way he did. Involving you in Hannah's death. But it's finished now, I promise. You don't have to listen to him. He won't work through you again.'

'Work through me?' I heard amusement in her voice. 'Work through *me?*' she said again. 'You think Conor worked through me?'

'Of course I do. Well, he's your father.'

'What has that to do with it?'

I realised she was laughing at me. Until then, I'd thought her childish. Seen her just as Conor's daughter. But she was looking different now. No longer sad, pathetic, lonely, but mocking, powerful, very adult. She was standing between me and the pathway to the fort. As I watched, she retreated up the path, walking backwards a few yards so she could tower over me.

Until then, I'd not sensed danger. I'd been nervous on the path but I'd not been afraid of Em. But Em was looking different now. Dry-eyed, scornful – pitiless.

I swallowed, clutching at my throat, wishing that the rain would stop. Wanting to get out of there.

Em said, 'You think Conor would use *me?* You're stupid if that's what you think. Of course, I know that he's used you.'

'He may have. But he doesn't now.'

'He was using you to be a TV star. He always uses women, Brigit. The ones he sleeps with, anyway. That woman, Janice Seton, for instance. He sleeps with her when he's in London. That's so she will sell his paintings. And he used to use my mammy. She got pregnant, then he left her so that he could marry Hannah. She had money, that was why. But he didn't love her.'

The rain was easing off. In five minutes it would stop.

I told myself there was no reason to feel nervous of this creature. Em was tiny, fragile, thin. Just because she'd blocked my path, I shouldn't feel afraid of her. She was just a small, drowned rat. I didn't fancy rats that much but why should I be frightened of them?

She went on, fiercely now, 'He never loved the likes of you or any of those other women. But it's different with me. I knew that we'd get on together. That's why I came to Kilnaboy, so I could be there with my daddy. We trust each other, him and me. He despises other women, that's why he tells lies to them. But he would never lie to me. We're like that, the two of us. He's sure he can depend on me. He knows I'll always help him out.'

'The way you helped him to hide Hannah. Much good that's done you, Em. I was in the studio when you came in to get the wig. We have a video to prove that you pretended to be Hannah. I know you took the bubblewrap. I found some on the Flaggy Shore.'

Em picked up a jagged rock and juggled it between her hands. The path was lined with rocks like that. I felt a chill run down my spine. I knew I was a perfect target. I told myself not to be intimidated.

'Conor won't get that money now,' I continued. 'There's too much evidence to prove that Hannah died before her father.'

Em stopped juggling for a minute. 'That's what *you* think,' she declared. 'But you're stupid, aren't you, Brigit? Hannah didn't die that night. When Seamus Talbot-Kelly died, Hannah Byrne was still alive. Conor's going to get the money. Hannah didn't die that night. It worked out fine for us, you see. She died *after* Seamus died. I know, because I killed her.'

Talking now about what happened, I say I thought that Em was lying; either that, or she was mad.

That was what I thought, at first. But as Em continued speaking, I began to change my mind.

It all began the night when Conor went to check on Hannah. According to Em, he found her lying on the floor, surrounded by her lovely hair which he knew she'd cut off herself. She'd often threatened to do that. Hannah thought she *was* her hair because it was so beautiful. The act of taking scissors to it was tantamount to suicide.

Seeing her stretched out on the floor, believing she was dead, Conor retched, then panicked. He rushed downstairs to waken Em. He was weeping. 'Hannah's dead!' he kept repeating.

He was in a shocking state. He never thought about the money that he'd lose with Hannah dying. It was Em who thought of that. She knew Conor needed it, knew that he was running short. She'd heard him talking on the phone, eavesdropped, watched what he got up to, and she'd drawn her own conclusions.

While Conor was in such a dither, Em remembered Hannah's father and the money he would leave if she didn't pre-decease him. She made Conor drink a brandy. Told him he should listen to her, that she had devised a plan. It would be a gamble but if it worked – and it just might – Conor wouldn't lose the money from his wife's inheritance.

'*Listen* to me,' Em had said. 'This is what we're going to do...'

Conor listened, wept, protested. Finally, he saw the light.

The rest of it I had worked out. The borrowed wig. The bubblewrap. The journey to the Flaggy Shore. The hiding place – the flagstone shelf.

Em directed all of it. Conor hadn't been much help. He'd not only been upset, he'd carried on about the hair, as if the fact she'd cut it off was as bad as Hannah dying.

While Em was rolling Hannah up in bubble-wrap, Conor gathered up her hair.

'It must be kept,' he said to Em. 'I'm going to put it in a box,' and off he went to deal with that as if it was of great importance. Perhaps it helped him. Certainly, when he'd removed the hair, he did become more practical and even wrote the note for me.

As Em said to me, 'He knew that Seamus was near death. He saw the sense in what I'd said. He thought I was wonderful.'

'Sense? What sort of sense is this?' I said. 'You tell me that you murdered Hannah. But now you say that she was dead when Conor found her in her room.'

'Conor *thought* she died that night. But Conor got it wrong, for once. She was only in a coma. Hannah died the night Conor came back down from Inishbofin.'

That night, as Conor was on his way home, Em thought that she would check on Hannah.

At that stage she, too, believed that Hannah was already dead when she rolled her up in

374

bubblewrap. She only went to check on her in case the body had been found.

It was half past nine when she walked up the Flaggy Shore, relieved to see it was deserted. She wasn't really all that worried. She didn't think anybody would inspect the flagstone shelves. She reached them, feeling confident that she would find the body where she and Conor had left it.

The body wasn't there. Em was horrified. So it had been found, she thought. In spite of their well-laid plans, Conor would lose all that money. She was wondering what to do, thinking that there wasn't much, when she spotted something moving on the far side of the flagstone. It was large and silvery.

A creature from the sea, she thought. A silver seal? A stranded dolphin? Here, on this deserted shore?

Apprehensive, curious, she went to have a look at it. Then she realised it was Hannah, partly swathed in bubblewrap, crawling weakly up the beach, looking like a butterfly emerging from the chrysalis.

Em was shocked but not defeated. After a moment her mind began to work again. The situation, although desperate, might be turned to her advantage. Now at least, she told herself, nobody could say that Hannah died before her father. But the fact remained, she had to die. If Hannah lived, she'd talk. Demand to know what happened to her. Tell the tale to other people. Suspect Conor. Maybe leave him. Then he wouldn't get the money.

Hannah had to die – and quickly.

Luck, said Em, was on her side. Before she'd driven to the shore she'd been into Ballyvaughan where she'd met her supplier. In the boot of Conor's car was what she needed to kill Hannah. She even had syringes there.

She ran back and returned well-armed. Hannah hadn't moved very far. She was too weak to make much progress. Her face lit up when she saw Em crouching in the sand beside her. Em, she thought, was going to save her. She babbled words of gratitude. 'Aw, thank you, Em. You're very good.' She actually apologised for all the trouble she was causing – 'I'm sorry, Em. I'm really sorry. Conor will be cross with me. I drank too much. I tried to die.'

'Never mind about the drinking.' Em was filling a syringe. Beside her was her armoury – boxes of temazepam and some sparking Ballygowan. No alcohol. *She* didn't drink.

Hannah kept on talking to her. 'I saw them in the studio. I was looking through the window. He was making love to Brigit. I was sure I could trust her. That was why I tried to die.'

'Sit up a minute,' Em insisted. 'Take these pills and you'll feel better.'

How much temazepam would kill her? Em understood what drugs could do. She knew temazepam was mild. It was just a sleeping pill, manufactured legally. Benzodiazepines generally, unless you took a lot of them or washed them down with alcohol, didn't constitute a risk. But Hannah was an alcoholic. Her system had been ruined by drink. So she should be susceptible.

'Here. Drink some Ballygowan with them.'

376

'I want vodka,' Hannah moaned.

'I don't have vodka. Only water.' Stupid woman, Em was thinking. But Hannah was obeying her, gulping down what she'd been given. Hopefully, the pills would work. When Hannah started getting woozy, Em intended to inject her with some more temazepam.

She did so, thinking of her mother. Of how, if Conor hadn't married Hannah, he might well have married her mammy. Either way, hating Hannah helped Em then, and kept her going at the end when Hannah fell asleep forever.

The only problem that remained was where to put her body now till Conor came and they could dump it in the bay.

Finally, she left it there, partly swathed in bubblewrap, lying on the Flaggy Shore. She really had no other option. She couldn't lift the body up and put it back on the shelf.

Still, she didn't feel at risk. It was dark by then and rainclouds hid the moon and stars. She didn't think anyone would walk along the shore that night, and in another hour or two she'd be coming back with Conor. She wouldn't tell him what she'd done. She'd drop him off in Ballyvaughan. He could break into the boathouse. Grab an engine and some oars. Find a boat that they could use and join her at the Flaggy Shore.

She'd have Hannah's body ready to be put into the boat. She'd say, 'I dragged it off the shelf myself. It wasn't very heavy, Conor.' She would never, ever tell him that she'd had to murder Hannah, in case he became distressed. He was an artist, after all. He was sensitive by nature. That was why he'd gone to pieces when he went to Hannah's room and found her lying on the floor.

My own part in poor Hannah's death makes me hang my head in shame. Compared with what had happened to her, my need to regain self-respect seemed nothing but a selfish whim.

On the pathway, Em was juggling with the rock once more. When she spoke again, it was in a pensive voice.

'That was how I wanted it. But I made a big mistake. I won't do that a second time. I won't tell him about *you*.' Then holding the rock in one hand, she reached out for another one.

I was frightened, certainly. But over and above that fright were my emotions about Hannah. Her killer must be brought to justice. I mustn't let Em hurt anyone again. To do so would betray the woman that I had betrayed already.

'What was your big mistake?' I said, trying to sound unconcerned, more interested in what Em had done than what she'd do a second time.

She answered automatically. 'I wasn't going to tell him, Brigit. Conor needs to be protected. But when we went to Shannon airport, Conor had a row with me.'

Shannon airport, I was thinking. So they went to Shannon after all.

I didn't interrupt; I let her talk about the row.

It started off as just a tiff. Conor was annoyed with Em for talking about his plan to spend a few days in LA, with the result that I'd heard about it from someone else. He'd wanted to tell me himself. He ticked off Em for interfering. Said she was becoming bossy. Trying to take control of him.

Em was piqued by what he said. 'Bossy? Interfering? Me? But Conor, I am part of you. Look at all I do for you.'

Somehow it went on from there until she lost her temper and blurted out what she had done so Conor wouldn't lose the money. He was horrified, repelled. And Em, on seeing his reaction, told him that she was his daughter.

She'd been saving that one up as a present for the future but she thought she'd give it to him now so that he would be understanding and agree with her that she was truly part of him.

But he rejected her. He ranted, raved and told her that she'd have to leave the studio. She might, or might not, be his daughter. But that was beside the point. He wanted nothing more to do with her. What she had done was terrible.

'But it was for *you!*' wailed Em. 'So you could have that money, Conor.'

By then, they'd stopped outside departures. Conor took his suitcase out. He turned to Em and said, tight-lipped, 'I'll never speak to you again. When I come back from LA, Em, make sure you're not at Kilnaboy.' Then he walked away from her and through the automatic doors.

'He didn't once look back at me. That's why I had to punish him. But he'll be back, I know he will. He needs me. He depends on me. When he comes back from LA, Brigit, I know he'll be pleased to see me.' She sounded like a little girl.

'He's not in LA,' I said.

She stared at me in disbelief. 'He *is*. I dropped

him off at Shannon airport. Of course he's in LA. He wouldn't lie, not to me.'

'You're wrong. He lied to all of us about it.'

'He wouldn't lie to me,' insisted Em.

'No?' I took his passport from my pocket. I knew what that would do to her, remembering what it did to me. 'Come down and look at it,' I said. 'It's Conor's passport. Trust me, Em. He might lie to all of us but I'm not going to lie to you.' I held the passport out to her.

'He wouldn't lie,' she said again. But she'd put down the jagged rocks. As I stood there, she came towards me.

'Let me see it,' she demanded.

I put the passport in her hand. 'Notice that it's up to date. Conor's not in LA, Em. I can't imagine where he is. I only know he lied to you.'

She began to cry. She looked so young, standing there, with the passport in her hand. 'I can't believe he lied to me,' she wept.

I thought of Joe. I felt for her. But not for long. The memory of another woman who had also loved her father came between us.

Leaving Em in tears, I set off up the path again. I wasn't frightened as I climbed up to Cromwell's Fort. Without fear of Em, I walked on to *Beal na Brad*. The tide was coming in. Port Island would be cut off soon; as it was I had to wade across the inlet to reach Braud. There, I waited for a while, to see if Em would come after me. But she didn't reappear.

The inlet was now impassable. The star-shaped fort was playing the part for which Cromwell had designed it, acting as a moated gaol, the person who was trapped out there remained till the next low tide.

I walked on, keeping Closhkeem in my sights. Like Conor, I did not look back.

TWENTY-ONE

Halfway back reaction hit me. I felt desperately lonely. I was crying, I remember, when I reached the second cove.

And then something splendid happened. I'd been walking with my head down, feeling sorry for myself. Then I heard my name called out. I looked up and there was David, walking towards me on the sand.

At first I thought he was a mirage, then I saw the guards behind him. He was real, and so were they! My eyes filled up with tears again.

Asking how they'd tracked me down was way beyond me at that moment. But David told me anyway. The Creggan guards found Conor's car where Em left it in the car park. They got on to Guard McMahon. He let Clodagh Moran know and Clodagh, naturally, told David. He had been looking for me and knew that Hannah's car was gone. He got back to Guard McMahon and suggested he check at Creggan to see if the second car was there.

When Guard McMahon said it was, David got hold of Patrick and they both drove up to Creggan. At Day's Hotel, someone said they'd seen me making tracks for Cromwell's Fort. The guards knew I'd been at the cottage. They'd been there and met the boy who told them about Em and me.

'It's brilliant that you're here!' I said. It was all that really mattered.

At Day's Hotel, I had a bath, my clothes were tumble dried for me and later, when we got to Creggan, I made a statement to the guards.

Em had been picked up by then. The guards were waiting by the inlet as the tide was going out. They found her on the rock outcrop, hunched up, wretched, dripping wet. I don't think she'd budged an inch after I had gone away.

Later, when I told Louise, she found this aspect fascinating. She wanted to hear more of Em. But I didn't share her interest. The way the whole thing seemed to me, my relationship with Em had ended back at Cromwell's Fort. So I kept procrastinating. 'I'll come back to Em again.'

'All right then,' agreed Louise. 'But where was Conor all this while?'

Conor. When I talk about him now it is in a guarded manner. The power of him is with me still. Despite the fact that I am happy, it frightens me, to tell the truth. Compassion is a part of it. But today there is a difference. Where in the past I had pitied Conor because of his tie to Hannah, now she's unconnected with it and I simply pity him. Yet when the news about him broke, I can't remember feeling pain, or feeling anything at all. I'd gone down with laryngitis. Dr Moylan's medication blunted what I might have felt.

But that was all later. Before that, we pulled out of Creggan, Patrick travelling alone and David driving Hannah's car so he could keep me company. Not that we said very much. In no time I was fast asleep, curled up on the leather seat, unaware of roads and milestones, lakes and hedgerows, passing cars.

How ironic it seems now, to think I never saw that car. And David, as he passed the scene, didn't give much thought to it. The lorry had been towed away. There wasn't that much damage to it and the driver wasn't hurt, except for minor cuts and bruises. No one was in need of help. Nobody was standing around, commenting on what had happened. David soon forgot about it. He drove on, his thoughts elsewhere, wondering what we should do next. We couldn't stay at Kilnaboy, he reasoned, not after what I'd told the guards. On the other hand, we couldn't simply disappear. The guards might need to ask more questions. Should he look for a hotel? Should we both go up to Dublin and wait there until things were settled? That would mean a hotel too – at least, it would for David. Emer Brennan had gone home. He couldn't use her flat again.

All this was running through his head when I finally woke up, at which point we talked about it.

'It's late. We can't move out tonight,' said David.

'You're right. Let's go to Dublin in the morning. Mammy's in the clinic still. You can stay at Dalkey with me.'

'Guard McMahon should be told. He'll want to stay in touch with us. I'll phone him first thing in the morning.'

But it didn't work out like that. A fever set in overnight and I felt lethal by the morning. Dr

Moylan came at nine and warned that I should stay in bed. And then, before David could phone him, Guard McMahon phoned the house.

Clodagh broke the news to us. Naturally, she was upset. 'There's been an accident,' she said.

So we didn't go to Dublin. And we were there, in Kilnaboy, when Janice Seton came to the house. Her visit seems quite hazy now, the way it was when I was ill. But, logging in to memory, her image comes up on the screen and there is Janice once again, sentimental, arrogant, clad in black from head to toe, telling us the tragic story.

Some of it we'd heard before, from Clodagh Moran. 'The lorry driver was at fault,' she said. 'He was coming round a corner. Eighty miles an hour, they say. And driving on the left as well.'

Janice said that wasn't true. The lorry wasn't going too fast, nor was it on the left-hand side as it turned round that dangerous corner. And it was not the driver's fault. The villain was a tabby cat which scrambled underneath a gate and dashed in front of Conor's car.

'Poor, darling Conor,' Janice wept. 'He couldn't bear to run it over.' Instead, he'd swerved and lost control, smashing straight into the lorry. The impact killed him instantly. Janice emerged quite unscathed, though obviously deeply shocked.

Of course she had to talk about it, and tell us about Conor. She said she'd been in love with him. That she'd hoped to marry him when he and Hannah got divorced. It was on the cards for years. But Conor was so sensitive. So concerned about her drinking. 'Although he loved me, Brigit, he felt he couldn't just walk out, not until she'd stabilised. Naturally, I understood. But after Hannah died, well, we were free to be together. "I'll come to Kilnaboy," I said, knowing he'd need me. But Conor said I shouldn't, not yet. In October, possibly, after things had settled down. He said, "But come to Ireland, by all means. We can explore the west together. And we'll go to Inishbofin so you can see my real paintings".'

Janice knew about those pictures – Conor often spoke about them – and she was intrigued to see them.

She flew into Shannon where she was met by Conor. He hired a car for them. 'His Jaguar wasn't ready. He'd arranged a service for it but the garage let him down.'

If only Conor had had the Shell, that might have saved him, Janice said. Unlike the car that Conor hired, the Shell was robust. It might have lived up to its nickname. Conor might be still alive. Instead of which…

Janice broke down.

I didn't have the heart to tell her how mendacious Conor was, even when it came to cars. I didn't talk about myself. I didn't say, 'He used us, Janice. Love? He didn't know the meaning of it. Adulation? Yes, of course. Adulation turned him on. He needed it, from both of us. He couldn't have enough of it. But if he'd had his way again, we'd both be dangling on a string. You would sell his paintings for him and I would help him become a TV star. And if Hannah hadn't died, he'd be using her as well, living off the money that her father left to her. What fools we were, the three of us, to think that love and Conor Byrne had anything at all in common.'

I couldn't say those things to Janice. There had been enough destruction. Janice was more in love with Conor than I had ever been. Irritating as she was, arrogant as she could be, she didn't lack sincerity. And I knew what she'd have to face when Em was charged with Hannah's murder and Conor's part in it emerged.

What a bastard Conor was. And yet I say I pity him. Why do I feel compassion for him? He couldn't love – well, that's a reason. He couldn't love unless he had you in his power. If you were small and sick and frightened, maybe he would care for you, as he did for dogs and cats and maybe, despite all the odds, in a sense, for Hannah too. But Conor had his reasons for the way that he behaved, as I discovered later on. I already had a clue, lying on my bedside table, to what motivated Conor but I didn't come upon it until after Janice left.

The thread that led me back to Conor was supplied by David. It was a document of transfer which related to the cottage. As David told me afterwards, he'd had to wait some days in Dublin for it, which was why he stayed in the city. He had thought it was worthwhile, hanging around for evidence to prove that Conor had been lying, that the cottage wasn't his, or that he'd got it by foul means. He was somewhat disappointed to discover he'd been wrong.

'Me daddy's father's brother had it,' said the boy in Inishbofin, and that turned out to be quite true. His daddy's father's brother's name was on the document, though I didn't know his family name then.

When I saw the name on the document, it took a while to realise I'd come across it before. I rummaged in my memory. Found myself in Lorcan's house. I was early, Lorcan had said. I'll find a book to read, I'd told him.

Armed with *Irish Georgian Houses,* I'd sat on the sofa bed. Looked at pictures in the book. Come across a dedication which was in the Irish language.

The dedication was to Lorcan. A quotation had been added: *'Mar, maraionn cach an rud is anfa leis'.* I had been translating that when Lorcan interrupted me but I remembered what it meant. *'All men kill the thing they love.'* Oscar Wilde had said it first. The author writing it in Irish had been Diarmuid Esmond Darcy. And here now was his name again on the document of transfer. Diarmuid Esmond Darcy had owned the cottage before assigning it to Conor.

Rummaging around again, I conjured up the conversation between Lorcan and myself after I'd first seen that name.

'This book on Georgian houses, Lorcan. The author was a friend of yours?'

'Diarmuid Darcy? Yes, he was.'

'I don't think I've heard of him.'

'No? But then he died some years ago.'

Aha, I thought, a mystery here. Lorcan is concealing something. You can see it on his face. And there's sadness in his eyes.

Conor had no time for Lorcan. Hadn't liked my seeing him. I'd put it down to jealousy. But I had

388

got it wrong again. As usual with Conor Byrne, there was another motive.

I might have got it out of Lorcan but in the event it was Sheila Ferguson who put me wise about it.

Sheila had heard from her daughter Nuala Moylan that I'd been sick and she called round to see me, partly out of kindness, partly curiosity. Sheila loves picking up juicy stories as she flits from friend to friend. And why not? She lost her husband, then her voice, and only got the latter back. She might as well make use of it.

That day, she was doing the talking. She spoke of Conor and herself. Of how she'd honoured him at first. Her gratitude for what he'd done to help to restore her speech amounted, so she said, to love. When Conor said he needed money, she was happy to supply it. Investment in the studio, that was how he put it to her. She felt ennobled by her gesture. Later on he'd asked for more. A loan he'd soon repay, he said. Sheila had coughed up again. But Conor didn't pay her back. Instead, he tried to borrow yet again.

By then, the atmosphere had changed. Sheila had learnt more about Conor. She refused to lend the money. As she had said when we'd first met, she owed a lot to Conor Byrne but she had settled that account and no longer trusted him. She'd realised what a self-serving manipulator he was.

'How did you work that out?' I asked.

'Because of Diarmuid Darcy,' said Sheila.

She'd got the story from a friend, an editor at Celtic Press. The firm had published Diarmuid's books. The tale of his affair with Lorcan Burke had been an open secret there.

'Conor broke them up, you know. And when I mentioned Conor's name, Deirdre told me all about it.'

'Really? What exactly did she tell you?'

'Everything. You won't believe it! Conor won a scholarship – that was how he got to art school. His parents didn't have a bean. His father was an awful man. He hated Conor from the start. He found the artist in him threatening. According to what Diarmuid said, and what Deirdre told me later, he belted Conor as a child. They were ghastly, fearful beatings. He broke his arm on one occasion. They had him up in court for it. You can create a monster that way.'

Or a man who cannot love unless he has you in his power.

The man that Mr Byrne created set his feelings to one side when Diarmuid Darcy fell for him. They had met at Lorcan's house where Lorcan was instructing Conor. Diarmuid dumped his long-time lover. Conor gave him what he wanted. In return he got the cottage. He'd do anything for gain – he was always short of money.

'But Conor wasn't gay,' said Sheila.

'No,' I said. 'I'm sure he wasn't.'

'There was a girl around as well. They say she had a child by him.'

There was no escaping Em. Everything went back to her. Her real name was Mary Moriarty but I can't get used to that. When I talk about her now, I still refer to her as Em.

Em. I wish when I'd left her at the fort that had

been the end of her. But she had done her worst by then – to Hannah, and to Conor too. She told me she had punished him for snubbing her at Shannon airport. I hardly heard her at the time, being so concerned about myself. It never occurred to me that she could inflict a blow like that on him. Conor's life was over but his talent should have stayed with us. Em ensured that wasn't so. But then, she was a monster too, and monsters are destructive creatures.

It was Janice who found out when she went to Inishbofin. For her, it was a pilgrimage, that journey up to Conor's cottage to see his 'real' paintings, as he'd promised her she would.

At the cottage she met the sulky boy who asked what she was doing there.

'I've come to get the paintings that Mr Byrne left in this cottage,' Janice told him loftily. 'I'm going to put them in my gallery so that people back in London know how talented he was.'

But Em had made sure that couldn't happen. Before she went to Cromwell's Fort, she'd been busy with a paintbrush. She'd used all the oil paint up. The pictures were still on the walls, but all of them were over-painted.

'All I saw was white,' said Janice. 'Everything was painted white. Conor's paintings were ruined. That woman destroyed him, Brigit.'

Louise, when I told her, was appalled.

'But couldn't they have been restored?' she said. 'Surely Janice could have saved them? Called an expert in to help her?'

'She tried. It didn't work,' I said. 'Em used spirits on the pictures, *then* she over-painted them. There was no hope of saving them.'

'Did Em admit what she had done?'

'Not the murder. She only spoke about that to me. I think she felt she had triumphed because she'd destroyed her father.'

So that is why I pity Conor.

His memory doesn't seem to fade, despite the fact that I am happy. Despite the time that has elapsed since I went back to Ireland that time.

Much has happened in the meantime. Em's in gaol, where she belongs. She got off on the murder charge – the evidence just wasn't there and she had pleaded innocent. The drugs charge was another matter – she's going to be inside for years. Mammy has married Ivor Sheehan. He worships her, he really does. She's sitting on a pedestal and Ivor's looking up at her. I think she's a bit bewildered. She'd thought that women worshipped men, that pedestals were just for them. But Mammy's also happy these days. She no longer snipes at me and I'm more tolerant of her.

Ivor's daughters aren't bad either, quite OK as sisters go, though not as splendid as Darina. How could they be, I ask myself, now I know more about Darina and what she did to protect me?

It all goes back again to Joe and his involvement in that scam. Oh, yes, he was involved all right, despite what he proclaimed in court and Lorcan's optimistic view. Fergal Dillon told the truth about the shares that Joe had held. Joe's shares, he'd said, were held in trust, they were not in his name. A declaration to that effect was issued to him afterwards. The guards had searched his home and practice but had failed to find the papers.

No wonder, since Darina had them. Joe had phoned her in a panic, saying, 'Go to Howth and get them. When you do, you must destroy them.' Darina says she thought of me, how hurt I'd be if Joe went down. So, much against her better judgement, she caught the bus to Howth.

When I'd dredged all this out of Mammy, on her honeymoon in London, I set off to see my sister to tell her that I'd finally grown up and that I'd always love her for trying to protect me. And I wanted to see Mikey too.

Mikey's so much better these days, since the Green Tree Spirit's gone. It was living in the oak tree, just outside his window. Mikey was so frightened of it that he couldn't talk about it, but he managed to tell me it was huge and sickly green.

It was the frog clock that did the trick. Green Tree Spirits are malign but they're terrified of frogs. The spirit that was in the oak tree took fright when we put up that clock and Mikey hasn't seen it since.

Darina's more relaxed as well. Robert's cut back on the golf – that's the story she tells me. I think there's more to it than that. Robert's secretary has resigned. I gather that she was very pretty and inclined to be flirtatious. Maybe Robert was unfaithful but, if so, it is over now and things have settled down again.

Which is more than can be said for Seamus Talbot-Kelly's wives and their claims on his estate. The lawyers are still working on it, seeking justice for their clients, but it may take years and years before the matter is resolved.

Meanwhile, Em is where she should be, serving out her prison sentence.

And I am where I should be too, living in New York with David. We got married in the spring. Louise says she can't believe it. But, as I said, I'm happy now.

Despite Conor? you might ask.

Despite Conor, I will answer, and the fact I think about him virtually every morning. Blame it on the cat, I say. An alley cat has adopted us. I tell myself I only feed it because it keeps rats at bay. As I'm dishing up its breakfast, as it hovers around me, spitting, I can't but remember Conor who, with all his fearful failings, died so he could save a cat.

I think of Conor and of shadows. I see the shadow of a man who might be any age. Who might be tall or small or fat or possibly emaciated. I can't tell the shape of him because the sun, and Conor too, has been playing tricks with him.

But I know who that figure is, who cast his shadow on those paintings. I know it is Conor's shadow. The shadow that he must have feared, created by his father's beatings.

I was luckier, I think, in the father that I had. Joe was not the hero I created when I hadn't yet grown up. He took part in shady dealings. He cheated me with Lorcan's stories. Joe was not a moral man. He was Harlequin. Cunning, twisted, witty, agile. But, like Harlequin, he intended to amuse me. In his way, I think he

394

loved me. And when I think of other fathers, I don't think that Joe's so bad. At least he didn't wallop us.

I've let him off the hook at last. I'm not demanding anything. He doesn't have to be heroic. I've the measure of him now. He's shifty but he's very charming. And, after all, he *is* our father.

Darina doesn't want it back so I still wear his signet ring.

The publishers hope that this book has given you enjoyable reading. Large Print Books are especially designed to be as easy to see and hold as possible. If you wish a complete list of our books please ask at your local library or write directly to:

Magna Large Print Books
Magna House, Long Preston,
Skipton, North Yorkshire.
BD23 4ND

This Large Print Book for the partially sighted, who cannot read normal print, is published under the auspices of

THE ULVERSCROFT FOUNDATION